Redwall
Mossflower
Mattimeo
Mariel of Redwall
Salamandastron
Martin the Warrior
The Bellmaker
Outcast of Redwall
Pearls of Lutra
The Long Patrol
Marlfox
The Legend of Luke
Lord Brocktree
Taggerung
Triss
Loamhedge
Rakkety Tam
High Rhulain
Eulalia!

Castaways of the Flying Dutchman
The Angel's Command
Voyage of Slaves
The Great Redwall Feast
A Redwall Winter's Tale
The Tale of Urso Brunov
Seven Strange and Ghostly Tales
The Ribbajack

BRIAN JACQUES

Illustrated by DAVID ELLIOT

PHILOMEL BOOKS

PHILOMEL BOOKS
A division of Penguin Young Readers Group.
Published by The Penguin Group.
Penguin Group (USA) Inc., 375 Hudson Street, New York, NY 10014, U.S.A.
Penguin Group (Canada), 90 Eglinton Avenue East, Suite 700, Toronto, Ontario M4P 2Y3,
Canada (a division of Pearson Penguin Canada Inc.).
Penguin Books Ltd., 80 Strand, London WC2R 0RL, England.
Penguin Ireland, 25 St. Stephen's Green, Dublin 2, Ireland
(a division of Penguin Books Ltd).
Penguin Group (Australia), 250 Camberwell Road, Camberwell, Victoria 3124,
Australia (a division of Pearson Australia Group Pty Ltd).
Penguin Books India Pvt Ltd, 11 Community Centre, Panchsheel Park,
New Delhi - 110 017, India.
Penguin Group (NZ), 67 Apollo Drive, Rosedale, North Shore 0632,
New Zealand (a division of Pearson New Zealand Ltd).
Penguin Books (South Africa) (Pty) Ltd, 24 Sturdee Avenue, Rosebank,
Johannesburg 2196, South Africa.
Penguin Books Ltd, Registered Offices: 80 Strand, London WC2R 0RL, England.

Published simultaneously in Canada.   Printed in the United States of America.
Design by Semadar Megged.   The text is set Palatino.
Library of Congress Cataloging-in-Publication Data is available upon request.
Jacques, Brian.
Doomwyte / Brian Jacques ; illustrated by David Elliot.   p. cm. — (Redwall)
Summary: The Redwallers face some of their most dangerous villains yet in a treacherous
hunt for long-lost treasure.   [1. Animals—Fiction. 2. Buried treasure—Fiction. 3. Fantasy.]
I. Elliot, David, 1952– ill. II. Title.   PZ7.J15317Do 2008   [Fic]—dc22   2008000662
ISBN 978-0-399-24544-2
1 3 5 7 9 10 8 6 4 2

For PFC Donald Reas Axtell,
a true warrior.

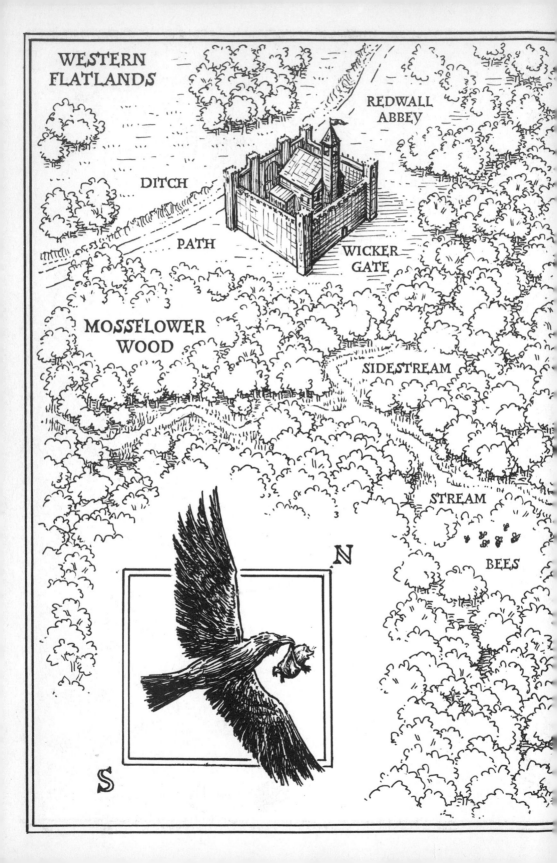

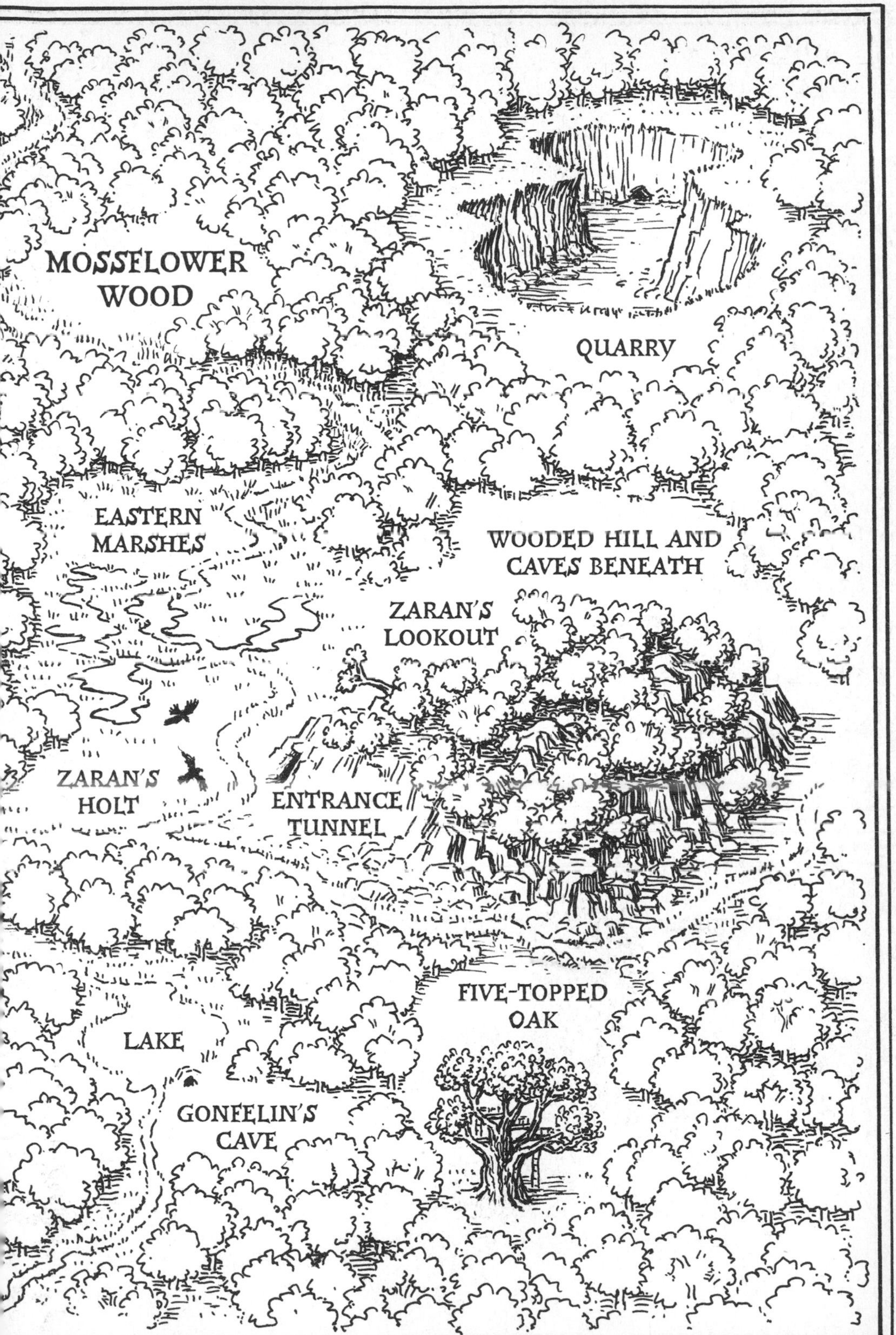

MOSSFLOWER
WOOD

QUARRY

EASTERN
MARSHES

WOODED HILL AND
CAVES BENEATH

ZARAN'S
LOOKOUT

ZARAN'S
HOLT

ENTRANCE
TUNNEL

FIVE-TOPPED
OAK

LAKE

GONFELIN'S
CAVE

PROLOGUE

The warm days are past, the dry dust has settled, those long-dead summers, a dim memory, small birds have flown south, cold eastwind is dreary, so come ye and sit by the fireside with me. Let's add a good log, stir up the pale ashes, 'til they glow crimson gold, twixt the grey and the black, I'll recall to you my adventurous young seasons; together, my friend, we'll go journeying back. Meet my comrades long gone, whom I'll always remember, I hope when I've joined them, you've learned what it means, that a story passed down can live on forever. I'm the Teller of Tales, and the Weaver of Dreams. . . .

BOOK ONE

The Raven

They danced and twinkled in the woodlands at night . . .
those little lights.

1

Blustery and wild were the days of late spring, wet and windy, with little sign of more placid weather. Thus it was that night, when Griv sought shelter from battering rain and buffeting winds out of the east. Redwall Abbey was the perfect place. Tossed about on the dark skies, like a scrap of black-and-white rag, the magpie caught sight of the imposing building as she was swept high over the swaying green of Mossflower woodlands. Skilfully she went into a steep dive, tacking and sidesweeping on drenched wings. Homing in on the Abbey's west face, Griv sought shelter on the leeside, out of the gale.

She made an ungainly but safe landing upon the sandstone sill of a second-storey dormitory window. What attracted the magpie to that particular spot was the welcome golden light, slanting narrowly from between wooden shutters. Ruffling and grooming her wet plumage, Griv edged along the sill until she was securely lodged, twixt stone and timber, in a corner.

Ever curious, she peered through a slim gap in the shuttering. There were creatures inside, young mice, moles, squirrels and hedgehogs. One, a mouse, only slightly older than the rest, was speaking. He was relating a story to his audience, who were listening intently, hanging upon his every word. From her perch on the window ledge outside, Griv listened also. . . .

The narrator, a young mouse named Bisky, was in full dramatic flow. Leaping up on the little truckle bed, he made a number of gouging gestures above his head. Bisky held out his other paw as though he were thrusting a dagger, relating avidly to his goggle-eyed friends, "One, two, three, four! Prince Gonff stole the four precious stones, which were the statue's eyes. Aye, mates, old Gonff popped 'em out, just like that, robbed the eyes from the great Doomwyte Idol!"

A Dibbun hedgehog (Dibbun is the name given to the youngest Redwallers) interrupted curiously, "Why did 'e doo'd that?"

Frintl, his older sister, sighed impatiently. "'Cos 'e wuz Gonff the Prince o' Mousethiefs, dat's why, sillyspikes!"

Bisky was accustomed to Dibbuns butting in—he carried right on with the story. "Well, there was all manner of 'orrible vermin chasin' after Gonff, but he just laughed, ha ha, an' he escaped 'em easily. . . ."

"Wot bees ee gurt Doodley whoit eyeful?"

Bisky looked down at the tiny mole who had poked his head out from beneath the bed. Moles speak with a curious accent, but Redwallers can always understand them. The young mouse smiled. "It's the Great Doomwyte Idol, a big statue with four eyes. They're actually precious stones, that's why Gonff the Prince of Mousethieves stole 'em."

The mole Dibbun, who was called Dugry, nodded solemnly. "Ho urr, Oi see. But whurr did zurr Gonffen take ee h'idol's h'eyes to?"

Bisky spread his paws wide. "Right here to Redwall Abbey he brought them!"

Dugry thought about this, before asking, "Hurr, then whurr bees they?"

The young mouse explained patiently, "Nobeast knows where the eyes of the Great Doomwyte Idol are, 'cos Gonff hid 'em."

The little hogmaid Frintl posed a question. "Hah, an' I don't s'pose you know where they are?"

The storyteller shook his head. "No, 'cos they're in a very secret place, but someday I'll find 'em, just see if'n I don't!"

A young squirrel, Dwink, who was the same age as Bisky, chortled scornfully. "Yah, wot a load of ole pieswoggle! You made it all up, big fibberface Bisky!" He hurled a pillow, which caught the young mouse in the face. Bisky flung it back, but missed.

" 'Tisn't pieswoggle, Samolus told me it was true!" Dibbuns like nothing better than a pillow fight at bedtime. In the wink of an eye the dormitory was transformed into a noisy battleground. Babes and young ones squealed with merriment as they flung and swung pillows at each other.

Outside on the window ledge, the magpie Griv had heard everything. Regardless of the stormswept night, she flew off, headed for a place where her information might prove profitable. Griv, like most magpies, always had an eye to the main chance.

Back at the dormitory, the pillow fight was at its height, as was the noise. Redwall Abbey's Infirmary and sick bay were on the same floor as the Dibbuns' dormitory. Brother Torilis, the Herbalist and Infirmary Keeper, did not bother to knock. Flinging the door open, he strode straight into the scene of chaos. His paw shot up, catching a pillow in mid-flight. A hush fell over the entire chamber, broken only by a volebabe falling from the top of a wardrobe onto a bed, where he lay at rigid attention. A few small feathers and wisps of pillow stuffing drifted silently to the floor, as every young eye became fixed upon the tall, saturnine figure of the squirrel Herbalist. His voice was quiet, but loaded with menace.

"What is going on here?" No answer being expected, or given, he continued, "And who, may I ask, is responsible for this riot?"

The bleak gaze of Torilis swept the dormitory, coming to rest upon the hogmaid Frintl. She could no more resist Torilis's stare than a baby chick confronted by a hunting serpent. Frintl's chubby paw shot forth, pointing at Bisky. Words bubbled forth unbidden from her.

" 'Twas him, Brovver, a-tellin' fibby stories, he's the one wot started it, honestly, Brovver!"

The Infirmary Keeper turned swiftly on the culprit. "I might have known. You, as one of the older dormitory creatures, ought to know better. You should be setting an example, instead of behaving like a madbeast!"

Bisky bit his lip at the injustice of it. Dwink was the one who had started the pillow fight. He tried to explain. "But Bro—"

Torilis's harsh tone cut across his words sharply. "Silence! Not another word, you young savage! Directly after breakfast tomorrow you will appear on Abbot's Report!"

Bisky knew there was no point in protesting. Nobeast, particularly a young one, would dare argue with the grave-faced Brother Torilis. Instead, he contented himself with glaring at Frintl.

With a final strict instruction, the Infirmary Keeper swept from the dormitory. "Straight into your beds, and go to sleep immediately, all of you!"

As the door slammed shut, Dwink curled his lip at Frintl. "Why couldn't you keep yore mouth shut?"

The hogmaid began to blubber and babble at the same time. " 'Twasn't my fault, soon as he looks at me like that I can't help it. . . ."

Brother Torilis had not gone straight back to his sick bay chamber, he had paused outside the dormitory door. Now his voice rang out like thunder. "One more word and you'll all be up in front of the Abbot tomorrow. Silence in there!"

The dormitory became immediately quiet, some of the more nervous Dibbuns trying hard not to breathe aloud.

On a moonless night, Mossflower Wood could be a daunting prospect, particularly for travellers who were not familiar with its thickness and diversity. It was made doubly eerie by the storm. In the total darkness, anybeast roaming abroad could be easily unnerved. Winds wailed through the crowded avenues of massive tree trunks. Sometimes the gale rose to a sound like that of a tortured beast, whilst often it subsided to a dirgelike moan. Driving rain caused foliage and twigs to bend in a mystical dance. The patter of raindrops upon broad leaves was said to sound like some phantom, creeping up behind the unwary wanderer. All in all not the best place to be, the woodlands on a stormy night.

These thoughts had occurred more than once to Slegg and Gridj, as they stumbled and floundered their way through Mossflower. The two rats had been lost for almost a day and a night. Their object was to reach the western seashore, which Slegg seemed to know all about. Gridj, the younger rat, was regretting he had ever listened to his companion, and was telling him so in no uncertain terms.

"Which way now, mate, straight ahead, eh? Go on, cabbage brain, straight ahead you said. Huh, an' we been goin' straight ahead, all day an' 'arf the night. Aye, straight ahead in circles!"

Slegg took an optimistic view of their troubles. "Lookit, mate, yore only a young un yet, leave it t'me, I got experience, y'see. If'n we just push on straight ahead, we're bound to arrive at the seashore sooner or later. I allus sez, no matter where ye are, yore on land, right? So, if'n ye walk straight ahead, then ye've gotta arrive at a seashore."

Gridj sat down on the saturated loam, figuring he could

7

not get any wetter than he already was. "Well let me tell ye wot I allus sez, scraggynose. I allus sez when yore lost in the dark, an' yore follerin' yer tail round in rings, then ye may's well sit right down an' wait'll daylight, when ye can see where yore goin' proper. But don't yew lissen t'me, go on, straight ahead. I'm stayin' here!"

Slegg carried on a few more paces, then halted. Shaking his head forlornly, he turned, walked back and sat down with his companion. Animosity had been growing between the pair, so each one held his silence. A short time elapsed, then Slegg felt compelled to speak. He did so in a sulky tone.

"Yew called me cabbage brain, an' scraggynose. That ain't right, I never called yew nothin'."

Gridj sniffed. "Well, I ain't sorry, see. Wot would yew call anybeast wot got ye lost, eh?"

Slegg shrugged. "Dunno, I'm no good at name callin', I was brought up decent. Wish I was back 'ome right now, or mebbe sittin' in a liddle cave by the seashore, on nice, warm, dry sand, wid a fire, too. Cookin' all kinds o' fishes in a pot, lobsters an' cockles, an' crabs. . . ."

Gridj pointed an accusing paw. "Yew said cockles wasn't fishes. Lissen, mate, do ye really know wot yore talkin' about? I mean, did ye ever go t'the seashore? Tell the truth!"

Slegg had never set eyes on saltwater. Instead of answering, he broke out into a song, which he had learnt from a searat when he was younger. His harsh unmelodious voice rang out into the storm.

"Come take a stroll down by the strand,
aye haul in close to me,
ye'll live a life so free an' grand,
just sailin' on the sea.

There's flatfish an' dogfish an' codfish, too,
there's big jellyfish galore,

to fry to roast or boil in a stew,
wot beast could ask for more!

So come on, messmate, shun the land,
the sea runs deep an' blue,
with beaches full o' golden sand,
a-waitin' there for you.

There's halibut, herring, haddock an' dabs,
they jumps right out o' the sea,
cockles'n'mussels'n'limpets an' crabs
an' a whale for you'n' me!"

Slegg was about to launch into another verse, when Gridj halted him with a sharp jab to the ribs. He winced. "Yowch! Wot did ye do that for?"

The younger rat muttered an angry reply. "Y'don't know who might hear ye, give yore gob a rest!"

Slegg blew rainwater from his snout. "There ain't the sound or sight of anybeast round 'ere. Huh, I'd be glad t'see 'em if'n there was!"

Gridj's reply was to clamp a paw about Slegg's mouth. "Ssssshhh!"

Slegg freed his mouth indignantly. "Don't yew start shushin' me, I kin talk whenever I like. Yore gettin' a bit too big for yore tail!"

Gridj pushed the older rat's face to one side, whispering, "Will yew stop blatherin' an' look over yonder? Over that way, wot can yer see?"

Slegg blinked hard as he peered between the rainswept trees. "It's a light! Wot's a light doin' out 'ere in the middle o' the night?"

His companion rose stealthily. "I dunno, let's go an' take a closer look. Come on, go quietly. That means keep yore big trap shut!"

Slegg got the last word in, hissing, "An' yew, too!"

They advanced cautiously toward the light, which was little more than a pale, glowing flame. It seemed to hover at eye level, but as the rats came closer, it brightened slightly, and began moving away from them.

Slegg whispered in his friend's ear, "Wot d'ye make of it, couldn't be a campfire, could it?"

Gridj was openly scornful. "Hah, have you ever seen a movin' campfire, idjit? Looks t'me like some kind o' lantern. Maybe it's showin' us the way to someplace warm an' dry?"

Slegg blew rainwater from his snout tip. "Warm'n'dry eh, I ain't arguin' with that. C'mon, mate, let's foller the liddle glimmer!"

They hurried forward, but the pale flame flickered, then disappeared. Gridj gave his companion's tail a vicious tug. "See wot ye've gone an' done, thick'ead, yew frightened the pore liddle light away, dashin' at it like that!"

Slegg retaliated by stamping on his mate's tail. "Lissen, swinkylip, I've took all I'm gonna take off'n yew. Now stop pickin' on me or I'll chew yore ear off an' spit it out where ye won't find it, see!"

The hostilities were about to escalate—Gridj was pulling a club from his belt—when the light reappeared. It emerged from behind a beech tree, where it was joined by a second light. Both lights twinkled to and fro, as if performing a dance.

Slegg gurgled happily, "Hawhaw, lookit, the liddle fellers are dancin' fer us!" He held out his paw, hoping that one might alight on it, but the pale flame wavered, moving away again.

As the two rats raced after the dancing lights, a third flame appeared, then a fourth. They stayed just out of reach, weaving merrily around one another. Slegg made an awkward swipe at the nearest flame; it evaded him, wisping off to join its partners. Gridj gave a snort of irritation.

"Leave 'em alone, stoopid, if'n ye try to grab 'em they might fly off alt'gether!"

But Slegg ignored him and chased after the twinkling lights, crowing like an infant. "Cummere, liddle mateys, ole Slegg won't 'urt ye, come to me now, I knows ye won't burn me. Stand on me paws an' I'll carry ye for awhile."

He chased the four flames with outstretched paws, bumbling and stumbling as he dashed headlong through the storm-buffeted woodlands. Almost mockingly, the quartet of eerily glowing lights stayed nearly, but not quite, within the rat's reach.

Gridj, not relishing being left alone amidst the night-dark trees, chased after Slegg, calling, "Yore gonna git lost good'n'proper if'n ye don't slow down, I warn ye!"

Then Gridj tripped on a protruding root and went down face-first. Spitting out dirt, and pawing mud from his eyes, he peered about into the rainy gloom. "Slegg, where are ye?"

The older rat's reply seemed to come from directly ahead. It was the cry of a beast in trouble. "Gridj . . . mate . . . O 'elp me, I'm guuuuurrrrggghhh!"

There was no sight of the four pale lights. Gridj went forward on all fours, shouting, "Wot's 'appened, mate? Slegg, are yew alright?" Alarm bells went off in Gridj's head as he felt his paws beginning to sink into the suddenly soft woodland floor. Pulling himself loose, he scrabbled backward until his back encountered a purple willow. Grabbing a bough of the tree, he hauled himself upright, staring in horror.

The four twinkling lights were flickering around Slegg's head. He had run straight into a swamp, and was sinking at an alarming rate. Frozen with horror, Gridj could only watch as his companion's head, illuminated by the lights, sank further. Slegg's final gurgle was stifled by a fearful sucking noise, then he was gone forever.

Rigid with terror, Gridj watched the lights sweep around him. Frightened out of his wits, he babbled, "Stay away from me, wot d'yer want, why did ye lead me pore mate inter the swamp like that, we weren't doin' ye no harm, we was only goin' t'the seashore, 'twasn't our fault we got lost. . . ."

Cruel claws seized Gridj, ramming his head hard into the tree trunk. A net was thrown over him and secured tightly. Through the net holes he gazed, half-stunned, at the pale lights dancing closer.

A harsh voice hissed, "Hakkah, the Doomwytes have got you now, rat!" His head was banged against the tree trunk again. Gridj fell into the dark pit of senselessness, all hopes of visiting the seashore gone forever.

2

Brother Torilis rapped briefly on the Abbot's chamber door before entering. He bore a steaming beaker to the bedside. "Good morning, Father Abbot, did you sleep well?"

The Abbot of Redwall, a fat, old, hairy-tailed dormouse named Glisam, sat up slowly, removing his tasselled night-cap. Sighing, he gazed out into the grey dawn. "Not much change in the weather, Brother."

Torilis placed the beaker on the table, close to paw. "That wind has died down. 'Tis not a cold day, but still raining, I'm afraid, Father."

Abbot Glisam got creakily out of bed, lowering himself gingerly into his favourite armchair. "Rain and the rheumatiz go together, y'know. My poor old joints are creaking like a rusty gate."

The Herbalist moved the beaker closer to Glisam. "That's why I brought you musselshell and agrimony broth. You'll feel better once you've taken it."

Glisam used his nightgown sleeves to protect his paws against the hot beaker. He pulled a wry face as he took a perfunctory sip.

"Sometimes I think I'd be better off just putting up with the rheumatiz. This stuff tastes foul, absolutely horrid!"

Brother Torilis ignored his Abbot's protest. "You must

13

drink it up, every drop. Sea otters brought those mus-selshells all the way from the north beach rocks, and I scoured the ditchsides to get that agrimony. The broth is a sovereign remedy for rheumatism in older creatures. Drink!"

The fat, old dormouse kept sipping under the pitiless eye of the stern squirrel. When the last drop was drained, Glisam tossed the beaker down on the table. "Yakkkblech! Rotten broth, it'll kill me before it cures me, mark my words, Brother!"

The Abbey's head cook, Friar Skurpul, came bustling in, a jolly mole in his prime season. "Burrhoo, zurr h'Abbot, Oi bringed ee a candy chesknutter, hurr, 'twill taken ee narsty taste away!"

Glisam gratefully accepted the candied chestnut. Cramming it in his mouth, he munched away at the sweet tidbit. "Mmm mmm, thankee, friend!"

The good Friar helped his Abbot get dressed. "Yurr naow, this un's a noice clean habit. Oi warmed it on ee kitching oven furr ee, zurr."

Glisam nestled into the clean, warm garment. "Ooh, that's comfy, better than all those stinky concoctions for rheumatiz. I feel better already!"

Brother Torilis merely sniffed. "That will be my broth working. Shall we go down to breakfast, Father? You have to hear young Bisky, I put him on report last night."

Leaning on Torilis and the Friar, Abbot Glisam went haltingly downstairs, speaking his thoughts aloud, mainly to Skurpul. "Dearie me, what's poor young Bisky been up to now? I do so hate to sit in judgement, dishing out penalties and punishments, especially to young uns."

Torilis kept his eyes straight ahead, declaring firmly, "Well, that is one of the duties of a Father Abbot. Things can't always be candied chestnuts and warm robes, can they?"

Glisam patted the Brother's paw. "You're right, Torilis,

thank you for reminding me of my responsibilities. You know, sometimes I wonder about being Father Abbot of Redwall Abbey. Mayhaps I might have been better suited as a cook, a gardener or even a Gatekeeper."

Friar Skurpul chuckled. "Nay, zurr, you'm bees a h'Abbot, an' gurtly beluvved boi all, hurr aye!"

No matter what the occasion, Glisam seldom lacked an appetite. He shuffled eagerly to his seat at top table. Redwall's Great Hall was packed with mice, squirrels, hedgehogs, moles, otters and sundry other woodlanders. Everybeast rose as the Abbot came to table and recited morning grace.

"Throughout each passing season,
in fair or stormy weather,
we live, work, eat and rest,
in Redwall here together.
Attend ye to this day's first meal,
in friendship, truth and peace,
enjoy the fruits of honest toil,
and may good fortune never cease."

There was a clatter of benches as the Redwallers seated themselves. Helpers were busy lighting extra lanterns to brighten the hall; outside it was still raining and overcast. Between the tall fluted sandstone columns, long stained-glass windows echoed to the continued patter of rain-drops. Water running down the panes of many-coloured rock crystal glass created a liquid pattern of various hues, casting a soft rainbow effect upon the worn stone floor. The Abbot gazed at it, letting his thoughts wander. It was many seasons since he had been appointed to his exalted position, but he was still a humble beast, the first dor-mouse ever to reign as Father of the legendary Abbey. A squirrelmaid server broke into his reverie.

"Mornin', Father, will ye be takin' some oatmeal?"

Glisam nodded. "Half a bowl please, Perrit."

She measured it from a steaming cauldron on her trolley. "Honey, too, Father?"

Glisam smiled at her, she was extremely pretty and neat. "Oh, yes please, and some nutflakes if you'd be so good, Perrit. Hmm, and mayhaps a few slivers of fruit."

Deftly, she dribbled clear golden honey on the oatmeal, adding flakes of almond, chestnut and hazelnut, topping the bowl off with some crystallised slices of apple, pear and autumn berries.

The Abbot dug his spoon in, stirring it all up. "Thank you, that's just the way I like it!"

Duty servers went back and forth between the diners, distributing the delicious fare for which the ancient Abbey was so renowned. Bread in different shaped rolls, farls and loaves, hot and crusty from the ovens, honey or preserves to spread upon it. Oatmeal, scones and savoury pasties were passed to and fro amidst the beakers of fruit juice and hot herbal teas.

Sitting on the Abbot's right, Rorgus, the Skipper of Otters, used his keen-edged dagger to peel a russet apple in one winding, unbroken ribbon. He murmured to Glisam, directing his gaze to a solitary figure seated apart at the edge of the bottom table, "Torilis tells me that young Bisky's got hisself in the soup agin, Father. On report, ain't he?"

The Abbot accepted a slice of the russet apple from the otter's bladetip, and nibbled on it. "Aye, I'm afraid he is, Skip. Why can't that young scamp behave himself?"

Friar Skurpul's older brother, Foremole Gullub Gurrpaw, seated on the Abbot's left, emitted a deep bass guffaw. "Ahurrhurrhurr! A 'coz ee'm young, zurr, they'm young uns allus a-gittin' in trubble, 'tis gudd fun. Wot bees the point o' bein' a young un if'n ee carn't git into trubble, I arsk ee!"

Abbot Glisam poured himself some hot mint tea. "Well,

let's hope the trouble Bisky got into isn't too bad. Then I won't have to come down on him with a heavy paw."

After breakfast, Abbot Glisam went down to Cavern Hole. It was not as huge as Great Hall, but still quite a comfortable, roomy chamber, frequently used by Redwallers. At present, Samolus Fixa was the only beast there, busy renovating a well-worn table. Samolus could repair anything, hence the tag, Fixa, which he had earned in bygone seasons. He was a mouse of indeterminate age, old, but very spry, and always active, with a sharp, intelligent mind.

Abbot Glisam sat in a corner niche, which had a cushioned ledge. When the weather outdoors was not good, he could often be found there, usually enjoying a post-breakfast nap. He spoke to Samolus. "Giving that table the tidy-up treatment, eh, Fixa?"

The old mouse put aside his mallet and pegs. "Aye, Father, this is still a fine bit o' furniture, almost as old as you or I."

Glisam smiled. "I didn't think anything was that old, friend, even a table. Still, you're making a fine job of it—is it almost finished?"

Samolus pressed the tabletop hard, trying to shake it. "Almost, Father. I've put new pegs between the joints and spruced it up with my little block plane. Nice wood, a good piece of elm." He smoothed the top with his paw. "See the grain, it'll look twice as pretty after a fair rubbing with beeswax, 'twill be good as new!"

The Abbot was about to take a closer look at the elm topgrain when Brother Torilis entered, beckoning curtly at the pair who were following. "Step lively, you two, come on. Stand up straight in front of Father Abbot, shoulders back, chins up!"

Glisam raised an eyebrow at the Brother. "You told me there was only onebeast on report."

Torilis glared at the young squirrel, Dwink. "This one

chose to pick an argument with me. He became insolent, so I put him on report, too."

Bisky blurted out, shaking his head vigorously, "It had nothin' t'do with Dwink, I started it, Father!"

Dwink pointed a paw at himself, raising his voice. "Don't listen to him, Father, I whacked him with a pillow, that's wot started it all. I just got fed up of hearing Bisky tellin' fibby stories!"

Torilis stamped a sandalled footpaw on the floor. "Silence, you'll speak only when you're spoken to!"

Bisky ignored the Brother, turning his wrath on Dwink. "They're not fibby lies, that was a true story about Prince Gonff. I know it for a fact, see, 'cos my ole grandunk told me, ain't that right, Samolus?"

The Abbot stood up, waving his paws until order was restored. He shook his head in bewilderment. "What is all this about, will somebeast please tell me?"

Torilis replied dramatically, "Father, it's all about a noisy pillow fight in the dormitory!"

Abbot Glisam scratched his bushy tail in agitation. "Well, who's 'Grandunk,' and what's he got to do with it?"

Samolus placed himself between Torilis and the accused pair of young ones. "I'm Grandunk, least that's wot Bisky calls me. Aye, an' he's every right to. From wot I've heard I think I can reason this out, Father. So let's calm down an' I'll tell ye wot I know of it, eh?"

Torilis drew himself up to his full height, glaring down his nose at Samolus Fixa. "We are here on a matter of an Abbot's Report. I don't see what it has to do with the like of you!"

"Brother!" Glisam interrupted sharply. "Hold your tongue, please, and don't speak to Samolus in that manner. Let's all sit down and hear what our friend has to say. Samolus?"

The old mouse bowed. "Thank ye, Father Abbot." He took up the narrrative. "My family goes back to the very founding of Redwall Abbey. I have made a record of it from

18

Sister Violet's archive collection in the Gatehouse. Martin the Warrior, our hero and founder, had, as you know, a lifelong companion, Gonff, the Prince of Mousethieves. I can trace my descent right back to the family Gonffen, as they later became known. During my research it became evident that young Bisky was also from a distant branch of the Gonffens. Two or three times removed, I believe, but still in the same bloodline of Prince Gonff."

There was quiet snort from Brother Torilis.

The Abbot cast him a reproving glance. "Brother, if you have other chores to attend, kindly leave us. Obviously you are cynical of our friend's claims, but I for one believe him."

Torilis arose, stalking frostily off. Bisky and Dwink exchanged grins as their Abbot spoke.

"Carry on, Samolus, this sounds most interesting."

The old mouse tugged his tail respectfully. "With yore permission, Father, I'll carry on workin' as I tell the tale. Marvellous how a job can help a beast like meself t'think clearly!"

All three listened intently as the story unfolded.

Bedraggled, wet, hungry and cold, Griv the magpie flew in circles. She had been flying all night; due to the storm, she had been blown off course several times. Now she was lost. Thankfully, the wind had subsided, but there was still heavy rain to contend with. On an impulse, Griv soared high into the dreary grey skies, searching the ground below until she found her bearings. There off to the left was the huge, rocky, forested mound. Winging to one side, the magpie zoomed down to where a meandering stream skirted the smaller foothills. Griv made an awkward landing in the lower boughs of a downy birch. With the quick, jerky head movements common to magpies, she righted her perch, giving voice to several harsh cries.

Four carrion crows appeared, as if from nowhere. Three stopped on the streambank, whilst their leader landed on the bough, alongside Griv. His hooded head cocked to one side as he addressed the magpie aggressively. "Haaark! What does the longtail do in this place?"

Griv was not intimidated, she rasped back at him, "Garraah! My business is with the Doomwyte, Korvus Skurr. He alone awaits my news."

Veeku, leader of the carrion crows, smoothed his shiny black plumage with a sharp beak, as if considering Griv's words. Then he nodded once. "Haark, you will follow us!"

Close by the stream, in the base of the hill, was an opening. Thickly growing reedgrass almost hid it from view. Escorted by the crows, Griv flew inside. It was a winding tunnel—they were forced to land and walk the remainder of the way. The filter of outside daylight died away as they progressed along the tunnel; a few torches and firefly lanterns illuminated their path. Rounding a bend in the rockwalled passage, Griv gasped at the sudden onslaught of sulphur fumes. The atmosphere became extremely humid, a sickly green glow bathed the tunnel in eerie light. Strange noises echoed from further ahead, like liquid boiling in a giant cauldron. This was interspersed with squeals, grunts, shrieks and the harsh chatter of big birds.

Griv and her crow escort emerged into an immense cave. The sight resembled some infernal nightmare from the brain of a madbeast. High up in the poisonous, mistwreathed recesses of the vast ceiling, water dripped from limestone stalactites. Further down, the walls glistened with crusted filth, rotting matter spotted with violently hued patches of fungi. Heaps of protruding, decayed and yellowed bones were piled up against the lower walls, quivering with a life of their own, as spiders and cockroaches hunted the countless squirming, wriggling insects who inhabited the nauseous debris. All around this hideous scene, birds were perched everywhere. There were a few magpies, like Griv, but the rest were dark carrion birds, jackdaws, choughs, crows and rooks. It was the crows who outnumbered the others.

The centre of the cavern floor was dominated by a large lake, which occupied more than half the total floor area. Its waters emanated clouds of yellowy green steam from the constantly bubbling liquid morass. Deep within the earth, some primeval, volcanic force was heating the water with its phosphorescent vapours. There were no seasons in the cave, only constant heat, and misty green opalescence.

There was an island in the middle of the lake, which gave the illusion of having no foundation, seeming to hover in the mist. The centre of this island was a lime-stone hill, surmounted by a monolithic statue of polished black obsidian. It was a monumental work, depicting a huge raven, with a snake draped about its neck. The reptile coiled several times around the raven's neck, ending up circling its host's head in the manner of a crown. Both the face of the raven, and the snake above it, contained eyeless sockets.

Veeku, leader of the carrion crows, was about to lead Griv toward the island, when the roll of a large drum boomed out. Veeku spread his wings, holding the magpie back. A party of a dozen crows and rooks came hurrying by. These were followed by several toads and lizards, all armed with sharpened bulrush spears. At the centre of the strange group a net was being hauled along. It contained Gridj, the unfortunate rat, who, with his late companion, had been wandering lost in the previous night's storm. Immediately, all the inhabitants of the cave began chanting. "The Wytessss! Wytessssss! Korvussssss!" Again the big drum sounded. A silence fell over the cave. One of the toads poked the captive with its bulrush spear, causing him to wake up moaning.

A harsh-voiced crow called out, "Karrah! We bring thee an outsider, O Korvus Skurr!"

As carrion birds go, the raven is one of the largest. However, Korvus Skurr was the biggest of all ravens. He looked even bigger with the live smoothsnake decorating his head as a crown. Korvus Skurr appeared directly beneath the statue—with one mighty swoop he made it from the island onto the cave floor, with hardly a full wingspread. Stretching up almost onto talon point, he spread his awesome wings, displaying their dark iridescence. His subjects greeted this with their coarse, grating tribute, making the cave echo. "Krahaaaaaah! Skuuuurrrrrr!"

Korvus turned to the four crows. "A gift from my Wytes, show me this outsider!"

The four hauled the net up, so that Gridj could be clearly seen, holding on to the meshes in an attempt to stand upright. The raven tyrant came close to the net, peering in at his captive. Just one glance at Korvus Skurr was enough for Gridj. The huge raven, with his heavy, murderous bill and wicked dark eyes was enough to unnerve anybeast.

The serpent he was wearing as a crown shoved its blunt nose toward the prisoner, tongue flickering as its beady reptilian eyes surveyed him. Gridj was immediately reduced to a blubbering, whimpering wreck.

"Oww, don't 'urt me Yer 'Ighness, I ain't done nothin' wrong, it was Slegg's fault, 'e led me astray through yore territ'ry. I was lost, just tryin' t'find me way out of it, that's all, I swear on me mother's whiskers!"

At a signal from Korvus, the toads grabbed the net, opening it at the top. They dragged Gridj up, so that his head was exposed, then retied the net, leaving him still imprisoned, but with his head free.

Terrified into silence, the rat stood trembling. Korvus paced up and down in front of his captive, then suddenly snapped out, "Kraaak! Where are the Eyes of the Great Doomwyte?"

Gridj was surprised for a moment, but he replied as respectfully as he could, "Wot d'yer mean, 'Ighness? I don't know nothin' about no eyes, on me honner I don't."

Korvus moved like lightning, latching his lethal beak onto Gridj's ear and wrenching his head so that he could see the statue on the island. "Behold the Great Doomwyte! Where are its eyes?"

Wincing under the pain of the raven's beak, Gridj wailed, "Waaaah! I never seen that thing afore, Yer 'Ighness, I don't know wot yore talkin' about! Believe me!"

The raven released his prisoner as the snake hissed, "Hold him where I can sstare into hisss eyesss!"

With talon and beak, a gang of carrion birds held Gridj upright and motionless. Two toads scrambled up the net and gripped his head, pulling back the rat's eyelids, forcing him to look.

Korvus came close again, allowing the smoothsnake to come eye to eye with Gridj. The flickering tongue was touching Gridj's nosetip as the serpent spoke.

"Nobeast can lie to Sicarissss. I sssseek the truth in your eyessss, let me gaze into your hidden secretsss!"

Gridj had no choice, gripped tightly as he was, his stare forcibly held upon the reptile. Slowly, slowly, Sicariss weaved a pattern with her head, moving from one side to the other. The rat's eyes began following, until they were moving automatically. Sicariss moved even closer, whispering strange, sibilant things to Gridj. His mouth scarcely moved, but low words were coming from it in a kind of sighing monotone.

The snake halted her interrogation by drawing back, and tapping her chin lightly on the raven's beak. Korvus allowed Sicariss to take up her perch upon his head plumes. She whispered to him, "The beast isss not from these partsss, he knowssss nothing of the Eyessss, he issss brainlesssss!"

Korvus Skurr took off. Flying into the sulphur-laden fumes of his cave, he circled, casting his swift, dark eye on those awaiting his pronouncement. Landing gracefully on the island, directly at the base of the statue, he made two choppy movements with his beak. One at the rat, still imprisoned by the net, the other to the steaming, bubbling pool. The cave echoed to the din of eager carrion birds. "Rakaaah! Skurr! Rakaaaah! Skurr!"

Gridj was still in a trance as the toads looped a rope

23

through the net and knotted it. He hardly felt himself being dragged to the rim of the pool. The constantly boiling water of the bottomless lake woke him—he gave one long, agonised scream. It cut through the cawing and harking of carrion birds, then he was gone, plunging down into the scalding depths of opaque green.

Veeku, the crow leader, tugged on the rope, watching the thermal action of the water bobbing the net-enveloped carcass of Gridj around beneath the surface. He turned to Griv the magpie. "Kraak! We will feast well tonight. Come, I will take you to Korvus Skurr now."

Outside, the driving rains continued to pound the forested hillside which housed the Doomwyte's domain. A dark beast moved like a storm shadow along the hillslopes, restless, ever alert. Ceasing its labours of digging away at the hillside, moving rocks and hacking at roots, the strong, sleek creature took up its post, like a sentinel upon the huge mound. Watching, waiting, planning, as its fierce, vengeful eyes gazed at the cavern entrance— the only way in and the only way out of the raven's foul realm. The dark beast stayed motionless, always watching, waiting, planning.

3

In the warmth and comfort of Cavern Hole, Abbot Glisam, Bisky and Dwink sat listening to Samolus Fixa talking as he worked upon restoring the old table. For all his long seasons, the sprightly old mouse seemed to have perfect recall.

"Aye, they were three lifelong pals, Martin the Warrior, Gonff the Mousethief and a mole called Dinny. Though ye could say they were four, 'cos there was Gonff's lovely wife, the Lady Columbine. Be that as it may, I'll go straight to wot I knows of the Wytes."

Dwink scratched at his bushy tail. "What are Wytes, what do they do, sir?"

The Abbot replied as Samolus searched through his box for a scribing tool, "I learned about Wytes from an old owl I once knew. Nobeast can say for certain what a Wyte is. It could be bird, reptile or some type of vermin, one has never been caught, or found dead. From what I've gathered, a Wyte is a sort of flickering light, which lives in the woodlands. They say that it can lead travellers astray."

Dwink interrupted, "You mean make 'em get lost, Father?"

Abbot Glisam settled both paws into his long sleeves. "Aye, completely lost, or gone forever. There's no record of anybeast turning up again, once they've been enchanted away by the Wytes."

Bisky snorted. "Hah, all 'cept Prince Gonff. No Wyte would ever steal him away, eh, Grandunk?"

Samolus had found his scribe. He began marking out a design upon the tabletop with its sharp, little iron spike, not taking his gaze from the work as he answered, "That's true, but ole Gonff, he weren't silly enough to go off followin' Wytes, 'twas a totally different thing wot led him to their lair." Samolus paused to resharpen his scribe point with a file.

The Abbot enquired, "How do you know all this, where d'you keep all the research you say you've collected? Did you make notes?"

The old mouse tested the scribe point on one pawpad. "'Tis not just notes, Father, it's reasonin', ponderin' an' keepin' yore wits about ye. Oh, I've got lots of notes, the main two bein' Dinny's mole scrolls an' Lady Columbine's diary. I don't doubt ye'd like to see 'em. Right, then, come along wi' me. I've done enough 'ere for awhile, my eyes gets tired easy these days."

Abbot Glisam opened the Abbey building's main door. It was raining hard. He stared glumly out across the lawns and flowerbeds, to the western outer wall. On one side of the threshold gate stood the small Gatehouse. Pulling up his hood, Glisam complained, "Do we really have to go all the way over there in this downpour, just to look at some records?"

Dwink hopped eagerly from one footpaw to the other. "Oh, come on, Father, if'n you run we'll get there in no time." The young squirrel grinned cheekily. "I'll race ye, Father Abbot!"

Glisam shook his head ruefully. "Alas no, Dwink, my running seasons are long gone."

Samolus went into a sporting crouch. "Here, young un, I'm about the same age as our Abbot, I'll race ye. . . . On y'marks, get set—go!"

26

They shot off into the rain like two arrows.

Glisam chuckled. "Just look at them go! Who d'you think'll win, Bisky?"

"My old grandunk of course, Father, he can still beat me, an' I'm a faster runner'n Dwink. Come on, Father, watch ye don't slip on the wet grass."

Paw in paw, the old dormouse and his young friend shuffled off into the curtains of sheeting rain. If they could not be bothered to skirt puddles, they simply trudged through them. The Abbot suddenly did a little jump, causing a splash. He laughed.

"Good fun, really, isn't it? I can't remember the last time I had a good old splash and splosh."

Bisky kicked out, sending a sheet of water widespread. "Let's sing the Dibbuns' rainsong, Father!"

It was just as well that Brother Torilis was not there to witness the undignified performance: young Bisky and the Father Abbot of Redwall Abbey, roaring the song as they cavorted happily about in the rain.

"When the clouds are cryin' rain,
we run outdoors an' play,
splash an' splosh about in pools,
splash an' splosh all day!

Jump about an' wot do y'get,
'tis only rain, you just get wet ,
get wet as y'like an' it's alright,
then we won't need a bath tonight!

Splashin' here an' splashin' there,
splishin' sloshin' everywhere,
sloppy sandals soakin' fur,
up to bed you naughty pair!
Splish diddly splash splash . . . splosh splosh!"

Young Umfry Spikkle, the big hedgehog Gatekeeper cum Bellringer, called from the Gatehouse doorway to Bisky and the Abbot. "Come in h'out that there rain afore youse catches a dose h'of the chewmonia, 'urry up. Sam'lus an' Dwink 'ave been 'ere awhile, waitin' for ye."

Bisky stood aside, letting the Abbot enter first. "Who won the race, Umfry?"

Dwink showed himself, drying his handsome brush off with a towel. "Huh, your ole grandunk, that's who!"

Samolus could be seen within. He was trotting about in small circles, his eyes twinkling. "Glad I ain't young no more—got no energy, these young uns today, heeheehee!"

Umfry was still a youngish hog, a simple type who was not overburdened with learning. However, nobeast ever remarked on this, because he was a big hedgehog of prodigious strength. He tossed the newcomers a warm towel apiece, and poured two beakers from a kettle resting on the hearth. "Youse drink this down, h'its coltsfoot an' burdock tonic. Mind now, h'its 'ot!"

Samolus stopped jogging. "Be a goodbeast an' give me a lift up t'the rafters, Umfry. I've got some stuff stowed up there that we need to look at."

Umfry lifted the old mouse over his head, as though he were merely placing a book back on a high shelf. "I never knew you was 'idin' stuff up there, Sam'lus, wot sort o' stuff is it?"

Reaching into a recess where two rafters crossed, Samolus brought out a parcel of scrolls, and two books. "Oh, it's just some ancient records. Nothing that'd interest you, Umfry."

The burly hedgehog placed Samolus carefully on the gatehouse floor. Samolus tossed the parcel on the table. "Ole records, eh? I never been able t'make spike or snout o' that written stuff, h'it's like a pile o' wriggly worms t'me."

Abbot Glisam patted the Gatekeeper's hefty paw. "I'll have to see about reading lessons for you, young fellow. Meanwhile, you just sit quiet and listen while Samolus reads to us."

The old mouse took up a beautifully bound little vol-

ume, the front of which was adorned with a skilful drawing of a dainty flower. "See, this is a columbine, just like
Gonff's wife's name. It was her diary." He leafed slowly
through the pages of neat, close-written script.

"Ah, here 'tis, listen to this. . . ."

I could tell that Gonff had been stealing again. As soon
as he came in last evening. It made me feel very anxious
for him. My Gonff is no ordinary thief, he'd never steal
from good creatures, but if he takes a fancy to something
owned by a foebeast, a vermin or any evil creature, then
he'll steal it. I didn't say anything, knowing that he'd
tell me all about it, sooner or later. It was a warm summer evening, we took supper on the banks of the Abbey
pond, with some of our friends. Martin the Warrior was
off on a quest, so I sat with my Gonff, and our dear mole
friend Dinny. It was he who noticed that all was not well
with Gonff.

"Yurr zurr, you'm not a scoffen ee vikkles much. Wot
bees up with ee, zurr Gonffen, you'm gone aseedingly
soilent. Coom on, mate, owt wi' et!"

Gonff took us both to a quiet corner of the orchard,
not wanting any other Redwaller to hear what he had to
say. It was a strange tale he related.

"A few nights back I was out on one of my rambles, in
Mossflower Wood, when I saw an odd thing. Two little
lights, pale, flickerin' flames, dancin' about in the darkness, as pretty as you please. At first, I felt like going to
see just what they were, but something warned me not
to show myself, so I stayed hidden, in a yew thicket.

"Then I spotted the stoat. He was a fat, raggedy vermin, swiggin' away at a big flask o' grog. I could smell
the stuff, even from where I was, it was foul, probably
made from bogweed an' withered berries. So I watched
Mister Stoat, he was bumblin' along, bumpin' into everythin' an' singin' a vermin drinkin' song that'd curl yore
ears. He caught sight o' the two little flames, the fool.

29

Gigglin' like a Dibbun an' offerin' 'em drinks o' grog, he goes staggerin' off after those tiny lights. I stayed where I was for a moment, then went off quietly, followin' t'see what'd happen.

"Now I know my way round Mossflower better'n most beasts, an' I could tell that we were near to the eastern marshes. Not a place that any creature with a grain o' sense'd go wanderin' about in the dark o' night. I stopped on firm ground an' saw it all. The lights led that ole raggy stoat on a right merry dance, jiggin' about, just out of his reach. Round an' round they danced him, then they took off, straight over the marshes. Before I could do anythin', the stoat chased after the two lights.

"Needless t'say, he went down into the swamp like a stone. Right up to his chin, an' sinkin' fast he was, with the two little lights hoverin' over him. I couldn't quite make it all out, but they seemed t'be whisperin' to the stoat. Somethin' about whites, hissing softlike, it sounded like . . . Wytessssss!

"Then he was gone, under the mud, never t'be seen again. I've never liked vermin as y'know, but I felt a bit sorry for the stoat, bein' murdered in that horrible way. I say murdered, because that's wot those two pretty little flames did to the pore fool, lured him off an' murdered him. So I decided to trail the lights an' see where they went. Two points east an' one point south they headed, or as otters'n'shrews say, east sou'east! Then it was me that felt foolish—the tiny flames vanished altogether, just afore dawn.

"Aye, there I was, trailin' empty air, I began to doubt I'd ever seen those two little lights. So, I had a bite o' brekkist, a drink from a stream an' climbed an elm tree to get my bearin's.

"There's some nice country over that way, parts I've never seen. But I recognised the big hill over to the east, I'd seen it before, but never been there. Huge high mound,

30

all covered in trees an' woodland. Did those little flames go to the hill? I decided to go an' take a look myself.

" 'Twas a stretch o' the paws, I can tell ye! Daylight was beginnin' to fade when I made it to a stream runnin' round the base o' the main mound. Things seemed to grow thicker in that part, there was no shortage of growin' vittles. Apples, pears, nuts an' berries, all up an' ripened, well before autumn. It felt warmer, too, just like those places the ole sea otters tell about, beyond the sunset, over the great seas. Just then I hears birds, cawin' an' cacklin', carrion birds, crows an' the like, four of 'em. I saw them flap by, they didn't spot me. Next thing they were gone! Crossin' the stream, I found the place. An entrance, all grown over with reeds an' trailin' vines. Well, bein' a Prince o' Mousethieves, I'd never turn away an' leave it unexplored, so in I went!

"It was a long, twisty, rock tunnel, more than paw deep in streamwater. After awhile there was a few lit torches, an' firefly lanterns, hangin' from the walls. The air became close an' hot, awful smelly, too, like rotten eggs. Then I came round a sharp bend and into a cavern—it was so massive that it could have held Redwall Abbey an' all its grounds inside! Everything was in a sort of green light. There were carrion birds perched every where, reptiles, too, lizards, toads, grass snakes an' birds flyin' round up near the ceiling. It was a dangerous place to be, so I hid behind a big heap of bones.

"Suddenly the cave became alive with noise, birds cacklin', toads croakin' an' a big drum bangin'. A gang o' the carrion an' reptiles came in, draggin' a net with two creatures trapped inside it. They lugged it to this big lake, in the middle of the cave. There was clouds o' the green mist comin' off this lake, it was bubblin' like a cauldron over a fire. There was an island at the centre of the lake, with a statue on it. The thing looked like a huge black bird, with a serpent coiled on its head, like a crown. But it was the eyes of the statue that caught my attention. Four of 'em, great, glitterin' jewels, two red for the bird, an' two green for the snake. They shone like fire, twinklin' an' dazzlin' like stars!"

Bisky whispered to Dwink, "The Eyes of the Great Doomwyte, see, I told you it was true. . . ."

Samolus silenced Bisky with a glare. He turned back to the ancient diary as Umfry Spikkle interrupted eagerly, "Wot 'appened next, Sam'lus, tell h'us more!"

Abbot Glisam reprimanded the big Gatekeeper mildly. "Hush now, Umfry, give Samolus a chance."

The old mouse turned the yellowed pages slowly.

"Then a giant crow, with a snake curled about his head, just like the statue, came flyin out o' the mist. All the birds an' reptiles started chantin', 'Rigvar Skurr! The Wytessss! The Wytesss!' Then the big drum set off to boomin' again. From where I was hidin', I could see that the two trapped in the net were Guosim shrews, friends of Redwall. But there was nothing I could do to help them. It was horrible wot happened to those two pore beasts, too awful to tell ye."

Samolus paused as he turned the page. "Lady Columbine takes up the story now."

My Gonff would speak no more about the fate of the Guosim shrews. He sat quiet awhile, breathing in the sweet scent of the orchard before he spoke again.

"How lucky we are to be living in this beautiful Abbey, able to breathe clean air, and see the sky above. Just the thought of that cave gives me the shivers, but some good came out of it. Everybeast has to sleep sometime, that was when I took my revenge on those evil ones, for the cruel way they slew those shrews. I stole what seemed to me their most treasured possessions, and escaped the cave without being noticed. For am I not Gonff, the Prince of all Mousethieves!"

Bisky clapped his paws with delight. "Ha ha, good ole Prince Gonff, he swiped the eyes out o' the statues!"

Samolus tweaked the young mouse's ear. "Excuse me, who's telling this tale, me or you?"

Smilingly, the Abbot corrected him. "Lady Columbine, I think, friend. You're only the reader."

Samolus sniffed. "Good, then perhaps you'll allow me to carry on with my reading. Right, back to Columbine."

Gonff produced a cloth bag from his jerkin, and gave it to me. There were four stones in it, each the size of a dove's egg. They were brilliant, two as red as embers in a winter night's fire, the other two as green as sunlight shining through a mossy pool.

"These are for you, my dear," said Gonff.

However, I could not think of accepting such gifts, and gave him my reason for refusing. "If these jewels are the eyes of the statue you told me of, then they have seen many evil deeds. I could not wear them, touch them, and I feel very uneasy just looking at them. You must put them somewhere where they will never again be seen. Someplace where they will not bring danger to Redwall. If their owners ever find out it was you who stole the eyes of their statue, it could bring death to our Abbey. They are stones of ill fortune!"

Samolus closed the book. "So there you have it, Father, the tale young Bisky told was mostly true, with just a few words of his own invention to make the recital of it more thrilling. Is that not right, young un?"

The young mouse shrugged self-consciously. "Aye, just as ye say, Grandunk. But wot happened to the Eyes of the

33

Great Doomwyte? Did Prince Gonff ever tell where he'd hidden them?"

Abbot Glisam let his curiosity show. "Indeed, it would be very interesting to know. Is there nothing in Lady Columbine's book?"

Samolus shook his head. "Nothing at all, Father, she never mentions the subject again. But do you see this other book, and these scrolls, that I had hidden in the rafters? Well, this book belonged to Gonff, it's one long riddle from beginning to end. As for the scrolls, they're the mole Dinny's notes."

Dwink chimed in brightly, "Please, sir, could we have a look through them, maybe we could find some clues. . . ."

Abbot Glisam perked up suddenly. "What fun that would be. May we look, Samolus? I don't suppose there'd be any harm in just looking. Who knows, we may even find the jewels."

The old mouse willingly placed the material on the Gatehouse table. "Be my guest, friends. I've taken a good peek through 'em meself an' had no luck. So if you think ye can translate the scribbles of a mousethief, an' the squiggled ramblin's of a mole, yore welcome to 'em!"

Bisky leapt upon Gonff's journal. "Leave this to me, pals, I'll find those jewels!"

Abbot Glisam forestalled him, by gathering up the lot. "Of course you will—straight after your kitchen duties, and lunch. Is it still raining outside?"

Umfry poked his spiky head outside the Gatehouse door. "Aye 'eavier than h'ever, Father. We'll 'ave to put these towels h'over us an' run for it."

Carrying the records between them, they donned towels and dashed over the waterlogged lawns, through the pelting, wet curtains of rain.

Abbot Glisam took charge of the volumes and scrolls. Samolus and Umfry went to visit the wine cellars, which were jointly run by Foremole Gullub Gurrpaw and Umfry's grandfather, Corksnout Spikkle. Old Corksnout was

34

the biggest hedgehog who ever lived, or so they said. An injury in a bygone battle had robbed him of his nose, but the ever resourceful Samolus fashioned him a new one from a keg cork attached by a string to his headspikes. Even Umfry was dwarfed by the size of his grandfather. Bisky and Dwink both reported to Friar Skurpul in the kitchens, where they were assigned duties.

The mole Friar looked them up and down. "Hurr, young uns, you'm bees soaken frum ee rain. Hmm, 'ow wudd ee loike a job on ee warm uvvens, pullen owt breadloaves. That'll dry ee!"

Gratefully the pair hastened to join the oven crew, and began using long wooden paddles to retrieve freshly baked items. They joined in with their mates, singing what they termed the "Oven Shanty." Helping on the ovens was a chore enjoyed by all the young Abbeydwellers. Side by side, they wielded the long beech paddles, roaring out the verses lustily, like sea otters aboard ship.

"Vittles don't get cooked by themselves.
Ho paddle away, mates, paddle away!
Paddle 'em from the hot oven shelves,
then paddle in plenty new vittles oh!

All fresh an' crusty that's the job,
Ho paddle away, mates, paddle away!
Each farl an' loaf or twist an' cob,
there's nowt like new baked bread oh!

Step lively now an' paddle those pies,
Ho paddle away, mates, paddle away!
Some scones for the Abbot, a nice surprise,
an' maybe a raspberry tart oh!

Who bakes such wunnerful things as these?
Ho paddle away, mates, paddle away!
With onion gravy an' bubblin' cheese?
'Tis Redwall's kitchen crew oh!

So heave an' ho an' paddle oh.
Kick open that door an' load in more,
afore we're all done paddlin' oooooooohhhh!"

Frintl placed a big plum cake on Bisky's paddle. She smiled sheepishly at him. "Sorry I snitched to Brother Torilis about you, I just couldn't help myself."

Bisky smiled as he shot the cake along the oven shelf. He wiped a paw across his brow cheerfully. "It turned out pretty well for me, don't fret, matey!"

4

Contrary to popular hopes, the rain didn't stop after lunch. If anything it seemed to increase, driven by a gusting east wind. This meant that the young ones, and particularly the Dibbuns, could not play outdoors. The molebabe Dugry and his trusty aide, a tiny squirrelmaid called Furff, were leading a band of their companions to the main Abbey door, until they were confronted by Skipper Rorgus. The brawny otter gave them a comical scowl.

"Shudder me rudder, I've caught a band o' deserters!"

None of the Dibbuns feared Rorgus, they thought he was quite amusing. Furff wrinkled her snub nose at him. "Wot's bandazerters?"

Rorgus allowed Furff to clamber up until she was perched on his shoulder, then he winked at her. "A band o' deserters, me liddle darlin', are scamps who run away when their friends need 'em."

Molebabe Dugry began the ascent of Skipper's legs. "Burr, we'm b'aint runnen 'way, zurr, us'ns jus' loikes t'goo owtsoide an' get soaked wet in ee rain!"

Rorgus clasped a paw dramatically to his brow. "Haharr, don't go, mates, ye'll all be drowned out there. Parts o' that lawn are flooded deeper'n yore liddle heads. Stay indoors, I begs ye!"

A very tiny mouse spread his paws wide. "I soona get drownded. Wot us do in 'ere, eh, nuthin'!"

Skipper crouched down, looked left and right, squinting one eye, and beckoned them close. He spoke in a secretive whisper to the Dibbun band. "Nothin'? You mean pore ole Skipper's goin' t'be all on his own up in that dormitory?"

The very tiny mouse whispered back to Rorgus, "Worra you do up inna dormitty?"

The otter confided in a low, urgent tone, "I gotta ship up there, ready to set sail right away. I'm goin' on a trip until this rain stops an' I finds a rainbow. But I needs a crew—anybeast knows where a pore Skipper can find strong, trusty beasts?"

There was an immediate clamour of volunteers. A moment later, Rorgus was labouring up the stairs, laden down by his clinging crew. Abbot Glisam, who had overheard everything, smiled as he watched them go.

"I think our Skipper should keep them amused. You know, I'm not sure who enjoys that otter's games more, him or the Dibbuns."

Violet, the jolly hedgehog Sister, shook her head. "A table turned upside down, with one o' my good bedsheets for a sail. Those liddle uns do 'ave fun!"

Samolus nodded wearily. "So they do, Sister, an' what pray will we get. A table for me to fix, an' a torn bedsheet for you to mend. That'll be Skipper's ship!"

Glisam agreed with both his friends. "Aye, that's how it usually ends, but you wouldn't begrudge the babes a bit of enjoyment on a rainy day, would you now?"

Sister Violet adjusted the fussy embroidered cap she always wore. "Gracious me, Father, I'd be the last one to complain. In fact, I think I'll go to the kitchens and make a small parcel of provisions for those poor mites on their long voyage."

Stifling a chuckle, the Abbot turned to Samolus. "I'm glad they won't go hungry. So, my old friend, what'll we do with the rest of our day?"

Samolus scratched his tail, as if it were a weighty decision. "Hmm, let me see. Ah yes, I thought we might join our young friends, Bisky, Dwink and Umfry, just to sort out Prince Gonff's journal, and find where he hid those precious jewels."

They gathered in the cellars to begin their research. Apart from the sounds of Corksnout and Gullub Gurrpaw working amongst the barrels, it was relatively peaceful. Using a barrelhead as a table, they sat near a forge, where the Cellarkeepers burnt old cask staves to make charcoal. It was pleasantly warm amidst the fragrant aromas of charred oak, October Ale, maturing wines and fruit cordials.

Abbot Glisam tossed Gonff's journal to Bisky. It was an ordinary, green-covered volume, with an elaborate letter *G* written on it to denote its owner. The Abbot shook his head.

"I glanced through that during lunch. One thing's certain: Gonff might have been the Prince of Mousethieves, but he was nowhere near as neat and concise as Lady Columbine. The whole thing is a frog's dinner, just look at it!"

With Dwink and Umfry leaning over both his shoulders, Bisky did. At first he tried to study the notes carefully, but he ended up merely riffling through the worn and dog-eared pages.

"I see what you mean, Father, how is anybeast supposed to make tail or snout of this? It's a mess, a jumble of scribbles and silly little sketches."

Dwink took the book, opening it at the centre pages. "Aye, it's a hotchpotch alright, but listen to this:

'Red'n'green green'n'red
gouged out of an idol's head
spurned by flower red'n'green
for the evil ye have seen
where are they, four magic lights
seek for them in vain, ye Wytes.'"

Samolus took the book. "I've read this bit a few times over the seasons, 'tis one of the few bits that makes sense. At least it confirms that Prince Gonff stole the stones and hid them. It also verifies Columbine's version of the story."

Umfry stared hard at the words, rubbed his eyes and enquired, "How d'ye make that h'out, Sam'lus?"

It was Bisky who explained it to Umfry. "Look at the line, 'spurned by flower red'n'green.' Columbine is the flower, red and green are the jewels. Remember what she said in her diary. Lady Columbine refused to take the stones from Gonff, so he hid them."

Samolus glanced over at Bisky. "Well spotted, young un, do ye see anything else there? Take your time, go on, study the book."

The Abbot interrupted, "While you're searching, keep this in mind. It would be excellent if we stumbled immediately on where the stones are buried, or hidden, but I don't think that will be the case. We know Gonff's book is a mess of scribbles and sketches, none of them have much connection with the other. So, I think the exact location of the four stones will come out in due course. However, first we must establish which area they would be in."

Dwink was frankly baffled. "What are you sayin', Father?"

"He's sayin', young sir, that ye've got t'find the rough location. In the Abbey, or in its grounds, maybe out in the woodlands, or on the west flatlands. Find the approximate area, d'ye see now?"

They all turned to see Umfry's grandfather, Corksnout, leaning on some kegs behind them. The giant Cellarhog had been listening, as had his assistant, Gullub Gurrpaw.

Abbot Glisam bowed slightly. "Thank you, friend, maybe you'd like to help out here. That's if you and Gullub aren't too busy with your cellarwork."

The mole produced a tray, setting it down in front of them. On it were a few cheese wedges and a knife, three jugs and enough small sampling beakers to go around. He tugged his snout respectfully, as moles do. "Us'ns wudd be durlighted to join ee, zurr h'Abbot. May'aps you uns cudd 'elp uz, too."

Corksnout explained, "We've just broached three new barrels of fine October Ale, Father. Now we're judgin' which one we should use first. We'd appreciate your opinion. There's some cheese to nibble a'tween sups." Reaching over, he tweaked Umfry's chinspikes. "Aye, an' you, young hog, you can spend an hour or two down here everyday. Yore eddication has been sadly neglected. Startin' tomorrow, me'n Gullub will be teachin' ye to read an' write."

Umfry pulled a face, then set to with his friends. They applied themselves wholly to the ale and cheese. Old Samolus went at it with a will. "By the seasons, this is a good, nutty-tastin' ale! Er, wot's wrong with you young uns, not drinkin'?"

Bisky took a small taste, then screwed his face up. "I think we're a bit young to judge October Ale, sir, haven't you got any sweet cordial, or Strawberry Fizz?"

Gullub chortled as he tilted a firkin into a clean jug. "Hurrhurr, try summ o' moi danneloin'n'burdock corjul, likkle surr, be that'n sweet enuff furr ee?"

Bisky swigged it gratefully. "Oh, that is nice, Mister Gurrpaw, but we're not getting much solving done like this, are we?"

Corksnout had been riffling through Gonff's journal. He stopped at one page, placed a dainty, little pair of rock crystal spectacles on his cork appendage and peered closer at the script. "I don't know much about this Prince Gonff, but I'll say this, he must've been an aggravatin' little beast. See wot ye make o' this. . . .

"The bird has no buries, the snake no red meals,
two bruise and two mere lads, where are the nests O?
A pincer those five hid them well!"

41

The huge Cellarhog gave a scornful snort, which blew his cork nose up between his eyes. Dwink giggled. Corksnout adjusted the nose quickly, glaring at the young squirrel. "What'n the name o' my ole grannie's spikes is all that nonsense supposed t'mean, eh?"

Dwink replied meekly, "P'raps it's a riddle, sir."

Umfry grinned cheerily at his big grandsire. "H'I thought you would've guessed that, Granpa."

Corksnout clenched his paws and ground his teeth, as he searched for words to berate the pair.

Abbot Glisam defused the situation by addressing Umfry. "Oh, I've no doubt that your grandfather had guessed that as soon as he saw it, he's a lot smarter than most creatures. But it does sound like a load of nonsense, doesn't it? That's because it *is* a riddle, you see. Riddles are supposed to sound like that, or there wouldn't be much fun in trying to solve them. Now, you bright young uns, any ideas?"

Dwink and Umfry sat dumbly, staring at their beakers. Only Bisky had anything to say.

"Like Mister Spikkle said, Father, it's nonsense, the words are all mixed up, they don't make sense."

Samolus drained his beaker, and filled it from another jug. "Hah, then 'tis up to us to unmix those words, so they do make sense. Someone read it out again, please."

The Abbot obliged, speaking slowly and clearly.

"The bird has no buries, the snake no red meals,
two bruise and two mere lads, where are the nests O?
A pincer those five hid them well!"

Putting aside his beaker, Samolus began pacing the floor, giving rein to his powers of reason. "Right, let's keep this in mind. We're searching for the jewels that Gonff hid, long seasons ago. So, let's take this bit by bit. It's a message, cleverly designed by Gonff. We've got to be just as clever to solve it. I suggest we all look at it together, see which words look out of place and what clues they contain."

Glisam, Samolus, Bisky, Dwink and Corksnout sat study-ing the lines. Not being able to read, Umfry was at a loss. Gullub picked up the scrolls, which had been written by Gonff's molefriend Dinny. The kindly Cellarmole took Umfry to one side, away from the rest. "Yurr, maister, Oi'll read ee owt summ molescript."

Meanwhile, something occurred to Bisky as he looked at Gonff's writing. "Either Prince Gonff was an awful speller, or I've missed somethin' on this first line."

Dwink enquired, "Why so?"

Bisky tapped the page. "Look here, 'The bird has no bur-ies,' surely that's not right. If a bird had no berries to eat, that would be spelled like *berries*, the sort that grow on trees. But the way it's written here, that's like somebeast having to dig a grave. He buries the body, see what I mean?"

Corksnout nodded. "Yore right, young un, so why's it spelled like that, eh?"

Samolus ventured, "It could be an anagram."

Gullub suddenly began waving the piece of scroll parch-ment that he had been reading. "Hoourr! Nannygrammer! Et sez yurr ee Gonffen cudd make nannygrammers!"

Umfry scratched his headspikes. "Wot's a nannygrammer?"

The Abbot explained. "The correct name is an anagram. If you split the letters of a word apart, and put them back together so they spell a different word, that's an anagram. Maybe the word *buries* means something else."

Dwink took a charcoal stick and began using the barrel-head as a writing board. "Er, how do I split *buries* up?"

Samolus made a suggestion. "The best way to write it is to form the letters in a circle, like this."

They looked at it. Bisky shook his head. "Still looks pretty much mixed up, I can't see a new word."

The Abbot's eyes were twinkling. "Look closer, Bisky, think what we are searching for."

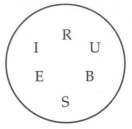

Dwink took a guess. "The eyes that Prince Gonff stole?"

Corksnout shouted out the solution. "Rubies, it's rubies!"

It was Bisky's turn to snort at the big Cellarhog. "Well, thanks for shouting it out, I almost had it before you started yelling. Rubies, eh."

Corksnout shuffled his huge footpaws. "Sorry, I got excited. Go on, you can have the next one."

Dwink looked baffled. "Wot next one?"

Samolus whispered in his ear, "I'd guess it'd be 'red meals.'"

Dwink murmured out of the side of his mouth, "Why d'you guess that?"

Bisky had been eavesdropping; he grinned from ear to ear. "Ha ha, I know wot 'tis without puttin' the letters in any circles. It's emeralds!"

The Abbot's expression was one of complete surprise. "Great seasons, how did you guess that so quickly?"

The young mouse winked broadly. "It just suddenly came to me, Father. Rubies was the first one. We're looking for red stones and green stones, two of each. So I thought, rubies are red, what jewels are green? I looked at the words *red meals*, and it sprang out at me. Emeralds!"

Corksnout rubbed his big paws together in a business-like manner. "C'mon, c'mon, wot's next, mates?"

Samolus read the next line out. "'Two bruise and two mere lads, where are the nests O?' Give me that charcoal and I'll write it down. I think 'two bruise' first, eh, Father?"

Abbot Glisam looked secretly pleased. "Don't write 'two

bruise,' just 'bruise' on its own. In fact I've got it, no need to write it down—"

Dwink sprang up. "Bruise, buries, same letters. It's rubies again."

Bisky chuckled. "So it is. Two rubies and two mere lads. Hah, mere lads. Sounds like an anagram of red meals. Emeralds! Two rubies and two emeralds. What's the rest? 'Where are the nests O?'"

Corksnout puffed out his chest, declaring, "That ole Prince Gonff wasn't so smart, tryin' to baffle brains like ours. Huh, rubies an' emeralds are jewels, they're precious. 'Nests O!' My grannie's spikes, that's stones, precious stones!"

Gullub Gurrpaw left off reading the mole scrolls and took his friend severely to task. "Oi wishes ee'd stop a-showtin' owt ee arnswers an' give they'm young uns a charnce, zurr. They'm'll lurn nawthen iffen ee doan't give 'em no h'oppertunery!"

Corksnout was mortified. He sniffed so hard that he unseated his false nose, almost swallowing it. Stalking off down the cellar floor, he called huffily, "I was only tryin' to help, but I'll get on with me own work, there's plenty for me to do, thankee!"

Umfry pointed an accusing paw at Gullub. "You've h'upset 'im now, Mister Gurrpaw!"

The mole gave a gruff bass chuckle. "Eem doan't loike wurkin' alone wi' cumpany abowt. Ole Corky'll coom back anon, mark moi wurd, zurr!"

Dwink wriggled excitedly. "Just one more line to solve!"

Abbot Glisam read the final segment out. "'A pincer those five hid them well.'"

Umfry began to complicate the issue. "Five 'idden well! Wot five, h'I thought we was h'only searchin' for four stones. H'another thing, wot's h'a pincer doin' h'in this riddle?"

Corksnout must have been listening. He called out from the corner where he was working, "I've got a fine pair of

45

pincers, for grippin' hot iron hoops when I 'ammers 'em into shape!"

Gullub smiled as he shouted back to his friend. "They'm pincers bees called tongs, zurr!"

The big Cellarhog strolled back to join them. He was wielding a pair of tongs. "Well, I've allus called 'em pincers, just like my dad did."

To avoid further argument, the Abbot agreed. "I knew your dad, so if he said they were pincers, that's good enough for me. Pincers they are!"

Corksnout donned his tiny glasses again, peering at the line on the page. "A pincer those five hid them well? That says *pincer*, not *pincers*. Wot are ye babblin' about pincers for?"

5

Without any warning there was a panicked squeak from outside the cellars. The young squirrelmaid Perrit came tumbling in, flinging her apron over her face, a sure sign of distress in little maids. She shrilled at them, "Eeeek! Father Abbot, Mister Sam'lus, come quickly!" She started running willy-nilly, but Corksnout swept her up in his strong paws.

"Now now, missie, wot's all the fuss about?"

Perrit peeked over her apron hem, she began babbling like a brook. "Oh, sirs, Skipper Korgus says for you to come to the big gate right away 'cos carrying birds tried to steal likkle Dugry!

The entire party went thundering up the cellar steps and across Great Hall. Samolus panted to Bisky as they ran together for the main Abbey door, "Carrying birds? I think the young un must've meant carrion birds. The robbin' scum!"

Slamming the doors open wide, they rushed out onto the rainswept lawns. Across at the outer threshold gate there were several creatures grouped about something. Running just behind Bisky and Samolus, Umfry Spikkle hooted out in alarm. "Hoi! Who opened the main gates, get 'em shut!"

Molebabe Dugry was being comforted by Sister Violet, who had the little fellow wrapped in a shawl, rocking him to and fro. "There there now, my dearie, the big, nasty bird has gone. Shame on him, tryin' to steal you away like that!"

Dugry seemed none the worse for his ordeal. He jabbed the air with a tiny paw, yelling gruffly, "Eem gurt naughty burd carried Oi roight h'up inna sky. Roight, roight 'igh h'up Oi go'd!"

Abbot Glisam arrived panting. He leant on Skipper, gasping for breath. "Whoo! What's been going on here?"

The Otter Chieftain pointed to the glittering bundle of dark plumage, slumped in the gateway. "'Twas a crow, Father, big, ugly bird. Tried to fly off with one of our Dibbuns."

Samolus ventured close to the bird. "Never heard o' that afore. Wot stopped it?"

Skipper Rorgus nodded to the gatehouse door. "He did, right in the nick o' time, too."

The door opened to reveal a mountain hare, clad in a green-and-lilac plaid kilt and tunic, with silver buttons at cuffs and collar. His fur was patched white and tan. Slung on his back was an odd instrument, resembling a fiddle. In one paw he carried a short, curved bow, fashioned from bone. The hare strode languidly over to the fallen bird. He turned the carcass over with a deft shove of one massive footpaw. There was a slim, flightless metal rod protruding from the crow's chest. Placing his footpaw on the dead bird, the hare tugged until the rod came free. With a grimace of distaste he tossed the rod to Bisky.

"Here, laddie, would ye be sae kind as tae wipe ma arrow clean, Ah cannae abide dirty shafts!" From the lace ruffles at the hem of his tunic sleeve, he drew forth a daintily embroidered silk kerchief which gave off the scent of heather and lilac. Wiping it fastidiously over the paw which had held the metal rod, he twirled the kerchief, making an elaborate bow as he introduced himself. "Guid day to ye, even though the weather is a wee bit inclement. Ah'm the Laird Bosie McScutta o' Bowlaynee, at y'service!"

The Abbot inclined a brief bow in return. "My pleasure, m'Laird, I am Glisam, Father Abbot of Redwall Abbey. My thanks for your brave and prompt action in saving the life of a Redwaller."

Accepting the cleaned-up shaft from Bisky, the hare slotted it into a built-in quiver, which formed the arm of his fiddle-like instrument. He shook Glisam's paw. "Ach, away with all that m'Laird stuff, ye can call me Bosie, or just plain hungry. D'ye no serve afternoon tea at this place?"

Glisam smiled. "Forgive me, of course we do, Bosie. Come, you'll be our honoured guest for what you've done. I hope little Dugry has thanked you."

Bosie set out for the Abbey, paw in paw with Glisam. "Land sakes, there's no need for that. Ah wouldnae be much o' a Warrior Minstrel if Ah let a crow scoot off with a wee molebairn. Ah was comin' doon the path outside when Ah heard the ruckus. Then who should be flappin' o'er yon wall but a roguey of a crow, with the bold, wee Dugry in his bill. So Ah dropped him wi' a single shaft. Bein' a thrifty beast, Ah never use more than one arrow on carrion like yon rascal. So, this is the braw Redwall Abbey. Ah've heard lot's o' guid things aboot it, especially the vittles."

The Abbot squeezed his new friend's paw. "I pride myself on saying that you won't be disappointed, Bosie!"

Back at the gate, Umfry was about to lock up, when Corksnout indicated the slain bird. "Don't shut yore gate yet. Lend a paw to sling this one into the ditch, the insects will make short work of him. I ain't hangin' about to dig holes for villains. You take the talons, an' I'll take the head. C'mon, young Dwink, you, too, grab a wing. Bisky, you get the other wing. Right, lift!"

As they manoeuvred the carcass across the path, which

ran north to south outside the Abbey, Corksnout spoke. "Y'know, I've been thinkin' about that word, *pincer*. I'll tell ye wot I think, it's an anagram of Prince."

Umfry chuckled. "Yore a clever ole grandad, I would 'ave never guessed that, would you, Dwink?"

The young squirrel replied airily, "Oh, I prob'ly would have, sooner or later. Wot are you grinnin' about, Bisky?"

His friend's grin became even wider. "I've solved it, or at least I think I have. Thanks for guessing that pincer was really Prince, Mister Spikkle. Right, let's put it all together, this is how it goes. . . ."

They paused on the edge of the ditch, listening as the young mouse explained.

"'The bird has no rubies, the snake has no emeralds, two rubies and two emeralds, where are the stones? A prince of thieves hid them well!' That's it!"

Corksnout grasped Bisky's paw and shook it heartily. "Yore right, young un, those two words after pincer, or Prince, *those five*, they're an anagram which comes out as . . . of thieves. But how did ye guess?"

Bisky explained, "I just kept repeatin' the lines as we'd solved them. Then when you said Prince, it all fell into place!"

The big Cellarhog cautioned them both. "Now don't ye go tellin' ole Gullub that I solved the pincer word, or he'll be gettin' all in a tizzy with me, moles are funny creatures sometimes, y'know."

Dwink released his hold on the dead bird. "I wish we had a mole with us now, I'll wager he'd dig a hole for this villain quick enough."

Umfry shook rainwater from his spikes. "We h'aint diggin' a buryin' 'ole, are we, Grandad?"

Corksnout shook his head so emphatically that his false nose wound up behind his ear. "We certainly ain't! I'll toss him in the ditch, wot the insects don't get will be gone by tomorrow. This rain'll flood the ditch an' wash everythin' away." He tipped the saturated jumble of feathers that had once been a crow over the edge of the ditch. Marching away without a backward glance, Corksnout called to the young ones, "Best put a move on, or afternoon tea'll be all gone."

Umfry hurried to catch him up. "Er, why's that?"

His grandfather was well versed in the habits of other beasts. "'Cos we got a hare to feed, have ye ever seen one o' those lollop-pawed rascals scoffin' vittles?" The three young friends confessed that they had not. Corksnout stepped up his pace. "Well ye've got a surprise in store!"

When they had gone, the dead crow stirred, but not of its own volition. Two other carrion crows that it had landed on top of emerged from the ditch, leaving their slain comrade. They were part of the mission to kidnap a Redwaller. Shaking mud from his plumage, the smaller of the two spoke fearfully.

"Kraaah, we cannot go back and tell Leader Veeku that his plan failed."

The larger crow disagreed. "Yakkarr, we have more to report. Did you not hear the earthcrawlers tell how a Prince of Thieves stole the Eyes of the Doomwyte? They must be hidden inside the big stone house!"

The smaller bird blinked his quick, dark eyes. "Karray, you are right, brother, we will tell him this!"

A moment later they were two dark shapes, flapping off into the pounding rain.

Beyond the great cave, which contained the eyeless statue, lay another cavern. Not as large as the main chamber, but still of an impressive size. This was the inner sanctum of Korvus Skurr, and his serpent, Sicariss. The interior was silent, save for the constant dripping of water. Firefly lanterns and smouldering torches made it a place of sinister elongated shadows. The climate was more temperate—it was not suffused by green mists from a volcanic pool. However, it did boast its own expanse of water, deep, still and icy cold.

The raven tyrant perched on a rock, overlooking the subterranean lake. He stared down into its translucent depths, watching the pale, sightless fish and other small reptilian denizens which dwelt there.

The snake, coiled on Korvus's head, stared unblinkingly at the long, sinuous bulk which was threading upward through the water. "Sssseeee, our Welzzz comesssss."

Even the tyrant, Korvus Skurr, was cautious of the monster fish. He drew back slightly from the edge of the rock on which he was squatting.

The fish was truly an impressively hideous sight. It was a wels, that fearsome giant member of the catfish family. It halted, staring up at the bird and snake, its mighty length trailing down into the icy waters. Two wide-spaced eyes, twin black beads, ever on the watch for prey, loomed close to the surface. The wide, blubbery, blue-tinged lips, moving constantly, opening and closing, caused two long barbels on the upper jaw to move in concert with the four lesser ones beneath the lower lip. The monstrous fish stayed momentarily hanging there, its fins rotating slowly. Then it leapt clear of the pool arching as it sped back down. A pale, plump frog, which had strayed too close, vanished into the big fish's jaws.

Korvus peered at the reflection of Sicariss in the pool. "Did Welzz speak again?"

The smoothsnake reared slightly, so that it was looking into the raven's eyes. "He ssspoke asss alwayssss, of our ancessstorsss, Rigvar Sssskurr and Sssssumisssss!"

The raven's voice was flat and harsh. "Ayakk! Are we forever to bear the guilt of the blinded Doomwyte? The dust of seasons and the mists of time have long blown away. Our fathers' fathers could not even recall when Rigvar Skurr and Sumiss were alive, why should we?"

Sicariss adjusted her coils, tightening briefly around the head of her host. "Becausse they were the onessss who let the eyessss be ssssstolen. It isss we who musssst get them back."

With a quick, angry movement, the raven pecked one of the snake's coils, which was close to his beak. This caused Sicariss to relax the pressure on Korvus's head. She hissed soothingly, "We have done more than any other before usss. For do we not know the name of the thief who ssstole the eyesss? Prince Gonff, a mere earthcrawler."

The raven tyrant groomed his breast plumage irately, shifting the snake's grey-brown coils as he did. "Aye, a mousethief, thousands of seasons gone now. All we have is stories told by other young earthcrawlers in the Redstone house. Mayhaps more will come to light if Veeku's crows capture the storyteller and bring him back here to us."

Time inside the caverns was not marked by the passage of day or night. Korvus Skurr and Sicariss waited impassively, brooding over the still surface of the dark pool. It was some moments before Veeku, leader of the crows, called out from the small passage between the two caves, "Harrakk, my birds bring word from the Redstone house for the mighty Korvus!"

The raven hopped down to the pool's edge. "Bring them here to me!"

An escort of rooks and choughs brought the two crows forward. Veeku took his place beside Korvus. "Mighty One, my birds did not capture the one who told stories, but they bring useful information."

Sicariss hissed, "Let them ssspeak for themselvesss!"

The two crows prostrated themselves, with outspread wings, in front of Korvus. The larger of the two spoke. "Hakaaarr! Our brother captured a young one from the Redstone house, but he was slain by a strangebeast and flung into a ditch. There were many Redstone creatures there, we had to hide, or we would have been slain also. But we heard their words, O Mighty One."

Korvus Skurr raked the stone floor with his fearsome talons. "Speak then, tell me what they said."

The two crows relayed the solution of the puzzle, as best they could, speaking alternately.

53

"Bird has no rubies, snake no emeralds. . . ."

"Where are the stones, hidden well by Prince of Thieves. . . ."

They waited in silence, not daring to look up.

"You heard thosssse wordssssss?"

Veeku spoke for both his crows. "If that is what they said, then that is what they heard."

Korvus lowered his head, allowing Sicariss to slither down onto the mossdamp stones. "See if they speak truly."

The smoothsnake positioned herself in front of the larger crow. "Look into my eyesssss . . . look deeeeeeep!" The bird was compelled to obey. He stared in fascination at the two gold-rimmed, black-beaded reptilian eyes. The snake's head moved back and forth as it intoned, "Deeeeeep . . . look deeeeeeep! All you have to fear isssss death itsssself. . . . Sssspeak to Sicarisssssss!"

The carrion crow fell immediately under the snake's spell. He spoke slowly in a dreamlike voice. "We were afraid for our lives . . . hid in the ditch. Those were the words I heard. I wanted to return . . . wanted to report words to Leader Veeku."

The snake's tongue flickered toward the other crow. "And thissss one, what did he want? Ssssspeak!"

The larger crow replied automatically, "He did not want to come back, but I said we must."

With eye-blurring speed, Sicariss whipped her coils about the smaller crow's neck and began bunching her muscles, constricting in a death grip. Korvus turned to look at Veeku. The crow leader clacked his beak.

"Kayaah, there is only one reward for disobedience!"

The smaller crow flapped and rent the air with his claws, gurgling. Then he went limp. Sicariss swiftly loosed her victim, sliding slowly up the big raven's outspread wing until she regained her former position on the tyrant's head. Korvus went back to his perch on the rock, nodding to Veeku.

"Welzz awaits him."

The carrion crow leader thrust the dead one into the pool's icy waters, leaping back as the monster fish struck.

Veeku waited until Korvus was finished watching the revolting spectacle, then spread his wings in salute. "Yarrra, Great One, this lowly bird awaits your orders."

The raven and his snake seemed to hold a whispered conversation. Then Korvus turned to Veeku. "This time I will send my Wytes to the Redstone house, they will bring me what I want. You will go with them, but stay outside the place. This is what I want you to do, listen carefully."

Outside it was still raining, with no sign of a break in the dull, brooding clouds. The dark beast lurking on the hill outside the caverns had watched all the comings and goings, of both birds and reptiles. No movement from below escaped its fierce, vigilant eyes. Whenever there was no activity from below, the mysterious creature would continue its demolition of the heavily forested slope, using tools it had fashioned roughly, digging and gouging implements. Beneath its jet-black coat, the beast's sinews and muscles flexed and strained as it attacked the rain-soaked earth, levering loose rocks and boulders, and severing tree roots. It was a formidable task for one creature alone, but the worker toiled on doggedly. It might take seasons of labour, but the dark beast would accomplish the task, because it was driven, regardless of its own life, by the quest for vengeance!

6

That strange mountain hare, the Laird Bosie McScutta of Bowlaynee, was highly impressed at the magnificent spread of afternoon tea laid out in Great Hall. Having been introduced to all and sundry, he shook Friar Skurpul's paw soundly. "Och, ye had nae need tae put on a special spread for me, mah guid fellow."

The Friar grinned cheerily. "Nay, zurr, Oi b'aint dun nawthin' speshul furr ee. This'n yurr bees moi yooshul arternoon Abbey tea."

Abbot Glisam patted the seat on his right side. "Please sit down and help yourself, Bosie."

Everybeast present stared in amazement as the warrior bard applied himself unsparingly to the food, commenting between mouthfuls. "Is that nutbread ye have there, aye, an' celery cheese, too? Jings, there's nought like it, wi' a dab o' honey, some slices of apple an' a leaf or two o' lettuce. Ah'm verra partial tae it, ye ken."

Using the nutbread as a base, Bosie built himself a sandwich of epic proportions. "Mmmff gruch grrulp! Would ye like tae pour me a beaker o' yon mint tea, mah wee lassie?"

The squirrelmaid Perrit obliged willingly. "Careful, sir, it's hot. There's October Ale or Pale Summer Cider, if you'd like something cooler."

Hot mint tea did not seem to bother Bosie, he swigged off the beaker at a single gulp. "Weel, that hit the spot nicely. Ah'll take a tankard o' yore ale, an' mebbe one o' yon cider. Och, Ah'm thinkin' 'twould be a sensible scheme, if'n ye were tae hire me as wee bairn rescuer tae your Abbey. Would ye no consider it, Father?"

Glisam sliced into a warm scone. "I'd not deny you the position, if you so wish it, friend. Though it isn't every day you'd be called on to rescue Dibbuns from carrion birds."

Bosie ploughed through a plum pie reflectively. "True, true, but if'n yer foes knew that Laird McScutta o' Bowlaynee was guardin' the entire Abbey, och, the rascals would be afeared tae come near. Anybeast knows Ah'm a braw, bonny warrior o' wide repute. As for mah needs, Ah'd bother ye little, Father. A place tae rest mah heid, an' six square meals a day—not countin' snacks an' supper ye ken, we McScuttas are noted as frugal creatures. So what d'ye say?"

Abbot Glisam buried his nose in a beaker of pennycloud cordial, trying hard not to burst out laughing. Calming himself, he turned to Sister Violet, seated nearby. "Hmm, that sounds fair enough, what's your opinion, Sister?"

The jolly hedgehog Sister replied promptly, "Oh no, don't drag me into it, Father, go and ask Friar Skurpul, vittles are his responsibility. Er, excuse me, Laird Bosie, I see you own a musical instrument. Perhaps you'd like to play or sing for us."

The hare left off licking an empty meadowcream bowl. "Aye, 'twould be mah pleasure, marm. Clear the floor!" With a bound he was up, tuning his fiddle-like instrument. Holding it at waist height, he drew the short bow across its strings. Bosie launched into a pleasant, lively air. The lyrics were hard to understand, being in the Highland dialect. As he sang, Bosie danced a jig, his huge footpaws and flailing legs whirling at odd angles. The music was so lively

57

that many Redwall paws began tapping, particularly the Dibbuns, who considered themselves the very cream of dancing beasts.

"A braw wee beastie tramped o'er the hill,
Red Jemmie was his name sir,
tae pay some court tae a bonny young maid,
who dwelt hard by the burn there.
Sae skirl the pipes an' rosin mah bow,
an' Ah'll sing all the day,
is the wit, the heart or the belly tae rule?
Ah canna truly say.

Bold Jem he came tae the wee lassie's door.
'Are ye within, mah darlin'?'
She yelled, 'Awa' ye roguey scamp,
how dare ye come a callin'.'
Well skirl mah pipes an' rosin mah bow,
och, are ye afear't tae play?
Does a girlie's nay mean yea mayhap,
or does her yae mean nae?

She's barred the door on puir young Jem,
she's spinnin' by the fire,
an' left him langin' in the cauld,
far frae his heart's desire.
So skirl mah pipes an' rosin mah bow,
'tis aye mah golden rule
that Ah will sing an' dance an' woo,
but Ah'll be naebeast's fool!

Now Ah'm awa' tae mah wee bit hame,
havin' suffered enough ill will,
an' Ah've commandeered yore mammy's pie,
frae off yon windowsill.
Aye, skirl mah pipes an' rosin mah bow,
Ah'll relish every bit,

for 'tis many the maid may rule mah heart,
but mah belly commands mah wit!"

Brother Torilis picked up two Dibbuns, who had been cutting a fancy jig upon the tabletop. Stern-faced, he wiped honey from the little ones' footpaws before placing them down on the floor. "Really, Father Abbot, do we have to put up with this sort of rowdiness at mealtimes? All this shouting, singing and dancing, it isn't very dignified. I think it sets a bad example!"

Glisam, who was still applauding the music and dance, shook his head. "Oh no, Brother, it was such good fun. I vote we give Laird Bosie the job!"

Any objections Brother Torilis attempted were drowned out by cheering Redwallers and squeaking Dibbuns. Bosie put away his instrument. Spotting a half-plate of scones, he sat down and attacked them vigorously.

"Mmmf grmff sninch! Mah thanks tae ye all, Ah'll do mah best tae be worthy o' the task!" He waggled his long ears at Brother Torilis. "An' you, mah friend, practice smilin', but watch yore face doesnae crack an' fall off!"

Torilis stalked off in a huff, whilst Bosie helped himself to what was left of the spring vegetable soup. He winked at Bisky and Dwink. "A wee word of advice, laddies: Always see the table is well cleaned afore ye leave it!"

They sat watching him in openmouthed awe.

Corksnout addressed Umfry. "D'you see wot I told ye, ole Bosie's a beast to be reckoned with, whether fightin', singin' or eatin'. Pore Friar Skurpul is wot I say."

Umfry could only shake his head and mutter, "Six square meals a day, not countin' supper h'or snacks?"

Gullub Gurrpaw, who besides being Cellarmole was also Foremole, Chieftain of Redwall Abbey's mole community, sat down between Bisky and Dwink. "Well, zurrs, did ee solven ee riggle?"

Corksnout butted in swiftly. "Oh yes, of course they did,

an' without any 'elp from me, I might add. Go on, Dwink, you tell Foremole Gullub about it."

The young squirrel explained, "Well, we worked out that pincer meant Prince, from then on it was easy. A Prince of Thieves hid them well!"

"Hurr, that wurr sloightly easy. . . ." Gullub wrinkled his velvety brow, casting a wry glance at his cellarmate. Corksnout returned the mole's look indignantly.

"I never breathed a single clue to 'elp those young uns, may my spikes fall out if'n I did!"

Bisky threw a paw to his mouth in comic alarm. "What's that rattlin' noise?"

The Cellarhog quickly inspected the floor behind him. "Where, what rattlin' noise?"

Dwink, Umfry and Bisky stifled their giggles.

Foremole Gullub poured Corksnout a tankard of October Ale. "Thurr ee go, matey, Oi knows you'm did et with ee best of attentions, hurr so ee did!" The mole turned his attention to the young ones. "Naow, you'm lissen to Oi. Et may be summat an' et may be nought, but Oi've found sumthen that you uns moight be interested in."

Bisky sat up alertly. "Golly, sir, is it another riddle?"

Bosie peered over the rim of the soup bowl he was licking. "A riddle, is it, Ah'm pretty guid at riddles, ye ken. What goes underwater an' never gets wet?"

Even Umfry knew that old puzzle. "A h'egg in a duck's tummy, sir."

The mountain hare sniffed. "Och, ye're far tae clever for yore own guid, laddie!" He rose, wiping his whiskers fussily on his scented silk kerchief. "Ah've a mind tae acquaint mahself with this braw place. Mebbe ah'll start wi' a tour o' the kitchens."

Abbot Glisam was at his side with alarming haste. "Kitchens? My dear Laird, there's a whole Abbey to view before we get to the kitchens. Allow me to be your escort, you'll find Redwall a fascinating place, I'm sure."

Corksnout caught the Abbot's urgent nod. Rising swiftly, he joined Glisam, so that they had Bosie hemmed in on both sides. The big Cellarhog steered the hare toward the stairs. "Er, may'aps ye'd like t'see the dormitories?"

Gripping Bosie's paw, and treating him to a beaming smile, the Abbot interrupted, "What a splendid idea, you'll need a place to sleep of course. Now tell me, d'you mind sharing a room, or do you prefer to be alone?"

Bosie tried hanging back, but Corksnout took a firm grip on his other paw, propelling him stairward. The Laird Bosie McScutta of Bowlaynee found himself outmanoeuvred, but he continued to plead his case. "Och, Ah'm nae bothered where Ah lay mah heid, any auld bunk'll do for me. But Ah'd be well pleased tae view those kitchens, aye, an' the larder, too, Father. There's nought like a well-stocked larder, ye ken!"

However, the Abbot was determined not to let the gluttonous mountain hare loose upon either kitchen or larder. He and Corksnout practically frog-marched their guest up the stairs.

Bisky, Dwink and Umfry grinned as they watched the unwilling Bosie being taken to inspect the sleeping accommodations.

Samolus seated himself next to them, observing glumly, "Huh, that lollop-eared rascal didn't leave much afternoon tea. Mark my words, he'll eat us out of house'n'home afore yore much older."

Bisky nodded. "No doubt he will, but y'can't help likin' Bosie, he's good fun. You stay here, Grandunk, I'll go and get you some vittles from the kitchen."

The old mouse toyed with some crumbs on the tabletop. "I'll get some later, thankee." He beckoned them close, dropping his tone. "I've found another clue, would ye like t'see it?" Three heads nodded eagerly. Samolus tapped a paw to the side of his nose. "Foller me, young mateys."

Samolus rapped on the Infirmary door. Behind him the three young friends stood looking nonplussed. Dwink had a horror of infirmaries and sick bays; he twiddled his paws nervously. "What're we doin' here, there's nothin' wrong with me. I don't like this place!"

Samolus was about to reply when the door opened. He found himself gazing up into the stern face of Brother Torilis.

"Yes, what can I do for you?"

The old mouse forced a tight smile. "Well, it's er, like this, Brother, er, er . . . can we borrow ole Sister Ficaria for awhile? 'Twon't take long, an' we'll bring her right back."

The tall, sombre squirrel frowned at the little party. "Is this some kind of foolish prank?"

Samolus spread his paws disarmingly. "Oh no, Brother, we just need t'borrow her for a bit."

The saturnine Infirmary Keeper glared at Samolus. "Borrow Sister Ficaria. . . . Borrow? No, you may not, she has important work to attend to. Go away!" He was about to slam the door in their faces, when a small, high-pitched voice called out from within.

"Wait'll I get my stick. Wait, I'm coming!" A moment later a tiny mouse scooted out, carrying a walking stick, which was totally unneccessary.

Bisky offered her his paw, renewing the request. "Might we borrow ye for a bit, marm?"

Old Sister Ficaria beamed a twinkling smile. "What a handsome young mouse, of course ye may." She looked over the rims of her tiny glasses at Torilis. "I'm sure you can do without me for a few moments, Brother. Won't be long!" Leaning on Bisky's paw she trotted off along the corridor. "'Tis just down here. My, my, isn't this all exciting. Pay no heed to Torilis, he means well!"

Old Sister Ficaria's room was above the Dibbuns' dormitory, a cosy, medium-sized bedchamber. She invited them in. "Sit anywhere, friends, I shared this room for many,

many seasons with Miz Laburnum. There's only me here since she passed on. Hmm, that was awhile back, fifteen, twenty seasons. Who knows?"

Samolus installed her in a woven osier armchair. "Sister, it's about the Pompom rhyme. You remember, the one you told me about."

Umfry Spikkle looked totally bemused. "Pompom?"

The little old Sister smiled at him."Yes, that's the one, do you know it, too?"

Samolus crouched in front of her, holding both her paws to focus the Sister's attention. "No, he doesn't, there's only you who knows the rhyme. Can you say it for us please?"

She stared at Samolus as if seeing him for the first time. "You're quite old, aren't you?" Then the Sister patted Bisky's paw. "But you're very young, and very handsome, too. I saw a picture of Prince Gonff once, you look very like him. You're not Gonff, are you?"

The young mouse smiled back at her. "No, Sister, my name's Bisky. I'd love to hear you say the rhyme."

Folding both her paws, and holding up her chin, Ficaria looked as though she were about to recite. Then she went off into an explanation. "Miz Laburnum was very old indeed, you know. She was the Abbey schoolteacher. Every lesson, every song and every rhyme she knew, Miz Laburnum wrote them down in her manuals."

Dwink leant forward eagerly. "Which manuals, Sister, where are they?"

Ficaria began fidgeting with the tassels on her shawl. "All gone now, all gone. The hot summer, about ten seasons back, or was it twelve, no matter. It was the sun, you see. I left my glasses on the windowsill one afternoon, when I went down to tea. Brother Torilis said that the sunrays magnified through the glasses. That's what caused the fire. Quite dreadful, but they managed to put it out. As for Miz Laburnum's manuals, all gone, every one of them. But I remember things that were written in them, that Pompom poem." She seemed to drift off, staring into space. Suddenly she began reciting.

"Pompom Pompom, where have my four eyes gone?
There's a key to every riddle,
there's a key to every song,
there's a key to every lock,
think hard or you'll go wrong.
Pompom Pompom, who'll be the lucky one?
What holds you out but lets you in,
that's a good place to begin.
What connects a front and back,
find one, and then just three you'll lack.
Pompom Pompom, the trail leads on and on."

Old Sister Ficaria stopped speaking. Samolus held up his paw to the others, lest she start again. However, that was all she had to say. They sat awhile in silence, then Ficaria glanced coyly at Bisky. "Did you like my poem, Prince Gonff?"

Without correcting the ancient mouse, Bisky clasped her frail paws warmly. "It was a very nice poem, Sister, you did it beautifully. Now, you see those two friends?" He gestured toward Dwink and Umfry. "Well, they are going down to the kitchens to bring something nice for you. Tell them what you want."

Sister Ficaria brightened up. "Hot mint tea, with honey in it, lots of honey. Oh, and if Friar has some of those wonderful almond biscuits, I'd like one or two, and perhaps a damson tart, please."

Samolus nodded to Dwink and Umfry. "You young uns run along now, me'n'Bisky'll stay with the Sister. I'll get some parchment an' charcoal. Mayhaps she'll say the lines again, I'll copy 'em down this time. Right, Sister?"

Ficaria stared fixedly at Samolus. "Yes, I'd do that if I were you, sir. Being as old as you are, it would be wise to record the poem, before you forget it!"

Samolus glared at Bisky as he went to fetch writing materials. The young mouse was spluttering to hold back his laughter.

Old Sister Ficaria cheerfully recited the poem again, fortified by honeyed mint tea, a plate of Friar Skurpul's special almond shortbreads and a daintily latticed damson tart. Studiously following her every word, Bisky wrote the lines down neatly. Dwink listened to his friend rereading the entire thing. The young squirrel waved his tail rhythmically to and fro. "It sounds just like a Dibbun thing, you know, the sort of chant they do when they're playing games."

Umfry agreed. "Like h'a sort of singsong rhyme. Maybe that's h'exactly what h'it was, d'ye think so, Sister?"

Sister Ficaria's small crystal spectacles had slipped awry on her nosetip; the little old mouse had dozed off. Samolus took a rug and covered her gently.

"Hush now, let's go downstairs to study this."

7

They went to Cavern Hole, where Samolus set about re-
pairing a chair seat. Bisky watched his granduncle artfully
weaving dried reeds and stripping away broken ones. "Tell
me somethin', Grandunk, how did you come to find out
about this rhyme?"

Samolus trimmed the reed ends with his sharp blade.
"Oh, 'twasn't too hard, though it happened quite by ac-
cident. When I was readin' through Lady Columbine's
diary, she wrote that as a joke, she often called Gonff the
Pom. When he asked her why, she kept him in the dark.
Then one day he guessed, the first letters. Prince of Mousethieves . . . Pom!"

Samolus inspected the repair he had completed. "There,
that should do! C'mere, young Bisky, make yoreself useful.
See this soft moss pad, it's full o' beeswax an' lavender.
Give this chair seat a good rubbin'. It'll give it a nice shine,
a sweet scent an' keep the reeds supple."

Bisky obeyed, but continued with his questions. "You
found out that Pom stands for Gonff's title, what happened then?"

The old mouse sheathed his sharp blade carefully.
"'Twas some time back, beginnin' o' spring. I was in the

sick bay, fixin' up a new shelf for all those potions an' pots of ointment. Huh, that Brother Torilis, always has a face on him, like a fried frog. He never spoke a word t'me, or offered me a bite to eat or drink. So, I worked away an' kept meself to meself.

"After awhile I noticed little Sister Ficaria, sittin' in a corner hemmin' sheets she was. Guess wot, she was chantin' that poem as she stitched away at her work. Said it three or four times she did. I never thought any more of it, 'til this mornin'. I was on me way to brekkist, an' I stopped at the big tapestry picture of Martin the Warrior in Great Hall. I always look at Martin's eyes, have ye ever noticed anythin' about 'em?"

Bisky looked up from his task. "Aye, they seem to follow you wherever you go."

Samolus winked at the young mouse. "That's right! Well-noticed young un, yore a Gonffen sure enough. Anyhow, I stood there, starin' at Martin, an' he's starin' back at me, an' I thought, good ole Martin, he was Gonff's best friend, aye, Gonff the . . . I was goin' t'say Gonff the Prince of Mousethieves, when I suddenly said that word. Pom! Now don't you young uns make fun o' me, but I gives you me word. Martin's eyes twinkled, an' Sister Ficaria's rhyme shot straight into me head. That was when I knew the words meant somethin' special! Dwink, read it out."

The young squirrel took up the parchment.

"Pompom Pompom, where have my four eyes gone?
There's a key to every riddle,
there's a key to every song,
there's a key to every lock,
think hard or you'll go wrong.
Pompom Pompom, who'll be the lucky one?
What holds you out but lets you in,
that's a good place to begin.

What connects a front and back,
find one, and then just three you'll lack.
Pompom Pompom, the trail leads on and on."

Umfry appeared quite elated, his spikes stood up straight. "Did ye hear that, it says, that's a good place to begin, what connects a front and back?"

Dwink hazarded a guess. "A middle?"

Bisky shook his head. "No, no, you're lookin' at the wrong bit. Start at the line which goes, 'What holds you out but lets you in, that's a good place to begin.'"

Dwink frowned. "It doesn't make sense, I don't know anythin' that holds me out but lets me in."

Umfry provided the answer quite unwittingly. "Huh, 'cept a door, h'I think."

Samolus raised his eyebrows. "Is that what ye think, Umfry, I wonder why that is?"

The hulking young hedgehog gave his reasons eagerly. "'Cos the words are all about keys, an' that's what ye need to h'open doors."

Samolus had already solved the riddle, but he wanted the young ones to think for themselves. "What's your answer, Dwink?"

The squirrel screwed his face up in concentration. "Er, er, I think it's right, wot Umfry said, I mean. An' a door's the only thing that needs a key."

Samolus sighed. "Yore right, it is a door, but the words tell ye of other things that need keys. A riddle, a song and a lock. So think about this, what can hold you outside, or let you inside?"

Dwink replied, "Is it a door, Mister Sam'lus?"

The old mouse turned his attention to Bisky. "Of course it is. Can you tell us why? Come on, think!"

Bisky could explain his reply, and he did. "A door connects front an' back. Back door, front door. But we need a key for the door. Even then we won't find the four Eyes of the Doomwyte. Next to last line, find one, and just three you'll lack. Right?"

Samolus sat down on the newly repaired chair. "Right, but at least it's a start. Now, where would we find door keys, eh?"

Surprisingly, it was Umfry who spoke out. "But there h'aint no keys h'in Redwall, an' I should know, 'cos h'I'm the Gatekeeper!"

Samolus looked dumbfounded. "Great seasons, young un, yore right! In all me time at our Abbey I've never seen a door with a key'ole an' a key to fit it. We've got doors you can bar, an' doors ye can bolt, but I've never seen one ye could turn a key on!"

Dwink shrugged. "So wot's the use of this riddle if'n we're lookin' for a door that locks with a key, an' there ain't one in the whole bloomin' Abbey?"

Bisky had a suggestion to make. "Suppose it's a door to a cupboard, or a wardrobe, or, or, somethin' like that?"

Samolus pondered the idea, then rejected it. "No, I don't think so, leastways I've never seen a locked cupboard. As for wardrobes, most of them have a curtain instead of a door. It looks like we're stuck on this puzzle, mates, unless . . . "

Umfry stared at the old mouse expectantly. "Unless wot, sir?"

Samolus explained, "Unless we put the question to every creature in Redwall. Somebeast's sure to know. Listen now, here's what we do. . . ."

By dinnertime that evening, Abbot Glisam felt he was close to the end of his tether, as did Corksnout Spikkle, and one or two others. Glisam watched the Laird Bosie McScutta of Bowlaynee bounding off to his chosen room, calling cheerily, "Ah'll be back in the twitch of an ear the noo. It doesnae take me long tae freshen up an' change for dinner!"

The Abbot slumped down on the stairs, sighing. "At least it doesn't look like he's escaping to inspect the kitchen and larders again!"

Corksnout clenched his powerful paws. "Did ye see the number o' barrels an' kegs that he opened in my cellars? Sniffin' an' samplin'. I tell ye, Father, 'twas all I could do to stop meself reachin' for a bung mallet an' sendin' him off for a good afternoon nap with a sharp tap!"

Skipper Rorgus shook his head and chuckled, "Stap me rudder but ye can't help likin' Bosie, can ye now. He's an amusin' beast, aye, an' good company, too. Even though ye can't understand everything he says."

The Abbot smiled ruefully. "I suppose you're right, Skip, he does possess a certain charm. Ooh, I think my old bones are setting, lend a paw here please or I'll end up stuck fast and miss my dinner."

Taking hold of the Abbot's paws, Skipper and Corksnout hauled him up off the stairs. On the way into dinner, Samolus caught up with Glisam, and had a whispered word with him. The Father Abbot nodded understandingly.

"Of course, friend, you have my permission."

Dinner at Redwall was always a pleasant and lively event. Before the Abbot arrived at top table everybeast was already seated, listening to a rendition of a Dibbun song. This was performed by a notorious crew known as the D.A.B. (Dibbuns Against Bedtime). They were a raucous bunch of infants, constantly in rebellion against authority. A very tiny mousebabe conducted with a spoon as they sang. What they lacked in melody, they made up for in enthusiasm, particularly the small moles' bass section.

"Life is 'ard for likkle Dibbuns,
anybeast can tell us off,
an' they makes us swaller fizzicks,
every time we sneeze or cough.
Us gets sent t'bed too early,

baffed an' scrubbed wiv soap an' brush,
an' if us sez we don't like it,
they scrub 'arder an sez 'Shush.'
Mind dat langwidge, watch dose manners,
don't talk back an' walk don't run,
all sit still an' don't be naughty,
for us Dibbuns dat's no fun!"

Resplendent in dress kilt and fresh ruffles, Bosie turned up to accompany them on fiddle. He sniffed away an imaginary tear, sending out waves of fragrance as he dabbed both eyes with his silk kerchief. "Och, aren't they dear, wee, bonny beasties!"

Brother Torilis upbraided the mountain hare. "Hardly. I'd advise you not to encourage them."

For answer, Bosie jigged around Torilis, bowing his odd instrument gaily.

"Och, were ye no a babby once,
ye hairy auld yahoo?
Ah'll bet yore kinfolk got a fright,
when they set eyes on you.
Ye must ha' lived up in a tree,
on gruel an' mouldy bread,
a-hauntin' all the countryside,
until the neighbours fled!"

Skipper Rorgus beckoned Bosie to sit alongside him. "Ahoy, mate, join me here, an' don't be teasin' pore Brother Torilis. He can't 'elp bein' the way he is. Some o' the young scamps round here needs a creature like Torilis t'keep 'em in line."

Bosie reached for a plate of carrot'n'onion pasties. "Ach, the auld misery, Ah cannae take tae a beast who doesnae know how tae smile." As the hare selected a pasty, Torilis rapped his paw, making him release it.

The Brother chided Bosie, "Don't touch until the Father Abbot has said grace!" The mountain hare's ears stood rigid; he was about to reply when Glisam began the grace.

"We who toiled with right good zeal
for the food that makes this meal,
let us pause and spare a thought,
without good cooks, 'twould taste like nought.
To Friar Skurpul and his crew,
our heartfelt thanks we give to you!"

The Redwallers applauded this new grace, and the one it was directed at. Friar Skurpul covered both eyes with his flour-dusted paws, shuffling to and fro, in the way moles do, when acknowledging a compliment.

"Burr nay, Oi wurrn't doin' n'more than moi dooty!"

Then Abbot Glisam made an announcement. "Friends, if anybeast owns or possesses a key, Samolus Fixa would like to see it. Also, if you know of any door in our Abbey which would require a key, please let Samolus, Bisky, Dwink or Gatekeeper Umfry see where it is. Oh, and there'll be a reward for whoever finds the key, or the door. Thank you, please enjoy your dinner!"

The very tiny mousebabe's paw shot up as he piped out, "Pleeze, Farver H'Abbit, can us stay up late to look for doors'n'keys pleeze?"

Glisam sat watching the tiny mousebabe, scrambling up onto his lap. "No, I'm afraid you can't, little one." The Abbot rubbed his eyes wearily, knowing what was coming as the mousebabe stuck out his lower lip.

"But why, Farver?"

"Because you have to go to bed."

"But why, Farver?"

"Because you're only a babe, and you need your sleep."

"But why, Farver?"

"So you can grow up big and strong."

"But why, Farver?"

Sister Violet came to the Abbot's rescue, sweeping the tiny mousebabe up in her paws. The fat, jolly Violet knew how to deal with Dibbuns, particularly those of the D.A.B. gang.

"Gracious me, who wants to go roamin' round a dark ole Abbey all the night? Can't ye hear that rain lashin' away at our windowpanes? Some o' those stairways an' passages can be cold an' draughty on a night like this. I knows where I'd sooner be, snug an' warm in my nice, soft bed, aye, an' that's exactly where I'll be soon. Plenty o' time on the morrow to go a-rummagin' an' searchin' about, liddle un, you mark my words!"

All the time she was speaking, Sister Violet was gently stroking the mousebabe's head. As a result he had fallen asleep. She crept off to the dormitory, carrying him carefully.

Bosie called out to Glisam, "What's the reward tae be, Father?"

Skipper nudged him. "Keep yore voice down, matey, or you'll waken the babe."

The Abbot replied in an exaggerated whisper, "A special Redwall Abbey fruit trifle that Friar Skurpul has promised to make."

Murmurs of delight echoed about Great Hall. Friar Skurpul's special Redwall Abbey fruit trifle was a legendary delicacy.

All through dinner, speculation was rife as to where the mystery objects might be found. Everybeast seemed to have his or her theory about the location.

"Yurr, they'm'll be unner ee grownd, buried sumplace."

"I think that key'll be high up, mebbe in the top attics."

"Garn! Nobeast's been up there in twenny seasons!"

"All the more reason the key will be hid there."

"Might not be hidden, there might be a door up in the attics with a lock to it."

"Ho aye, zurr, an' ee key sticken roight in ee key'ole. Hurr, pull moi uther paw!"

Umfry Spikkle confided to Dwink, "H'I think that key might be h'in my gate'ouse, but tomorrow'll be plenty o' time to start searchin' for it. The rain's too 'eavy h'outside, h'any room h'in yore dormitory, mate?"

The young squirrel nodded. "Aye, there's a spare bunk or two, but won't that leave the Gatehouse unattended, Umfry?"

The hulking young hedgehog snorted. "Huh, there h'aint been a sign o' life passin' the threshold, not since this rain started three days back, h'its quiet enough h'out there."

Abbot Glisam yawned. "Dearie me, I can't seem to keep my eyes open."

The Laird Bosie took out his odd fiddle. "Aye, 'tis this weather, ye ken. A wee drap o' sunlight on the morrow will liven us up again."

Corksnout and Foremole Gullub began shepherding the Dibbuns off to their beds. Even the notorious D.A.B. gang did not complain. It seemed that most Redwallers felt heavy-lidded and languid. Bosie played a beautiful, slow air, which conjured up scenes of quiet, heather-strewn glens, with tranquil streams wending through them. One by one, everybeast drifted off upstairs, until there was only the mountain hare and Samolus Fixa, keeping each other company amidst the flickering shadows cast by guttering candles and fading lanterns.

The old mouse slumped back in his cushioned chair. "Great soakin' seasons, will ye lissen t'that blinkin' rain out there, will it never stop?"

Bosie continued playing, with his eyes closed. "Och, 'twill cease when it has a mind tae, mah friend, an' nary a moment sooner, Ah'm thinkin'."

Outside in the rainswept, clouded night, across the water-logged lawns and drooping beds of daffodils, late snow-drops, early periwinkle and purple pasque blooms, a single, silent, pale light floated in over the threshold wall.

It was soon followed by a second. Between them they slid back the well-greased bar of the main gates. With scarcely a creak, the outer gates opened a mere fraction. That was enough. At ground level, and slightly higher up, the eerie lights shimmered in, half a score of the mysterious flames, undimmed by the downpour. The Wytes had come to Redwall Abbey.

8

If (seasons forbid) there were ever a competition to find the loudest snorer in all Mossflower, Umfry Spikkle would win, paws down. Even as a tiny babe he was renowned for his nocturnal snoring. In his wisdom, Father Abbot Glisam promoted the young Umfry to the Gatehouse at the first opportunity. That way, it was only on placid summer nights, with a breeze drifting in from the west, that he could be heard inside the Abbey. In the dormitory that night, the soothing sound of raindrops pattering on the shutters was rudely shattered. Umfry had begun snoring.

Everybeast was wakened by his stentorian efforts, including the Dibbuns. The tiny mousebabe roared, "Good an' my gracious, I fink someun betta chop off 'is snout. Thatta stop 'im, I fink!" Even well-aimed pillows did nothing to halt the snoring Gatehouse Keeper's noisy slumber.

Then the dormitory door flew open, to reveal the dreaded figure of Brother Torilis, holding a lantern. "What is that horrific din?"

Molebabe Dugry pointed a small digging claw at the culprit. "Thurr ee bees, zurr Bruther, ee'm a-snoren. Boi 'okey Oi b'aint hurred nuthin' loik et!"

Brother Torilis was experienced in snoring problems, particularly in hedgehogs. Producing a small jar of rosehip syrup from his night pouch, he poured some over the sleeping Umfry's footpaws. Torilis prodded the hedgehog's gently rising stomach twice, with a thin piece of rowan wood. Umfry promptly curled up into a tight ball, as hedgehogs do. A moment later he was sleeping soundly, and silently.

Dugry wrinkled his tiny button snout. "Wot did ee do, zurr?"

The Infirmary Keeper explained briefly, "Smeared his footpaws with sweet rosehip syrup, and made him curl into a hogball. He won't be snoring again tonight, just sucking his footpaws. Now back to sleep, all of you, and not another sound!" Within moments of the Brother's departure, everybeast was back, sleeping peacefully—with the exception of two, both Dibbuns.

Furff, the infant squirrel, watched the very tiny mousebabe creeping toward the door. She shook a warning paw, whispering, "Back inna bed or Bruvver'll choppa tail off!"

But the mousebabe was not easily deterred. "I gonna finda key an' winna big big tryfull!" Like a flash, Furff was out of bed and with him.

"I cum wiv ya, Furff likes tryfulls!"

Having found the Gatehouse deserted, the group of Wytes flickered across the lawns to the Abbey's front door. Two of the pale flames landed on the simple latching device, weighing it down. The others waited patiently until the door creaked ajar. Silent as a breeze wending amidst gravestones, they drifted inside.

Samolus and the Laird Bosie were still seated at the dining table in Great Hall. It was peaceful in there, a place of shadows and dim light. Both creatures' eyelids were drooping, their heads nodding forward, paws loosely clasping tankards, which now held only the dregs of good October Ale.

Samolus felt the draught from outside. Shivering, he scowled. "Brr, feel that, somebeast's left the blinkin' door open. Those young uns, you'd think they was born in a field!"

Bosie watched him shuffling over the worn stone floor. "Ah'm no feared o' a wee draught. Och, if ye hail frae the Highlands ye get tae know what cold really is, mah friend!"

Samolus shut the big door, rattling it to make sure it was properly closed. "Maybe you come from the Highlands, but I'm from Mossflower. We value our warmth an' comfort in this Abbey, mate!"

Bosie upended his tankard, finishing the last drops. "Ach well, Ah'm awa' tae mah bed, just like yon beastie up there, the noo!"

Samolus paused, halfway across the hall. "What beastie, where?"

Bosie gestured with the fiddle he had picked up. "Ah thought there was somebeast carryin' a candle up the stairs a moment ago. Ye couldnae tell who 'twas, all Ah saw was the candlelight. Look, there he goes again!"

This time Samolus saw the light. "It must be a Dibbun, searchin' for the key. But how did a Dibbun get hold of a lit candle? They're not allowed anythin' that'd be dangerous. I'll get the little rascal!" He bounded for the stairs, with the mountain hare following at a more leisurely pace.

"Och, the wee mite cannae do much damage wi' a candle, the place is made o' stone." Any further debate was cut short by a piercing scream from the upstairs corridor.

"Yeeeeek! The fire 'as got me! Eeeeeeeeh!"

Bosie overtook Samolus, bounding upward, three stairs at a time. Doors began slamming open, the night peace was broken by cries.

"Wot's goin' on out there!"

"Who's doin' all the yellin'?"

"Lookit them lights, is the Abbey on fire?"

Bosie caught sight of the mousebabe. He was floating toward the stairs, a short distance above the floor. With two stretching leaps, the hare caught up with the screaming Dibbun. Grabbing him, Bosie seemed to jump up and down hard, several times. Sister Violet, flopping about in slippers and nightgown, trundled toward a window, bellowing.

"Whooooooo! It's tryin' to take pore liddle Furff away. Heeeeelp!"

The tiny squirrel was floating, suspended between two of the lights. They fluttered about, as if trying to open the wooden window shutter. Bosie was moving faster than anybeast, knocking Sister Violet to one side as he fitted one of his metal shafts to the bow of his fiddle. The shutter flew open, blowing rain into the passage. Both lights were halfway out of the window, still holding on to Furff, when Bosie fired the metal arrow. There was a harsh, anguished croak. One of the Wytes released its hold on the Dibbun. The other one, unable to sustain the burden alone, let Furff go. She landed on the open windowsill with a bump.

Charging forward, Bosie grasped the little squirrel's tail and nightgown, grabbing her back inside. As they both fell flat upon the floor, several more lights flew out of the window, into the rain-slashed darkness. Breathing heavily, Samolus arrived on the scene. Staring out into the night, he wiped rainwater from his eyes.

"What'n the name o' fur'n'whiskers? There they go, the lights are all gathered round one, as though it's havin' trouble floatin'!"

Bosie passed Furff to Abbot Glisam, who had just come trundling up. "Aye, it'll have problems floatin', or flyin' should Ah say. Yon were braw big birds, bigger'n yon carrion Ah slew outside yore gates. Anyhow, Ah hit the scum, Ah know Ah did!'"

Skipper Rorgus and Corksnout came running to the Abbot's side. The Otter Chieftain brandished a throwing javelin in a businesslike way. "The rest o' those lights went out by the main door downstairs, Father. They were too quick for us. Straight over the lawns they floated, an' right out the big west gate, which, by the way, was lyin' open."

The young squirrelmaid Perrit was calling from the far end of the passage. "I've got the mousebabe, he's not hurt. Yurrrk! What is this thing, someun bring a lantern!"

After Bosie had saved the mousebabe, he had sped straight on to rescue Furff. The pretty squirrelmaid had picked the mousebabe up and crouched against the wall, hugging him tight to her. Close by, there was something writhing sluggishly for the stairs. Brother Torilis hurried up, holding a lantern. Placing himself between Perrit and the thing, he stooped forward, peering through the lantern light. It was a snakelike reptile, dull brown, with a single thin, dark stripe along its spine. The features looked more lizardlike than serpentine. Bosie had jumped on it several times, with devastating force. The reptile was fatally injured, but still dangerous. It tried to coil and strike at Torilis.

"Don't move, Brother, stand very still!"

Thwack! Skipper despatched the thing, with a sweeping blow from his javelin. It slumped like a wet piece of cord. The otter Chieftain looped the coils around his javelin with a skilful flick. "A slow worm? Sink me, 'tis a few seasons since I clapped eyes on one o' these. This rascal was a full-growed feller. Ahoy, lookit the head, it's shinin', with a kind o' light!"

Bosie knelt down to inspect the head. "Och, so 'tis, Ah've never seen ought like it!"

Corksnout, who was standing behind the hare, made another revelation. "Aye, the bottom o' yore footpaw's shinin', too, Bosie. How does it feel, hot?"

The Highland hare snorted. "Ach, it doesnae feel like anythin'. It must've come frae when Ah did a wee jig on yon beastie's skull. Er, ye dinna think 'tis poison, do ye, Brother?"

Torilis inspected the faint glow on Bosie's footpaw pads. "It's not poison, only if you were to lick it off. That's what is called a phosphorescence, probably some mixture of mineral compounds. If you come along to my sick bay I have an herbal wash that will clean it off."

As if fearing to walk normally, Bosie hobbled off with Torilis, thanking him, and apologising also. "Weel, Ah'm sorry Ah made mock o' ye earlier, friend. Ye're a right braw beastie, an' finely learnit. Lissen the noo, frae this very-day, iffen anybeast speaks ill of ye, or mocks ye, they'll answer tae the Laird Bosie McScutta o' Bowlaynee. Ye can tak' mah word on that!"

When the excitement had died down, Abbot Glisam bade everybeast to assemble in Cavern Hole, where he addressed them.

"I think it would be wise for us all to spend the remainder of the night down here. Bisky, Dwink, would you please see that there are plenty of blankets and pillows brought in. Sister Violet, keep a good fire burning in the hearth, please. Samolus, I'd like all doors and window shutters secured, and bolted where possible. Skipper, take Corksnout, Gullub Foremole and some molecrew with you. Our Abbey must be searched thoroughly, make sure there are no more strangebeasts within the grounds, or this building. Only Friar Skurpul and anybeast on breakfast duty is authorised to leave Cavern Hole. Settle down now and try to get some sleep. Thank you!"

The Redwallers began occupying every ledge, nook or comfortable place they could find. Before he departed with the search party, Corksnout had a word to say.

"Er 'as anybeast seen that grand'og o' mine, Umfry?"

Dwink staggered in, carrying a load of cushions. "Umfry? Hah, he's curled up in the dorm, fast asleep an' still lickin' rose'ip syrup off his paw, sir."

The big Cellarhog nodded grimly. "Righto, young un, when he wakes, tell 'im t'wait in the cellars. I wants a word or two with an idle Gate'ouse Keeper who leaves the main gates swingin' open at night!"

Far from settling down to rest, a festive atmosphere

81

pervaded Cavern Hole. Abbot Glisam retired to a corner, not wanting to spoil the happy mood. He reasoned that it would help to dispel any fears of strange lights haunting the Abbey. Sister Violet started up the singing, whilst the incorrigible D.A.B. showed off their jigging prowess. The song took the form of a repeating line, which required a clever singer. Sister Violet held her own. She had a pleasant voice, though she was pleased when others joined in. None of the older Redwallers attempted the dancing; this was the speciality of the Abbeybabes. Dibbuns can be very athletic, and quite competitive. It was not a jig for the fainthearted. Jumps, turns, somersaults, backflips and special pawshuffles were executed energetically. Two old moles on flute and side drum accompanied Sister Violet and the singers.

"Well there was an ole hogwife who dwelt in the
    wood.
The wood the wood, oh summer be good!
And this is the song she'd sing.
I eats plum pudden an' gooseberry pie.
Oh pudden an' pie some more says I!
I'm as happy as bees in blossom trees.
Those bees in trees do as they please!
Whilst the birds fly up in the sky.
The wood the wood, oh summer be good!
Oh pudden an' pie some more says I!
Those bees in trees do as they please!
'Tis better to laugh than to cry!"

Outside, the searchers braved the rain-drenched night, after securing the main outer gates. Bosie went through the gatehouse for a second time, accompanied by Corksnout. The mountain hare looked around admiringly. "'Tis a braw wee hoose, but there's naebeast here, eh, Corkie?"

The huge hedgehog ducked as he went through the

doorway. "Right y'are, Bosie, let's search the orchard. Leave the pond area to Skipper'n'Gullub."

The gluttonous hare stepped out with a will. "Lots o' guid fruits in yon orchard, eh?"

Corksnout blew rainwater from his replacement snout, which landed over his left eye. "Never mind the good fruit, mate, you just look for the bad foebeasts!"

Bosie grinned. "That's a grand trick ye do wi' yore auld nose, could ye teach me how tae do it?"

Corksnout searched in his broad apron pocket. "Certainly, just let me find my bung knife, an' I'll cut yore nose off an' carve ye another. . . . Hi, where are ye runnin to? Come back, mate!"

Up in the Belltower two shining, dark eyes watched the searchers below. This was one Wyte who had vowed not to return to the reeking cavern without a live captive.

9

The rain stopped falling an hour before dawn, making the daybreak beautiful in its serenity. Daylight showed the skies in banded layers of pink and pearl grey, with smooth cloud banks illuminated gold underneath by the rising sun. Birds were trilling everywhere as blossom and leaf raised their drooping faces to the growing warmth. Five ravens, weary and bedraggled, landed in the branches of the birch tree, outside the cave entrance. Veeku, leader of the carrion crows, looked them over with a keen, observant glance. He bowed in a servile manner to the ravens. "Kraah, my Lords, the Doomwyte awaits you!"

Korvus Skurr did not wish to confront his brothers from an exalted position in the yellow-fogged atmosphere of the big cave. With Sicariss perched upon his head, the big raven stalked about at the edge of the dark pool. He watched four of the ravens carrying the fifth one between them. They were all capable-looking birds, but none as tall and powerfully built as Korvus, the leader of the brood. They laid the injured bird down at the poolside. Korvus could plainly see the thin metal arrow protruding from the back of his left wing.

"Garrah, who did this to ye, Murig?"

The raven managed to lift its head. "Yaark! 'Twas a long-legged earthcrawler, who lives in the Redstone house. I am hurt bad by this thing."

The smoothsnake reared up, standing like a diadem on the head of Korvus. Sicariss swayed as she hissed at the ravens. "Ye are not Wytessss, ye are sparrowsssss, where isssss the captive?"

Frang, the eldest of the raven brothers, clacked his beak dismissively. "Kaach! We were lucky to leave the Redstone house with our lives. Those earthcrawlers are fierce fighters, they do not like their eggchicks being taken. See what they did to Murig?"

The smoothsnake slithered down from Korvus's head to confront Frang. She glared icily at him. "Foolsssss, you could not catch one earthcrawler between you. Idiotsssss!"

Frang, who had been in charge of the mission, was not afraid of Sicariss. He cocked his head scornfully at the serpent. "Yaaaark! Your Snakewytes did nought to help us. They won't get back here until evening, slow, useless worms!"

Sicariss reared up as if she was preparing to strike the raven. Frang did a warlike hop, flexing his talons. Korvus Skurr swooped down between them, wings spread.

"Rakkachurr! Fighting amongst ourselves will get nought done. Six of you went to the Redstone house, but I see only five returned here. Where is our brother Tarul?"

Murig, the injured raven, attempted to rise, but he flopped back awkwardly, head drooping, eyes clouding over. "Kaah! Tarul stayed. . . ." Murig got no further. In his fall to the ground he had landed on the protruding metal shaft. A feeble rattle issued from his beak. He lay dead.

Korvus hurried to his side, prodding at him with his powerful beak. "Garrah! What of Tarul, where is he? Speak!"

Sicariss began coiling around the tyrant bird's head, hissing, "Murig will sssspeak no more. He goesss to meet Welzzzzzz!"

Korvus Skurr shook the snake from his head with a

85

quick, angry jerk, berating her stridently. "Harrrakah! No brother of Skurr will be eaten by that monster. We will feed Welzz your slow worms when they return. I have spoken!" Folding his wings, and puffing out his chest, the tyrant swaggered up to his perch above the pool.

Sicariss followed him, appeasing her host as she slithered back up to the crown position. "Your word issss law, the voice of Korvussss Ssskurr mussst be obeyed in all thingssss!"

Korvus turned his beaded eyes upon Frang. "Yarrr! What became of Tarul?"

Frang explained, "Harrah, he is hidden inside the Redstone house, your mission did not fail."

Preening his feathers, the tyrant raven spoke to Sicariss. "Kraaah! You see, my Wytes serve me well. This is good. You will speak with the Welzz, find out what the omens say."

Korvus Skurr may have thought that he was ruler absolute of his sinister world, but it was the smoothsnake who was the one that dictated most of the policies. Sicariss was a mistress of intrigue, she bent Skurr to her will by preying on his vanity, his greed and most of all upon his superstitious nature. Sicariss would stay out of reach of the monster catfish, hovering over the pool, as if listening and conversing with Welzz. The fish would swim up from the depths. Whenever Sicariss appeared, it usually meant feeding time. It would wait there, visible to onlookers, the wide, ugly, barbeled mouth opening and closing constantly. Korvus believed that it was the spirit of his underworld realm, and that it spoke to him through Sicariss. Secretly, the raven was afraid of Welzz. Once anything, living or dead, went into the pool, it was devoured in the most revolting way.

Korvus closed his eyes, pretending to doze, as Sicariss communicated with the giant fish. The smoothsnake knew of the raven's fear, feeling through her coils the tension beneath his luxuriant plumage. Accordingly, she prolonged the supposed interview, until she heard Korvus murmur impatiently. "Krraaah, what does he say? Tell me!"

Sicariss made her report, knowing that Korvus would accept that it came from Welzz. If the snake felt he was going to be disagreeable about things, she could back up the demands with warnings, dire threats and predictions of doom. Sicariss contracted her coils lightly about the raven's head, indicating that she was ready to transmit the wisdom of Welzz. Back on his perch, Korvus dismissed all within hearing. He listened intently to the snake's sibilant whisperings. The four remaining raven brothers, and a few carrion crows who waited in attendance, withdrew to the far side of the cold, gloomy cave. Perched upon the ledges, they watched the ill-matched couple. At times they hissed and cawed violently, whilst at other intervals their heads were close together, as if in agreement.

It was a long time before they were finished conferring. Korvus Skurr signalled to Veeku, leader of the carrion crows. He hopskipped across the cave floor, with a quick, bouncy gait. Veeku paid heed to his instructions, then winged off to the sulphured atmosphere of the main cavern, in preparation for the announcement.

Noon shadows were starting to lengthen in the sunny day outside, when the three slow worms arrived back. They were ushered into the big cave by an escort of choughs and jackdaws. The trio of reptiles coiled together at the edge of the steaming lake. Hemmed in by their guards, they instinctively knew trouble was brewing for them when the drums began rumbling. However, they stayed passive, knowing there was no escape from the judgement which was about to descend upon them.

The drumbeats rose in volume and tempo until the high cave, with its noxious, decaying odours and slime-encrusted walls, echoed with their intensity. Every bird and reptile gathered around the boiling, sulphurous lake, chattering, hissing and cawing.

"Warrahaarr! Attend ye the Mighty Korvus Skurr and his crown, Sicariss!"

The drums stopped, and the chatter died immediately. Birds and reptiles stood in frozen silence, staring toward the centre of the mist-shrouded lake.

Boom!

As the echo of the single drumbeat died, the tyrant raven and his smoothsnake appeared. They seemed to float in the mist which surrounded the base of the eyeless, ancient likenesses of themselves.

The cave's inhabitants chanted, "Rakaah Skurr! Rakaah Skurr! Sicarissssss! Rakaah!"

Veeku launched into his pronouncement. "One of our Wytes has been slain, by the earthcrawlers of the Redstone house. . . ." An audible moan ran through the listeners, then the carrion leader continued, "Great Lord of Doomwytes, the Mighty Korvus Skurr has commanded that there will be a new flame in the woodlands tonight." Veeku raised his beak toward the vast, high ceiling. "Go to your Master and receive the Mark of the Wyte!"

A young raven, quick of eye and fleet of wing, swooped down from the gloomy recesses. He landed on the central island, in front of Korvus Skurr. Carved in the base of the Doomwyte statue was a shallow basin; it glowed with the strange light of some liquid which floated in it. Sicariss whispered an instruction to the young raven. Holding forth his right wing, he dipped it into the basin, holding it in the glowing fluid whilst the snake chanted.

"Thissss isss the Mark of the Wyte,
thisssss issss the light of the Wyte,
if the light ever diesss or fadesss
that isss the end of your daysssss!"

The young bird stayed with his right wingtip immersed in the liquid, until a nod from the serpent bade him remove it. Korvus Skurr spoke then.

"Harraaak! There are always seven Raven Wytes, you are one of us now. Gaze into the eyes of Sicariss!"

The smoothsnake moved like lightning, wrapping her coils around the initiate's neck, drawing him close, so that her eyes were but a fraction from his. Sicariss stared intently into the newcomer's eyes, holding him there until he appeared to go limp. Korvus bowed, pausing until Sicariss had resumed crown position on his head, then he spoke again.

"Yarraaak! Will you live to serve the Doomwyte? Will you die in its service? Will you slay at the will of the Great Doomwyte?"

The young raven's gaze was fixed on the stone idol. He croaked tonelessly, "I live, I die, I slay, for the Doomwyte!"

Now Korvus turned his attention to the three slow worms, who lay at the lake's edge, guarded on all sides. The tyrant's voice was harsh. "Yakkaaarraa! These worms left one of my Wytes to die in the Redstone house. They disobeyed the command of their Master. One of them will get to meet Welzz. The choice is yours, my brother."

Hissing wildly, the three slow worms coiled about one another, intertwining at the lake's edge. The new Wyte flew at them, seizing the head of one in his cruel talons. The victim's strength was not a fraction of the raven's; with a savage wrench he tore it clear of its companions. The slow worm writhed helplessly as the Wyte soared off to the smaller cave, amidst a loud cawing and hissing of applause from the onlookers. The two remaining slow worms tried to wriggle off, until Veeku clacked his beak at the guards.

"Heekaah, into the lake with them!"

The carrion birds pounced upon the unfortunate slow worms gleefully. There was no love lost between them and the reptiles, whom they considered the lower orders in their caverns. Sicariss watched the two former reptile Wytes writhing in agony as they sank into the boiling waters. She looked down from her head perch, expressing her disapproval to the tyrant raven.

"There wassss no need to ssssslay all three wormsss, one wassss enough. Now we have lossst three more Wytessss."

But Korvus was unrepentant, and determined to assert his authority. "Hakkah! Who needs worms? If we are to bring back the times of our greatness, the eyes must be returned to the Doomwyte. Have ye not said so yourself, many times?

"We cannot defeat the creatures of the Redstone house in battle, they are secured within their fortress. Stealth and skill are not enough, fear is needed now. Once fear is instilled into the mind, defeat is certain to follow. Fear is the most powerful of all weapons!"

Sicariss tried bringing her influence to bear on the Doomwyte Ruler. "I have many snakesss, sssslow worms, grassss snakessss, even sssmoothsnakessss, ssssuch assss me. Snakesss can be fear itsssself, Mighty One."

Korvus shook Sicariss roughly from her perch to the ground. "Yaaaaaark! Only my ravens can be trusted to regain the Doomwyte Eyes. No more reptiles, toads, lizards or snakes. . . ." Here he paused, then spoke out as though struck by a sudden inspiration. "Except one particular snake."

Assuming that Korvus was speaking of her, Sicariss hissed gratefully, "Your word issss my command, Mighty One, you will not regret choosssing Sicarissss!"

The big raven clacked his beak dismissively. "Kachah! Who needs you, I was speaking of Baliss!"

Sicariss recoiled in horror at the dreaded name. "Balissss! What would you want with that monsssster?"

The raven's dark eyes glinted wickedly. "Haaaark! Who better to bring fear to the Redstone house than Baliss the Evil One? Go, bring him to me!"

Outside the caverns, from a vantage point on the wooded hillside, the dark beast sat watching the scene below as evening descended.

Griv the magpie and her mate Inchig flew slowly, close to the ground. They followed the sluggish progress of three reptiles, two grass snakes and a fat toad. Griv had learned all the gossip amongst birds and reptiles concerning the mission, but Inchig had not. As they perched in a woodland clearing, waiting for the reptiles to pass, Inchig was full of curiosity.

"Aaakh! Why are we going to the old quarry?"

Griv pecked at a passing ant. "*They* are going to see Baliss the Slayer. *We* are only going to see that they obey orders."

Inchig seemed to shrink close to the grass. "Baliss? Yarrak, I'm not going near that monster!"

Griv moved aside to let the reptiles pass. "Garrah! We don't have to, all we do is watch. Otherwise I'd have just flown south, and kept on flying. They say that Baliss is ancient, and blind, but still the most dangerous adder in the land. I heard Sicariss say that the blood of the great Asmodeus runs in his veins."

Inchig ruffled his plumes as he shuddered. "Kiiirrrh! Who will dare speak to such a mighty serpent?"

Griv devoured another ant, nodding after the reptiles. "The grass snakes, I suppose." She sniggered wickedly. "The toad is nothing but a food offering."

10

Frintl, the young hog, had already crept out of Cavern Hole for a quick outing. She was about to pop out of the main door, when Skipper Rorgus, coming in from the orchard, caught her. He sent the young hogmaid back to Cavern Hole, where she would have to wait with the others until the breakfast bell sounded. Frintl went back, but only after she had gossiped with a few of the kitchen helpers.

Dwink roused himself from the mossy ledge, which he and Bisky had occupied overnight. He yawned, gazing around at the Dibbuns and young ones, most of whom were still asleep in the quiet warmth. Frintl was chuckling to herself as she stole back into the temporary dormitory. Dwink's voice startled her. "Where've you been, missy?"

Picking up her blanket, Frintl began folding it. "Oh, I just went outdoors for a stroll, it's a lovely mornin', nice 'n'bright."

Umfry Spikkle entered; rubbing his eyes, he smiled dozily at the hogmaid. "G'mornin', Frintl."

She pursed her lips primly. "Not for you it ain't, Master Spikkle. Father Abbot wants t'see you, an' not after brekkist, but soon as yore up an' about. Sister Violet jus' told me!"

Umfry sat back, nursing his head in both paws. "Spikes'n'Spikkles, suppose I'm in for h'it!"

Bisky hopped down from the ledge, bringing Dwink with him. "Never mind, mate, we'll go along with ye, an' put in a good word, if'n we get the chance."

Abbot Glisam had decided to see Umfry out in the orchard. The gorgeous spring morn and the bright, blossoming trees did little to allay his dismay. Glisam turned to the group of elders who had joined him, shaking his head sadly. "Oh dear, I detest having to sit in judgement on others, especially young uns. I don't like it at all."

Umfry's grandsire, Corksnout Spikkle, sat down on an upturned barrow. "Yore too soft-'earted, Father, best leave this t'me. I was supposed to see the young rip down in my cellars earlier on, but young Frintl said he was sleepin' sound. So if ye'll allow me I'll have a stern word with 'im."

Glisam smiled gratefully. "Thank you, sir, I'm obliged."

Brother Torilis sniffed, issuing a disapproving sound. "Hmph!"

The Laird Bosie, who was also in attendance, held out a spotless, scented kerchief. "Here, mah friend, blow yore snout if'n ye've got the sniffles." He watched Torilis stalk off stiffly, then winked at Glisam. "Och, was it somethin' that Ah said?"

Umfry plodded into the orchard, flanked by Bisky and Dwink. He bowed to the Abbot, who pointed to Corksnout.

"I think it's your grandfather who wants to hear what you've got to say for yourself, young un."

Corksnout glared at Umfry. "Well?"

Dwink immediately spoke out. "It was my fault, I said that he could sleep in our dormitory last night, 'cos of how bad the weather was. It's a long walk t'that Gate'ouse through all the wind an' rain . . . an' all that. . . ."

His voice trailed off, so Bisky cut in. "I told him to stay indoors, too, sir, he might've caught a cold an' the sniffles, y'see."

93

Corksnout's gaze moved from one to the other. "I ain't speakin' to either of you two. So, young Umfry, wot's yore excuse for leavin' the main outer gate open an' unguarded last night, eh?"

Umfry shuffled his footpaws, mumbling, "The gate was shut an' barred when h'I left it, sir."

Samolus added, "He's prob'ly right, it must've been the intruders that opened it."

Umfry took a grip of himself. Standing up straight, he spoke out loud and clear. "Maybe h'it was, but that's no h'excuse, 'tis my job h'as Gatekeeper to guard that gate. Well, h'I didn't. So h'I'll 'ave to h'ask ye to h'accept me h' apologies, 'twon't 'appen again, sir!"

Foremole Gullub Gurrpaw nodded approvingly. "Hurr, well spaken, zurr, wot do ee says, Corkie?"

The burly Cellarhog stroked his chin. "Well said right enough, but something, 'as t'be done about it, so this is my judgement. Umfry, yore relieved of gatekeepin' duties 'til I says. As a punishment, ye can clean the cellars out, from top to bottom. Sweep, 'em until there ain't a sign o' dust nor cobweb anywhere. All the stock must be restacked, every barrel, keg, puncheon, cask an' firkin, neat'n'tidy. Dwink an' Bisky, you confess to encouragin' Umfry to desert his post?"

Both the young creatures stood to attention. "Aye, sir, we did!"

Corksnout nodded grimly, then adjusted his nose, which had slid into his mouth. "Right, then you can 'elp Umfry with the task!"

Abbot Glisam sighed with relief. "Well, that's that! But who'll mind the gate?"

Foremole Gullub raised a huge digging claw. "Hurr hurr, that'll be Oi, zurr, ee gurt bed in yon gatey'ouse bees the mostest cummfibble wun Oi ever see'd in moi loife."

A smile played around the Father Abbot's lips. "As long as you don't neglect your duties by snoring all day in it. Permission granted!"

Dwink twirled his bushy tail. "When do we start our job?"

Corksnout stood up from the barrow, fixing the trio with a severe stare. "How about right now this instant!"

Umfry's jaw dropped. "But wot about brekkist?"

Gullub beckoned toward the Abbey. "Cumm ee with Oi, may'ap ee Froir wull make you'm up ee packed vikkles."

Samolus watched them trotting off happily. "There goes three good young uns, proper friends!"

Bosie waggled his ears. "Aye, ye ken the way they helped each other oot? Och there's nae much wrong wi' them!"

Friar Skurpul greeted the friends at the kitchen doorway. "Goo'day, likkle zurrs, you'm cummed to 'elp Oi at ee ovens furr awhoil?"

Foremole Gullub came trundling in behind them. "Hurr, Oi'm afeared they'm b'aint a-worken at ovens t'day, Froir. Thurr bees tarsks furr 'em a-cleanen owt ee cellars. Straightaways, too, an' they'm b'aint havved a taste o' brekkfust yet."

The kindly Friar ladled out three beakers from a cauldron. "Yurr now, set ee doawn an sup moi leekybean soup, whoilst Oi pack summat furr you'm pore stummicks!"

Foremole Gullub helped himself to a tankard of the savoury soup, and a small crusty loaf. He waved to them as he left the kitchen. "Goo'bye, Oi'm off t'moi Gatey'ouse. Hurr hurr, you uns have fun in ee cellars!"

The cellars at Redwall Abbey were ancient, and widespread. Bisky placed the big food parcel, which the Friar had made up, on a barreltop table. He smiled ruefully. "There's enough cleanin' work down here to keep us busy for a season or two, I think!"

Dwink had already begun inspecting the contents of the parcel. "Good golly, mates, ole Skurpul's packed enough to keep us fed for twice that long. Look, apple'n'blackberry turnovers, cheese'n'onion pasties, a full rhubarb crumble, scones, honey an' salad. Anyone for brekkist?"

Umfry sighed. "Not just yet, Dwink, we'd best make h'a start with the cleanin' first."

"That's the spirit, young uns, work first, eat later!" Corksnout stood in the cellar doorway. "I'm just off to Great 'All for brekkist. But I'll be back t'see 'ow yore goin' on with the task. Now you'll find brooms, mops, pails, dusters an' so on, outside o' my room over there. Bend yore backs t'the job at paw, an' we'll get on fine t'gether."

Bisky saluted the big Cellarhog. "Right, sir, where'd you like us to start?"

Corksnout pointed. "Right at the far wall o' the back cellar. Move all the barrels, dust 'em, make sure the bungs are tight an' check 'em for leaks. Brush all the floor an' walls, then restack the barrels." He strode jauntily off, humming a tune.

Umfry mopped imaginary perspiration from his headspikes. "H'I feel tired jus' lissenin' to that ole hog!"

Dwink had gone back to checking their food. "I've just noticed somethin'. Friar Skurpul never gave us anythin' to drink."

Bisky was grinning broadly, winking at Umfry. "I wonder why, got any ideas, mate?"

Umfry did not see the funny side of things. He shrugged. "Prob'ly 'cos we're h'in a cellarful o' drinks. Come on, let's get the brooms h'an make a start!"

The back cellar was a fair distance from the main chamber. Lanterns had to be lit there before they could see anything clearly. Even then it had a slightly morbid atmosphere, full of shapes and shifting shadows. Barrels, casks, kegs and firkins were stacked in rows, from ceiling to floor. Umfry moved to the far corner, tapping a heap of standing barrels with his paw.

"These are empty h'ale barrels. Let's dust 'em h'off."

Bisky made a sensible suggestion. "Aye, we can roll 'em out into the passage. They'll be ready then, for the next October Ale brewing."

They worked steadily at the barrels, with Umfry singing
a little song he had learned from his grandad.

"Ye can't do no more than a good day's work,
to earn a good day's feed,
so bend that back an' when yore done,
some grub is wot you'll need!
There ain't no room for idlebeasts,
nowheres about this place,
if ye sit about an' shirk yore chores,
you'll end with an empty face!

Keep goin' it ain't lunchtime yet,
don't dare pull tongues at me,
a cellarbeast must earn his bread,
the vittles here ain't free!
A drop o' sweat an' soon I'll bet,
you'll see that I was right,
with a back that's sore an' a dirty paw,
you'll sleep like a hog all night!"

Having returned from breakfast, Corksnout looked in.
He gave a nod of approval which knocked his nose askew.
"Hollo, that's the way, me jollybeasts. Shift those last two
barrels out, then take yore lunchbreak. Here's some elder-
flower an' bilberry cordial for ye to drink."
They moved the remaining barrels out into the passage
in a burst of energetic speed, then sat down to lunch.
Where the friends were seated was practically in the
dark. The next pile of barrels blocked out the lantern light.
Umfry groaned. "Ooh, me pore back's breakin', get h'up
an' move that lantern, so's h'I can see where me mouth is
h'an' put some vittles h'in it!"
Bisky perched on a sack of sand, which was used for
breaking the fall of barrels from the pile. He scoffed, "Get
up yourself, y'great lump, I'm tired, too!"

Umfry made no move to stir himself, but turned his persuasive charms on Dwink. "That's a h'awful way to talk to h'a beast with 'is back broke. You'll move the lantern, won't ye, Dwink?"

The young squirrel replied indignantly, "I'd move me footpaw round yore fat, lazy bottom, if it wasn't all covered with spikes!"

Umfry felt around in the gloom. He found an open half-sack of corks and flung one at Dwink. It went straight into Dwink's open mouth.

"Yaggsplooh! Who did that?"

Looking the picture of innocence, Umfry pointed at Bisky. "He did, h'an' 'e threw one at me, too."

Dwink flung himself upon Bisky, who retaliated by doing something the young squirrel could not abide. He tickled the tip of Dwink's bushy tail. "Yowoostoppitgerroff!" Bisky was hurled onto Umfry. Dwink jumped on top of them both. Chortling, tickling, pinching and yelling, the three friends rolled about in the lantern-lit gloom. Recklessly they cannoned into the heap of barrels, which rumbled and shifted.

"Look out, they're fallin'!"

The empty barrels made a noise like a pile of bass drums, as they thundered and bumped about the cellar. The noise continued a short time, then ceased. Dwink felt about in the darkness, calling, "The lantern's gone out, are you two alright?"

After a good deal of coughing, and hawking up dust, Umfry answered, "My skull's broke, but h'I'm sittin' h'on a rhubarb crumble, so h'I'll be h'alright!"

Dwink scrambled up, tripped over a barrel and landed in Umfry's lap. "Where's Bisky?"

Umfry spoke through a mouthful of crumble. "Dunno."

Bumbling and stumbling his way out into the passage, Dwink grabbed a lantern from the wall and hurried back, yelling, "Bisky, mate, where are ye, speak t'me!"

He was answered by a stunned mutter. "Nuuuunhhh!"

"H'over 'ere, h'I've found 'im!" Umfry yelled.

Dwink held the lantern up, scrambling over heaped barrels to the far angle of the wall. Umfry lay atop two barrels, pointing down. "Fetch that lantern—'e's down there!"

In the shifting shadows of the swinging light, Bisky could be seen. He had fallen down some kind of hollow in the floor, his footpaws sticking up in the air.

Dwink found a bracket in the wall and hung the lantern on it. "Stay still, mate, we're comin'. Umfry, come on, let's move these barrels so we can get at him!"

Forgetting their aches and stiffness, the two friends thrust the barrels wildly aside, until a space was cleared.

Bisky sounded much recovered as he shouted, "Down here, lend a paw, look what I've found!"

It was a small flight of five stone steps, running away into the corner. Down in the stairwell, Bisky hauled himself upright, his eyes glittering in the lantern light as he pointed to an ironbound door. The young mouse was yelling. "Look, it's a door, a door with a keyhole, and guess what?" He held an object up, his voice hoarse with excitement. "I've found the key!"

11

It was still night, but not more than two hours before dawn. The magpies, Griv and Inchig, perched on the tussocked rim of a deeply carved depression. This was the old quarry; it had been the habitat of adders, back into the mists of time. Far below, the two grass snakes and the toad wended their way over the quarry floor, skirting thistlebeds and large pools left by the heavy rains.

Inchig cocked his head on one side, curiously. "Raaak! Is this where the giant Baliss lives?"

Griv indicated an area, overgrown with hairy bittercress and white deadnettle, at the foot of the north quarry wall. "Karrah! There are many hidden entrances behind those weeds. Baliss dwells in the caverns and tunnels over that way."

Inchig watched the three reptiles threading their way through the vegetation. Swelling his chest, the male magpie strutted about on the rim. "Kayyar! Are we supposed to go down there also?"

Griv eyed him humorlessly. "Yikk! You can, if you are foolish enough. I am staying here, to do what we have been sent here for. To watch and wait."

Inchig's chest deflated, he squatted down by his mate. "Haayak! We must obey orders."

The toad blinked, gazing into the black hole which confronted them. Everything about the entrance reeked of
danger. The strange, musty odour, complete silence and
impenetrable darkness. He began to waddle backward but
was jolted to a standstill, by vicious butts from the snakes'
blunt snouts. Previously, the grass snakes had ignored
their fat, bloated companion, merely making sure it was
with them, and travelling in the right direction. The unwit-
ting toad, had of course, been deeply hypnotised by the
skilful Sicariss. However, faced with the mysterious black
entrance hole, the toad grew fearful. The grass snakes also
had their orders. They fiercely set upon the frightened creature, hissing, and nipping with their fangs. The unfortunate victim was left with no alternative; it hopped forward
in ungainly fashion, to escape the slashing teeth. Straight
into the hole, falling awkwardly down a dark, steep slope.

The grass snakes retreated a short distance. There they
writhed and curled into grotesque attitudes, lying frozen
in that manner. Feigning death is considered a good defence by grass snakes, when threatened with danger.

The toad had reached the bottom of the sloping tunnel. Feeling something nearby, it, too, tried to remain
completely still. It was, however, betrayed by its pulsing
throat, which seemed to have gained a life of its own. Now,
a large but delicately forked tongue caressed the toad's
skin. A disembodied voice whispered almost soothingly,
"Baaaallliiissssssss!" Then a heavily scaled body shot forward, enveloping the victim in its irresistible embrace. In
less time than it had taken the wretched toad to slide down
the underground slope, there was no trace that it had ever
existed. Nothing, save for the sated hiss, which echoed
about. "Baaaalllliiiissssssssss!"

Dawn filtered slowly over the quarry. Early sunlight
touched the clifflike walls, with their banded layers of
buff and dull red sandstone. The two magpies were still

perched on the quarry rim. Griv was dozing, but Inchig had wakened with the early sunrays. He ruffled his feathers, clacking his beak irritably.

"Kraak! What's going on down there, how long have we got to wait? There's no sign of this monster serpent, no movement of any kind. Look at those two grass snakes, they're not moving at all. Mayhap Baliss slew them, sneaked up in the dark, with his poison fangs. What d'you think?"

Griv was annoyed at being disturbed from her nap. "Rakkahakk! Have ye never seen grass snakes playing dead before? Why don't you do as I'm doing, just be still and watch. When something happens, it'll happen without all your grumbling. Now be still!"

Inchig was about to obey his irate partner, when he spied movement below. He began hopping about, spreading both wings, and fanning his tailfeathers. "Chakkach-akka! Something happens, see, see!"

Griv stared at the scene below in horrified awe.

From the tangled vegetation camouflaging the entrance hole, a head emerged, a huge, spade-shaped thing, his sightless eyes two milky, bluish-white orbs. Baliss halted, probing the air with a forked, viperine tongue. Then with smooth rapidity the mighty serpent slithered forth into the open. The snake was a nightmarish sight, dark brown, with the *V* shape at the base of his skull connecting to a broad zigzag pattern, which ran the length of his back. Bunching powerful scaled coils, the reptile reared high, head moving in a lazy, swaying arc. The flickering tongue explored the still morning air. Ignoring the grass snakes, in their twisted mock death poses, Baliss began crossing the quarry floor with a sinuous, unhurried grace.

Inchig was jigging about frantically, cawing and cackling aloud. "Karrakah! Look at that serpent, Griv, see the size of him! How long d'you think he is? Akkarr! He must be as thick as a great oak limb!"

Griv had risen onto her talons, berating Inchig. "Fool, shut your beak, be silent, noisy idiot!"

Baliss halted, again rearing his monstrous head. He pointed directly at the magpies on the rim. "Wingbirdzzzz, why does Korvussss sssend ye here?"

Inchig ceased his frenzied dance; he shot Griv a befuddled look. "Harraah! How does he know Korvus Skurr sent us?"

Baliss provided the answer. "Who but the raven would sssend carrion, wormzzzz and a croaker to my domain?"

Griv came to the very edge of the rim, noting that the head moved to mark her progress. "Hayyakh! Our Chieftain would speak with ye. If ye follow us and the grass snakes, we'll take you to him."

Baliss nodded, dropping his bulky coils to the ground. "I know where your masssster livezzzz. Go now, tell him Balissssss will meet with him. Tomorrow noon at the sssstream, where hisss guardzzz wait in the birch tree. I will sssspeak to Korvussssss. Go!"

Griv glared at her mate, as Inchig babbled, "Yakkarah! So, we can go now, good! But what about those grass snakes?"

The giant adder began returning across the quarry floor. Both magpies heard his departing remark. "Go, Balisssss will take care of your grass snakessssss."

Inchig watched with bated breath, as the huge serpent slithered toward the death-feigning snakes. Griv dealt him a smack with her open wing. He scowled. "Ayyakk! What was that for?"

She readied her wing for a second blow. "Raahaak! Our work is done here, ye heard Baliss. Go!"

As they winged their way back, Inchig was still curious. "Karra! D'you think those snakes will get away with playing dead?"

Griv cackled, "Yakyakyak! They will until Baliss shows them real death!"

Inchig gasped in disbelief. "Raah! A snake eating snakes?"

Griv set her gaze on the dew-kissed distance. "Yahaar! That evil beast would eat anything!"

News of the secret door and the key being discovered in the Abbey cellars spread swiftly around Redwall. Plus, of course, the rumours, which were mainly put about by Dibbuns.

"H'Abbot sez we not t'go down in Mista Spikkle's cellars, case Googlybeasties gets uz!"

"Burr, wot bees Googlybeasters?"

"Ho, great hooj vermints, wiv teeffs an' twenny claws!"

"Gurr, bees that roight, Sissy Vi?"

Sister Violet was not about to encourage Abbeybabes to venture down to the cellars alone. She nodded. "Well, if'n Father Abbot says so, I s'pose 'tis right enough. Go an' wash those paws now, afore lunch."

As it was a warm, sunny day, the Dibbuns dashed off toward the Abbey pond. This was as good an excuse as any for getting wet and paddling about. Sister Violet lumbered after them, wheezing.

"Walk, don't run, wait for me, yore not allowed around that pond on yore own. Dugry, come back here!"

A committee of Redwall Elders was assembled in the orchard to question Bisky, Dwink and Umfry. Bisky related the events of the incident. Having finished, he stood watching the Abbot studying the rusty, old iron key, holding it up for inspection.

Samolus was jubilant at the discovery. "Aye, that'll be the very key the riddle spoke of. I'll wager it fits that door like my ole grandad's nightie fitted 'im!"

The Laird Bosie brushed a dust speck from his cuff. "What'n the name o' crimmens has yer auld grandad's nightgown tae do wi'it, did et have a keyhole?"

Brother Torilis sniffed audibly. "Sheer foolishness, an' oldbeasts' tales, that's all it is. The door's probably rusted too badly to open."

Samolus cut in on him sharply. "A door rusted too badly to open, Brother? I'd say *that's* a bit o' sheer foolishness.

Leave it to me, there's nothing in this Abbey I can't put right, from a wobbly table leg to some rusty, old door. And as for oldbeasts' tales, where d'you suppose you gained most o' yore knowledge of herbs an' cures, eh?"

Brother Torilis was taken aback by the old mouse's verbal attack. Samolus was still facing him, his jaw jutting forth truculently.

Skipper Rorgus placed himself between the pair, in an attempt to calm the situation. "Steady on, mateys, this is only a friendly parlay. Let's keep it that way. Father Abbot, wot's yore view on doors'n'keys?"

Abbot Glisam had already formed an opinion, ever since the three young ones had told of their discovery. The excitement and happiness in their eyes was enough for him. "Friends, there's no question about it. These three scamps must find what lies beyond the door. . . ." Glisam got no further—he was smothered by Bisky, Dwink and Umfry, hugging, patting and paw shaking.

"Good ole Father Abbot, thankee kindly, sir!"

"H'I knew you was h'our mate, Father, h'I jus' knew h'it."

"An' I promise we'll clean out the cellars as soon h'as we can, Father!"

Bosie extricated the Abbot from the trio's embrace. "Haud on there. If'n yore bound tae gang through yon door, Ah'm comin' wi' ye. As protector an' warrior o' Redwall an' its beasties, 'tis mah right!"

Skipper pounded the mountain hare's back. "Well spoken, bucko, I volunteers to come with ye!"

Samolus was still ready to argue with anybeast. "Well, you lot ain't goin' nowhere without me. Any objections?"

Foremole held up a sturdy digging paw. "Ee'll need a trusty moler with ee, if'n you uns bees axplorin' unner they'm cellars."

Glisam shook his head in admiration of the Foremole. "You can't argue with good, sound mole logic. I think it's a sensible idea. Er, just one more thing, I think we've got enough for the task now, otherwise we'll have the entire Abbey wanting to come along."

The remark was greeted with general laughter.

Perrit the squirrelmaid approached; smiling prettily she curtsied to the Abbot. "I hope they're not thinking of going now, Father, I think they should wait until after lunch."

Bosie winked at her. "Och, yer right, lassie, who'd go anywhere wi'out a wee bite o' lunch!"

Bisky was so excited that he was hard put to gobble down some late spring vegetable soup, and a portion of turnip, leek and parsnip pasty. He tried taking in all the information which was being given to him and his friends. Some of it was good and practical advice.

"You'll need lanterns. Make sure they're properly filled and trimmed."

"Oh, an' some flint steel and tinder in case the lights get blown out."

"Ropes, too, you'll need ropes, they always come in useful."

Friar Skurpul wrinkled his snout at Bosie. "Hurr, an' sum vikkles, juzz to keep ee goin', zurr."

Bosie flourished an elegant bow to the Friar. "Mah thanks tae ye for thinkin' o' the main essentials, sir, yer a paragon among beasties, Ah'm thinkin'."

Early afternoon found the party gathered in the back cellar. Lanterns illuminated the scene as they sat on the floor watching Samolus. At the bottom of the stairs, the old mouse was working on the rusted doorlock. Bisky, Umfry and Dwink were reciting the rhyme which Sister Ficaria had recalled. They chanted aloud:

"Pompom Pompom, where have my four eyes gone?
There's a key to every riddle,
there's a key to every song.
there's a key to every lock,

think hard or you'll go wrong.
Pompom Pompom, who'll be the lucky one?
What holds you out but lets you in,
that's a good place to begin.
What connects a front and back,
find one, and just three you'll lack.
Pompom Pompom, the trail leads on and on."

The head of Samolus appeared from the stairwell. He held a mangled iron bar in one paw, rubbing dust and rust flakes from his face with the other. His aggressive mood had not yet worn off. "Hoi! Can you keep it quiet up there, I can't hear myself think. Sound really echoes down there, y'know!"

Skipper thumped his rudder in a soft, sympathetic manner. "Looks like ye ain't havin' much luck with that door, Sammo."

The old mouse gritted his teeth, declaring his determination to the Otter Chieftain. "I needs to concentrate, Skip, a bit o' quiet is all I asks. I'll crack it, you'll see. Might take me a bit o' time, but an ole iron door isn't goin' to defeat Samolus Fixa. No sir!"

Abbot Glisam placed a paw to his lips, beckoning the three young ones and Bosie to follow him. Up into Great Hall they went, wondering what Glisam wanted. The old dormouse trundled across the hall, explaining as they went.

"You young uns, stay with me. Then if Samolus can't open the door, he won't be able to blame you. Dearie me, he has got himself into a bit of a tizzy. Now, Laird Bosie, what do you know of Martin the Warrior?"

The hare answered as best he could. "Is that not the beastie who had the job o' Abbey Warrior afore me? Ah'm told he's lang departed, Father. But Ah've seen his likeness over yonder. Aye, an' a braw bonny laddie he looks, too. Ah wouldnae like tae meet him as a foe in battle!"

They arrived at the recess where the great tapestry was

displayed. There was Martin, the very spirit of Redwall Abbey, woven expertly, by loving paws, to stand through all seasons. He was depicted in full armour, with his legendary sword. Courageous, confident and heroic, with vermin enemies fleeing in all directions to get away from him.

Bisky had seen the tapestry almost every day of his life. He often wondered how anybeast could look so tough, yet carry in his eyes a twinkle of humour and kindness. The young mouse had tried often to emulate Martin's expression, until one day, Brother Torilis suspected he was suffering from some form of rictus, and physicked him thoroughly with pungent herbal medicines. Bisky broke off his reminiscences, to hear what the Abbot was saying.

"A warrior with the responsibility of protecting others should carry the best of weapons. Now I know, Bosie, that you have your fiddlebow thing, with the little metal shafts, but in a confined space, fighting paw to paw, for instance, a sword is more useful, would you agree?"

The mountain hare nodded, but with no great enthusiasm. "Ah'll grant ye there's those who fancy the blades. Ah've fought afore now, armed wi' a claymore. Ach, but they're unwieldly things, Father. Besides, Ah doubt ye'd own sich a thing."

Glisam went to the wall to one side of the tapestry. He took the blade from the silver pins which held it, passing it to Bosie. "This is the sword of Martin the Warrior. Long ago in the mists of bygone times, it was made by a Badger Lord at Salamandastron, from a piece of a star which fell from the sky. You may borrow it, to fight in defence of our Abbey and its creatures."

The Laird Bosie McScutta of Bowlaynee took it. Testing its weight and balance, he inspected the sword from the bloodred pommel stone, to the plain, black-bound grip, over the elegant, flaring, crosstree hilt and down the channelled and embossed blade. The entire weapon shone with a radiance of its own, sharp as a midwinter ice storm, pointed like a deadly needle.

Bosie swung it, revolving the sword in a figure-eight motion. He flipped it back and forth until the blade gave out a high-pitched whine. Whipping it down to floor level, he spun it in a blinding arc of steel, leaping over the blade nimbly. Banging to a sudden halt he thrust the blade at Bisky's face, stopping it a hairsbreadth from the young mouse's nose. Whirling about, Bosie charged full-tilt at Umfry, yelling, "Bowlaaaayneeec awaaaaa!"

The young hedgehog stood frozen, immobile, as Martin's sword neatly clipped a single spike from between his ears. Bosie halted his performance by holding the sword to his lips and kissing it. "Oh, mah babbies, 'tis a braw blade, an' Ah think Ah've got the hang of et now. By mah sporran, yon Martin didnae have much bother bein' a warrior wi' a weapon sich as this beauty!"

The Abbot was full of admiration for Bosie's prowess with the sword. "That was superb, but you said that you weren't one for swords. Unwieldy things, so you said?"

The Highland hare shrugged. "Aye, true enough, Father, but Ah'd ne'er felt a bonny blade like this afore. Let's go an' take a peek at how our friend Samolus is getting on with yon door."

They were halfway down the stairs when a loud boom rent the air. Hitching up his habit, Glisam hurried the pace. "What was that? I hope nobeast has been hurt!"

The door had been knocked flat. Samolus was dusting off his paws; he appeared to have cheered up somewhat. Skipper and Corksnout were busy hauling a barrel back up the little flight of steps.

Samolus told them how he had solved the problem. "Hah, 'twould've taken me more'n a day to move that lock. So I rolled a barrel of October Ale at it. Sometimes there's nought like brute force to get a result, aye, plus a big drop of good October Ale!"

Corksnout heaved the barrel upright. "Huh, first time my ale's been used as a batterin' ram. Don't seem any the worse for wear, though, do it?"

Bisky stood on the fallen door, sniffing the air of the dark, rough corridor that stretched out in front of him. "That's strange, the air down here seems quite fresh. You'd have thought an old, sealed-up tunnel like this would be smelly, musty and dank."

Samolus joined him. "Hmm, yore right. So, what d'you think we should do, stand here sniffin' the air, or get on with the search for the Eyes o' the Doomwyte?"

It was a rough and tortuous tunnel, twisting and dipping unexpectedly. Sometimes the walls were natural rock, but mostly they were earth, with roots of trees protruding downward. In places, the going was wet and sloppy, where stream- or springwater seeped through.

Bosie and Samolus led the way, with Bisky, Dwink and Umfry following. Skipper Rorgus and Foremole Gullub were rear guard. Holding their lanterns, they pressed onward into the narrow world of looming shadows and hanging roots.

It was Skipper who posed the question: "Ahoy, mateys, ye don't mind me askin', but have we got any clues t'go on?"

Foremole chuckled gruffly. "Hurhurr, et do sounds loike ee gudd question, zurrs, elsewhoise we'm bees a-wunderin' willy an' nilly!"

Bosie halted at a spot where the passage widened a bit. "Let's halt here an' see what we've got. You young uns, recite the poem again tae us."

Dwink recited the lines, slowly and clearly.

Samolus scratched his chin. "We've been through most o' that, 'twas all about the door an' the key, that's been solved. Give me the last four lines, Dwink, maybe they mean somethin'."

The young squirrel recited:

"That's a good place to begin.
What connects a front and back,
find one, and just three you'll lack.
Pompom Pompom, the trail leads on and on."

Skipper questioned the leading line. "What connects a front an' back. What's that supposed t'mean?"

Umfry explained, "We h'already solved that, 'twas h'a door, that's the connection. Front door, back door."

The Otter Chieftain continued, "Must be the next bit. 'Find one and just three you'll lack.' Sounds to me like we're searchin' for just one o' the jewels. Then there's all this Pompom stuff. Where does that leave us?"

Bisky crouched with his back against the tunnel wall. "Nowhere, I s'pose, it says the trail leads on an' on, but it doesn't give any clues on where to search."

Foremole wrinkled his button nose. "May'aps that bees wot'n we'm got to do. Go on an' on, fullowin' ee trail."

Samolus patted the mole's back. "Yore right, mate, we go on an' on, to see where it leads us. Who knows, it might take us right to the Doomwyte's Eye!"

Bosie had something to add. "Ah ken what ye say, though 'tis mah opinion that we should search this passage for more clues as we go."

Bisky sprang upright. "Sounds like good sense t'me. Right quick march, or should I say slow march an' keep yore eyes peeled!"

They seemed to have been marching for an age. Dwink stumbled, bruising his footpaw on a piece of flint. He complained, "You'd think whoever built this tunnel, they could have at least put a smoother floor to it."

Foremole Gullub answered, "Hurr, 'tworrn't nobeast builded this un, it bees ee tunnel wot's allus been yurr, zurr. Could've bee'd summ unnerground stream wot dried out longen ago."

Samolus, who was slightly ahead of the rest, called out, "Come an' look at this, mates!"

The old mouse was standing at a forked junction, where the tunnel divided, going two ways. Samolus began to get peevish again. "So, the trail leads on an' on, eh? Two bloomin' ways!"

Foremole opened one of their supply packs. "Sit ee daown an' eat, zurrs. Vikkles bees guud furr ee brains, Oi allus says."

Bosie plumped himself on the ground. "Och, yore a guid, wise mole, that's the best suggestion Ah've heard t'day!"

They ate in silence, glancing from one fork to the other, until Bisky spoke. "So, wot's it t'be, carry on together, or split up?"

Skipper was in no doubt. "No sense in comin' this far, an' havin' to leave one tunnel unexplored. We're best splittin' into two parties, mates. Now, how d'ye split seven up?"

Foremole Gullub had a suggestion. "Oi'll stay by yurr, wurr ee tunnels splitten, you'm go three uppen wun way, three uppen t'uther."

Bosie shrugged. "Ye cannae argue wi' that, though maybe auld Gullub should go with one party, an' I'll bide here, just tae keep guard on the vittles, ye ken."

Samolus shook his head. "You guardin' vittles? Huh, an' who'd we leave here t'guard you, my greedy friend? No, you can come with me an' Dwink. Skip, you take Bisky an' Umfry with ye. Right, which one do ye fancy, left or right?"

The otter Chieftain had an idea. "We'll let Martin's sword choose. Give it a whirl, Bosie."

Placing the glistening blade flat on the ground, the Highland hare spun it. The swordpoint stopped spinning, facing to the right tunnel. Foremole gave the verdict.

"You'm bees ee sword carrier, zurr, so take ee the path et points to."

Umfry started off down the left passage. "We'll h'all report back 'ere later h'on, good luck." Without further ado they went their separate ways.

Foremole sat by the ration packs, with one lantern for illumination. He watched the lights of both groups until they were out of sight, hoping none of his friends would come to any harm.

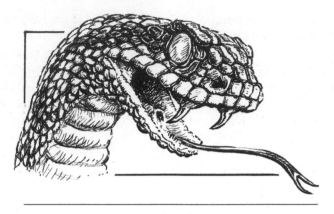

12

Korvus Skurr had not been outside his cavern for a full season. However, on this particular day he emerged into the bright sunlight at midmorning. The raven tyrant perched high in the birch tree on the streambank, surrounded by carrion birds. Veeku, the crow leader, shared the same branch with Korvus. It was an altogether odd scene—the black birds, normally rending the air with their cackling and harsh cries, were silent. All eyes were turned north, watching the treetops. Veeku spotted the two magpies first. "Kraah, I see them, Mighty One!"

Griv and Inchig landed on a lower limb, gazing up at Korvus. Inchig waited quietly, leaving the announcement to Griv.

"Kayaah! Baliss will be here when the sun is high, Lord!"

Korvus was not wearing the smoothsnake, Sicariss, draped about him. The reptile had chosen to stay within the underground retreat. The big raven closed his eyes, as if enjoying the day's pleasant warmth. He spoke to Veeku, ignoring the magpies now that they had told him what he wanted to hear.

"Kraaak! When the blind one arrives, you will have all your carrion guarding the cave entrance. I think Baliss will not try to get by them, after I have talked with him."

114

Veeku gazed impassively ahead. "Arrah, it shall be as ye command, Lord. I will await your signal!"

The sun rose to its zenith over the weird tableau below. There was little breeze, hardly a leaf stirred, only a damp rustle in the grass on the streambank. Korvus came alert as he saw the faint movement on the ground. He clacked his beak at Veeku, that was the signal. Immediately the drums from inside the cave entrance began pounding; there was an urgent flapping of birds' wings. The host of Korvus Skurr blocked the cave mouth completely, barring entrance to anybeast.

Slowly, majestically, the reptile's great, spade-shaped head arose from the grass, stretching upward, with its forked tongue sensing the atmosphere. The drumming ceased, everything was silent once more. Seeing the monstrous apparition rising against the birch trunk, Korvus mounted to a higher branch. Baliss spoke.

"Birdsssss! Sssso many birdssssssss!"

The raven was distinctly nervous, he chattered, "Yakkarraah! Nobeast can pass into my caves!"

The giant viper withdrew slightly, coiling at the bottom of the birch, his milky, sightless eyes pointed at the spot where the raven's voice had issued from. "Why doesss the mighty Sssskurr ssseek Dalissoooo?"

The raven regained his composure. "Hayaah! Come, and I will tell you!"

Launching himself from the tree, Korvus Skurr soared away, flapping noisily, so that the adder could track his movement. When he was sufficiently out of earshot, Korvus swooped down into the fork of an elm, waiting until Baliss arrived. Not wanting to linger with the fearsome snake, he came straight to the point.

"Arrakaa! Those earthcrawlers in the Redstone house need to fear my name. They must know Baliss is with me, they will learn the meaning of terror. You can do this."

The reptile's head swayed back and forth. "Balisssss knowssss all creaturessss fear him, even the great Sssssskurr.

But why do you do me thisss honour, what isss my reward to be?"

Korvus cocked his head from right to left, as if he feared being overheard. He lowered his voice. "Arrah! When the Eyes of the Doomwyte return to their rightful place, you will be rewarded. I will command my carrion birds to drive out every reptile from my caves. Frogs, toads, lizards, slow worms and grass snakes. They will be yours to treat as you please."

Baliss coiled and uncoiled languidly, a sign that he might be pleased with such an arrangement. "Thesssse reptilessss, what are their numberssss?"

Korvus Skurr spread his wings wide. "Yahaarr! Like the leaves which grow on the trees!"

The monstrous snake glided slowly off, his final words causing the raven to shudder. "Remember thisss: If you play me falssse, Balissss can make your death lassst half a sssseasssson!"

Not since the great snake Asmodeus had there been a serpent so feared in all Mossflower. Long seasons had done nothing to affect the huge reptile's power, speed or venom. Moreover, the blindness that had been visited on Baliss had only served to enhance all the snake's other sensory skills. In short, it created a creature that was totally fearless and fearsome, with no natural enemies, only victims.

Korvus Skurr was well satisfied with his plan. He flew off, back to his netherworld of caves, ignorant of one puny smoothsnake. It had lain coiled above his head, disguised by the billowing foliage of the stately elm tree. As soon as Korvus winged away, the little snake began her slithering descent from the elm trunk. Sicariss was no mere head ornament—she, too, had her eyes and ears in the strangest of places.

Other eyes had also witnessed what took place outside the caverns. High on the hillside, the dark beast saw it all.

116

The mysterious watcher drew a strange sword slowly back and forth over a whetstone slab. Little did Korvus Skurr or his scheming smoothsnake know that they were being observed by a creature who was planning their destruction, no matter how long it took. The double-bladed sword hissed softly as it was drawn over the whetstone, sharp and dangerous as the fangs of any reptile, when held in the paws of the dark avenger.

Tarul the raven Wyte had stayed concealed in the Belltower of Redwall Abbey. Stubborn determination kept him there; he had sworn to himself not to leave the Redbrick house without taking with him a prisoner. One of the small earthcrawlers they called Dibbun. But things had not gone well from the start.

First there had been the rain, when hardly anybeast stirred out of doors. His spirits brightened with the arrival of fair weather. However, he soon found himself out of position, isolated in the Belltower, whilst the Dibbuns played, either in the orchard, by the pond or near the Gatehouse. They were generally well watched also.

This Belltower was not a good place, Tarul thought to himself. At least four times daily he had to cower in the furthest corner, with his head tucked tight beneath one wing. This was because of the burly hedgehog called Spikkle. At set intervals he would come in to ring the twin bells, at midnight, dawn, high noon and sunset. For a long time after each session of peals, the Raven Wyte's head would resound with bell echoes.

But that was not all. It was hunger and thirst which beset Tarul most of all. Once he had been about to sample the fruits of the orchard, when he spied the long-eared one strolling in the grounds. Tarul feared him greatly, having seen the damage he could wreak with his strange weapon, which fired sharp, metal sticks.

So he remained in the Belltower, growing gaunt with

starvation, and ill with headaches, but still foolishly obstinate. Thinking of the praise he would gain, from being the most daring of Wytes.

Then one morning, the burly spikehog did not appear to ring the dawn bells. Tarul stirred his bedraggled feathers hopefully. Believing that his luck was about to change, he posted himself by the upper window of the tower, eagerly awaiting any development. Throughout the golden spring morn he watched the grounds below. The chance came at midday, when most of the Redbrick house dwellers gathered in the orchard to eat lunch. Both his hated foes, the spikehog and longears, accompanied by a party of others, left the orchard, hurrying off indoors.

Then two of the Dibbuns finished lunch and trolled off across the lawns, totally unwatched by elders. Excitement bubbled in Tarul's chest when he saw where they were heading. Straight to the belltower! Hopping about eagerly, the Raven Wyte positioned himself slightly above both bells, ready to pounce. Luckily, the door below was ajar and both the little creatures entered with ease. It was Furff the infant squirrel and the very tiny mousebabe. They went straight to the trailing bellropes, seizing one apiece, tugging for all they were worth.

Tarul decided quickly. He could only manage one captive, in his weakend state; so, he would swoop down, slay the squirrel and capture the mousebabe. Being the smaller it would prove far less difficult. The raven stifled his cackles, listening to the pair below.

"A lunchertime be gone now, worra use us ringin' bells?"

The very tiny mousebabe tugged even harder, still with no result. "A case anyone doesn't not knows it lunchertime. Cummon, lazytail, pull 'arder willya!"

"I are pullin' 'arder, but no bells aren't ringin'!"

Then the unexpected happened. Sister Violet had seen the Dibbuns leave the orchard. She went after them. Tarul had missed seeing her, through hopping about in delight. The plump, jolly hedgehog tippawed up, surprising both Dibbuns.

Furff gritted her little teeth, still heaving on the bellrope. "Grrr, us ringin' a bells fer lunch, Sissy Vi!"

The hedgehog Sister reached above their paws, taking a firm grip on both ropes as she assisted the Dibbuns. "Oh well, you'll need to be a few seasons older, and eat all yore veggibles, just like me. C'mon now, all together. One . . . two . . . pullll!"

Babongbongggg!

The brazen rims of the Matthias and the Methusaleh bells (named after two long-gone heroes) struck the Raven Wyte either side of his head. Tarul died with the echo of the joint peals ringing through his skull. He toppled from the beam he had been perched upon, like a dark bundle of tattered rags plunging from the top of the Belltower. Sister Violet had the presence of mind to glance upward. She saw the falling object, and pushed both Dibbuns back against the wall.

Shielding them with her flowing habit, Violet stared in dumbstruck horror at the slain raven. The very tiny mousebabe peered from under the garment's wide hem. "Huh, no wunner d'bells wuddent ring."

Unaware of the drama that was being enacted in the Belltower, both parties of questers carried on their search in the gloomy underground tunnels. Skipper, Bisky and Umfry plodded along the left passageway, constantly avoiding entangling roots, dripping water and rough chunks of flint, which stuck out at every angle. Umfry spoke his thoughts aloud as they pressed onward.

"Huh, 'ope we don't lose h'our way back, we must've come miles h'out o' the way."

Skipper chuckled. "We can 'ardly lose our way back, 'cos this is the only tunnel we've travelled along."

The burly, young hedgehog was still not convinced. "But suppose h'it splits two ways h'again, h'I bet it'd be h'easy t'get lost then, eh, Bisk?"

His young mousefriend scoffed, "If that happens, Umf, we'll fret about it then. Yore a proper ole worrywart, mate!"

Skipper sniffed the atmosphere. "The air seems t'be gettin' fresher down 'ere. Are you thinkin' wot I am, young Bisky?"

Umfry interrupted, "You mean that there's a way out h'into the fresh air h'up yonder somewheres!"

The Otter Chieftain held his lantern up, winking at Bisky. "Our Umfry ain't as green as he looks. Mark my words, that hog'll go far someday!"

Umfry sat down where the floor was dry, massaging his footpaws. "H'I've gone far h'enough for one day, thankee, Skip. Let's take h'a liddle rest."

Bisky and Skipper joined him. From where they were seated, the passage before them appeared to run straight, without any twists or turns. Resting his chin on both paws, Umfry declared gloomily, "Huh, this blinkin' tunnel must go h'on forever!"

Bisky squinted into the passage as he consulted the Otter Chieftain. "How good are yore eyes, Skip?"

Skipper shrugged. "Not as good as they used t'be, why?"

Bisky pointed down the tunnel. "Somewhere along there I thought I saw a glint o' light. Might've been a sunray shinin' through!"

Umfry wrinkled his snout after a perfunctory glance. "H'I can't see anythin' from 'ere."

Bisky was already up, hurrying forward, with Skipper following, upbraiding Umfry as he went.

"Shift yoreself, spiky bottom, let's go an' investigate!"

Bisky raced ahead, shouting, "I was right, it's daylight, comin' through a hole in the ceilin'. C'mon, mates!"

The young mouse put on an extra burst of speed, outdistancing his companions. He arrived in the golden-moted shaft of light. A shadow passed overhead. Cupping paws about his mouth, Bisky called out, "Lend a paw up there, we're from Redwall Abbey!"

A carved rock about the size of an apple, attached to the end of a long, greased line, struck Bisky on the side of his head. He slumped forward, half-stunned, the line whipping round his body. Several other similar lines hit him, snaring the young mouse completely. A multitude of paws hauled him swiftly up through the hole. Shrill voices chanted jubilantly, "Yikyik! Gorramouse! Yeeeeeeeh!"

Skipper could not make out what was going on up ahead. Hearing the sounds, he dashed toward the shaft of light. Not being as fast, Umfry stumbled behind, calling anxiously, "Where's Bisky gone, 'as somethin' 'appened to 'im?" Almost at the spot, Skipper skidded to a halt.

Dark shapes were pouring through the hole, lots of them. Another cry rang out. "Hiyeeeh! There's more, gerrem, gerrem!"

Suddenly the passage was crowded with foebeasts. In the gloom, Skipper could not make out who, or what, they were. Acting instinctively, he hurled his lantern at their front ranks. Turning, he grabbed Umfry. "Out of here, mate, quick!"

Phut! A plumed splinter of wood shot the otter just above his right footpaw. Kicking it out, he pushed Umfry into a headlong run.

"There's too many of 'em. Get goin' or we're finished!"

Both otter and hedgehog fled for their lives, with the screeching mob at their heels.

"Yeeeyeee! Gerrem, catcher 'em! Hiyeeee!"

BOOK TWO

A Prince's Descendants

Was there ever such a thieving tribe?

13

The passage to the right was not only pitch-dark, but it began going downhill sharply. Bosie was in the lead, he dug his footpaws in and held on to the damp rocky wall, calling advice to Samolus and Dwink. "Och, iffen this gets much steeper, we'll fall doon tae who knows where. We'd be best tae rope oorselves taegether."

Dwink passed the rope, which they looped about their waists before continuing. It was just as well that they were roped together, because Dwink slipped. Dropping his lantern, the young squirrel gave a yell of dismay as he shot past his companions. Samolus was too late to stop Dwink. He bumped into Bosie.

"Grab the rope, stop him!"

The rope played out, then tautened. Bosie grabbed a rocky protrusion, bracing himself, steadying Samolus by pinning him against the wall. They both stared downward, watching Dwink's lantern light disappearing into nothingness. Dwink's voice came up to them, tight and urgent.

"Don't let me go, hang on to the rope, I'll try an' climb up. Don't let go o' that rope, keep a tight hold!"

By the light of Bosie's lantern, both he and Samolus could see that they were on a narrow rim. Below them yawned a wide, massive hole, a pit which looked bottomless. The mountain hare shouted to Dwink, "Are ye alright doon there, laddie, d'ye want us tae pull ye up?"

Dwink's answer carried a touch of indignation. "I'm a squirrel, y'know, I can get myself up."

Samolus could not resist a wry rejoinder. "If'n yore so nimble, then how did ye manage to fall down there, eh?"

Dwink was about to reply when a booming voice interrupted, "Beware the eye of death and the pit of lost beasts! Go back now, or die! Woooooooooh! Baliss!"

Dwink scrambled up onto the ledge like a shot. He huddled behind his two friends. "Who said that?"

The phantom voice echoed out again. "Your fate is sealed if ye do not turn back now. I am the Eye of Death, I see all, heed my warning! Woooohoooohhhhhh! Baliss!"

Dwink was frightened. He whispered to Samolus, "There's nothin' for us down here, we'd be better doin' wot the voice says an' turnin' back!"

The mountain hare, however, was made of sterner stuff. Clipping Dwink's ear lightly, he called into the dark void, "Ach, away wi' ye! Eye o' Death mah grannie's apron! Ah'm the Laird Bosie McScutta o' Bowlaynee, a braw warrior, an' frit o' naebeast. If'n Ah'm no mistaken, ye have the voice o' a bird. So hearken tae me, auld Deatheye, d'ye see mah blade?" He waved the sword of Martin in the lantern light, adding as it shimmered and shone in the gloom, "Lissen, mah friend, Ah'll clip yore wings wi' this bonny thing, aye, an' send ye intae yer own pit!"

A soft, green light appeared at the far arc of the narrow ledge. As it travelled closer, the light increased in brilliance. Samolus swallowed hard as it approached them.

"Great seasons, what creature has an eye that size?"

Bosie nudged him, none too gently. "Haud yer wheesht, y'auld ninny, let's see what it has tae say for itself!"

It waddled hesitantly out of the darkness, a tawny owl, holding a great emerald in its beak. Dropping the jewel, it placed one of its fierce four-taloned claws on the precious object before addressing Bosie. "Clip my wings, would you, sir? Alas, that has already been done. I am condemned to a life of walking, a sweep of your blade to my throat would come as a mercy to me. My name is Aluco, welcome to my world, such as it is. Pray tell, what are you doing down here?"

Samolus, whilst feeling pity for the owl, could not restrain his curiosity. "We could ask you the same question, Aluco."

The tawny owl heaved a hooting sigh; he appeared ready to explain. However, his head swivelled, almost full circle, and his dark eyes shone alertly. "I could tell you, friend, but I haven't the time. Quick, they're coming!" He began shuffling away along the ledge.

Bosie called after him, "Who's coming, what are ye talkin' aboot?"

Aluco came back to retrieve his stone. "The Painted Ones from above the other tunnel. I don't know why they've chosen now to attack me, but their numbers are many, we must hide. I have a den over the far side of this ledge. They never venture there, follow me!"

The yells and screeches of the foebeasts could be heard, echoing down the tunnel as Dwink spoke. "From the other tunnel, you say? We've got three friends who went searching up there, and a mole, waiting at the junction of both passages!"

Bosie began climbing back up the slope. "So ye see, we've got tae go an' help 'em. Ah dinnae care how many o' they Painted Ones are abroad, Ah'm bound tae aid mah friends!"

Aluco scrambled up to the hare's side. "Then count me in, better a quick death than dragging my life out in this place. Besides, if we can make them retreat back to the left tunnel, I've got a trap laid that'll keep the fiends off our backs. Follow me, I know my way round down here."

Unfortunately the tawny owl, not being able to fly, slowed things down considerably. Aluco trundled along the rocky corridor with his newfound friends stumbling impatiently in his wake. The high-pitched screams of the Painted Ones grew louder up ahead.

Anxious to find out what was going on, Bosie pushed past the owl. "Ah best make haste afore 'tis too late!" He hurtled onward, up the tunnel, toward the sound.

A lantern glimmer showed ahead. It was Foremole Gullub and Umfry, between them they were supporting Skipper. The Otter Chieftain was limping badly.

The cries of the foebeast were almost drowning out every other sound as Bosie reached Skipper's side. "Och, whit ails ye, laddie?"

The brawny otter winced grimly. "No time for chatter, mate, git us out o' here, there's a mob o' savages on our tails!"

Aluco hove into view, with Samolus and Dwink illuminating the way with lanterns. The tawny owl beckoned urgently. "Back, back, to the ledge. My den's on the far side of it. I'll see if I can face them off whilst you escape!"

Bosie saw the mass of dark shapes pouring at them out of the gloom, yelling, screeching and shouting. Drawing the sword of Martin, the mountain hare stood alongside the tawny owl. "Ah'm with ye, bucko, nae beast'll say that the Laird McScutta left others tae fight his battles!"

As the rest of the party rushed Skipper off to safety, Aluco picked up a lantern, muttering to Bosie, "They fear me, let me show you." Holding the big emerald in front of the lantern light, the owl gave vent to a blood-chilling cry, which resounded around the passage. "Whoooh! Baliss the Eye of Death sees all! Whooooeeeeh!"

The Painted Ones suddenly fell silent, milling about, as if unsure of what to do. Aluco whispered to Bosie, "Let's start retreating slowly whilst they're still." The vermin mob stayed motionless for a moment, then they were forced to come forward, as the front ranks were shoved by those behind them. Bosie whirled the sword, his blade weaving an eerie green arc in the emerald light. Then he roared out his warcry. "EulaliaaaaBowlayneeeee! Ah'm the slayer frae the mountains! EulaliaaaaBowlaynee! Ah'll send ye all tae Hellgates! Yaaaahaaarrrrr!" Aluco bellowed out his Eye of Death challenge as Bosie carried on with his battle rant. It seemed to have the desired effect. They backed hastily off, still delivering dire threats.

But it did not last. The pair were almost safely on their way, when the Chieftain of the Painted Ones shouted out angrily, "Gerrem! Killem afore they 'scape! Chaaarge!"

Then the owl and the hare were running for their lives, as the vermin mob stampeded forward after them.

Aluco's den was a cul-de-sac at the far side of the deep pit. Going in single file along the narrow ledge, which circled the abyss, the friends helped Skipper along, whichever way they could. Gasping and panting, they took shelter behind a palisade of stubby stalagmites, which fronted the den.

Taking his knife, Samolus cut strips from his tunic, passing them to Gullub, Dwink and Umfry. "Gather stones an' pebbles, there's lots of 'em about, this cloth should do to make slings. Skip, stay here an' rest yoreself, we can't leave Bosie an' Aluco to face those villains alone. Come on!"

Skipper attempted to rise, but his leg flopped uselessly under him. He thrashed his rudder in frustration. "Garrr! That dart they stuck me in the footpaw with has deadened my blinkin' leg!" Hauling himself upright on a stalagmite, he pointed. "Ahoy mates, here they come, gimme a sling, will ye!"

Bosie and Aluco reached the narrow rim with the vermin hard on their paws. The owl directed his companion, "Take the left ledge, I'll go right. Watch out for any darts they shoot at you, they're dangerous!"

The hare was a short way along the ledge, pushing his back hard against the rocky wall, as he tried to not think of the bottomless void yawning in front of him. A Painted

One ventured out onto the ledge, loading a dart into a hollow blowpipe. He leered wickedly at Bosie.

"Yikahee, getcher now, rabbet, Gadik never misses!" A chunk of limestone struck him on the neck. He gave a choking gurgle, and plunged headlong into the pit.

Samolus's voice called out cheerily, "I never miss, either, scum. Step up, who's next?" This was followed by a salvo of slingstones, as the defenders called encouragement to Bosie and Aluco. "You'm goo easy naow, zurrs, us'll give 'em billyoh 'til ee bees safe!"

The vermin gathered on the rim's edge, with their Chieftain egging them on. "Shoot, shoot! Stoppem! Yikikik!"

Skipper grabbed up a lantern and shook it. "Give me space, mateys, this 'as still got oil in it!" Holding himself upright on the stalagmite fence, he swung the lantern back and forth with his powerful rudder. The still air whooshed as he hurled the lit lantern. Up it went, streaking across the dark pit like a comet. The vermin were too tightly packed on the far rim to avoid it. The missile came down with a crash amongst them, its rock crystal prisms shattering, spraying blazing vegetable oil over the heads of the foebeasts. The screams were deafening; three fell, blazing, into the black abyss. A second lantern followed, thrown by Foremole Gullub's mighty digging claws. Dwink was about to hurl a third lantern, but he was stopped by Umfry.

"Don't throw that un, h'it's the h'only light we got left!"

Bosie and Aluco scrambled into the safety of the cul-de-sac. The hare put up his sword. "Mah thanks tae ye, friends, Ah reckon that's given the blaggards somethin' tae think aboot!"

The far rim was in chaos, more vermin were falling into the pit, as the mob scrambled to get away from the flames. The Chieftain was screeching unmercifully, lying flat on his back as he tried to extinguish a smouldering bottom and tail.

A green-and-black-painted female garbed in vines and withered vegetation took charge. She charged about with a long blowpipe, issuing orders. "Back, back, alla ye! Take Chigid with ye!"

Aluco pointed a talon. "That's Chigid, their leader. He took me captive and pulled my pinions to stop me ever flying. What a pity the flames never slew him, the evil little rat!"

Dwink watched the enemy retreat from the rim. "Is that what Painted Ones are, rats?"

The owl nodded. "Aye, small, wild tree rats. They don't like anybeast to know what they really are, so they paint themselves all green and black, and wear many kinds of vines and plants to disguise themselves. But there's lots of them, they're cruel and vicious!"

Tears popped unbidden to Umfry's eyes. "H'and they've got pore Bisky, our mate!"

Skipper placed both paws against his brow in despair. "Aye, 'twas my fault, I couldn't stop 'em!"

Bosie patted the otter's stout back comfortingly. "Ach, ye canna blame yerself, Skip, Ah'll wager ye did all ye could tae save the young un. But dinna fret, Ah'll rescue Bisky frae yon vormin rogues. Aye, an' Ah'll make 'em weep bitter tears for their wrongdoin's, ye have McScutta's word on it!"

Aluco gave the hare a withering sideways glance. "Bravely said, sir, and when, pray, is all this going to happen, eh?"

Umfry interrupted, spikes a-bristle with righteous wrath, "H'as soon h'as possible, h'in fact right now!"

The tawny owl's huge eyes widened. "Excuse me saying, but do you think that's wise?"

Dwink sprang up, fitting a rock to his sling. "Wise? There's no time t'worry about bein' wise, we've got to save our pal Bisky from those fiends!"

Foremole Gullub shook his head at the young squirrel. "Ee owlyburd b'aint no fool, you'm lissen to 'im, zurrs!"

131

Knowing that mole logic could not be disputed, Samolus agreed with Gullub. He bowed to Aluco. "Carry on, friend."

The owl puffed out his chest feathers, launching into an explanation. "I know this may sound dreadful, but forget about saving your friend for a moment. Our main problem is how to save ourselves. Think about it. Just up that tunnel there's a whole army of Painted Ones, thirsting for our blood. Believe me, you wouldn't last the wink of an eye. I know their leader, Chigid, he's been injured by the lantern flames. That one won't rest until your skinned carcasses are hanging from his five-topped oak tree. I was a captive of the Painted Ones for many seasons, I know how they think. They'll be sworn to avenge themselves against you at all costs."

Samolus had a question. "But how did you escape from them? And one other thing—where did you get that Doomwyte Eye, the big, green jewel you carry?"

Aluco placed the stone where the lantern light reflected its verdant fires. It was the size of a pigeon's egg, completely smooth and highly polished. "'Tis a long story of how I escaped those savages. However, I jumped into the hole, near the five-topped oak. With twoscore Painted Ones pursuing me, I went in a mad scramble. I'd never been in the tunnels before, so I just plunged blindly along, not knowing where it would lead me, and totally in the dark. I was beginning to tire, out of breath, they were coming fast, almost right on my tail. The front runners were carrying blazing torches. Just around a bend, I ran smackbang into a locked door. I must have hooted and screeched aloud with pain and shock. Right at that moment they came racing round the bend, holding up their torches. The tunnel was suddenly filled with green light from the stone, which was fixed to the center of the door. What with that, and the dreadful noises I was making, they turned and fled. I could hear them shouting, 'Baliss! Baliss!'

"I was very frightened, having heard of the great serpent Baliss. So I lay still there for awhile. When nothing happened I rose, and picked up a torch which one of my hunters had dropped. Blowing the torch back into flame again, I looked around. There was myself, a locked door and the great, green jewel, but nought else. I sat there a long time pondering, until I solved the puzzle. That door must have been the gate to the serpent's lair. The Painted Ones must have thought Baliss had slain me.

"Well, I was not waiting around for the serpent to devour me, so I picked up the torch, took the green stone and hurried off. Whenever I thought there were Painted Ones lurking in wait, I began hooting and yelling out 'Baliss.' It must have worked, because they left me well alone. I found a place to hide, on the other side of the pit. I've lived alone there, until you came along, friends."

Dwink looked sympathetically at the tawny owl. "It must have been dreadful, down here in the darkness, with nothing to eat."

Aluco blinked his great eyes, almost coyly. "Oh, I wasn't exactly starving, I'm quite vengeful myself, you know. If one can hunt, there's always a meal to be had, though one can't be too choosy."

Umfry gazed at the owl in horrified awe. "Y'mean you ate Pain—

Tactfully, Samolus cut across Umfry's question. "Well, I never! So that's where the green stone was, attached to the back o' that door. Hah, an' we knocked it flat an' trampled over it to search the tunnels. The door wasn't an entrance to a snake's den, Aluco, it comes out in the cellars of Redwall Abbey."

The tawny owl gave a long, hooting sigh. "Redwall Abbey, if only I'd known! D'you think they'd have let me in? I'd dearly love to visit there."

Foremole Gullub stroked the owl's flightless wing. "O' course, zurr, you'm cudd make yurr 'ome thurr with us'ns, iffen ee so desoired!"

Aluco seemed overcome with gratitude. "Oh, thank

133

you, friend, it would be wonderful, a real dream come true. Thank you so much!"

Dwink loaded a stone into his sling. He shot it pointlessly off into the dark abyss. "I'd save my thanks if'n I was you, mate. We've found the jewel we came for, shiny, useless thing! All this searchin' for the Eyes o' the Doomwyte, what's it got us, eh?" Usually an easygoing young squirrel, Dwink surprised them all with his angry outburst. "It's got us trapped here, miles underground, by a mob o' savage vermin. An' wot about my pal, we don't even know if'n he's dead or alive. That's wot huntin' for some stupid jewel has got us!"

He grabbed up the big emerald, shouting, "Down that deep hole, that's the best place for this thing. I never want t'see it again!" He swung back his paw to throw the Doomwyte Eye, when a well-aimed kick from Bosie's swift paw sent him flat on his back. The mountain hare picked up the gem, holding Dwink down with his paw.

"Ach, nae so fast, laddie. Ah've been figurin' a plan tae get oot o' here. This wee bauble is part of it. So, do Ah take it yore with me, or do ye all want tae set there, wi' faces like auld biddies who've burnt the oatcakes?"

Skipper grasped Bosie's free paw. "Here's me heart an' here's me word, mate, we're with ye!"

The mountain hare adjusted his fine lace cuffs. "Gather ye round an' hearken tae me, braw beasties, here's how we'll do the deed!"

14

Sometime in the late evening, Bisky regained his senses. A searing pain in his tailtip caused the young mouse to cry out in anguish. He was being bitten by a rat of about his own age, a Painted One. Bisky assessed his situation at a glance. His forepaws were strung to an overhead limb, high up in a massive five-topped oak tree. The tree rat bit him again, sniggering at its own joke.

"Yikkachikka, I eatin' you, mousey!"

Fortunately, Bisky's footpaws were unbound. He kicked out hard, catching his foe in the stomach. The vermin lost his breath in a loud *whoosh*, falling from the bough where he was perched. He hung by his long tail from the smaller branches below, wailing. "Waaaaah! Mouse tryna kill Jeg, 'elpeeeeelp, Mammeeee!"

An older female, presumably Jeg's mother, came rushing through the foliage, accompanied by three other ratwives. She snapped an order at her companions. "Gerra likkle Jeg backup 'ere, 'urry, 'urry!" Whilst they scrambled to do her bidding, she set about scratching viciously at Bisky's ribs. "Juss yew ever raise a paw t'my Jeg agin, an' I scratch yer 'eart out, an' yer eyes, too, d'yer 'ear?"

The young mouse arched his back in agony, but she continued raking until he called out aloud, "Stop, I hear ye, please stop!"

The torment ceased as she helped the others to haul her son up. Having wiped away his tears, they sat him on the broad limb, a safe distance away from Bisky. They all began stroking and comforting the young Painted One, as they glared at the captive.

Bisky studied them; he had heard of Painted Ones before, but this was his first face-to-face encounter with the savage vermin. They looked like primitive throwbacks of some bygone age, small for rats, but very wiry and agile. Their teeth were filed into sharp points, and their snouts pierced with bone ornaments. Painted Ones covered their bodies with heavy plant dyes, black and dark green. All sorts of straggly vegetation, weeds, vines, leaves and creepers, draped about them like kilts and cloaks, completed the camouflage. Bisky judged by the rustlings and comings and goings all about that there was a great number of the vermin in the five-topped oak, and other nearby trees. All in all, a fierce and barbaric tribe.

Jeg's mother, Tala, hugged her son close, peering maliciously at Bisky. Jeg stuck out his lower lip, in a sulky manner. "Dat mouse hurted me stummick, an' I weren't doin' nothin' to 'im!"

Bisky shouted an angry reply. "Ye rotten liar, you were biting me!"

Tala seized a long willow withe from one of the others, and slashed Bisky across his face. "Shuddup, who asked yew t'speak, mouse?"

Jeg set up a blubbering wail, a ruse he often used to get his own way. He pointed a grimy claw at Bisky. "Badmouse! Yew should be slayed! I want 'im killed, Mamee Tala, let Jeg kill d'badmouse!"

Tala stroked her son's scraggy ears, murmuring soothingly. "Nono, yore Dadda Chigid never said nothin' about killin' d'mouse, yew'll haveter ask 'im!"

Jeg went into a real tantrum then. Wrenching himself free

of his mother's embrace, he climbed into the foliage, and began hurling down twigs and leaves. "My dadda's the Tribechief, I'll tell 'im all about yew's lot. Letting' d'mouse hurt me stummick, an' not lettin' me kill 'im. Yore a bad mammee, yore all bad. My dada will beat yew all for bein' nasty t'me!"

Bisky flinched as an acorn hit him in the eye. Blinking up at the spoiled young vermin, he found himself murmuring, "I'd like to leave you a day with Brother Torilis, huh, he'd soon teach you a few manners!"

Tala went off to the tunnel hole, to watch for her husband's return. She took some of her companions with her, leaving three to guard the prisoner.

Bisky tested his bonds by tugging them. They were too well tied for any escape to be possible. He tried them again, but after receiving another slash from the willow withe, he gave up. The young mouse hung there, with bowed head, trying to ignore his bruises and scrapes, wondering how his friends were faring.

Back at Redwall Abbey the two Dibbuns, Furff and the very small mousebabe, had become the hero and heroine of the season. Sister Violet had denied any part in the death of the big raven inside the belltower. Besides being a fat, jolly hedgehog, she was also very tenderhearted, and could not admit a part in the death of anybeast, friend or foe. So, it was left to the two Dibbuns to claim the notoriety, which they did, with absolutely no pretence to modesty, or truth. The raven had been displayed out by the main gate prior to being consigned to the ditch outside. Redwallers viewed it, with awed observations as to its size and ferocity.

"Buhurr, jus' lukk at ee talyons on yon burd!"

"Aye, and the beak, too, imagine getting a peck off that?"

The tiny mousebabe, draped in a cloak which was ten sizes too large for him, strutted shamelessly back and forth, keeping the onlookers at bay. He waved a ladle, his chosen weapon, and a pan lid, which served as a shield, cautioning everybeast, "Don't not better get too close, y'might get hurted!"

Furff was in her element, she had appropriated one of Friar Skurpul's vegetable skewers, which she kept jabbing in the direction of the raven's carcass, muttering darkly, "Good job Umfry wasn't ringin' the bells, the big bird woulda gotted 'im!"

It was not long before Brother Torilis appeared on the scene, complaining to the Abbot, "Really, Father, how long is this disgusting spectacle to continue? Wouldn't it be wise to remove that object from the premises? It makes me sick just looking at it!"

Abbot Glisam was forced to agree with Torilis. "Aye, Brother, I thought I'd just let our Dibbun warriors bask in the glory for a moment or two. Mister Spikkle, will you help the Brother and me to haul this thing out and tip it into the ditch?"

Corksnout tugged a dutiful headspike at Glisam. "Aye, Father, but I kin do it meself, no reason for you two gennelbeasts to soil yore paws, leave it t'me."

Brother Torilis breathed an inward sigh of relief, knowing he would loathe touching the dead raven. "Thank you kindly, Cellarhog, I'm obliged t'you."

The tiny mousebabe interrupted gruffly, "That bees our job, me'n'Furff, we drag 'im out!"

Judging the size of both infants to the raven, the Abbot hid a smile. He took both their paws. "I've got a much better idea, why don't we honour our two warriors with a feast by the Abbey pond, eh?"

No second bidding was needed. The two raven slayers, surrounded by a host of their friends, stampeded off in the direction of the pond, roaring and whooping. "A feast, a feast! Redwaaaaaallllll!"

Brother Torilis followed in the Abbot's wake, still with a note of complaint in his voice as he watched the charge of the Dibbuns. "But what about bedtime? It's evening already." He was almost knocked flat from a buffet on the back by Sister Violet.

"Oh, you can go to bed right now if you're tired, Brother. We're going to the feast!"

Abbot Glisam winked at the jolly Sister. "Well said, friend, come on, I'll race you!"

Torilis cast a stern eye at their receding backs, then continued with his own measured pace.

Friar Skurpul had already been told about the feast, he had the orchard laid out wonderfully. The squirrelmaid Perrit had set out all the food on woven rush mats. Not having to sit on chairs at table was a novelty for the little ones. Moreso, when the Abbot and elders joined them on the grass. Friar Skurpul caused much merriment amidst the Abbeybabes by addressing the Father Abbot as though he were a naughty Dibbun.

"You'm moind yurr manners, Glisam, an' keep ee paws clean, moi laddo. Dugry, keep yurr eye on that un an' doan't let 'im go a-jumpin' abowt!"

Abbot Glisam's reply caused further hilarity. "What, me jump about? It'll take four of you to lift me back up onto my paws after this!"

Even before they had taken a bite of the delicious food, the Dibbuns were up and dancing, pulling mock bellropes and stamping their tiny footpaws to an impromptu song. The very small mousbabe roared out the lines, which (with a lot of help from Sister Violet) he had composed. What it lacked in melody and meter, the song made up for in raucous exuberance.

"Ho we make'd the bad bird fall down dead,
Fall down dead! Fall down dead!
We pulled onna ropes an' he falled on his head,
Faaalled . . . on . . . his . . . head!
The naughty bird was goin' to eat us all,
Eat us all! Eat us all!

'Til us pulled the ropes an' make'd him fall.
Riiiight . . . on . . . his . . . head!
Y'won't see that ole bird no more
'Cos his head went crack onna Belltower floor.
Bing bong! Ding dong! Boom crash bang!
The bird falled down anna bells all rang!"

Out at the main gate, Corksnout Spikkle was hauling the raven's carcass out to the ditch. The taloned limbs stuck out stiffly. Facing the bird's carcass, the big Cellarhog took one in each paw, and began pulling. His imitation cork nose slid down beneath his chin as he strained away. Adjusting it, Corksnout mopped his brow, turning to address his thoughts to the dead bird. "Whew! I didn't figger on you bein' so 'eavy. Still, ye are . . . beg pardon, I mean was, a fine, big lump of a featherbag. Huh, I should've let the Father an' Torilis 'elp me."

Standing in the open gateway, with his back to the ditch, the burly hedgehog carried on his one-sided conversation with the dead raven. He was totally unaware of the monstrous head rising up from the ditch behind him. The senses of Baliss had caught odour and movement. The giant snake's blue-marbled eyes filmed over as he reared high and struck with lightning speed.

Down in the tunnels, Chigid, Chieftain of the Painted Ones, was seething with wrath and pain. The pain, from blazing lantern oil searing his tail and nether parts. The wrath, to destroy the beasts who had inflicted such agonising embarrassment upon one of his lofty position. Standing at the rear of his band, he berated them, until the tunnel walls echoed to his scorn.

"Yaaar yigalig! Idjits! Cowwids! Get back down d'passage, charge an' killem! Killem all, skin 'em, burn 'em like they burn Chigid. Chaaaarge!"

Pushed forward by the back ranks, the front and centre

Painted Ones went, stumbling and tripping toward the ledge, which circled the deep abyss.

Behind the stalagmites which fronted Aluco's retreat, the friends heard the foebeasts' warcries. "Yeeeee! Gerrem! Killem! Yeeeeeeeeh!"

Skipper shielded the light from their last lantern, muttering grimly, "Belay, mates, sounds like we got vermin tryin' t'pay us a visit. Are yore slings loaded?"

Dwink's paws were shaking with nerves, but he replied boldly, "Aye, I've got four stones in mine!"

Bosie patted the young squirrel's back. "Yer a braw laddie. Remember now, don't shoot 'til I give ye the word. That goes for all o' ye!"

Foremole Gullub nodded sagely. "Hurr, Oi 'opes ee plan wurks, zurr!"

The Highland hare replied blithely, "Och, it'll have tae, 'tis the only one Ah've got."

The yells of the enemy sounded louder now, closer. Umfry Spikkle began twirling his sling rapidly. "Do we lets 'em 'ave h'it now?"

Samolus tweaked Umfry's snout. "Patience, young un, just do as Bosie says, wait!"

The roar of charging Painted Ones reached a crescendo. This was suddenly interrupted by screeches of dismay, and shouts to halt. "Yaaagh, stopstop! Gebback, back!" Having the excellent sight of an owl in darkness, Aluco whooped exultantly.

"Whoohoo! A load of the villains went straight over the rim, into the pit!"

Bosie began whirling his sling, remarking, "Aye, spilt lantern oil is verra slippy, Ah'm glad they'd forgotten that. Right, mah buckoes. Shoot!"

Each of the defenders had in his sling as many stones as it would hold. They rattled off a hefty volley at their adversaries. Bosie was yelling, "Load as fast as ye can, mah bonnies. Dinnae stop!" Turning aside, he whispered

141

to the tawny owl, "Aluco, can ye see one that ye could capture?"

With his huge eyes dilating, Aluco pointed. "Actually I can see two of the scum in trouble over there. One has fallen stunned at the rim, the other is clinging to the side of the pit."

The hare smiled admiringly. "Ah wisht Ah had your eyesight. D'ye no think ye could clamber out an' get one of 'em?"

Aluco responded promptly, "Just don't hit me with any of those stones, and I'll collar both the blaggards, and bring 'em back here." He scuttled out onto the narrow rim, which encircled the pit. Foremole Gullub followed.

"Oi'll cumm with ee, zurr, jus' to lend ee a paw."

Skipper lofted a slingful of stones at the far side. "Good luck, mates, hurry now, we'll give ye coverin' fire. Don't fret, we'll aim high!"

The loss of their front rank into the abyss, coupled with the savage rain of stones, caused the Painted Ones to retreat momentarily. Aluco hooked the whimpering vermin who had been clinging to the edge. One heave of the owl's huge talons lifted him onto the rim. Stunning him with a quick wingsweep, the owl began hauling him back. Foremole seized the other Painted One by his tail, dragging him along backward. "Yurr, you'm cumm with Oi!"

Hearing no further warcries from the opposite rim, Bosie called a cease-fire. They sat the two prisoners in the lantern light. Both the painted tree rats huddled fearfully together. Seizing both their ears, Samolus gave them a sharp twist, to gain the vermins' attention. Bosie drew Martin's sword, playing the point between his captives' snout tips.

"Pay heed tae mah words, ye scruffy omadorms. Now, ye have two choices. One, Ah throw yer ears, tails an' paws intae yon endless pit, after choppin' 'em off. The rest of ye will follow at a leisurely pace. Och, what a pity, Ah can tell ye dinnae fancy that at all. So, are ye ready tae lissen te mah second option, which'll mebbe save yer worthless lives?"

Two black-and-green-tattooed heads nodded furiously.

Chieftain Chigid's mood was not improved when he saw his minions come scampering back empty-pawed. He laid about them with a rock tied to a thin rope. "Yeeeyakkah! Shoopid, daft idjits, wot 'appened?"

One venturesome voice dared a reply. "Chigid, it was slippery down there, an' oily, d'front uns slid inta the big 'ole. They throwed lotsa stones an' driv uz back. We couldn't gerrat 'em!"

Chigid gritted his pointed teeth, snarling, "Dead'eads, git sand an' soil, spread it onna oil. Cheechaah! I gotta do everythink meself, cummon foller me, I'll show 'em!"

Even before Chigid and his following had reached the rim, the screams began. The sounds were of Painted Ones in excruciating pain. Sobbing, screeching, wailing and pleading piteously. It had the desired effect—Chigid and his band halted, the fur on the scruffs of their necks rising in horror, as the cries continued.

"Heeeeek! Yowaaaaargh! Oh no, pleaze, mighty Baliss! Owowowooooow! No, pleaze, don't do that! Yeeeeek!"

A horrified whisper ran through the vermin ranks.

"Baliss 'as gorrem, the giant serpent Baliss!"

"Baliss is torcherin' 'em t'death slowly!"

The howls broke into sobbing moans. "Oh noooo, Baliss, mercy, pleaze! Arraaaaagh!"

Chigid seized the nearest beast to him, and began throttling the unfortunate. "Baliss? You never said nothin' about Baliss!"

One of the vermin pointed a quaking claw. "Lookit, Chief . . . Baliss!"

The screams had ceased. From across the abyss they could see the great, glowing, green eye. Now an awful hiss sounded, echoing around the rim. "Balissssssssss! I sssssmell painted ratssssssss!"

It was more than any vermin's nerve, including Chigid's, could stand. They stampeded into a disorderly retreat, everybeast for himself, each scrambling to be first back up the tunnel. Chigid, being the Chieftain, rushed to his former position at the rear, which had now become the front. Everybeast feared Baliss—a bunch of vermin in an underground tunnel more than most, as it turned out.

Aluco shook Bosie's paw firmly. "An excellent plan, sir, it worked perfectly."

Wincing, the Laird of Bowlaynee extricated his paw from the owl's talons. "Och, think nought of it, now let's get oot o' this neighborhood whilst the goin's guid!"

A lot of the numbness had left Skipper's footpaw, though he still limped a bit as Foremole Gullub assisted him back along the tunnel. Both the captive vermin, now bound together by slings, were made to march at the head of the group. Bosie followed behind, jollying them along with his swordpoint.

"Lead on, mah bonny scum, if'n there's any chance o' an ambush, ye'll be the first tae get it, ye ken."

It took some time, but they finally reached the spot where the tunnel split two ways, one straight on to the Abbey, the other, which was now on their right, to the place where Bisky had been abducted. Foremole sat back down on the rock where he had previously waited.

Aluco perched beside him, gesturing up to the low ceiling, which he could almost touch with his wingtip. "See the hollow up there? Well, that was left when this rock fell." He gestured to the big boulder where he and Foremole were perched. It had left a sizeable dent in the tunnel roof. The tawny owl continued, "I brought that down, by scraping round its edges. Nearly killed myself in the process."

Samolus held the lantern up. "Why are you tellin' us this, friend?"

Aluco shrugged. "I was thinking of blocking that tunnel completely, so that the Painted Ones couldn't use it to get at me. But I didn't, because without the odd vermin to sustain me, I would've starved down here. But we could block it now, and stop them ever using the tunnels again."

Bosie nodded. "Aye, a braw plan, laddie, if'n we did it now yon vermin wouldnae bother us further."

Gullub stood atop the boulder, tippawed. He inspected the dented rift, nodding knowingly. "You'm roight thurr, zurr, all ee'd need wudd be to shift this yurr stone, an' ee roof'd cave in. Hurr, 'twuddn't take much, Oi c'd do et moiself."

Samolus spread his paws expressively. "Then do it, an' let's have a safe passage back home. What d'ye say, friends?"

Skipper cast any further doubts aside. "Right, mates, get further down the tunnel, out o' the way. Gullub, you jump as soon as it starts to move."

Aluco eyed the two Painted Ones hungrily. "What do we do about these two villains?"

Bosie pointed to the tunnel that led to the Painted Ones' camp. He gave both vermin a parting prod with his sword. "Ah'll count tae three, if'n yore still here then Ah'll give ye tae the owl. One . . ."

With their forepaws still bound, the two vermin fled, bumping into each other, down the tunnel.

Foremole Gullub set his huge digging claws into the earth around the stone slab, bellowing out, "Clear ee tunnel, she'm goin' to collapse!"

They ran back, flattening themselves against the rock walls. Foremole Gullub gave a mighty heave. Nothing happened. He gave another, nothing happened again. Moving his digging claws to another position, the stout mole leader pushed upward and tugged down hard. There followed a grating rumble of rock, soil and timber. Gullub leapt, tucking himself into a ball, he rolled off down the tunnel.

Whuuump! Boom! Cruuuunch! Whoooosh!

Aluco was knocked flat by the blast of displaced air in the confined space. Suddenly everything was dark and filled with choking dust. Shielding their faces, the friends stayed put until silence fell over the scene. Skipper came forward, coughing as he held up the lantern. Bosie looked up and gasped.

"Great seasons o' salt'n'soup, will ye no look at that!"

The tunnel was completely blocked by soil, rubble, rocks and the mighty trunk of a dead beech tree, which had dropped through the tunnel roof.

Samolus polished the dust-coated emerald on his tunic. "Nothin' could get past that, ever! Ah well, mates, let's get back to dear old Redwall, it's just down the passage a short way. Homeward bound, eh, Skip?"

The Otter Chieftain turned to Dwink, who was standing staring at the dust-coated ground. "Aye aye, mate, wot's up with you, me ole cove?"

Tears coursed down the young squirrel's grime-covered face. "We just cut off our last chance of rescuin' pore Bisky, I'll never see him again!"

Bosie threw a paw about Dwink's shoulders. "What's all this nonsense yer talkin'? The moment Ah get back tae the Abbey, an' fortify mahself wi' a bite o' dinner, Ah'll rescue Bisky for ye, never fret. Cheer up, mah bonny laddie!"

Dwink's tears flowed afresh. "But we don't know where he is!"

Bosie dusted off his, by now, filthy lace cuffs. "Ach, away wi' ye, yon vermin will be holdin' Bisky in the ten-topped oaky tree, or someplace like that."

Aluco corrected Bosie, "It's the five-topped oak, that's where they held me prisoner."

Skipper ruffled Dwink's ears. "Aye, an' anybeast who can't find a five-topped oak in the woodlands needs his no-topped brain a-seen to!"

15

Still bound to one of the upper boughs of the five-topped oak, Bisky flinched as a pebble struck his ear. Jeg, son of Chigid, the Painted Ones' Chieftain, flung another pebble. This time, Bisky saw it coming—he managed to duck his head, avoiding the stone.

"Cheeheehee! I getcha next time, mousey, knock yer eye out with dis un." Jeg was perched in the top terraces of the oak, trying to conceal himself amidst the foliage, but Bisky could see him.

The young mouse had complained to his three female guards, but the only response he got was a slash from a willow withe. Other than that, the guards ignored him. Sitting where none of the stones would hit them, they chattered and gossiped. This left the young mouse at the mercy of his tormentor. He never saw the next pebble coming, it rapped his bound paw. Luckily Bisky's paws were so numb from the tight bonds, he hardly felt it.

Allowing his dislike of the young Painted One to show, Bisky called to him scornfully, "Well, that one never knocked my eye out, thick'ead. Stonethrower? Huh, you couldn't hit water if'n ye were standin' up to yore neck in a lake!"

Jeg was not used to being talked to thus. Bouncing madly

about in the top foliage, he showered down twigs and leaves, also a few badly aimed stones. "Mousey mousey shoopid face daffnose mousey!"

Despite himself, Bisky could not help grinning at the infantile rant. He continued baiting Jeg. "Shoopid face daffnose? Dearie me, I'd learn to talk properly if I were you. Maybe you will, when yore not a baby anymore, little Jeggsy weggsy!"

It was more than Jeg could stand. Howling with rage he launched himself down upon Bisky, pummeling and kicking his helpless victim. The biggest of the female guards hauled Jeg off, shaking him roughly.

"Yeecheeh! Yore mammee said leave 'im alone!"

Jeg bit her paw fiercely, escaping from her grasp. He raced back to his former position, wailing and weeping through pure temper, as he spat at Bisky and the guard who had intervened. "Yew hew! Jus' wait, my mammee an' dadda Chigid kill ya for hurtin' me, you shaked me, hard!"

The guard stayed silent, averting her eyes. It was dangerous to make an enemy of the young tree rat. Because of who he was, Jeg usually got his own way in all things. Slowly he began descending from the foliage, a spiteful glint in his eye as he neared Bisky. The young mouse swallowed hard, trying to stay calm.

Suddenly a shrill yell rang out. "Yeeeh, Chigid back! Chigid back!" Painted Ones appeared from seemingly everywhere, hurtling down through the branches, taking up the cry. "Chigid back Chigid back! Yeeeeeeeeh!" Jeg and the guards were caught up in the melee, joining in the shouting as they sped earthward. Bisky heaved a massive sigh of relief at his unexpected salvation.

Holding his hairless bottom and scorched tail, Chigid tried to salvage some dignity as he was hauled upward through the boughs of the five-topped oak by all the females of his tribe. He did his best to appear as an injured warrior. "Yaggaah! Getcha paws offa me, I'm injured inna

148

war!" They spread soft tree moss and dead grass on a broad limb to accommodate him. However, sitting was out of the question, so Chigid lay flat on his stomach.

Tala, his mate, tried to apply a few dockleaves to the burns, murmuring soothingly, "Hayaah, does it hurt ye?"

The Chieftain gritted his filed teeth. "Idjit, shall I burn yore tail so ye can find out?"

Wisely, Tala got out of the way. Jeg came bounding up, throwing himself on Chigid, he shouted, "Dadda back!"

"Agaaarh! Gerroff!"

The Chietain landed his son a savage kick. It caught Jeg under the chin, stunning him. He toppled from the bough, falling to the woodland floor, where he lay senseless. Chigid glared about at those attending him. "Gemme barkbrew, then let me sleep!"

From where he was bound to the overhead limb, Bisky had witnessed the whole incident. He was satisfied that his friends had wrought some damage amongst the Painted Ones, and glad that the tree rats had taken no more captives. Also he was particularly pleased that Jeg had been taught an unexpected lesson. Now the stiffness in his limbs, and the excruciating pains in his tied-up forepaws blotted out everything.

Sleep eluded the young mouse. As darkness fell, he closed his eyes and hung his head. Feeling the heat, and breathing woodsmoke from a fire on the ground below, his senses started to reel. Bisky had almost drifted into a limbo, where he felt nothing anymore. Then his chin was jogged upward, as a wooden ladle was thrust against his mouth, accompanied by a guard's command: "Drink now, you drink, mouse!"

Gratefully, he slurped down water until it slopped from his chin. The ladle was removed, and a thick, soft root was shoved between his teeth, with another order. "Eat, if it fall yew get no more!"

Pushing his chin to one side, Bisky trapped the root against his shoulder. Holding it there he gnawed hungrily, identifying the taste as a wild parsnip. He had never eaten raw parsnip before, nor had he ever fancied the vegetable much. But it tasted good, he devoured the lot, including the green-fronded parsnip top. With his stomach gurgling, the young mouse finally lapsed into sleep.

Once during the night, he was awakened by excited cries. Opening his eyes he saw four flickering lights, flittering about the woodland floor below. Painted Ones were shouting, "Wytes! Gerrem Wytes, shoot darts!" There was quite a hullabaloo, though it did not last for long, receding off into the thicknesses of Mossflower. Bisky was too weary to take it all in, he drifted back into slumber.

Again during the night, the limb he was bound to began to bounce up and down. Dreaming he was back in Redwall's dormitory, Bisky imagined it was Dwink, jumping on his bed. He muttered drowsily, without opening his eyes, "Get back to yore own bed afore Brother Torilis comes."

Dawn was streaking the sky, and birdsong echoing through the trees. Bisky coughed as smoke from the cooking fires below seeped up his nostrils and into his mouth. A voice alongside him murmured in his ear, "Aye aye, mate, 'ow long've you been strung up 'ere?" Tied next to Bisky in similar fashion was a spiky-furred young beast, wearing a multistriped headband, a short kilt and a broad, buckled belt. The stranger nodded at him, continuing in a gruff voice, "They brung me in durin' the night, wot's yore name?"

Bisky felt less alone in the creature's company. "I'm called Bisky, from Redwall Abbey. I expect you've heard of Redwall?"

The newcomer winked almost cheerily at him. "Aye, expect I have. They call me Dubble, I'm a Guosim shrew, an' proud of it. Ye know wot Guosim means, don't ye, Brisky?"

Bisky winked back at him. "Name's not Brisky, it's Bisky. Pleased to meet ye, Drubble. I know wot Guosim means, first letter of each word. Guerilla Union of Shrews in Moss-flower. Right?"

The shrew grinned broadly. "Right, an' me name's Dubble, not Drubble. Tell me, 'ow did these blaggards catch ye?"

Bisky tried making light of his predicament. "Oh, I was explorin' some underground tunnels when they cracked me over the head, an' knocked me out cold. When I woke up, here I was. Wot about you, mate?"

Dubble stated flatly, "Arguin' with Tugga, that did it."

The young mouse was curious. "Who's Tugga?"

His shrew friend replied, almost in disbelief, "Y'mean you've never 'eard o' Tugga Bruster, big Log a Log of all the Guosim?"

Bisky could only shake his head. "No, I'm sorry, I haven't. Tell me about him."

Dubble snorted. "Huh, tell ye about Tugga? You lot at Redwall must lead a sheltered life if'n y'aint 'eard o' Tugga Bruster. Don't ye even know the famous song, Bisky?"

The young mouse admitted he did not, causing Dubble to break out into song.

"No shrew in the territory's as tough
as Log a Log Tugga Bruster,
'cos when he swings that big iron club,
he's a dangerous ole skull buster.
Oh, Tugga Bruster, Tugga Bruster,
he'd face any gang o' vermin they could muster,
he's full o' muscles hard an' wide,
one day I saw a fox decide,
to slay hisself by suicide, rather
than face ole Tugga Bruster!
Oh, Tugga Bruster, Tugga Bruster,
he won't put up with brag or bluster,
he can kick a stoat clear outta his skin,
or use a ferret as a duster,
good ole Tugga Bruster!

Oh, Tugga Bruster, Tugga Bruster,
he can fight all day, without the slightest fuss, sir,
so if yore a rat I'll tell ye that
one blast of his breath'd knock ye flat,
'midst shrews he's an aristocrat,
he's the Log a Log Tugga Bruster!"

Bisky chuckled. "He sounds like a real terror to me."

Dubble stared bitterly ahead as he answered. "Aye, an' he's my dad, too!" Bisky remained silent, waiting until the young shrew continued. "That's how I got meself tied to a branch alongside you, mate. Huh, that Tugga, always on at me, naggin' an' lecturin', an' clippin' me over the lugs. I can't do anythin' right accordin' to him. Can't use a logboat paddle, can't steer a craft, can't wield a Guosim rapier. Hah, you'd think to 'ear him I can't do a single thing to his likin'. Anyhow, I put up with it fer long enough, then I spoke back to me dad. One word led to another, an' next thing we were in the middle of right ole barney, me'n' Tugga. So I told him wot he c'd do with his Log a Log title, an' his logboats, an' his whole blinkin' tribe!"

Bisky's voice was no more than a murmur. "So you left home an' walked off, Dubble?"

The young shrew nodded. "Aye, off I went in a ragin' temper. Got meself lost, the first night out. I was wanderin' round the woodlands, like a bruised beetle in the dark. Then I sees a couple o' pretty liddle lights, twinklin' round, just ahead o' me. So I followed 'em, fool that I was, I let the bloomin' things lead me straight into a swamp. I was about to shout out for 'elp, when this crowd o' painted ragbags came swingin' outta the trees. They dragged me out o' the mud, an' tied me up like a parcel o' vittles.

"I tell ye, Bisky, I don't know wot they were usin' as weapons, some sort o' poisoned darts, an' blowpipes. They shot at one of the twinklin' lights an' downed him. Straight into the swamp he went. I could tell by the cries it was a bird, a raven, I think. Huh, that's one bird wot won't lead no more pore, lost beasts astray!"

Bisky tried moving his paws, to get the circulation going. "We've had trouble with those twinklin' lights at our Abbey, they're called Wytes, and I think their leader is called a Doomwyte. Dubble, d'ye think that yore dad an' the rest o' the tribe will come lookin' for you?"

Dubble turned his eyes skyward. "Yore guess is good as mine, Bisky. Though if'n they do, I can just imagine wot Log a Log Tugga would say." Dubble impersonated his father's deep, gruff voice. "Runnin' away from the tribe, gettin' lost, then lettin' yoreself get nabbed by tree rats. Yer not fit t'be rescued, young un, a disgrace t'the Guosim, that's wot ye are. Oaks'n'apples 'elp this tribe if'n you ever get t'be Log a Log one day!"

Further conversation was cut short by the arrival of Jeg and some of his cohorts. Jeg was carrying a willow switch, which he immediately slashed across Bisky's shoulders.

As the young mouse arched his back with pain, Dubble yelled at Jeg, "Ahoy, snotnose, enjoyin' yoreself are ye? You shouldn't be painted black'n'green. No, yellow'd be the right colour for you, stinkin' coward that y'are!"

Squealing with rage, Jeg began flogging Dubble. "I killya for that, killya! Yeeeeh!"

Bisky roared at the top of his lungs, "You rotten worm, if'n I was loose I'd slay ye with my bare paws, ye spineless scum!"

The noisy cacophony roused Chigid, who had been having a lie in, to heal his injuries. He came limping along the bough, accompanied by his mate, Tala, and several guards. Seizing the switch from his son, he tossed it down onto the cooking fires below, chattering at him. "Yikkiirrr! Stoppit, they're my pris'ners!"

Jeg glared at both captives. "Yaaarrr! I wanna kill 'em, they callin' me bad names!"

Chigid glared at Jeg, baring his pointed teeth. "I say

153

when we kill 'em, not you. Much work t'be done round 'ere, vikkles t'be got, that's pris'ners' job!"

Tala interceded on her son's behalf, calming Chigid. "Hayaaah, Chief injured, go now an' rest. Let Jeg take these beasts to gather vikkles!" She indicated three of her female companions. "Yew go with Jeg, keep a good watch on the mouses."

Chigid touched his scorched tail gingerly as he limped off, cautioning Jeg. "Yew lose 'em an' I skin ye good!"

Shortly thereafter, Bisky and Dubble were unbound and lowered to the woodland floor. There they were roped together by their necks, each being fitted with a hobble on their footpaws that had a boulder tied to it. Both were still as yet unable to get their forepaws working.

Jeg ordered the three guards to wait, whilst he vanished into the trees. He was back shortly, carrying fresh switches, which he issued to the minders. Making whippy noises with his own switch, the young Painted One smirked wickedly at his captives. "Yeeheee! You find plenty berries, fruits, eggs an' fishes. Lots o' vikkles, or ye get punished bad!"

Dragging the rocks to which they were hobbled, the pair lumbered awkwardly off. Dubble managed to murmur to Bisky, as they fell behind slightly, "Keep yore eyes an' wits peeled for a chance, any chance. Don't be afeared of slayin' 'em if'n ye have to."

The young mouse replied out of the side of his mouth, "Don't worry, mate, I won't be scared of finishin' the job, if'n it comes down to them or us!"

Swish! Jeg's switch caught both their paws. "Sharrap an' get movin', ye slackers!"

Dubble actually smiled at Jeg. "That's a nice liddle whip ye've got there, sir, 'twould come right out both yore ears if'n I was to stuff it up yore nostrils."

Jeg raised the switch, but something in the Guosim shrew's eyes warned him not to strike with it. To save face, Jeg slashed at some dandelions, knocking the flowering heads from their stems. He called to the guards, "Yekka! Keep these two movin'!"

The three guards were not as vindictive as Jeg. Bisky found that if they kept a reasonable pace, their trio of minders did not goad them.

Travelling through the late spring woodlands, they came upon a copse where, in a shaded spot, mushrooms grew in abundance. Under the watchful eyes of the guards, and Jeg, who lounged in the low branches of a maple, the two captives picked mushrooms. After awhile, Dubble began digging amidst the grass. One of the female guards prodded him with her switch.

"Wotcha doin'? Yer supposed t'be pickin' mushrooms."

The young shrew sniffed at his paws. "Radishes, there's wild radishes growin' here."

She pulled a face. "Yaaah, don't like radishes, leave 'em where they are."

Just to assert his superiority over the group, Jeg called out from his perch, "Dig some radishes out, my dadda likes 'em. You 'elp 'im, mousey, go on!"

Bisky joined Dubble at the digging, muttering to him, "I don't like radishes, either, mate, wot are we scrabblin' with our bare paws in the dirt for? Pickin' mushrooms is much easier."

Dubble showed him a sharp flint shard he had dug up. Stowing it swiftly in his belt, he winked at Bisky. "Just keep diggin' an' see if'n ye can find a good, sharp flint like I've got, then hide it quick. Nothin' like a flint shard for cuttin' these ropes, or a few Painted Ones' throats, when we gets the chance!"

Jeg threw a twig at them, calling, "Where's the radishes yer diggin' for, eh?"

Bisky suddenly came upon a keen-edged flint, shaped almost like a small knife blade. He shouted back, "Haven't found 'em yet, but there's radishes round here somewheres if'n my mate says there is."

Jeg climbed down from the maple, and came to see

155

for himself. Casting about with a footpaw, he sneered, "Yeeecha, ain't no radishes growin' here, waste o' time diggin'. The mushrooms'll do, let's git back t'the camp wid them. Move yerselves!"

On the journey back to the five-topped oak, Bisky whispered to his companion, "I found a sharp flint, it's hidden in my tunic. What's the next move, mate?"

Dubble's lips hardly moved as he replied, "Wait'll tonight, once it gets dark an' all the scum are asleep—that's when we make our move!"

16

On the rock overlooking the deep pool where the Welzz lived, Korvus Skurr perched in sombre silence. His snake, Sicariss, lay coiled on the far side of the pool. Korvus was curious as to why the smoothsnake had not been perching, crownlike, on his head of late. However, the tyrant raven had not questioned the reptile. She would talk to him sooner or later, but the silence between the evil pair was becoming uneasy. Korvus adjusted his stance, affecting to appear unconcerned as he spoke casually. "Karraaah, have ye not consulted with the Welzz today?"

Sicariss stayed mute, letting her eyes cloud over.

When the raven spoke again he sounded more commanding. "Yekkarr! Has the Welzz been fed?"

Sicariss gave her sinuous head the smallest shake.

The raven clacked his heavy beak. "Rrraaakk! That's why the Welzz has not spoken. Feed it!"

There was veiled insolence in the snake's reply. "Shall I feed it a black bird?"

Hopping down from the rock, Korvus advanced angrily on Sicariss. "Yakaaah! My birds are not to be fed to that thing! Are there no prisoners, did my Wytes bring nothing back?"

Sicariss unfolded her coils lazily. "Wytesss are your businesss, not mine."

The raven stopped just short of her; he sensed that Sicariss was brooding about something. But still he avoided asking her, instead, he rapped out his orders. "There are plenty of fat, old toads in the other cavern. Tell my crows to bring one here to me!"

Sicariss knew that Korvus Skurr could be dangerous when he was disobeyed. She slithered off to do his bidding.

No sooner had the smoothsnake departed for the sulphurous outer cavern than Veeku, leader of the carrion crows, came winging in. Landing alongside Korvus, he waited obediently.

The raven tyrant fixed him with his piercing dark eyes. "Rakkah, have my Wytes returned?"

Veeku bowed his head. "Mighty One, they are back."

Korvus spread his wings irately. "Ayaaaark! Then where are they?"

The crow backed off slightly, still with bowed head. "They are outside, perched in the branches of the birch tree, but they will not enter your caves, Lord."

This was something that Korvus Skurr had never before encountered. "Gaaraaakuh! Why is this, Veeku?"

"Mighty One, I know not. . . ."

The spread of the mighty raven's wings almost knocked the crow flat as Korvus launched himself into the air. "Yakkaaah! I will speak with my Wytes." He hovered over Veeku momentarily, lowering his voice. "Have Sicariss watched, listen to what she says, follow where she goes. Do this secretly, my trusty Veeku." He flapped off, leaving behind a puzzled crow leader.

Veeku had reported truly. Outside, by the stream, four ravens perched in the branches of the downy birch, silent and brooding. Korvus landed next to Frang, the senior bird. "Reekah! Greetings, brother, why do ye not come inside?"

158

Frang did not use any formal title as he replied, "Two Wytes have flown to Hellgates. . . . Slain!"

Korvus made a noise of surprise. "Whaaaark! Two, ye say?" He stood wordless, waiting for Frang's explanation.

The senior raven stared straight ahead as he reported. "Our brother Purz was killed by poison darts. It was the Painted Ones who slew him." Now he turned and looked his Chieftain in the eye. "We saw the serpent Baliss eating our brother Tarul. You should never have enlisted the Evil One's aid!"

Korvus was bewildered at this turn of events. "Yakkar! Where did ye see this thing happen, Frang?"

The senior raven's tone was loaded with accusation. "In the ditch outside of the red house. None of the earthcrawlers could have killed Tarul, he was daring and brave. Only Baliss could have done the deed. The monster will kill and eat anything that moves. Nobeast can rid us of him!"

The news, totally unexpected, momentarily stunned Korvus. It was Frang who snapped him back to reality, by stating boldly, "Heyaaar! 'Twas not a wise thing, sending for Baliss, ye should not have done it!"

Korvus was in such a rage that he hopped about clacking his beak against the tree trunk. "Harrrrakarakk! I am the Great Doomwyte, nobeast tells me what to do, I give the orders!"

Frang moved back to stand with the other three ravens. Facing up to Korvus, he grated flatly, "Yagarr, then ye did the wrong thing, we are all in danger from the poison-fanged one!"

The tyrant Chieftain stood glaring at him, holding his silence whilst trying to seek a reply.

Frang and three Raven Wytes stared back at him, unafraid. The realisation of his position struck Korvus Skurr. He was the biggest, and strongest, of all carrion, but they were four to one. He was outside of his underground realm, with no mystique surrounding him. No sulphurous

159

clouds, or snake crowning his head. No pounding drums and prostrate reptiles awaiting his every word. Turning, he strode off in a haughty manner, cawing dismissively. "Hurraak! I will think on your rebellious words. You will wait on my decision!"

"Hayaaah, then make it soon, we will not wait around to be slain by Baliss!"

Korvus did not turn, aware that it was Frang who had spoken. The Great Doomwytc knew he had been challenged. In a short space of time he had three new troubles. First, Sicariss, and her hostile manner, which he could not fathom. Next came his own Raven Wytes and their ultimatum to leave him. And finally, the biggest problem of all, the blind monster, Baliss, and the pact he had thoughtlessly made with him.

Korvus flew inside, through the horrific cave, with its sulphur-laden atmosphere, boiling lake and dripping walls. Insects scuttled through the heaps of rotting offal and yellowing bones. Winging over the eyeless monolith of the Doomwyte, he glided into the inner chamber. There in the cooler dimness he landed by the deep pool. Purposely, Korvus alighted close to Sicariss, hunching himself, so the smoothsnake could climb up and coil around his brow. She slithered away from him, coiling further around the edge of the pool. Attempting to make conversation, the tyrant nodded at the watery depths. "Rakkah, has my Welzz been fed?"

Sicariss replied indolently, "A fat, old toad, jussst asss ye ordered."

Puffing out his chest plumage, the big raven swaggered to the rim, staring down into the water. "Harrr, and did he tell ye any secrets that I should hear?"

The snake stretched, then coiled loosely, as though she was about to take a nap. "Welzzzzz had wordssss for you. . . ." She paused, adding almost mockingly, "O Mighty One."

On the high, wooded hillside, the dark beast stopped toiling at some tough, ancient hornbeam roots. The mysterious creature watched the Wytes quarreling with Korvus Skurr. Leaving the others still perched in the downy birch, Korvus strutted back into his caves. Wielding the double-bladed sword, the dark beast went back to work on the tree roots, glad that Korvus had not been injured, or slain by his own creatures. The fate of the Doomwyte Chieftain would be decided not by any bird. It was reserved for only one. The dark watcher.

Down in Redwall Abbey's cellars, the jolly Sister Violet wielded a bung mallet, cautioning Brother Torilis as she swung it. "Now hold that spigot still, Brother, but mind yore paws. Hold it at the bottom, there, that's right!"

They were broaching a fresh barrel of Corksnout Spikkle's renowned Strawberry Fizz. Violet dealt the spigot a resounding *thwack*. Pink liquid sprayed everywhere as the barrel was broached. Speedily, she dealt the spigot several more blows, until the wide end was seated, and the spray halted.

Brother Torilis gasped, wiping liquid from his face, then stood with his paws widespread, and a look of dismay on his sombre features. "Ugh, just look at me, Sister, I'm saturated with that sweet, sticky cordial, absolutely soaked!"

The plump hedgehog Sister chuckled. "'Twas all in a good cause, Brother, our Dibbun heroes called for more, and so they shall have more, lots more. Thirsty liddle warriors!" She watched the effervescent pink drink bubbling into a wooden pail set beneath the spigot tap. "Golly goodness, I do like a sip o' Strawberry Fizz m'self. Even though it tickles the throat on the way down. What about you, Brother?"

Torilis shuddered. "Dreadful stuff, far too sweet for my taste. I'd sooner have cold mint tea. Huh, after I've changed this robe and taken a bath. What are you looking at me like that for, Sister?"

Violet held up a paw for silence. "Shush, Brother, can you hear that booming noise?"

Torilis could hear the sound, he glanced nervously around the dimly lit cellar. "Probably something that only Cellarhog Spikkle knows about. Let's not loiter down here, Sister, the Dibbuns will be waiting for their Fizz."

Violet left the pail and hurried off to the rear chamber, holding up her lantern. "That'll be Laird Bosie's party, back from their search, Brother. Come and lend a paw with the doorbolt."

Between them they dealt with the stout bolt, which Corksnout had fitted to the repaired door. The pair were bowled over by a big, tawny owl who rushed up the small flight of steps. He was followed by the others, with Umfry close behind, shouting, "Somebeast's been pourin' Straw-bee Fizz, h'I c'n smell h'it. Hoho, let me h'attit!"

Flourishing Martin's sword, Bosie bowed elegantly. "Guid tae be back hame, marm, yer well, Ah trust."

Sister Violet was all a-fluster at the hare's gallantry. "Oh, indeed we are, sir, ye've arrived just in time. They're hol-din' a feast in the orchard for the Dibbuns, two of 'em slew one o' those big birds!"

Skipper Rorgus smote the floor with his rudder. "Well bully for 'em, I says. Come on, Aluco, mate, let's get ye vittled up with good Redwall fare!"

Brother Torilis addressed Samolus. "Where's Bisky? I don't see him with you."

Bosie put up his sword. "Och, cheer up, laddie, we'll be goin' tae rescue him as soon as we've taken a wee bite tae eat. Right, lead me tae the feast!"

They had just emerged from the main door of the Abbey when they heard the big west wallgate slam shut as Cork-snout Spikkle came bounding across the lawns, roaring and shouting. "Wahoooow! Get Brother Torilis! Ooooooh, hurry, quick! I've just been bitten by a monster serpent! Yawooooh!" The big Cellarhog was totally hysterical; his false nose had moved around on its cord, and was dan-gling from the back of his head. He was stampeding hither and thither, heedless of any fixed direction.

In his panic, Corksnout thundered over Torilis, not even noticing who he was. "Owowowoooh! The big snake bit me! Oooooh, it hurts! Wahaaah, I'm poisoned t'death!"

Skipper called to Bosie, "Quick, we've got to stop him afore he injures himself or any other beast. Get him, mate!"

Halting a large hedgehog of Corksnout's size was no easy task. However, it was the swift action of the hare and otter which accomplished it.

In a swirl of kilt, tunic and lace ruffs, Bosie threw himself flat in the charging beast's path, tripping Corksnout. The huge Cellarhog went headlong, scoring a path through grass and herbaceous border. Skipper fell upon the unfortunate, landing upon the big fellow's head. Corksnout was blowing out mouthfuls of grass, buttercups and daisies as he wailed aloud, "Gerroff me, can't ye see I'm dyin'? Ouchouch! The sting'n'the pain! Yaaaaaargh!"

Regardless of the bristling spikes, Skipper held on to the runaway bravely. He was joined by Bosie, Dwink, Umfry and Samolus, whilst Aluco hopped around them, hooting alarmingly. Brother Torilis sat down beside Corksnout's head, speaking calmly.

"Please stop all this howling and yowling, Mister Spikkle. If you've been really bitten by a poison snake, then the best thing to do is lie quite still. Dashing about will only make the venom circulate through your body quicker. So be a goodbeast and tell me how you were bitten, and where. Only then can I attend to you, sir!"

Through despairing sobs, the hedgehog managed some self-control as he explained, "I was just droppin' the slain bird into the ditch, outside the gate. Well, I managed to get him across the path, an' into the ditch, then I was turnin' away to come back inside, when *bang*! I was struck right on the rear, I was hit so bloomin' hard that I was shot forward, right through the gateway. The pain was like red-hot needles, I've never felt ought like it, Brother. I turned around an' guess wot I saw!"

Bosie shouted, "Tell us, laddie, tell us!"

Corksnout shut his eyes tight, as if trying to blot out the memory of the dreadful sight. "It was a great monster serpent, with 'orrible milky blue eyes, an' the dead raven hangin' from its mouth. I slammed the gate fast as I could!"

Brother Torilis nodded sagely, moving down to inspect his patient's rear end, which had a bald patch, devoid of spikes. He took a closer look, patting the area lightly.

Corksnout cried out piteously, "Eeyowch! That hurts somethin' fierce. Brother, I beg ye, let a pore ole beast die peaceable, I've been through enough torture, let me alone, please!"

Brother Torilis heaved a relieved sigh, then gave his diagnosis promptly. "Mister Spikkle, if, as you say, you had been bitten by a poisonous snake—an adder, in fact—of the size you describe, then you'd already be dead."

Umfry scratched his head quills. "Then why h'aint 'e, Brother?"

Torilis explained, "One, the snake could not have bitten him if its mouth was full of dead bird. Two, there are no bite wounds to be seen on our worthy Cellarhog. What occurred was that he was butted, with some considerable force. The strike was so powerful that it drove some bottom spikes inward. So, sir, it seems that I'll have to pull your spikes back out, before they fester in there."

Tears beaded in Corksnout's eyes, he wept with gratitude. "Seasons praise on ye, Brother. Oh, I'm goin' to live. Thank ye, thank ye!"

Torilis smiled, a rare occurrence for Redwall's Healer and Herbalist. "Don't thank me, Mister Spikkle, thank the fact that you have a bottom covered in spikes. Skipper Rorgus, Laird Bosie, would you kindly assist him up to the Infirmary, where I can work on him. I'd best take a look at you two also, you're both going to need some spikes drawn out of you."

The otter and the hare suddenly became aware that their

paws and faces had Corksnout's spikes protruding from them, which they had not noticed in the heat of the moment. Gingerly, they helped the Cellarhog upright.

Sister Violet praised them glowingly. "Oh, you were so brave and reckless, both of you. Is there anything you need?"

Bosie called over his shoulder, as they lugged Corksnout away, "Aye, marm, Ah'd be grateful if'n ye could fetch me a wee plate o' somethin' from the feast, an' a dram tae wet mah spikey lips!"

Skipper added, "Make that two, Sister, if y'please!"

Samolus enlisted the help of Dwink and Umfry. "Come with me, you two, let's go up to the west parapet. Best take a peep an' see if'n we can spot that giant serpent."

From the threshold of the walltop, above the main gate, they searched the path, the ditch and the flatlands below. There was no sign of either Baliss or the slain Raven Wyte. Abbot Glisam, having heard the reports from Aluco and Sister Violet, joined them. The old dormouse shuddered.

"Forgive me, friends, but snakes, especially adders, are the one creature I cannot abide. Just the name, snake, sends a trembling down my spine."

Samolus took the Father Abbot's paw. "Well, there ain't sign nor scale o' the villain now, so d'ye wish t'stand here shudderin', Father Abbot, or go back t'the Dibbuns' feast?"

Glisam took his friend's paw. "Let's go to the feast."

Lost to view from the Abbey, around a bend further up the ditch, Baliss was trying to consume the dead raven, in some considerable discomfort. The whole of the giant reptile's head was throbbing with pain. This was due to the spikes of Corksnout Spikkle, of which quite a number were embedded in the snake, owing to the ferocity and force of his strike on the Cellarhog. Baliss had no way of extracting the spikes. Several times the reptile left off his macabre meal, shaking his head violently, and butting at the ditchshide. This only caused the injury to worsen. Hissing savagely, he resumed eating the raven carcass.

Had Baliss not been blind the injury could have been averted, but the scents of raven and hedgehog combined to confuse the snake temporarily, causing what might have been termed self-inflicted wounds. Thus it was that fate had turned the cold, calculating hunter into a rapidly maddening monster, his whole snout and head pierced deep by the spikes of a simple hedgehog.

17

Anybeast could tell, by the scent of the woodlands, cease-less birdsong and the burgeoning of fruit, berry and flower, Summer had at last arrived, casting its stillwarm spell over Mossflower Country in placid eventide. Bisky and Dubble were exhausted by the time they arrived back at the five-topped oak. With boulders still hobbling them, burdened by the sacks of produce they had gathered, both awaited their captors' whim.

Tala, mate of Chigid, and mother of Jeg, threw down a rope sling from the upper boughs. "Lazybeasts, don't stan' there, load up vikkles!"

Under the watchful eyes of the Painted Ones, the prison-ers loaded the slings with the fruits of their foraging. They stood clear as the sacks were hauled up.

Jeg beckoned the guards to remove the hobbles from Bisky and Dubble, leaving them still anchored to each other by the rope halter around their necks. The young Painted One menaced them with his whippy switch.

"Stan' there, don't budge, or I make yer sorry!" The sling was lowered again, and bound jointly around them. They were hoisted roughly up onto the broad limb they had formerly occupied.

Dubble sighed wearily as the guards bound their forepaws to the bough above their heads. He appealed to them, "Oh come on, mates, y'know we can't escape. Why are ye stringin' us up like this agin?"

Jeg smiled maliciously. " 'Cos yer gotta stay like that 'til I says so!"

The young Guosim shrew snarled back at him, "Ye scringin' liddle worm, if'n my paws were loose I'd batter ye to a pulp!"

Jeg flogged at the defenceless Dubble with his switch, yelling shrilly, "Well, yer paws ain't loose, so I'll batter yew to a pulp. Stoopid watermousey!"

The willow switch snapped, leaving Jeg with only a short stub. Despite the beating he had taken, Dubble began taunting him. "Dearie me, broke yore toy have ye? Go an' cry to yore mammee for a new one!"

Jeg grabbed some mushrooms from the sacks. He hurled them at Dubble and Bisky angrily. "Hah! That's all the vikkles yew two are gettin'. I'll make sure ya starve t'death!" Shoving guards out of his way, the young tree rat dashed off into the higher foliage.

Bisky shook his head at Dubble. "If ye keep teasin' him like that he will end up beatin' you, or both of us, to death, mate. Why don't ye just let him be?"

The young shrew gritted his teeth stubbornly. "I've been punished by bigger'n'tougher beasts than that liddle spoiled brat!"

Bisky decided not to provoke his friend by arguing. Closing his eyes, he let his head hang limply.

Night's starry canopy descended over the woodlands. Both captives sagged, falling into an exhausted slumber. The Painted Ones had eaten; they did not bother lighting a fire down on the ground. Secure in their five-topped oak, and the surrounding trees, the vermin did not mount any guards. Each went to their own group, nestling in the forks of boughs, or huddling on broad limbs. Gradually the atmosphere slid into a relaxed drowsiness.

Bisky felt a footpaw kick him into wakefulness. It was Dubble, the shrew was ready and alert. He whispered to his companion, "Have ye still got yore sharp flint, matey?"

Keeping his voice low, the Redwaller replied, "Aye, for all the good it'd do us. How can I reach it with my paws bound up like this?"

Dubble shook his head. "I got the same trouble, friend. Mine's in me belt. I've got no chance o' getting' at it. Any bright ideas?"

For answer, Bisky reached out with his footpaws, by swinging them; he hit Dubble's stomach. His fellow captive gave an irate snort.

"Didn't Jeg beat me enough, have you gotta have a go!"

The young mouse cautioned him, "Keep y'voice down, mate, I've got a plan. Now, shove yore belly out toward me, so I can see that flint in yore belt."

Dubble obeyed wordlessly. Bisky started to swing his body to and fro, each time touching his friend's stomach. He could see the glitter of the flint in the starlight. Making an extra effort, he swung harder, grunting as his footpaws trapped the shard of flint between them.

Dubble hissed excitedly, "Hah, ye got a good grip on it there, mate. Well done, matey. Wot now?"

Arching his back, Bisky groaned in pain. "Ooohh, my paws are all swelled, with jiggin' about on this rope, it's really hurtin' me. Listen, I'm goin' to rest a moment afore I carry on."

The Guosim shrew gnawed his lip with concern. "Don't let go o' that flint, Bisky. Is there anythin' I can do t'help ye, bucko?"

Trying to ignore the stinging numbness in his tightly bound forepaws, the young mouse gasped, "Aye there's two things ye can do. When I give the word, suck yore stomach in. It'll make it easier for me to pull the flint out with my footpaws. Once I've got it I'll try a high kick. D'ye think ye could catch the flint in yore mouth if I could lift it that far, mate?"

169

His companion chuckled. "You just try me!"

With both footpaws tightly clutching the flint shard, Bisky gave the word. "Now!" Dubble inhaled, pulling in his stomach hard. The belt slackened, and Bisky swiftly tugged the flint free. He dangled back and forth, holding the flint, his face creased in agony.

Dubble muttered urgently, "Try an' swing yoreself up, mate, afore yore paws give ye too much pain. I'm ready, Bisky, swing now!"

With one last, desperate effort, the Redwall mouse levered himself forward, kicking upward. He lost the flint, it slipped from the grasp of his footpaws, revolving in the air. Dubble gave a small squeak of dismay as it struck the tip of his snout. However, he had the presence of mind to toss his head back, catching the flint shard neatly in his open mouth.

It was an effort for Bisky to raise his face; he smiled through the agonised tears which squeezed from the corners of each eye. "That was a good trick, mate, ye'll have to teach it t'me sometime."

Dubble never replied—he was busy mouthing the flint into a more useful position. Grunting with exertion he angled his neck awkwardly askew. Hoisting himself upward by his bound forepaws, he began sawing at the nearest rope.

Bisky murmured encouragement to the young Guosim. "C'mon, you can do it, cully, chop that ole rope to shreds, an' let's be shut o' this stinkin' place!"

Clenching the flint with his teeth, Dubble made strained grunting noises as he sawed furiously. It was a good, sharp-edged flint—strands rapidly twisted away from the rope. Then the shrew gave a mighty tug. He stared upward at the severed rope, hanging by one paw, grinning triumphantly.

"Good ole us, we did it! Stay there, I'll be with ye in two shakes of a newt's tail!"

Despite his pain, Bisky chuckled. "I'll stay here, seein' as I can't go anyplace until ye cut my ropes."

Once they were both free, the two friends sat awhile on the oak limb, waiting for the circulation to ease their forepaws. Bisky asked, "We've got a couple of hours afore dawnlight. Which way should we go when we get out of this tree?"

Dubble shrugged. "I ain't got a blinkin' clue, mate. I thought you knew yore way round this neck o' the woods. One thing I do know, though, we should get as far and as fast away from this place as we can."

Making their way down the five-topped oak was extremely perilous. Painted Ones slept in the most unexpected nooks of the big tree. Fortunately the tree rats were all heavy sleepers. In the lower terraces of the mighty oak, they came across Jeg. The young rat was curled up in a broad fork, alongside his mother and father, Chigid and Tala.

At the sight of their hated foe, Dubble's teeth began chattering with rage. Bisky threw a paw across his friend's mouth, whispering, "Not worth it, mate, we could be caught again."

The shrew allowed himself to be led away. Casting a final hate-filled glare at Jeg, he murmured, "Someday we'll cross trails agin. . . . Someday!"

The woodland floor felt good underpaw again—exhilaration coursed through the two friends' veins. Not being certain of any route or direction, they set off speedily into the thickest tree cover. Mossflower was completely silent, the heavy loam thick and soft underpaw, with the tree canopy overhead shielding any star or moonlight, making the woodlands a realm of total darkness.

Dubble laughed nervously. "If'n ye see any twinklin' lights tryin' to lead us someplace, ignore 'em mate, they're trouble."

Bisky gripped his friend's paw firmly. "They're worse than trouble, mate, they're Wytes."

It was still dark when they emerged into a clearing. Bisky splashed into a tiny streamlet which flowed through it. Immediately they threw themselves down, drinking the cold, clear water greedily. Bisky splashed some across his face. "Mmm, that feels good. I hadn't realised I was so thirsty, how about you?"

Dubble passed him a pawful of vegetation. "Look, watercress! It ain't much but it's good enough for hungry bellies. Wait there, let's see wot else is growin' roundabout. There's always a bit to be had around streambanks, even liddle ones."

Bisky ventured as far as the trees on the fringe of the sward, where he found a few mushrooms growing beneath some shrubbery. Dubble returned to the streamlet with other edibles he had gathered. Pepperwort, the leaves and stems of which had a hot but pleasant taste. He also had some wood sorrel, and a few half-ripe raspberries. They shared the results of their forage, lounging beside the tinkling streamlet.

Dubble lay back, patting his stomach. "Well, 'twasn't much, but at least it was somethin', matey. I tell ye, I'd give anythin' for a quick snooze right now, can't remember the last time I had a decent sleep."

Bisky was inclined to agree with him. "Me, too, I can't keep my eyes open. What d'ye say we find somewhere sheltered an' nap 'til daylight?"

Dubble stifled a yawn. "Right, lead me to it, bucko."

Following the stream out of the clearing, they searched for a likely spot. Bisky found it, an ancient black poplar. The tree was long dead and fallen flat. On closer inspection it turned out to be a hollow trunk. Dubble crouched low, scrambling into it gratefully. "We couldn't have found a better place for a liddle sleep than this, 'tis built for the job, mate."

Bisky crawled in beside him. "What d'ye mean, we? I was the one who found it, move over, mate, d'ye want all the room for yourself?"

The Guosim shrew grabbed a pawful of dry pulp and

tossed it at the Redwall mouse, giggling. "Oh, go to sleep an' stop moanin', swoggletail!"

Bisky retaliated with two paw loads of the pulp. "Swoggle-tail, is it? Well, take that, swinjeysnout!"

As young ones will, they fought playfully, laughing and shouting as they forgot their strange surroundings. The dark-cloaked creature who had been watching them since they left the clearing spoke in low tones to his band.

"Awright, get dem nets'n'clubs, soon as dey nod off we'll 'ave 'em. Norra sound now, speshully you, Gobbo, do yer 'ear me?"

The one called Gobbo replied indignantly, "Norra sound, 'ey? Yore makin' more noise dan all uv us put tergether!"

Bisky and Dubble gradually fell asleep, unaware how short their taste of freedom had been.

18

Evening shafts of red, gold and violet sunlight flooded through the long windows into the Great Hall, casting random patterns over the supper tables. Friar Skurpul and his staff were kept busy, serving a repast to the returned searchers, and their new feathered friend. Dibbuns crowded around to stare at Aluco. Never having seen a real tawny owl close up, they peppered him with questions.

"Hurr, Oi never see'd ee real h'owl, wot bees yurr name, zurr?"

"Farver Abbot sez you can make the *whoo hoo* noise, will ye do it for me?"

"I wish I could turn my head roun' an' roun' like you. Will ye teach me how t'do it?"

Abbot Glisam shook a paw at the little ones. "Would you please stop bothering Aluco and let him get on with his supper? Be off, shoo!"

The owl merely waved a wing at Glisam. "The little uns aren't bothering me, Father, not when there's vittles like these about." His huge eyes widened with pleasure as Friar Skurpul sliced off a portion from a big iron skillet on to his platter. "Thankee, Friar, Redwall food is the best I ever tasted. This is delicious, what d'you call it?"

The good mole smiled proudly. "'Tis ee cornmeal panny-cake, zurr, wi' hunny, chesknutters an' 'azelnutters baked into it. Oi b'ain't never cooked furr a h'owlyburd afore, Oi 'opes you'm loikes it, zurr."

Aluco was profuse with his praise. "Like it, Friar, great howls'n'hoots, I can't imagine living with anything so wonderful and not having it to eat ten times a day. It's absolutely super!"

Dwink and Umfry had wolfed their supper down in silence. They sat drumming the tabletop impatiently, not joining in the general enjoyment. Friar Skurpul chucked both of them under their chins with a floury paw. "Boi okey, young maisters, ee'll bringen on rain an' thunner wi' faces loike that. Wot ails ee?"

Umfry let Dwink do the talking. The young squirrel stared around him bitterly. "How can ye all sit there scoffin' an' laughin' whilst our mate Bisky might be held a prisoner, or even lyin' slain somewhere?"

Samolus interrupted stridently, "Now hold hard there, young un, didn't you hear Bosie say that as soon as we've had a bite to eat, we'd do something about Bisky? I'm concerned about him, too, y'know, he's my nephew!"

But Dwink was not about to be browbeaten. He came right back at Samolus, waving his paws around. "Well, where is Bosie, an' Skipper, too, for that matter? Doesn't anybeast care?"

"Och, did somebeast mention us, we're here the noo!"

Bosie and Skipper had arrived back from the Infirmary; both had poultices of dockleaf and sanicle bound round their paws. Pushing in next to Umfry and Dwink, the otter and the hare helped themselves to massive portions of bread, cheese, soup and salad. Bosie held up his bandaged paws.

"Will ye no look at what yon whey-faced torturer did tae us. Ah swear, 'tis the only time Ah've seen Brother Torilis smile, when he was pullin' Corksnout's spike from mah paws, wi' that long pair o' scissors!"

Skipper paused, with a soup bowl halfway to his mouth. "Aye, mate, ole Torilis did seem t'be enjoyin' hisself. But he got the job done well, I will say that for him."

The Abbot nodded his approval. "Pray tell, how is our Cellarhog faring, is he well?"

Bosie chuckled. "Aye, auld Corkie's lookin' bonny, though Ah'm thinkin' he won't be sittin' doon for a wee while yet. Brother Torilis pulled enough spikes out o' his behind tae fill a bucket."

Skipper tried to hide a smile. "Pore Corksnout, he looks like a big bumblebee, with his bottom covered in bandages."

Amidst the merriment which followed, Umfry was about to interrupt and enquire what Bosie intended to do about Bisky, when Perrit the pretty squirrelmaid came bustling in to make an announcement.

"Father Abbot, I was taking a stroll on the walltops, to see if the giant snake was still about, when I saw a lot of shrews at the main gate. I think they want to see you. Do we let them in? They're still out there."

Abbot Glisam nodded to Foremole Gullub. "The Guosim are always welcome at our Abbey. Unbar the gate for them, friend."

Threescore Guosim shrews strode into the Great Hall. Some of the Dibbuns ran and hid—they were a fierce-looking band. Spiky furred, with coloured headbands, they wore small kilts and broad, buckled belts. Each one had the traditional Guosim short rapier thrust in his belt. Other weapons—clubs, slingstones, bows and arrows and spears—were much in evidence.

Glisam met them with open paws. "Welcome to Redwall Abbey, friends, I'll tell our cooks to provide you with a meal and drink. Please sit. I am Glisam, Father Abbot of Redwall, how can we help you?" Redwallers vacated the supper tables; the Guosim were about to sit when their leader called out.

"Stand fast, all of ye, we ain't here t'feed our faces!" This was the Log a Log, Chieftain of the Guosim. He was no taller than the others, but powerfully built, having a hard potbelly and sporting a grey beard. He carried a long club made of solid iron. Swinging it over one shoulder he faced the Abbot aggressively. "I'm Tugga Bruster, Log a Log of the Northstream Guosim, an' I'm here to ask ye a question!"

Skipper immediately decided that he did not like either the tone or the manner of Tugga Bruster. He hurried forward, placing himself in front of Glisam. "Ahoy, bully, ye can ask wot questions ye like, but there won't be any answers until yore manners improve!"

Tugga Bruster held his club forward threateningly. "Out o' me way, riverdog, I ain't talkin' to you!"

Skipper whirled like lighting; his thick rudder struck the shrew's paws, knocking the iron club from his grasp. It rang out, like a hammer striking an anvil, as it hit the floor. Skipper clenched his paws. "Well, I'm Rorgus, Skipper o' the Mossflower Otters, an' I'm talkin' to you, watermouse!"

The Guosim shrew whipped out his rapier, yelling, "I'll send ye to Hellgates for that!"

It was Bosie's turn to step in now. He drifted in from the side, unknown to Tugga Bruster. As the Shrew Chieftain was about to lunge with his rapier, he was halted by the sword of Martin pricking his neck. The Highland hare stood poised, his tone leaving nobeast in any doubt. "Allow me tae introduce mahself, laddie. Ah'm the Laird Bosie McScutta o' Bowlaynee. Unlike mah friend Skipper, Ah dinna come tae the dance unarmed. So, let's talk. Ah'd advise ye tae put up yore blade, mine's bigger, d'ye see. Oh, an' tell yore clan not tae move a paw, or Ah'll lay yore heid on the floor an' play ball with it. Now, mah braw bucko, do we understand each other?"

Tugga Bruster thrust the rapier back into his belt. "I hear ye, rabbit!"

Zzzzzip! One deft stroke of Martin's sword sheared hairs from the shrew's beard. Bosie shook his head. "Tut tut, yore a hard one tae learn. Och, but ye'll find me a stern teacher. Now, state yore business."

Tugga Bruster backed off, his voice quivering. "Two things. Do ye keep Wytes at this place?"

Bosie leant on his sword, as if pondering the answer. "Ach, certainly not, what do ye take us for, rogues? Carry on, laddie, what's the other thing?".

The Shrew Chieftain asked in a more reasonable tone, "Has a young Guosim been seen hereabouts, goes by the name o' Dubble?"

The Abbot stepped out from behind Skipper; he had begun to put two and two together. "Do I take it that you think this young un, Dubble, has been captured by Wytes?"

The Log a Log nodded. "Aye, that's about it!"

Glisam beckoned to the tables. "All of you, and you, too, sir, please sit and take supper. Come on, Guosim shrews have always been friends of our Abbey. There's no need to create bad blood between us. Sit ye down now, please."

At a nod from their Log a Log, the shrews rushed to the table. Glisam made way for their leader to sit next to him. He enquired about the lost shrew. "Is Dubble one of your tribe, sir?"

Tugga Bruster nodded, as though it was hard to admit. "Aye, he's my son. We've come down from the North, this country is new to us."

The Abbot nodded understandingly. "It must be hard to have your own kin lost in a strange place, a dreadful feeling."

Skipper winked at Tugga. "When you've eaten yore fill, mayhaps ye'd like to join us. One of our own young uns, a mouse called Bisky, is missin'. He was snatched by the Painted Ones. I take it ye've heard o' those villains, eh, Tugga?"

The Shrew Chieftain set his jaw grimly. "Aye, what beast hasn't heard about 'em? Dirty, savage tree rats. There wasn't so many of the scum in my younger seasons, but they're in every reach of forest or woodland these days."

Samolus nodded agreement. "The gang we're after have their dwellings in an' round a five-topped oak, southeast of here. Who knows, maybe they've got yore son. Well, d'ye fancy joinin' us, Tugga?"

Tugga Bruster rose, adjusting the rapier in his belt. Shouldering his iron club, he called to the Guosim, "On yore hunkers an' join these goodbeasts. Y'can eat those vittles on the march, let's be off!"

In soft, dusk light the party left Redwall by the small east wickergate, heading straight into the verdant woodlands. Dwink and Umfry strode alongside a couple of shrews who were about their age, one called Marul, the other named Tenka. They chatted to one another in low voices. Umfry was curious about the Guosim way of life, which Marul tried to give him a flavour of.

"We lives mainly on the water, in logboats. You've got to be good with a paddle if'n yore a Guosim."

Dwink enquired, "Where's yore logboats now, mate?"

Tenka gestured off to his left. "Moored in a broadstream over that way, out o' sight."

He was silenced by Tugga, who had heard them talking. "Ahoy, silence back there, ye ain't out on a picnic. Shut yore gobs!"

The young Guosim promptly obeyed, but Umfry murmured indignantly, "Who does 'e think 'e h'is, givin' h'out h'orders left an' right?"

Samolus turned and tweaked the young hedgehog's snout before delivering a whispered caution. "He's a Guosim Chief, a Log a Log, an' whether ye like him or not, wot he says makes sense. Remember, you an' Dwink ain't in the Abbey now, yore out in woodlands by night. So ye keep yore eyes open an' your mouths shut, an' obey orders, see!"

Samolus went back to the rear of the band, where he fell

in step with Bosie. Skipper marched up front alongside Tugga Bruster; the Otter Chieftain had a fair idea of where the five-topped oak would be. Every once in a while pale moonlight showed through the gaps in the treetops, casting moonshadow on the woodland floor. Samolus nodded ahead. "Ah, I know where we are now, pretty soon we'll come to a clearing up yonder. Skipper will be able to take a bearing on the oak from there."

Bosie silenced the old mouse with a wave of his paw. "Wheesht, can ye not hear that sound?"

Samolus stood still, listening. "Aye, sounds like a sort of rustlin' an' thrashin', but I ain't certain where 'tis comin' from."

Bosie crouched low, letting the others march ahead as he listened carefully, down close to ground level. "Och, that could be more than one creature, comin' up from behind us. Ah think it's headed this way. You go an' tell everybeast tae get off to the right o' this trail. We'll lie low an' see what it can be, mebbe find out if 'tis followin' us."

Word ran swiftly along the column, whilst Bosie crept back along the trail to investigate. Dwink and Umfry obeyed the urgent signals of Samolus, as did the Guosim. The young Redwallers found themselves, along with Marul and Tenka, lying flat in a dried-up watercourse, to the right of the trail.

Now they could all hear the noise. At first it sounded like a stiff breeze, rushing low around the ferns and shrubbery of the woodland floor. But then they heard the sounds of twigs snapping, and some beast, or beasts, beating about amidst the vegetation. The noises grew closer, along with a slight musty odour, quite unpleasant, a bit like dead fish and old damp bark.

Dwink flinched slightly as Bosie dived in the dried watercourse beside him. The hare warned him to silence with a swift glance. Then the hissing could be clearly heard. It was Baliss!

The giant adder had been driven to madness. Leaving

the ditch outside Redwall, he had battered his wounded head against tree trunks, trying to rid himself of the many hedgehog spikes which had pierced his mouth, nostrils, face and snout. Some broke off under the pounding, others were driven deeper into the huge, blind reptile. Each wound became swollen and infected. With the double handicap of blindness and having no means of extracting the tormenting needles, Baliss became insane with agony. Having lost all sense of smell, and direction, the snake rampaged around the woodlands, hissing venomously, unable to do anything about his worsening condition.

Samolus watched, fascinated, as the thick, loathsome coils bunched and straightened like steel springs. Everybeast stayed motionless, unscathed, whilst the monster careened madly past the dry watercourse, along the trail and up into the clearing ahead. Samolus, his voice shaky from shock, stared at Dwink and Umfry. "See, ye never know wot ye'll run into at night in these woodlands. I hope you young Guosim realise that, too!"

However, Marul and Tenka, like the rest of the Guosim, had an all-consuming terror of snakes. The effect that Baliss had upon them was one of total fear. They lay shivering and moaning softly, unable to control themselves. Watching Tugga Bruster whimpering and cringing on the ground, Bosie turned to Skipper, remarking, "Would ye ken he was the braw beastie who was going tae run ye through with his blade this evenin'?"

The otter shook his head. "Aye, our Guosim mates won't be much use for awhile. But I'll tell ye, Bosie, that snake was actin' very strange."

The hare chuckled drily, holding up his bandaged paws. "Ah've nae doubt the beastie is, Skip, an' so would ye be if'n ye had half o' Corksnout's bottom spikes lodged in yore gob. Hah, Ah'll wager auld Torilis would laugh himself clear intae next season, if'n he could get his bonny big scissors tae work on that un!"

Baliss could be heard hissing and throwing himself

181

around the clearing up ahead. Knowing they had little to fear from the snake, providing they avoided him, the Redwallers set about trying to help the Guosim recover. Bosie hauled Tugga upright, shaking him soundly.

"Och, straighten yersel' up, laddie. No Chieftain should be seen blubberin' an' cowerin' in front of his own clanbeasts. Come on, get a grip o' yersel' afore I box yore ears for ye!"

That seemed to do the trick, the Guosim Log a Log recovered immediately, grasping his iron club and declaiming truculently, "Nobeast boxes Tugga Bruster's ears an' lives to boast of it, leggo o' me, I'm alright!" Ignoring the hare's broad grin, he went amongst his shrews, kicking them indiscriminately as he roared, "Up, ye lily-livered no-goods! Get formed into ranks, wot's the matter with ye, eh? 'Tis only an ole snake, it's gone now. Huh, I'd have bashed its brain out with me club if'n it'd tried to attack us!"

Skipper winked at Bosie. "Back to his usual modest shyness, ain't he!"

Bosie turned to Dwink and Umfry, who were shaking with laughter. "An' you two stop sniggerin'. Show some respect tae a braw Chieftain o' Guosim!"

19

Bisky was wakened as the world seemed to tumble and shake. The fallen hollow log that he and Dubble had chosen as their sleeping place was being shaken, rolled and generally banged about. Both friends scuttled out, straight into a sort of big bag. As they scrambled upright to escape, shrill, eager cries rang out from their captors.

"Don't jus' stan' there, sambag dem!"

"Awright, awright, keep yer tail on, I'm lukkin' fer me sambag, 'ere, Gobbo, giz yores!"

"O no, yer not getting' mine, lukk fer yer own!"

A loud, nasal snarl, obviously the leader's, broke in on the dispute. "Yew two, yer about as much use azza snail shell on a butterfly. Give uz that sambag 'ere!"

Two hefty blows knocked the prisoners unconscious.

Bisky awoke with a dull headache, which was not bad, considering the blow he had taken. As expected, he was bound back-to-back with Dubble, either side of a wooden post; also, they were both gagged. Craning his neck from side to side, Bisky viewed his surroundings. It was a long, low-ceilinged cave, with many wooden posts supporting it. The walls were decked with all sorts of what Bisky could only describe as rubbish. Dried fish skins, pieces of coloured stone, old earthenware beakers and wooden plates, all of which had seen better days.

Around small fires, dotted hither and thither, were gathered the scruffiest, weirdest bunch of mice Bisky had ever set eyes upon. Their scraggly fur was caked with mud and dust, and they were clad in tattered rags of barkcloth. The only weapons they seemed to possess were sausage-like sacks of sand, and tough, thin lengths of vine, with a wooden toggle attached to either end. The mice were constantly fighting and squabbling, over the most trivial things. Nobeast ever appeared to get hurt, but they would twirl their sandbags at one another, leaping about and exchanging the most colourful insults.

Every mouse's name ended in an *o*. Bisky heard them calling to one another. He tried to decipher some of the names—there was Gobbo, Bumbo, Tingo, then he gave up. Their accents were flat and nasal, and they spoke with a rapidity which was hard to understand. He watched two of them, the one called Gobbo and another called Tingo, disputing the ownership of a sandbag.

Gobbo shrilled, "Ey, yew, givvuz dat sambag, it's mine, I lost it!"

Tingo stood his ground belligerently. "Gerroff, dis sambag's mine, me ma made it fer me. Don't yew cum round 'ere tryna pinch my sambag, jus' 'cos yer lost yer own. Gobbo the slobbo!"

Tingo caught sight of Bisky watching them, and turned his irate attention upon the Redwaller. "Who are yew lukkin' at, pudden nose?"

Bisky tried to smile, shaking his head, to show he meant no harm or disrespect. Tingo swaggered over; twirling his sandbag, he glared coldly at the captive.

"One more lukk like dat an' I'll sambag yer good'n'proper, d'yer 'ear me, fliggle bottum?"

Bisky smiled and nodded several times. This did not appease Tingo, who began smacking the sandbag hard into

184

his pawpad. "I think I'll just give yer a smack fer laffin' at me like dat!"

He swung the sandbag, about to strike, when he was knocked ears over tail by a very fat mouse, who carried a weightier sandbag than the rest. He grabbed Tingo by the ear, hauling him roughly upright. "Lissen, bobble'ead, did yer search 'em like I told yer to, eh?" He held Tingo on tippaw by the ear as Tingo danced and complained.

"Owowow, leggo willyer, Da! We never found nothin' on 'em 'ccpt two ould slivers o' flint, dat's all!"

The fat one looked questioningly at Bisky. "Iz dat right, jus' two ould cobs o' flint, no treasure of any sort, eh?"

The one called Tingo answered, "I tole yer, Da, only two bits o' flint."

With hardly a glance, the fat mouse swung his sandbag. He struck Tingo in the stomach, knocking him flat on his bottom. The fat one scowled. "Who asked yew, sproutears? I'm talkin' to d'prisoner." He untied the gag from Bisky's mouth. But the young mouse kept quiet until he was spoken to.

The fat one scratched his stubbly chin. "Worra ye doin' in my territ'ry, Redwaller?"

The question caught Bisky off guard. "How did you know I'm from Redwall, sir?"

The fat one gave a humorless laugh. "Yer couldn't be from anywheres else, wearin' gear like that. I know all I need ter know, I'm Nokko, Pike'ead o' the Gonfelin Thieves. So, worra ye doin', playin' daft ducks inna holler tree on my land, wirra Guosim? Huh, I 'aven't seen one o' dem round 'ere fer awhile."

Bisky was intrigued by the name Gonfelin, but he answered truthfully. "I'm Bisky. The Guosim's called Dubble, I met up with him when we were captured by Painted Ones, sir."

Nokko dropped his sandbag, caught it on one footpaw, flicked it up and caught it neatly. "Painty Ones, eh? Y'must be soft in the 'ead, lettin' yerselves get catchered by dat lot. Before youse was caught, did yer 'ave any treasure wid yer?"

Bisky replied as Nokko was ungagging Dubble. "Treasure, sir, what d'you mean?"

The one called Gobbo had been eavesdropping on the conversation; he curled his lip scornfully at Bisky. "Wot does me da mean by treasure, hah! Loot, boodiggles, swipin's, pawpurse stuff, wot d'yer think 'e means, cabbage brain!"

Nokko shot his paw out. Latching onto Gobbo's nose, he twisted it until tears sprang from the victim's eyes. The fat Pikehead leader roared at him, "Worrav I told yer, muckmouth, stay outta things wot don't concern yer, awright?"

Gobbo did a frenzied dance of pain. "Owowowow! Awright, Da, leggo, willyer! Owowow!"

Nokko gave the nose a final, hefty twist before releasing Gobbo. He nodded, almost apologetically to Bisky. "Young uns, dey got no manners at all, 'specially sons an' daughters." He waved a paw at his tribe in general. "I've got enuff of 'em, I should know. I'll tell yer wot treasure looks like. Spingo, go an' fetch yer ma, tell 'er t'bring the jool."

Despite her rough attire, Spingo was the prettiest young mouse Bisky had ever set eyes upon. She shot him a brilliant smile as she tripped off down the cave. "Awright, Da."

Nokko could plainly see the smitten look on his captive's face. He flicked a paw toward his daughter. "Wish I 'ad more like my Spingo, pretty as the summer morn, an' good as the day's long. So keep yer mousey eyes off 'n 'er, she's worth more'n any jools to 'er ole da. Youse two don't look like rascals t'me. If'n I unties yer, will yer promise to be'ave yerselves?"

With a sense of relief, both Bisky and Dubble gave their word that they would behave. Nokko nodded to one of his sons. "Bumbo, cut 'em loose."

The Gonfelin Pikehead led them to a fire, with a caul-

186

dron bubbling over it. "Betcha could eat sumthin', eh, never knew a young un wot couldn't. Get some o' this down yer gullets." It was a thick oat and barley porridge, full of fruit, nuts and honey. An older female served them with stout wooden bowls, filled to the brim. She smiled at Dubble and patted his cheek, then went off to bring them drinks.

The Guosim shrew winked at Nokko. "Is she one of yore daughters, sir?"

Nokko helped himself to a bowl of the porridge. "Who, Fraggo? No, she's one o' me wives. Y'know, I've got that many wives an' young uns I've lost count, 'ow many wives an' young uns 'ave yew got?"

Dubble flushed, but before he could mumble a reply Nokko's daughter, Spingo, joined them. With her was an older mouse, who was still quite beautiful. Nokko patted her paw affectionately. "This is Filgo, me chief wife. See, Bisky, yer can tell where Spingo gets 'er good looks."

Filgo smiled quietly at the guests, nodding toward her husband. "Aye, an' it ain't from Nokko. His da used to use 'im t'frighten off spiders!" She sat next to Nokko. Spingo plumped down beside Bisky, bestowing him with another pretty smile. The young Redwall mouse was so overcome that he spluttered on his porridge. She thumped his back. "Eat slower, or you'll give yerself the collywobbles."

Nokko chuckled. "Go easy wid 'im, darlin', that un's a Redwall Abbey mouse, full of all kinds o' manners."

Gobbo, who was sitting nearby, scoffed. "I 'spect 'e's too good fer the likes of us!"

Nokko dealt him a lightning thud with his big sandbag, laying Gobbo out stunned. He lectured him needlessly. "Never know when t'keep yer gob shut, do yer. Well, let that be a lesson!"

Bisky was overcome with curiosity about the name of Nokko's tribe. "I hope you don't mind me asking, sir, but I heard you say that you and your mice are called the Gonfelins. Where did that name come from?"

187

The fat Chieftain proclaimed proudly, "'Cos Gonff the Prince o' Mousethieves was our ancestor. Gonfelins are all descended from him!"

Dubble interrupted, "How do ye know that?"

Nokko shook his sandbag at the shrew. "Yer a hard-necked beast, askin' a Pike'ead o' Gonfelins sumthin' like that. I know 'cos my da knew, an' his da afore 'im, right back to Gonff we go. So let that be the end o' the daft questions, awright?"

Bisky knew he was on dangerous grounds, still he continued enquiring. "Sir, I don't mean to give any offence, but Gonff came from Redwall Abbey, so why don't you live there? He and his wife, Lady Columbine, and Martin the Warrior all helped to build the Abbey, but I suppose you know that."

Nokko shrugged nonchalantly. "Course I did, I've even 'eard of Martin the Warrior, too. But I never knew Gonff's missus was called Lady Cumbilline. Nice name that, maybe I'll call me next daughter Cumbilline, or Cumbillino, that sounds better. Er, as fer livin' at Redwall, I believe we did, a long time ago. The story goes that our great-great-grandda's great-great-grandda didn't like bein' bossed about by Abbots an' Friars, an' elders. Any'ow, he didn't like takin' orders, so he left Redwall with his family, as far as I know."

Young Spingo wagged a paw at her father. "Ooh, Da, tell the truth, they was kicked out fer stealin'!"

Bisky looked at Nokko. "For stealing!"

Nokko thrust out his chin aggressively. "Well, wot's wrong wid that, Gonff was a thief, wasn't he? Nothin' wrong wid stealin', long as yer don't get caught. Bet you've stole stuff y'self, Bisky."

The young mouse shook his head. "Never, even though I'm a descendant of Prince Gonff myself. I'm no thief!"

Nokko upbraided him scornfully. "Yew, a descendant o' Gonff? Rubbish! Anybeast wid Gonfelin blood in their veins would draw rings around yer, even my pretty liddle

Spingo. Go on, darlin', tell this woffler wot bein' a Gonfelin's all about!"

Nokko pulled out a reed flute and began playing a lively little tune. Spingo leapt up, dancing and singing at the same time. She had a voice like a tinkling bell, and was light as sunbeams on her paws. She twirled around Bisky until his head was spinning.

"There ain't no lock nor bolt or key,
that could put a hold on me,
I can move like shadowy night,
free as a breeze an' twice as light.
'Cos . . . I'm a Gonfelin, a Gonfelin that's me!

I'll tell you, friend, that I believe
you don't know wot it is to thieve,
so better keep close watch on me,
I steal most anythin' I see.
'Cos . . . I'm a Gonfelin, a Gonfelin that's me!

I'll pinch the shell from off an egg,
I'll rob the wings right off a bee,
I'd steal the eyes straight out your head,
if you weren't watchin' me.
'Cos . . . I'm a Gonfelin, a Gonfelin that's me!

O make sure all ye have is yours,
count both ears an' all four paws
then check you've got an open mind,
an' see yore tail still hangs behind,
'cos . . . I'm a Gonfelin, a Gonfelin that's me!"

It was well danced and prettily sung. Bisky joined in the applause. Spingo bowed, flashed a smile, then sat down beside him again. Turning to her father, she enquired, "Well, Da, ain't yew goin' to show Bisky an' Dubble the jool that our ancestors were slung out o' Redwall for stealin' in the ole days?"

Nokko took an object from his wife, Filgo. It was carefully wrapped in fine moss velvet. He opened it slowly, exclaiming, "Jus' looka that, ain't it a beauty!"

Firelight cast blood-hued needles of colour into Bisky's eyes. He blinked. Even on first sight, he instinctively knew that the pigeon's egg ruby he was staring at could only be one thing.

One of the lost Eyes of the Great Doomwyte.

20

A pretty summer morn lent its freshness to Mossflower woodlands, with birdsong resounding through high-canopied trees. The Guosim band, together with the Red-wallers, had spent the night in the dried-up ditchbed, which had not proved uncomfortable. Tugga Bruster was up at the crack of dawn, bullying his shrews as usual.

"Up off yore laggardly tails, you lot. Marul, take six o' these layabouts, an' scout that clearin' up ahead t'see if'n that serpent's gone. Then report back 'ere t'me. Well, go on!"

The shrew Marul did not seem too pleased at the prospect. He chose six of his reluctant fellowbeasts, saluting Tugga Bruster as he paced back and forth. "Er, but suppose the giant snake's still there, Chief?"

The Guosim Log a Log chuckled mirthlessly. "Then ye'll run back 'ere twice as quick, won't ye? Stop tryin' to wheedle out of it, get yore paws movin'!"

Marul led the six off in a desultory fashion, all of them paw shuffling and lagging behind. Tugga Bruster worked himself into a fine temper, roaring at them.

"Call yoreselves Guosim, ye yellow-bellied, lily-livered ditherers. When yore Log a Log gives ye an order, ye jump to it! Now git up t'that clearin' afore I move yore bottoms with me warclub!"

He was swinging the iron club threateningly, when Bosie purposely bumped into him, sending the Guosim Chieftain sprawling. The hare made a flourish, waving the kerchief he carried in his sleeve.

"Oh dearie me, Ah'm sorry, Ah didnae see ye there. Och, silly me, allow me tae help ye up, sirrah!"

Tugga refused the proffered paw, and sat up fuming. "Should watch where yore goin', longears!"

Skipper, who was accompanying Bosie, pointed ahead. "We're just goin' t'see if that ole snake's moved hisself. No need for yore Guosim to go, mate, that is, unless ye'd like to come with us yoreself?"

Marul and the six Guosim gave a sigh of relief, and went back to the dried ditchbed. Tugga slammed his iron club against a sycamore. "I never told ye to go back there, now git up t'that clearin' an' look for the snake! Ye take orders from me, not some plank-tailed streamhound!"

Skipper's jaw was set grimly as he turned to Tugga. However, it was Bosie who interrupted. "Och, give yer auld tongue a rest, there's nae need for an army tae go tae yon clearin'. Why d'ye not take Skipper's advice an' come up there with us? Ah'm certain any serpent would-nae fancy tacklin' three braw beasties like we are."

The Shrew Chieftain snapped back at him, "I don't take orders, I gives 'em, an' I ain't goin' to no clearin' with you two, longears."

A dangerous glint came into the hare's eyes. His paw was on the swordhilt as he replied, "Where Ah come from Ah'm hailed as a Clan Chief. So Ah'll give ye a wee bit o' advice. Never order your tribe tae do somethin' that you're afeared tae do yerself, laddie."

Tugga Bruster was shaking with rage. He bellowed at Bosie, "I ain't afeared to do anythin' you can do, longears. I'll come with ye!"

Bosie took a step forward, eyes blazing. "Listen, mah

friend, if ye refer tae the Laird o' Bowlaynee as longears just once more, 'twill be a harsh lesson ye'll learn. D'ye ken?" Bosie signalled to Skipper. "Let's go tae this clearing', bonny lad, just ye an' me. We'll be better served without sich poor company. Leave him here tae give his orders!" The pair strode off, leaving an irate but speechless Log a Log behind.

Arriving in the clearing, they found it deserted, Baliss having departed sometime during the night. Skipper took an approving look at the greenswarded oasis in the woodlands. "Wot d'ye say, Bosie mate, 'twould be a great spot to take a leisurely breakfast, eh?"

The hungry hare beamed from long ear to long ear. "Och, ye took the words straight out o' mah mouth. Ah'll sprint back an' tell the others."

It was not strictly just a breakfast—everybeast knew this would be the one full meal they would have time for that day. Accordingly they made it a good one. Guosim cooks set up a cooking fire, and began unpacking most of the food provided by Redwall. Umfry and Dwink stood watching them. Umfry voiced his disappointment. "H'is that h'all they're going t'do, sit there stuffin' their faces all day?"

"Aye, I thought we was supposed t'be searchin' for Bisky, an' Tugga wotsisname's missin' son?"

Samolus butted in on their conversation. "You've heard the saying, an army marches on its stomach. You haven't? Well, let me explain. This is probably the last food we'll eat until tomorrow. Skipper tells me we're not too far from the five-topped oak. So, if there's to be a fight, it's better to die with a full stomach than an empty one. Eat hearty, you young uns!"

Guosim cooks baked flatbread over the fire. They were good at campfire food, it smelled delicious. Soon everybeast was tucking into baked apples, flatbread, toasted cheese and one of Friar Skurpul's heavy travelling fruitcakes. There was mint tea or pear cordial to go with it.

In a clumsy attempt to pay back Bosie for tripping him, Tugga Bruster feigned a stumble. Some of the beaker of mint tea he was carrying slopped over. It narrowly missed scalding the hare's head. The Guosim Log a Log made an exaggerated bow. "Ho dear, I'm sorry, are you alright, sir?"

Bosie merely nodded. "Ah'm fine, thank ye."

Tugga leered. "Almost scalded yore . . . long ears."

The hare rose, slow and deliberate. "Ah've taken enough from ye, defend yerself, shrew!"

Putting down his food, Tugga held up both paws, pads outward. He was smiling slyly. "I'd stand no chance agin that sword o' yores, Guosim rapiers ain't that long."

Bosie passed the sword of Martin over to Skipper. "Och, Ah'll no be needin' a blade tae deal with the likes of ye, cully!"

Tugga Bruster cast his rapier aside, commenting, "Aye an' I won't use my blade . . . just this!" Without warning, he charged, swinging his iron warclub.

Bosie, however, was ready. Skipping to one side he launched himself into a high sideways leap. The hare's powerful footpaws cannoned into the shrew's head, laying him flat-out, and stunned. It all happened so quickly that the onlookers were amazed.

Marul turned to Dwink, his jaw agape. "Sufferin' seasons, wot a kick!"

Dwink shrugged, as if he had seen it all before. "All Redwall warriors are good at their job, ain't that right, Skip?"

The Otter Chieftain nodded sagely. "Aye, mate!"

Marul was still greatly impressed. "I never seen anybeast do that afore, I wonder would Mister Bosie teach me how t'kick like that?"

Bosie retrieved his sword from Skipper. "Ye have tae be born with the footpaws tae do it, laddie, 'tis not a move ye'd learn overnight, ye ken." But Marul was not listening. He had suddenly sat down and was gagging, as though he were going to be sick.

Bosie looked at the young Guosim oddly. "Are ye alright, bonny lad, what ails ye?"

Skipper saw the trouble right away. Grabbing Marul, he spoke urgently to the hare. "It's those blinkin' Painted Ones, mate. Get everybeast back under the trees, quick!"

Throwing Marul across his shoulder, the otter scrambled back to the dry ditchbed, in the protecting cover of the trees. Everybeast followed, with Bosie arriving last, because he was assisting the half-conscious Tugga Bruster. Now they could hear the Painted Ones, calling from across the clearing, taunting and threatening.

"Yeeeheehee! We getcha!"

"Yeeheee, killya nice'n'slow!"

Bosie glanced up at the treetops on the far side of the clearing. He muttered orders, which were passed along amongst the Guosim. "Keep yore heads down! Look to yore bows, arrows an' slingstones. Watch the trees either side, Ah've a feelin' they're goin' tae circle round an' trap us in a pincer movement. Keep those eyes peeled an' wait on mah command!"

He turned to Skipper. "How's young Marul, is he hurt?"

The Otter Chieftain had laid Marul down; he was inspecting the Guosim shrew's still form. "He's dead, there ain't nothin' we can do for him."

Umfry could not believe what he had just heard. "Dead? But 'e was standin' talkin' to h'us not h'a moment back!"

Skipper pointed to Marul's throat. "See those darts, three of 'em. I was shot with one in the footpaw, back in the tunnel. I couldn't move me leg for almost a day, it was deadened. Those scum must tip their darts with some sort o' poison. Pore young Marul took three in his throat, cut off his breath. He choked, there was nothin' anybeast could've done to save him, nothin'!"

The news spread like wildfire. Shrews began chattering nervously. One rose, as if to make a break and run for it. Samolus tripped him, muttering angrily, "Do as Bosie says, keep yore head down an' arm yoreselves. Try to run, and they'll cut you down!"

Tugga Bruster had wakened sufficiently to learn what had taken place. He grasped his warclub. "We'll charge the villains!"

Skipper eyed him sourly. "Don't let us stop ye, mate, you go ahead an' charge, but ye'll be on yore own. See how far ye get!"

The Guosim Log a Log looked bewildered. "But wot'll we do, we can't lay here forever."

Samolus pointed to the trees, where the Painted Ones were hidden. "Take charge of your Guosim, watch those trees for any movement. Skip, Bosie, we need a plan."

The three Redwallers put their heads together, with Dwink and Umfry eavesdropping close by. They looked to Bosie, as the most experienced in those matters.

The hare looked from one to the other. "Council o' war, eh, easier said than done, mah friends. We need tae know how many o' the foe we're facin', an' a rough idea of when, an' how, they're goin' tae make their move."

Skipper agreed. "Aye, but we mightn't get much time to do it in. If there's a lot of 'em, they'll prob'ly try an' charge us. Though if there ain't so many, mayhap they'll try an ambush, a pincer movement, like you said, Bosie."

Samolus loaded a stone into his sling. "I wish we knew, it sounds like quite a bunch of Painted Ones, judging by their shouts."

The high-pitched taunting continued from the tree foliage across the clearing. An idea filtered into Dwink's mind—he decided to speak up.

"Er, 'scuse me, but could I say somethin'?"

Bosie looked at him curiously. "Say away, laddie."

Dwink broached his idea to them. "It's like this. I'm the only squirrel with this band, and I know I'm better amongst the treetops than any painted, little tree rat. I think I could steal up on them and capture one, bring him back here an' maybe you could get the information you need, eh?"

Samolus shook his head. "No, you're too young!"

Skipper scratched his rudder doubtfully. "Hmm, ye are only a young un yet, Dwink, an' it's very risky. Oh, there ain't much doubt that yore a good climber, I've seen ye myself, hoppin' round the Abbey battlements an' wall-tops. . . ."

Bosie cut in. "Och, let the laddie have a try, Ah was younger than him when Ah faced mah first war!"

Without waiting for further approval, Dwink grabbed the sling from Samolus. "This is a good, long sling, strong-lookin', too."

Samolus let him take it. "I made it myself, 'tis the best sling in Redwall, if ye'll pardon me saying."

Bosie smiled. "Then take it with ye, if'n ye feel the need o' such a thing. Och, where's the wee beasty gone tae?"

The young squirrel had scuttled off up a nearby elm.

Skipper winked at the hare. "I told ye he was a good climber. Let's hope he brings yore sling back, Mister Fixa."

Samolus heaved a sigh. "Aye, and himself with it!"

21

Veeku, leader of the carrion crows, perched near the rim of the boiling lake in the sulphurous atmosphere of the large cavern. He preferred it there of late; every bird or reptile in the domain beneath the tree-clad hill did also. Everybeast was avoiding Korvus Skurr. The Tyrant Lord of the Doomwytes held them all in disfavour. He remained in the darker, cooler rear cavern, brooding by the cold, bottomless pond, with only the huge, loathsome Welzz for company.

It was a futile exercise. The giant fish would not communicate with Korvus, no matter how much he fed it with live frogs, toads, newts and lizards. The longer Korvus Skurr stayed in isolation, dwelling on the disloyalty of his followers, the more dangerous he became.

His pact with Baliss was now common knowledge to all. He knew he had made a grave mistake by hiring the legendary slayer, but Korvus could not allow himself to lose face by admitting it. Accordingly, the situation got worse. Now no creature dared approach him, fearing his towering rages, and sudden fits of violence. Even his smoothsnake, Sicariss, had taken refuge in the noxious fumes of the main cavern. His once-faithful Wytes joined the crows, magpies and choughs, who mostly camped outside by the stream now.

It was close to evening when several crows, who had been out in the woodlands scavenging, came to perch in the downy birch outside.

Veeku was called from the bubbling lake—the crows had something to report. Winging out into the open, he perched on the topmost boughs of the birch, looking down on his minions. Veeku closed his eyes, waiting until one of the birds began.

"Kraaaak! My brothers and I have seen!"

The leader's eyes flashed open, transfixing the speaker with a sharp, inquisitive stare. "Kiiirrrraaaah! So, ye have seen?" It was the carrion manner of giving an underling permission to carry on; the crow launched right into his report.

"Kark! We saw the mighty poisonteeth Baliss. In the woodlands, south and west of here. Yarraaa! He is acting strangely, battering himself against trees and rocks, tearing up the earth, writhing and hissing. We think he has taken an injury."

Veeku switched his attention to another of the carrion for confirmation, snapping at him, "Grrakk! An injury, how did you know this?"

The second crow shuffled along the branch, spreading both wings expressively. "Korra! The head of Baliss is grown bigger, swollen, with many scars and sores upon it. By the way he hurls his body about, he looks to be driven mad!"

Veeku closed his eyes again, giving the matter much thought. When he had arrived at a decision, he clacked his beak at the two crows who had reported. "Korvus Skurr must hear of this. Yakkar! Follow me, you will tell him what you have seen!"

It was a frightening interview. Korvus menaced the three crows, pressing them for every scrap of information, hovering over them with his lethal beak ready to strike at eye or throat. They told him everything, the demeanour of Baliss, the extent of his wounds and the location where they had seen him. Korvus stood silent awhile, watching the shivering carrion, as his murderous, shining eyes bored into them. Then he spoke.

"Harrah! Leave me now. Veeku, tell my Wytes I would speak with them. Say it is my command that Sicariss attends me also!"

The tyrant raven was a clever schemer, he began planning. This news could restore his prestige, renew his power as ruler of the subterranean realm.

Sicariss coiled beneath a heap of reeking bones, which were piled against the slime-coated wall of the main cave. She had been listening at the entrance to the second cave, hearing all that went on. Sicariss did not trust the raven anymore, so she stayed hidden. Let Korvus Skurr do his own thinking from now on, see how far that got him, without the wisdom and counsel of his former oracle!

Out in the tranquil evening depths of Mossflower woodlands, the great adder Baliss lay on the bank of a shaded stream. The agony of his wounds had subsided to a mercifully bearable level. This had been achieved by immersing his head in the cold, clear streamwater. Gradually the flow cooled his hot, sightless eyes, seeping through his mouth, around the forked tongue and deadly fangs. Like most reptiles, the snake could hold its breath for long periods.

Baliss remained with his entire head submerged until a pleasant numbness engulfed him, relieving temporarily the unbearable pains. He repeated the operation several times, prolonging each period under water. At one point, Baliss was letting the water run through his mouth, lying there, with his jaws loose, feeling the current soothing his forked tongue, when he felt a tickle. It was a small lamprey, which had drifted in, and was attempting to attach its suckerlike mouth to the inside of Baliss's jaw. The serpent's fangs closed upon the unfortunate fish, he drew it out onto the bank, and devoured it, slowly, with great relish.

Uncoiling languidly, the huge reptile stretched on the

mossy bank, which was still warm from the day's sunlight. To look at Baliss, anybeast would have thought he was either dead, stunned or merely sleeping. That would have been a serious mistake.

Korvus Skurr had sent his remaining few Wytes out to seek Baliss. They were to watch the snake, and report back on his movements. If at all possible, Korvus wanted the serpent dead. He intimated this to his ravens, promising anybird who achieved this a mighty position, joint rule of the caverns and command over all who dwelt within them.

Soft night fell over the woodlands, with faint, far-off birdsong, echoing around the gently rippling stream. Four flickering lights illuminated the shade twixt moonshadows, as the Wytes winged low through the trees. They reached the spot where Baliss had last been sighted, and spread out to search the immediate area.

One Wyte, Frang, who normally led the others, perched in the low fork of an alder, waiting for the return of the others. He had not long to wait before the Wyte called Vugri returned. Keeping his cawing down to a minimum, Vugri pointed one luminous-tipped wing to where he had been. He leant close to Frang. "Raaak! I have seen the great serpent!"

Frang nodded for him to continue. Vugri hopped from one talon to the other, reporting eagerly. "Wakaaah! Yonder is a stream, Baliss is there. He no longer strikes his head against trees, or throws himself about as we were told. I saw him just a moment ago, I think maybe he is dead!"

Frang clacked his beak softly. "Yirkk! Show me." The sound he had made was one of disbelief. However, he still wanted to see for himself.

Both Wytes landed silently in the boughs of a wych elm. Vugri indicated his find with a nod. Down below them, and close by, Baliss lay in a patch of moonlight, the whole of his length unfolded, and limp.

Frang whispered, "Yaaark, ye could be right, the monster looks dead. Mayhaps the madness killed him, let us see."

With his stout, heavy beak he snapped off a twig. One powerful twist sent it spinning down at the snake. Frang's aim was good, it struck the reptile's head. Both birds were ready to fly for their lives, but the inert body did not even twitch a single scale. Frang clacked his beak in amazement, whispering, "Hayaaah, the great Baliss has gone to Hellgates!"

Vugri swelled his chest, emitting a loud, harsh cry. "Garraaakaaarr! What are ye whispering for, he is as dead as an old frog from the boiling lake!" He swooped down, cawing triumphantly. "Yiiihaaak! It was I who found him! I will tear out the poison teeth and take them back to Korvus Skurr, he will reward me well!"

Frang, the senior of the two Wytes, hurried after him. "Garrah! We will share the honours, brother!"

Vugri landed a hairsbeadth from the adder's lolling mouth. He struck at the venomous fangs.

But Baliss struck quicker.

Frang managed to swoop out of the dive he was making, wings fluttering wildly. "Kaaaarrrrraaaaagh!"

He winged madly off into the woodland night, as if pursued by golden eagles. The other two Wytes, hearing his terrified caws, left off their search and sped after him. All three remaining ravens headed for the caverns beneath the wooded hill. They were flying scared, stopping for nothing.

Veeku was almost toppled from his perch in the birch tree as the Wytes zoomed past him, crossed the stream and fled into the cave entrance. Torn leaves and strands of creepers fell into the water behind them. The carrion crow leader followed them at a more sedate pace.

In the waft of sulphurous air made by beating wings, Sicariss emerged from her hiding place, amidst the welter of bleached bones. Turning to the yellowed skull of a long-dead rat, she addressed it. "Ssssuch a hurry the Wytesss are in, and Veeku, too. To lissssten isss to gain knowledge, that isss the key to power, yessss!"

As the smoothsnake made her way to an eavesdropping session in the rear cavern, it seemed like the rat skull winked at her in agreement. However, it was only a cockroach passing through its eye socket.

Korvus Skurr listened to the ravens' reports, without comment. Veeku perched a safe distance away—it did not pay to be standing near the tyrant raven when he was hearing bad tidings. Unusually, Korvus showed no signs of violence or ungovernable wrath after he had heard the news. Watching the dark bulk of the Welzz, circling below in the deep pool, he spoke wearily.

"Haaaraaah! Even my Wytes have failed me this night. But who could expect the mighty Baliss to lie down and die, like any ordinary reptile?"

Frang ventured to agree, "Kahaar, aye, who, Lord?"

Korvus eyed him sourly, his voice heavy with scorn. "Yaaarr! You, for one. Get out of my sight, go on, all three of you!"

Frang and the remaining two Wytes obeyed promptly, relieved they had gotten off so lightly. Korvus changed his manner as he addressed Veeku.

"Waaark! My loyal commander of carrion crows, is it not a sad thing to be served by witless fools?" Veeku merely nodded, keeping his distance as the raven continued in a tired but affable tone. "Kraah! If I want anything done I must rely on you, Veeku, my strong right wing. Take the best of your birds on this mission, find Baliss, scout the monster out and observe him. Do not venture into danger, stay clear of the serpent. Send reports back to me on his movements. Will you do this for Korvus Skurr, old friend?"

Veeku was not fooled for a moment, but he spread both wings, bowing his head low. "Harrak, Mighty One, I will go myself to do thy bidding!"

Even the woodland songbirds did not serenade dawn's light within sound of the big, blind snake. Baliss had not rested or slept that night—the pains in his head were starting once more. When he found another stream he would

203

repeat the treatment of immersing his head in cold running water. It was the only thing which gave him temporary relief. Meanwhile, he was obsessed with one goal, revenge upon his enemy. Korvus Skurr was the cause of all his miseries, therefore, he must pay the price. The revenge of the giant adder was a fearsome thing to behold.

Vugri knew this only too well, though the biggest shock to the Raven Wyte was that he was still alive. A living captive of the most deadly creature in all Mossflower. Baliss had merely stunned him when he struck. The snake delivered not a bite, but a driving snoutbutt. When Vugri came to his senses, he made a painful discovery: one of his wings was broken, hanging uselessly at his side. He lay in frozen horror, staring into the sightless eyes of his captor.

Baliss reared, striking like lightning. The Raven Wyte managed a croaking gasp as he gaped into the open mouth hovering over him. Beads of venom pulsed into the fanged glands, and a forked tongue touched Vugri's eyeball, almost caressingly. He smelled the sickly sweet snake odour of death surrounding his head, and heard the sibilant voice.

"Life issss ssssweet, you wisssh to live?"

Vugri heard himself give a breathless sob.

"Y . . . y . . . yes." He ignored the twinging spasms from his broken wing, feeling the snake butting his back with a blunt snout, urging him to rise.

Baliss issued him instructions. "You will obey me."

With his heart beating almost in his throat, Vugri replied, "Yes, I will obey you!"

The snout of Baliss began driving him forward. "You will not try to essssscape, you will take me to Korvussss Sssskurr. Repeat that, to ssshow me you undersssstand the wordsss of Balissssss."

Vugri complied, though it took him some time to stammer out the instructions.

Sicariss concealed herself by the entrance to the inner cavern. She listened carefully, whilst Veeku repeated what he had heard and seen. Korvus Skurr strode jerkily back and forth, his chest plumage palpitating with the rapid beats of his heart. He turned suddenly.

"Arraaah! Where is the serpent now, tell me!"

Veeku blinked at the vehemence in his voice. "I flew back, Lord, to see he did not kill Vugri. He is forcing him to be his guide. They are not too far, but who could say how long he will take, Lord. He is making slow progress with Vugri as a broken-winged guide. Your Wyte is hobbling, but the serpent is with him all the way. What more can I tell you, O Mighty One? Baliss is coming!"

The watcher on the hillside above the cave entrance was still there. Ever vigilant, the dark beast saw all the comings and goings below. Besides any problems he had with reluctant carrion birds, a disaffected Sicariss and the threat of the approaching Baliss, the Chief Doomwyte remained unaware of the sable-furred mystery creature, hovering over him like a dark nemesis.

22

To a certain degree, Bisky and Dubble were allowed a limited freedom. No longer bound or gagged, they wandered around the Gonfelin cavern. The mousemaid Spingo accompanied them, proudly pointing out various facets of her home. Bisky was astounded to learn that the long, low dwelling was actually situated beneath a lake. Spingo pointed to the many timber columns twixt floor and ceiling, explaining in her curious accent, "I don't know who put these up. Ma always says it makes the ould place feel safer."

Dubble eyed the dwelling admiringly. "I tell ye, miss, you Gonfelins must be skilful beasts t'build a place like this!"

Spingo chuckled. "Nah, nobeast could've built this cave. The story is that they stumbled on it accidentally, when they was banished from Redwall. Talk about lucky, eh? There's only us Gonfelins wot knows about this cave. Da sez it's the best kept secret in Mossflower, we're safe from anythin' 'ere."

Bisky could not take his eyes off the mousemaid, she was so painfully pretty. He smiled at her. "Have you ever visited Redwall Abbey?"

Spingo shook her head ruefully. "No. But long, long ago

only the best thieves'n'warriors was ever allowed t'go to Redwall. Hah, they snuck in an' stole some great stuff. But my da's ole granda put a stop to it, said it was too dangerous, an' we should live our own lives. Ferget that Abbey, an' leave the Redwallers to theirselves. So, that's wot Gonfelins do."

Bisky sensed the regret in her voice, so he asked, "Would you like to go there someday, Spingo? I could show you around, you'd probably love it."

She was about to reply, when a clamour broke out up near the cave entrance. Spingo grabbed her new friend's paws. "Wot's all that kerfuffle about? C'mon, we'd better go an' take a look!"

Pikehead Nokko was trying to gain order from a crowd of Gonfelin mice, who were leaping about, yelling and brandishing their sandbags. Nokko walloped a few paws and backs, roaring at them, "Will youse shutyer gobs an' let Duggo make 'is report? Now shurrup, or I'll lay yez all out!" Most of the noise died down; Nokko pointed the sandbag at his scout and intelligence gatherer. "Now tell us wot yer saw, me ould son."

Duggo pranced about a lot, gesticulating as he delivered his summary in a speedy jumble. "Saw? I'll tell yer wot I saw, Da. It's those Painty Ones agin, in the clearin' not far from the five-top oak. The blinkin' blaggids, they're ambushin' some sherrews, jus' like that'n there!" He pointed to Dubble before hurrying on. "Aye, a whole gang o' sherrews, an' some others."

Nokko glared fiercely at him. "Wot others, son?"

The scout continued, "Well, Da, there's a big riverdog, a long-eared rabbet, a young treejumper an' a couple o' mouses, jus' like us an' 'im, wot ye catchered."

Bisky interrupted, "They sound like my friends, are they dead or wounded, tell me!"

Duggo shrugged rapidly, several times. "I dunno, never got close enough t'see, but there's enough Painty Ones t'make scragmeat o' yore pals! Loads o' the likkle rats, in the trees all round the clearin', they've got poison dart blowers, too!"

Bisky grabbed Nokko's paw. "My friends are in danger, and those shrews are most likely Dubble's Guosim tribe, you've got to let us go and help them!"

Nokko wrenched himself from the young mouse's grip. "Now 'old 'ard there, bucko me laddo, yew ain't goin' anywhere. . . ." He paused. "Oh no, not wirrout us! Arm yerselves fer war an' swipin's, Gonfelins! There's blood t'be shed an' loot t'be taken!"

Gobbo stared at his father oddly. "But, Da, we ain't the friends o' sherrews an' Redwallers. Wot's the point of gettin' injured or slayed fer them?"

Nokko seized his objectionable son, buffeting his ears soundly as he drummed home the lesson. "Lissen, mouth almighty, Painty Ones are our mortal foes, so anybeast who's an enemy o' them is a friend o' mine, see!"

Dubble could not help voicing his fears. "But I can't see ye defeatin' 'em with sandbags, sir."

Nokko chortled. "Hoho, we only uses sambags amongst ourselves. Gonfelins goes to war wid the real gear. Bring out the bows'n'lances, an' make sure yer carryin' stranglin' nooses!"

Bisky was in the vanguard along with Dubble and Nokko. Running at his side was Spingo, who, despite her da's orders, insisted on coming. Bisky was armed with a bow and a quiver of arrows, though he did not know whether he would be any good with them, never having been familiar with archery. As they charged through the woodlands, Bisky noted that even Spingo, besides toting a lance, was armed with a strangling noose. This was the other weapon, beside sandbags, which Gonfelins carried as a matter of course. He nodded at the tough, greased vine, with its bone toggles, which was looped about her waist. "Can you use that thing, Spingo?"

The mousemaid winked at him. "Been taught since I

was a babe, Da made me practice on raw veggibles, until I could cut through a big turnip. I've never had t'use it, but I'll wager I could take anybeast's 'ead off at the neck, if'n I had to, Bisky."

Nokko commented, "She could, too, my Spingo's a good liddle daughter, a rare beauty. Now belt up yer gobs an' get those paws a-runnin', or we might miss half the fun an' most o' the loot!"

Duggo, who had gone slightly ahead of the main body, halted and waved his lance. "The clearin's straight ahead, Da, we should be there soon. Wot's the orders?"

Nokko held up a double-headed hatchet, which he was carrying. "Halt 'ere! Duggo an' Twiggo, take a score apiece. Creep round the back o' the trees, get be'ind those Painty Ones an' lay low, wait on my warshout. Bisky, Dubble, Bumbo an' Gobbo, we'll charge the centre, then spread out into two wings. Righto, buckoes, lay low 'til Duggo an' Twiggo gets their crews inter position."

In the distance, the mocking chants and screeching threats of the Painted Ones grew in volume. Nokko ignored them, laying out the ground rules of Gonfelin warfare for the benefit of Bisky, Dubble and anybeast inclined to listen.

"Remember, Painty Ones are born cowards, sneaky rats who can't face up to a good, ould charge. So, youse stampede right in, give the scum a real batterin' until they squeals mercy. Then loot 'em out of 'ouse an' 'ome. All booty taken is t'be shared equally, that's an order!"

The Gonfelin Pikehead fixed his son with a hard stare. "Lissen t'me, Gobbo, one wrong move, or a word outta place, an' I'll come down on yer like a boulder on a butterfly. D'yew 'ear me?"

Gobbo nodded sullenly, avoiding his da's gaze.

Spingo felt her lancetip, whispering in a tremulous voice to Bisky, "Ain't never been in a battle afore, how 'bout yew?"

Buoyed up by her innocence, the young mouse pulled a

tough face as he lied. "Oh, I've done a battle or two in my time. Stick close to me, Spingo, I'll look out for you, me'n Dubble, that is. Right, mate?"

The Guosim shrew could see plainly that his friend was putting a brave face on things, so he winked at Spingo. "Aye, stick by us, miss, huh, Painted Ones don't bother us one liddle bit!" He fitted an arrow to his bowstring, testing its pull.

Bisky did likewise, just to show what seasoned warriors they were. Unfortunately, the shaft slipped, and the string pinged his nose.

Spingo suppressed a snort of laughter, but seeing the crestfallen look on her friend's face, she reached out and squeezed his paw affectionately. "Don't worry, mate, we'll get through it somehow, an' still manage a share o' the loot!"

Bisky restrung his shaft. "Oh, y'mean the swipin's, the pawpurse stuff and the boodiggles?"

Spingo smiled, hefting her lance lightly. "Now yore learnin' the Gonfelin way. Hah, we'll be callin' ye Bisko soon!"

From somewhere up ahead, two high-pitched whistles sounded. It was like the distress call of a small bird. Nokko rose, wielding his axe. "That's Duggo an' Twiggo, they've got their groups in position. Righto, ye thievin' bunch o' bloodswipers, up off yer hunkers, 'ere we go! Bisky'n'Dubble, youse take the right wing! Bumbo, take yore gang t'the left. I'm goin' in by the centre. Gobbo, stay be'ind me, an' behave yerself!"

Suddenly they surged forward, roaring, "Gonfeliiiiins! Gonfeliiiins!"

Knowing that the Abbey beasts might be someplace nearby, Bisky yelled at the top of his lungs, "Redwaaaaaaall! Redwaaaaaaall!"

Dubble added his own cries, hoping the Guosim could hear them. "LogaLogaLogaLooooogggggg!"

Skipper was first to see a familiar face amongst the mob of ragged mice that came rushing forward. He bounded up, calling, "Stow the plans, mates, here comes young Bisky, yellin' Redwall. It's a charge. . . . Redwaaaaaaallll!"

Tugga Bruster saw his son go hurtling by. He stood puzzled, watching. "Wot'n the name o' fur is a son o' mine doin' runnin' round with a pile o' raggedy mice?" He got no further—the flat of Martin's sword caught him smartly on the rump. Bosic roared at the Shrew Chieftain.

"Ach, ye ungrateful beastie, can ye no see, they're friends, come tae rescue us. Charge!"

In the trees, at the far side of the clearing, panic and consternation reigned amidst the Painted Ones. For the first time ever, they found themselves outnumbered. To make matters worse, they were also surrounded. Duggo and Twiggo were cutting off any retreat to the rear. In front, and to both sides, the clearing seethed with Gonfelin, Guosim and Redwall warriors.

Painted Ones were in truth only cowardly tree rats, whose fighting mainly consisted of ambushing lone creatures, firing darts at them from under cover of the high foliage. Their leader, Chigid, had no stomach for open warfare; this was more than he had bargained for. He raced back and forth amongst the foliaged terraces, seeking any means of escape whilst encouraging his fighters to make a stand. "Yeeeeh! Killem plenty, killem, killem!"

A flight of arrows buzzed upward, like vengeful hornets. Tree rats fell screaming, transfixed by the deadly shafts. This was followed by volleys of lances and slingstones. In their terror, the Painted Ones abandoned blowpipes and poison needles, even throwing away their stone-weighted ropes.

Chigid had no place to go but up. He scurried above the high branches, into the lighter twigs and offshoots. After only moments, balancing perilously amidst the fragile network, the inevitable happened. The twigs underpaw snapped. Chigid fell screeching to earth.

He landed with a sickening thud, which must have fractured many bones. Moaning softly, he sought to rise, holding out one paw as he sobbed, "Mercy . . . surrender . . . no kill Chigid. . . ."

Tugga Bruster brought his iron club crashing down on the Painted Ones' Chieftain. He was still raining blows on him when Samolus pulled him off the slain beast.

"What are ye doin', didn't ye hear him callin' for mercy and surrendering?"

Tugga Bruster tried bulling his way past Samolus, to get at Chigid's body. He was snarling. "Fool, ya don't show mercy to these scum. Kill 'em all, an' good riddance t'bad rubbish I say!"

Bosie saw what was happening; he bounded up, striking the club from the Guosim shrew's paws. "Ach, ye cowardly wee beastie, yer nae better than a tree rat yersel'. Look up, can ye no hear that?"

The Painted Ones had given up any idea of warfare since their Chieftain had fallen. They draped themselves over the high branches, wailing and moaning. Nokko, whom they had already been introduced to, leant on his war hatchet, shaking his head. "Yer can't fight scrinjin' beasts like that lot."

Tugga Bruster still thought that he was in the right. "Huh, says who? The only good painted rat's a dead un. I say finish 'em all off!"

Nokko grinned, winking at the Shrew Chieftain. "Lissen, mate, yew go a-slayin' all those Painty Ones, an' all yer'll get is wotever loot they've got on 'em. Wot gain is there in that, eh?"

Samolus liked the ragged Mousechief. "So, what do ye suggest we do, sir?"

The Gonfelin leader explained readily, "Well, me ould mate, wot I'd do first is to get 'em down outta those trees. Then I'd make 'em take us to their hideout, that five-topped oak. I'll wager they've got plenty o' loot stowed there, enuff fer us all to divvy up atween us. 'Ow's that fer an idea?"

Bosie nodded. "Sounds like a bonny scheme tae me. But ye still havnae told us what we do wi' yon bunch."

Umfry voiced a sensible suggestion. "H'if you'll h'excuse me sayin', I think h'it might be better to march the Painted Ones h'off from their 'ideout, right to the flatlands beyond Redwall."

Samolus was beginning to see the merit in the young hedgehog's idea. "Of course, then we scatter them t'the four winds on the open plains. Without a woodland full o' trees to hide in, and with no one to lead 'em, the Painted Ones'll be a threat to nobeast anymore."

Skipper chimed in, "Aye, then we can spend the rest o' the summer at the Abbey, with all our new friends, feastin' an' singin' to our 'earts' content, mates!"

Bosie brightened visibly at the mention of Redwall feasting. "Och, now that's what Ah call a canny scheme. Ah suggest we put it intae practice forthwith!" The Laird of Bowlaynee's enthusiasm squashed any arguments. Everybeast set up a hearty cheer.

Spingo latched onto Bisky's paw, overjoyed at the prospect of visiting Redwall. "Ain't it excitin', I'm finally gonna see where me ancestor Gonff came from!"

Bosie put up his sword, calling up into the trees, "Yore lives will be spared if'n ye come doon here now, wi'out weapons. Do ye surrender?"

There was no question, the goodbeasts had won the day.

23

Dwink had taken off into the trees at the near side of the clearing, with the hope of capturing a Painted One. If the venture were successful, Bosie and his friends could gain valuable information from interrogating the captive. The young squirrel wrapped Samolus's long sling about his waist, and set off about his task. Launching himself from a sycamore bough, he sailed through the air, landing heavily in the swaying branches of an aspen. Grappling awkwardly amidst the foliage, Dwink quietly reprimanded himself as he regained control of his balance. "Didn't judge that un very well, did ye mate? Out o' practice, that's yore trouble!"

He perched in the aspen for a moment, letting its swaying boughs settle, hoping nobeast had gotten wind of him. Dwink's quick eyes detected a movement in a stately elm, several trees from where he was. He moved stealthily, with a swift hop, skip and a jump, landing in the low branches of a spruce. Keeping his gaze trained on the elm foliage, he spotted more twitching in a high fork. Dwink smiled grimly, muttering under his breath, "Hah, that'll be a scout! Right then, ye painted vermin, let's see if'n we can't turn the tables on ye. Stop right there, I'm comin' for ye!"

Smooth as a streamripple, the young squirrel threaded

his way upward, until he reached the top section of the spruce. He was closer now, though he could not clearly make out his quarry. The telltale rustle of leaves told him the other beast was still there, but beginning to move in a sideways direction. Climbing higher, he dropped neatly down into the outspread limbs of a holm oak. Now he was next door to the elm. Unwinding the sling, he loaded it with a stone from his belt pouch. Some of the elm branches were almost touching the holm oak.

Scarcely daring to breathe, Dwink crossed from one tree into the other. His paws were trembling slightly, but he carried on upward, telling himself, "I'll show the blighter how a Redwall warrior operates!" When he was as close as he could get to the spot where he had seen the last movement of his foe, Dwink threw caution to the winds. Whirling his sling, he raced up the final boughs of the upper tree terraces, roaring the warcry: "Redwaaaaall!" He lashed out at the leafy screen with the loaded sling. *Whock! Thud! Wallop!* Leaves showered about his head as he plunged in. But nobeast was there.

The sling rebounded, jarring against his paw. "Yowch!" Dwink was wringing his numbed paw, when he caught sight of his enemy, off to the right. It was a Painted One, about the same age as himself. The tree rat snickered scornfully, loping off into the tall trees. Dwink went hurtling after him, blazing with anger that he had been fooled by a Painted One.

Now the foebeast seemed to be circling back by a roundabout route, not seeking to disguise his track by stealth or silence. Almost bursting with wrath, Dwink charged after him. Ahead he caught sight of a massive five-topped oak, rearing out of the woodlands. The Painted One went straight for it, bounding onto its broad limbs and springing upward. Dwink leapt onto the same branch where his foe had alighted. Whirling his sling, he shouted up into the high foliage, "I've got ye! There's no place to go but up now, is there, ye villain?"

Suddenly, from far off, a clamour rent the air, warcries, shouts and screams. Dwink halted for one brief moment, wondering why the Redwallers, and Guosim, had engaged with the tree rats. Out of nowhere a thin, tough rope came whipping; the stone attached to its end smashed into the side of Dwink's head. He collapsed, draped over the bough, senseless.

Jeg, son of Chigid, clambered down to view his work. He was beside himself with glee. He had finally done something worthy of a Chieftain's son, captured one of the enemy, single-pawed.

Snickering and giggling to himself, Jeg bound his captive viciously tight. Having accomplished this, he secured the rope's end to the bough, looped the remainder around the squirrel's footpaws and kicked him savagely. Dwink fell from the oak limb and hung, dangling upside down. Jeg climbed to the lower branch, where he stood facing Dwink, on a level with his face. He began swinging his unconscious victim to and fro roughly, sneering triumphantly.

"Yeeheeheehee! Well now, looka wot Jeg catchered, a shoopid treemouse. Wait'll Dadda comes back wid the rest an' sees wot I did. Don't ya see, daftbeast, dis is our territ'ry. Painted Ones knows every leaf an' every tree round 'ere. Didya think ye was gonna catcher me?" He struck Dwink's face with his open paw as he spoke. "Well, didyer, eh, didyer, bonebrains?"

Dwink gradually recovered his senses, only to find that the world was upside down. He was being jostled roughly, from side to side. He struggled to release his limbs as Jeg's face confronted him, grinning wickedly.

"Yeehee, awaked now, have ye?"

As he swung closer, Dwink acted instinctively, biting at his enemy. Jeg leapt back, avoiding the squirrel's snapping teeth. "Yaharr, missed me!" He spun Dwink around, jumping on his back and leaning down heavily, jerking him about painfully. "Wanna try agin, do ya? Heeheehee, Jeg's gonna have have fun wid this un!"

The added weight caused the young squirrel to gasp. "Ummff! Ye painted little coward, just wait'll I get loose!"

Jeg jumped down and faced, his prisoner. "But ya can't get loosened, can ya! Likkle treemouse, yore all mine, I kin do anythin' I want wid ya." Jeg broke off a twig; he began tickling Dwink's nose none too gently with it. The distant sounds of battle had ceased now. Jeg noticed it, too. He began taunting, "Ya friends are all slayed now."

Dwink snarled a reply. "Hah, that's what you think!"

Jeg's tone became almost reasonable. "Chah! My dadda's Chigid, big Chief, he got lotsa warriors, lotsa, lotsa dem. More'n yore friends got." He shook his head in mock sadness. "All ya pore mates be dead now, all slayed!"

Dwink came back stoutly, "Oh, no they won't, it'll be your scummy lot who'll be slain!"

Jeg struck him with the twig he was holding. He did not like being contradicted; a malicious gleam entered his eyes. "I say yore lot be slayed, not mine. One more word outta yore shoopid mouth an' I'll slay ya, treemouse!"

Aware of the peril he was in, Dwink wisely refrained from replying. But this only served to madden Jeg. He strode around his captive, lashing out with the twig, working himself into a dangerous rage.

"If I say they all be dead, then they all be dead, ooo! Heehee, no, yore right, they not all dead, you be still alive. . . . So?" Dwink smelled the tree rat's rancid breath as he leant close, speaking slowly and deliberately. "So you gotta get slayed, an' Jeg'll slay ya!"

Dwink felt himself go cold with fright. It must have showed on his face, because Jeg sniggered, and began enlarging upon his evil plan. "Now, wot's the best way to slay a silly treemouse, eh? Mebbee stick a blade in ya. Or loose der rope, an' let ya drop right down to the floor on yore 'ead, would ya like dat?"

Dwink dangled upside down. His ears were starting to ring with pressure; he felt dizzy and breathing was becoming an effort. Owing to the recent blow he had taken, the young squirrel began slipping back into a stupor. Jeg's voice receded into a distant drone. Jeg was in his element, describing in lurid detail various cruel methods of execution for his victim, each more sadistic than the last.

Wholly unconscious, Dwink found himself in the midst of a nightmare. His vision was clouded blood red, inhabited by purple and dark crimson foebeasts. He was still suspended by both footpaws. Painted Ones leant close, leering and grinning evilly as they whispered of the horrible fate that awaited him. Dwink felt close to death, alone amongst enemies, with no friendly face to reassure him.

Then he spied the light, a warm, golden radiance approaching him. The hideous images of the vermin faded, scurrying off into dark shadows. Suddenly, like a bright summer dawn, Martin the Warrior was with him. The legendary Redwall hero spoke soothingly through Dwink's fevered dreams.

"Your time is not yet come, be brave, young one. Friends are near, you must live. The Painted One is cursed to suffer a fate worse than anything he can devise for you. Live long, friend. . . . Live!"

Defeated and dejected, the Painted Ones were forced to descend into the clearing. They were disarmed, searched and ordered to be split into groups, each lot to be secured for safe conveyance to the five-topped oak. Samolus took charge of the operation efficiently.

"Nokko, form your prisoners in one tier. Rope 'em together by their necks, an' post guards round the villains. Skipper, Tugga, do the same with your groups. I'll take this last bunch myself!"

Tugga Bruster put in his objection immediately. "Who put you in command, eh? I ain't takin' orders off no ould mouse!"

Bosie placed a heavy paw, none too gently, on the Guosim Log a Log's shoulder. "Ye'll do as yore bid, bonnie lad. Ah've taken aboot all Ah'm goin' tae take from you. Samolus is takin' his orders from me, an' Ah'm commandin' this expedition. So, one more word against mah authority, an' Ah'll drop ye in yore tracks. Do ye get mah drift, bucko?"

Tugga Bruster saw that the Highland hare was not joking, so he swaggered off, bawling orders at his shrews. "Straighten the scum up, make sure those ropes are properly knotted! Dubble, where are ye off to, git back here, now!"

However, the young shrew had also taken enough from his bullying father. He joined Bisky and Spingo. "I'll go with you two, if'n ye don't mind." He trooped off with them both, as Spingo tipped him a mischievous wink.

"I know where the five-topped oak is, cummon, mate, we'll get there ahead o' the others, an' get first crack at the loot!"

Grinning, Bisky shrugged as he remarked to Dubble, "This maid's got loot on the brain, we'd best go along, just to see she doesn't land herself in any trouble."

Spingo shot him a comical scowl. "Lissen, Redwaller, you'll be in trouble if'n ye don't stir yore paws, now shift yerself!" They set off at a lively trot, which soon had Bisky and Dubble panting to catch up. The Gonfelin maid skipped ahead of them, singing a mocking little ditty.

"'Tis my belief if yore a thief,
you gotta get in quick,
don't hang about for others,
be nimble that's the trick.
'Tis no good of ye weepin'
when the loot's in other paws,
as any Gonf'lin'll tell ye,
it's better off in yores!
So don't be thick, just whip it quick,
an' take this tip from me,
with shifty paws, the treasure's yores,
'cos loot, ye know, is free!

219

So, don't be shy be sly,
an' don't be slow, but go,
grab all that ye can carry,
don't ever say yore sorry,
just steal the lot, don't worry,
be furtive, swift an' cute.
Grab! Catch! Swipe! Snatch!
All that lovverleee loooooooooot!"

Puffing and blowing, Bisky put on an extra turn of speed, muttering to Dubble, "I wonder what Abbot Glisam and Brother Torilis would say to that?"

Dubble stumbled into a bush; he emerged spitting out leaves and berries. "Who are they?"

The young Redwaller replied between gasps, "You'll find out when we get to the Abbey, mate!"

Spingo waved a paw ahead. "There's the oak, see!"

Bisky had always reckoned himself to be a good runner, but this Gonfelin maiden was something else. Spingo broke into an all-out sprint, careering off through the shrubbery and round the trunks of tall, ancient trees.

Jeg was crouching at the base of the massive oak, coaxing a small fire into life. He blew on it, adding dead pine twigs and dried moss until the flames spread. Looking up at the unconscious form of Dwink, hanging head down, the young tree rat gave an evil snigger.

"Yeeheehee! Wait'll ya see wot I've thought up, treemouse. I calls it Jeg's Warm Welcome. Heeheee!" He got no further, because something hit him from behind. Jeg went belly down onto the flames, due to Spingo leaping on his back. Using him as a springboard, the Gonfelin maid leapt up and caught a low branch. She was yelling happily.

"Yeehaarrr! I made it, first 'ere! Now where's all the loot hidden?"

Bisky and Dubble heard the screeches. Bulling through the undergrowth, they came hurtling onto the scene. Jeg was beating at his smouldering midriff, performing a crazy dance, he banged head-on into Bisky, knocking him flat. Even in his panic, Jeg immediately recognised his former prisoners. Hardly pausing to take breath, the tree rat bounded off into the woodlands.

Spingo was sawing away at Dwink's bonds with a small dagger. She called down to them, "Looka this, there's some pore squirrel strung upside down 'ere. Lend a paw, mates, mebbe he knows where the loot's hid!"

Bisky took one look. "Great seasons, it's Dwink! Wait there, Spingo, I'm comin'. Hang on, Dwink!"

Dubble grabbed Bisky's paw; his eyes were like chips of ice in a winter storm. "Did ye see who that was? Jeg, the dirty liddle scum who had us strung up in that tree!"

Bisky pulled free of his friend. "That's a Redwaller up there, I've got to go an' help him!"

The young Guosim dashed off, calling back, "Right, you do that, mate, I'm after that filthy villain. I took an oath I'd meet up with him again someday. See ye later!"

Between them, Spingo and Bisky used Jeg's rope to lower Dwink to the ground. They sat him against the oak trunk, ministering to him. Bisky bathed his friend's face with cool water, rubbing his paws gently to restore the circulation. Spingo took dried herbs from her satchel; she lit them from the remnants of Jeg's fire. When they began smouldering she shoved them under Dwink's nose. He was thrust, spluttering and coughing, into wakefulness. Bisky pulled a face as he caught a whiff of Spingo's reviver.

"Yurk! What d'you call those herbs, they smell foul!"

The Gonfelin maid shrugged. "Dunno wot they're called, but they always do the trick, mate. See, yore friend's as bright as a bumblebee now."

Dwink groaned, but managed a wry smile. "I'll live, though I thought I was a dead un for certain. Who's yore pretty friend, Bisky?"

Further chitchat was cut short. Bosie marched in, heading a veritable horde. Guosim, Gonfelins, Redwallers, plus the whole tribe of captive Painted Ones. The Highland hare saluted Bisky and Spingo. "Ah see ye've found wee Dwink, well done!" He turned to confront the other two Chieftains. "Now, mah bonnies, how do we find this loot?"

Tugga Bruster snarled, "Git that fire blazin' good an' leave it t'me. I'll make the scum talk!"

Skipper flexed his brawny rudder, glaring at the Guosim Log a Log. "Ye'll do no such thing!"

Nokko tossed a rope over one of the oak's lower branches. "Leave it to us Gonfelins, Skip. Jus' yew sit tight wid these Painty Ones 'til we get back. Hah, if'n there's any loot, boodle or swipin's up in that ould tree, my bunch'll find 'em!"

Within moments the ancient tree was swarming with small, raggedy mice, each bent on being first at the spoils. Scrabbling over one another, they argued and shouted in a manner that would have put even the Guosim to shame.

"Oi yew, gerrout me way, this is my branch!"

"Hah, who died an' left it ter yew, move over!"

"Who are yew talkin' to, big gob?"

"Big gob is it? Good job I left me sambag at 'ome, or yew'd be takin' a long snooze fer sayin' dat!"

"Yah, go an' sambag yer granny!"

Samolus placed both paws over his ears. "Such shocking language, what a dreadful row!"

Bisky was inclined to agree. "Aye, that it is!"

Bosie whispered confidentially to him, "Mind, laddie, that pretty maid ye've taken sich a braw shine tae, she's the roughest auld shouter o' the lot. Aye, a right pawful she is, Ah'm thinking!"

Tugga Bruster came swaggering up to Bisky, addressing him gruffly. "Hoi, you, mouse! Have ye seen my son Dubble around?"

The young mouse pointed. "Aye, he went that way, hard on the paws of a Painted One. Dubble has a score to settle with him."

The Guosim Log a Log shouldered his iron club. "I never

gave him leave t'go. A score, eh? I'll settle a score or two with that Dubble when he gets back here. . . . You, wot are ye starin' at?" Tugga Bruster's attention was caught by a Painted One glaring at him venomously. He pointed the club at her. "I asked ye a question, thick'ead, why are ye lookin' at me like that, eh?"

Tala, wife of the dead Painted Chieftain, Chigid, spat on the ground in front of the Guosim leader. "Yeeeeh, you da one wot kill my Chigid, I kill ya soon as I get the chance. Killya dead!"

Early evening sunlight was shafting through the wood-land foliage when Nokko and his tribe returned to earth. Umfry could not help remarking to Samolus about their trophies of victory. "Lookit that, Mister Fixa, did ye h'ever see such a pile h'of tatty rubbish. Huh, y'call that loot?"

Samolus nodded. "Indeed, that's what it appears t'be, but ye must remember, young un, one beast's rubbish is another's treasure. They seem happy with it."

Happy was an understatement, the Gonfelins were jubi-lant with their spoils. A few flagons of fur paint, which the tree rats decorated themselves with. Some blades, mostly blunt, broken or rusted. One or two blowpipes, darts and a vial of poison. Crude necklaces, bracelets and tailrings, plus the contents of a larder they had discovered.

Nokko was grinning from ear to ear. "This is the stuff, buckoes, I told yer there was plenny o' pawpickin's to be 'ad. Bosie, me ould scout, once we've 'ad supper I'll divvy the takin's up, fair shares for everybeast, that's the Gonfelin way. We may be thieves, but we're good, 'onest thieves. Spingo, Bumbo, pile all dat loot over yonder, an' stan' guard on it!"

Aided by Redwallers and Gonfelins, the Guosim shrews put on quite a nice supper, even cooking up the Painted Ones' larder supplies and serving it to them. Bosie was quite partial to shrewbeer, and the flat panbread which the Guosim were very skilled at making. Whatever was to

223

paw went into the panbread, preserved fruits, honey, nuts berries, fresh from the bush.

Not wanting to hurt Nokko's feelings, and speaking for allbeasts present by mutual agreement, Skipper raised his beaker and delivered a short speech. "Ahoy, mates, here's a toast to our friends, the Gonfelins. We'd never 'ave beaten the Painted Ones without their aid, so let's drink to 'em!" After toasting the Gonfelins' bravery, Bosie, who had been tipped the wink by Skipper, spoke further.

"Aye, an' wot reward can we offer tae sich braw beasties? Ah propose that we award Nokko an' his warriors all the loot tae keep for themselves!"

The ragged mousethief tribe cheered themselves hoarse. Nokko was moved almost to tears by his fellowbeasts' generosity. He sniffed loudly. "Wot can I say, buckoes, it's not offen yer come across real friends, an' proper mateys, but youse lot's the best o' the best. Right, Gonfelins, sing 'em out!"

A fine, baritone-voiced mouse sang the verse, whilst all the other Gonfelins joined in the chorus.

"One day a young Gonfelin was leavin' his home,
to seek for his fortune outside,
his pore fatty mother embraced him so tight,
crackin' two of his ribs as she cried.
    The code of the Gonfelins is ancient an' true,
      wot you've got is yores 'til I've swiped it off you!

'You whipped all the sheets off the bed, son,
an' the boots from yore granny, me dear,
but a pore mother's tears ain't worth nothin'
except when she's waterin' the beer.'
    The code of the Gonfelins is ancient an' true,
      wot you've got is yores 'til I've swiped it off you!

'You must promise to be dishonest,
out in that cruel world all alone,

when you dips yore paw into a pocket,
make certain it ain't yore own.'
    The code of the Gonfelins is ancient and true,
      wot you've got is yores 'til I've swiped it off you!

Well, the Gonfelin he kissed his ole mother so hard,
that he raised a big lump on her head,
'Farewell, Mother,' he cried, as she swooned at his side,
then he stole her best wig an' he fled.
    The code of the Gonfelins is ancient an' true,
      wot you've got is yores 'til I've swiped it off you!"

Roars of laughter were choked, as the listeners saw that Nokko and his tribe were quite overcome with emotion by their song. Some of the Gonfelins were weeping openly. The Guosim merely looked bewildered, but the Redwallers were forced to turn aside, one or two stuffing grass in their mouths to stifle ribald guffaws.

Wiping tears upon a ragged sleeve, Nokko announced solemnly to the assembly, "Er, that's our bestest song, we sung it to honour youse fer lettin' us 'ang on to the boodle. I want youse all t'know, that by yore kindness, you've done summat nobeast as ever done to a Gonfelin." He paused to blow his snout, then continued humbly, "You've stolen our 'earts!"

There was a stunned silence, then Bisky rose, raising his beaker and calling heartily, "Good health'n'long seasons to our mates the Gonfelins!"

24

Jeg's stomach was sore and smarting from the scorching he had received when he fell onto the fire. On running away from the five-topped oak, he had raced willy-nilly into the woodlands of Mossflower. The young tree rat hoped desperately that he would not be pursued by either of his two former captives. Jeg recalled beating the Guosim shrew with a willow withe; he shuddered at the hatred that had burnt in their eyes, especially the Guosim shrew—that one looked like a really vengeful beast.

He continued running, then paused, breathing heavily as he tried to catch any sounds of pursuit. However there were only the normal summer sounds—distant birdsong, the hum of bees and the odd noises of foraging insects. Having reassured himself, he continued at an easier pace, constantly touching his scorched fur and blistered flesh.

Jeg was at a loss as to how he could ease his discomfort, when he came across a woodland pool. The water was dark, it gave off a rank odour as he drew close. No good for drinking. Then his paws squelched into the layer of mud and sodden leaf mould—this was ideal. He sat down and began slapping it on his stomach. It was squelchy, cool, the ideal salve for minor scorching. Instant relief.

Before too long he heard sounds, which alerted him. Somebeast was on his trail, travelling fast, with no attempt at stealth. He glanced around for something to use as a weapon. There it was, a half-submerged tree branch. It emerged with a squelch as he tugged on it. The noises were distinctly nearer now, there was no doubt about it, somebeast was right on his trail, and coming fast. Jeg wedged the branch in a low tree fork and gave it a sharp jerk. The long branch snapped in two, leaving him with a fair-sized length, which he could use as a staff.

Dubble had a strong feeling that he was on the right trail of his foe. He dashed onward, hoping soon to catch sight of the Painted One. Seething for revenge, the young Guosim shrew never thought to act with caution. He ran straight into an ambush.

Leaping out from behind a sycamore, Jeg lashed out with his staff. The swinging blow would have stunned Dubble, but for a speedy reaction. Instinctively he threw up both paws, taking the major force of the staff upon them. He narrowly missed grabbing hold of the weapon, but Jeg was already striking again, this time from the other direction. Dubble was struck between neck and shoulder, he toppled off balance and fell.

The young tree rat was shrieking with delight as he thrashed at his adversary. "Yeeeheee, I killya this time, foolbeast, yeeeeheeee!" Some of the blows connected, others missed, thus was Jeg's haste to finish his enemy.

Dubble wriggled and rolled about furiously, his paws numbed by the initial strike of the staff. He pushed forward, grabbing Jeg's footpaw, and sank his teeth in savagely. The tree rat hopped about, screaming, as he tried to dislodge the shrew, but Dubble hung on grimly. Jeg kicked out at his head, but his foe caught the other footpaw, twisting it and laying him flat on his back.

This was the chance Dubble had been waiting for. Ignoring his various hurts, he threw himself upon Jeg, flailing away with all paws. Over and over the pair rolled, into the squashy compound of mud and leaf mould on the poolbank. Spitting stagnant water, Jeg managed to gain the upper position, forcing Dubble's head down into the mess. One mouthful sent the young shrew into an ungovernable panic—he bucked and jerked so wildly that he threw Jeg to one side. Dubble was up to his waist in the soggy bank morass. He was extracting himself, with some difficulty, when he saw Jeg, whom he had thrown up onto solid ground, take to his paws and run off. The young Guosim shrew yelled after him, "Ye can run, scumface, but-ye won't escape me. No matter wot it takes, I'll get ye!"

Thus began a second chase, this time it went in no particular direction. Jeg was really frightened now; he went in circles, sometimes going off at a tangent, dodging amongst the huge trunks of venerable woodland giants, and crashing through fernbeds, but always with Dubble close behind. Gritting his teeth, the Guosim pursued his quarry relentlessly, getting closer by the moment. Now they were running along a streambank, with Dubble almost on Jeg's tailtip. Both beasts were going so hard that they hardly noticed the low-flying crows between the trees.

Jeg had no time for such observations, running as he was, with the pursuer hard on his tail. Trying a swift ruse, he angled off amidst the trees, casting a backward glance to ascertain where Dubble was. It was to be the young Painted One's final error. Dashing along, as he looked backward, Jeg ran slapbang into a raven. The bird was hobbling along, dragging one wing. It squawked in alarm. Such was his speed that Jeg went tumbling, tail over snout. It was an unfortunate and fatal landing for the son of Chigid and Tala. Straight into a dark, moist, fetid opening. He managed one last horrified shriek, then the jaws of Baliss closed upon him like a steel trap.

Dubble saw the dreadful sight looming ahead of him. A

squawking raven scrabbling upright, and beyond that, the monstrous head of the great serpent. The Guosim shrew saw that it was not the reptile's forked tongue protruding from betwixt its lips. It was Jeg's limp tail. Skidding to a halt, Dubble turned and ran for his life. Emerging from the trees he hurried toward the stream, only to find himself suddenly hemmed in by carrion crows. With cruel, beady eyes glinting, and sharp, heavy beaks poised, the birds closed in on him.

After camping the night under the five-topped oak, the great march back to Redwall got under way. Once they were out of their immediate territory, the entire tribe of Painted Ones appeared very subdued, obeying commands without question.

This suited Bosie fine when they reached a broadstream bank. He had been walking in the vanguard, downwind of the captive band. Whether it was from their lack of bathing, or the noxious plant dyes which they were liberally daubed with, Bosie could not tell. The fastidious hare held a lace kerchief to his nostrils, to avoid the odour emanating from the conquered tree rats. Halting them on the edge of the broadstream, he pointed at the water.

Mayhaps ye'd like tae take a dip an' give yersel's a guid scrubbin'. It pains me tae tell ye that Ah cannae abide breathin' the same air as ye. So in ye go, ye braw wee stinkers!"

Skipper shook his head dolefully. " 'Tis the pore liddle fishes I pity, mate."

On the opposite bank, Bisky and his friends assisted Nokko and his Gonfelins, hauling out the freshly cleaned-up prisoners. Spingo remarked to her father, "Those Painty Ones don't look very scary, widout all that muck plastered over 'em, Da."

Nokko agreed. "Yer right, darlin', they ain't nothin' but a bunch o' skinny, wet rats. Hoi, yew, git back in an' scrub be'ind yer ears!"

Tugga Bruster threw Samolus a surly salute. "Is it alright fer me to cross with my Guosim now?"

The sprightly old Redwaller nodded. "Aye, go ahead."

Skipper watched the shrews wading through the stream. "Wot was all that about, mate?"

Samolus eyed the Guosim Log a Log shrewdly. "Bullyin', Skip. I've been watchin' Bruster. He's been bullyin' the prisoners, so I kept him over this side. I don't like that sort o' thing."

Bosie hitched up his kilt as he entered the water. "Och, yon Brusta would've slain those Painted Ones tae a beast if we hadn't stopped him. Ah tell ye, though, he's plain feared o' that ratwife, the dead leader's mate. If looks could kill, he'd be long slain, the way she glares at him!"

Samolus waded into the shallows, nodding. "Aye, she's a vengeful one, alright. The sooner we loose those rats on the flatlands an' Tugga Bruster parts company with us, the happier I'll be."

Skipper plunged into the broadstream, adding, "Right, mate, I've got a feelin' this whole thing could end badly, if'n we don't keep a tight rein on the situation."

Bisky, Dwink and Umfry marched alongside Spingo, being constantly plagued with questions and enquiries about their home. The Gonfelin maid was good company, and so pretty that they suffered her prattling gladly.

"So then, who's the Pike'ead at yore Abbey, eh?"

Umfry scratched his headspikes. "Wot's h'a Pike'ead?"

Spingo scoffed. "A Chieftain, my da's the Pike'ead of all the Gonfelins."

Bisky smiled. "Oh, I see, a leader. We have an Abbot, Glisam is his name, though I think he might object to being called a Pikehead. You'll like our Abbot, he's a friendly, wise, old dormouse."

Dwink interrupted, "You'll like Friar Skurpul, too, he's the best cook in all of Mossflower!"

Spingo nodded. "Sling beltin' nosh, can he?"

Dwink and Umfry were both mystified, but Bisky had come to learn a few Gonfelin expressions. He explained, "That means, does Friar Skurpul cook good food? Hah, let me tell you, missy, once you've tasted our Friar's breakfast, you won't be able to wait for lunch!"

Umfry's face took on a dreamy expression. "Nor h'afternoon tea, followed later by dinner, then supper. But best h'of h'all is Friar's feasts!"

Spingo looked the picture of wistful innocence. "I've never 'ad a feast, wot's it like?"

As if on cue, Dwink broke out into an old Redwall ditty.

"A feast is a feast, an' that's the least,
that any good beast can say.
You'll want it to start,
you won't want it to end,
but to go on many a day.
When you sit at the board, then rest assured,
you'll be most wonderfied.
Yore mouth'll water, you'll lick yore lips,
an' yore eyes'll pop open wide.
'The feast! The feast!' all goodbeasts cry,
'Just look at those vittles, oh me oh my!'
I'd sing you a ballad about this salad,
but that'd slow my pace,
now cut that cake, for goodness sake,
I'm dyin' to feed my face.
There's fruit an' bread, or cheese instead,
there's soup served by the pail,
ye can wash it down with Strawb'rry Fizz,
or rich October Ale.
There's pasties an' pies, 'tis no surprise,
there's puddens an' trifles galore,
an' meadowcream, like a buttery stream,
o'er crumble or flan to pour.
Choose cordial or wine, it all tastes fine,

231

so come on, one an' all,
we're goin' to attend a feast, my friend,
at the Abbey of Redwaaaaaaallll!"

Dwink had sung it so loud and fast that he ended up puffing for breath. When the surrounding applause was done, Spingo shot him a look of mock disappointment. "Don't they 'ave porridge? I like porridge." There was a moment's pause, then the friends broke into laughter. Nokko winked at Bosie.

"She's a maid an' a half, that un!"

Apart from the Painted Ones, the marchers were in high good spirits. Redwallers, Gonfelins and Guosim chatted together, laughing and singing. Tugga Bruster was, of course, the exception. Sullen and ill-tempered, he went out of his way to find fault with everybeast. Tala, mate of the slain Chieftain, Chigid, knew the Guosim Log a Log was avoiding her vengeful stare, so she began taunting him.

"Looka me, spikeymouse, I watcha alla time. First chance Tala gets, she killya. Oh yes, I creep up, all quiet, an' make worm meat of ye. Don't turn ya back, don't sleep, keep watch 'til Tala killya!"

Tugga Bruster began shaking with rage, gripping his iron club even tighter and panting rapidly.

Skipper tapped his shoulder, issuing a warning. "Don't even think of attackin' a captive, matey, or it'll be the last thing ye ever do. Unnerstand?"

The Guosim Log a Log blustered, lying loudly, "I wasn't thinkin' of attackin' nobeast, except that son o' mine. Huh, dashin' off without his father's permission. No manners at all, these young uns!"

Bisky had overheard the exchange. He murmured to Dwink and Umfry, "If Dubble isn't at Redwall by the time we arrive there, we'll have t'go an' search for him."

Spingo stated flatly, "Aye, an' I'll be comin' with ye, mate. But tell that ould Friarbeast t'save me lotsa feast grub, for when we gets back."

Umfry chortled. "Hoho, there's no h'arguin' with 'er, looks like yore h'included, miz!"

Night had fallen by the time they reached Redwall. Bosie pounded on the main gate. "Open up, will ye, 'tis the Laird o' Bowlaynee, with a braw company o' friends, an' many a rascally prisoner!"

Foremole Gullub Gurrpaw, who had been Gatekeeper that day, emerged from the Gatehouse, shaking his velvety head. "You'm must've smelled ee supper, zurr, they'm just settin' daown to et in Gurt Hall. Coom ee in!"

Everybeast trooped in expectantly. Abbot Glisam, who had been taking a pre-supper stroll, came hobbling over with the aid of a yew stick. The old dormouse straightened up slowly.

"Ooh, this back o' mine feels twice as old as me. Welcome back, friends, supper'll soon be on the table. Is everybeast safe and accounted for? Laird Bosie, who are all these vermin you have roped together?"

Drawing the sword of Martin, Bosie pointed with a flourish. "Och, allow me tae present the Unpainted Ones, Father, we had tae clean 'em up a wee bit. Ah'll dispose of 'em on the morrow, meanwhile we need a place tae keep 'em locked up safe."

The Abbot stroked his chin thoughtfully. "Hmm. Let me see. . . . Ah, the Belltower, it's built separate from the main Abbey. They can sit on the floor, and up the stairs. Top window there's far too high for anybeast to jump from. The belltower should be fine!"

Corksnout Spikkle volunteered to guard the captives. He ushered them into the tower, standing sentry over the single door, armed with his huge bung mallet. Corksnout issued stern commands. "Find somewheres to lay down or sit, an' not a peep out of anybeast. Oh, an' just let me hear one ding out o' those two bells, an' ye'll find out just wot this mallet's for, when it ain't bein' used on bungs!"

Nokko stared admiringly at the huge Cellarhog. "Now

if'n I was a Painty One, there's a beast I wouldn't mess wid. Dat big 'ammer of his makes a sambag look like a baby's toy!"

It was a strange experience for the Gonfelins, seeing inside Redwall Abbey. They had all heard of it, both in story and song, but for long generations no Gonfelin mouse had been inside the hallowed building. Their curiosity, however, was soon dismissed when they were introduced to their first Abbey supper.

Coveting a huge bowl of salad, a wedge of cheese and a fresh-baked farl, Bosie viewed them with awe, whilst repelling one or two of the raggedy mice from his own portion. "Och, will ye no' look at the wee terrors, Ah've never seen beasts shovin' vittles doon like that! Yowch! Away, ye fiend, that wee rascal bit mah paw!"

Glisam was being introduced to his new guests. Nokko shook the Father Abbot's paw cordially. "Me name's Nokko, Pike'ead of all Gonfelins, pleased t'meet ye, Abbo, sir!"

Bisky had to explain that all Gonfelin names ended with an *o*. Glisam smiled.

"Abbo, eh, I like it. Well, friend Nokko, allow me to present Brother Torilo, Friar Skurpo and our owl, Aluco."

The tawny owl bowed. "Actually, my name really is Aluco, so I could be considered as a Gonfelin, in an honorary sort of way."

Bosie raised his nose from the salad bowl. "Ah'm no bothered what ye call anybeast, as long as ye don't refer tae me as Bozo!"

Nokko spotted Bosie's one-string fiddle, the bow of which he also used for firing short metal rods. The Gonfelin inspected it, enquiring, "Is this thing a figgle, can ya play it?"

Amused by Nokko's mispronunciation, the hare nodded. "Aye, 'tis a fiddle right enough, an' Ah can play it. Do ye play the fiddle yersel', Chief Nokko?"

Shaking his head, Nokko passed the instrument to

Gobbo, adding, "No, I never learnt to figgle, but Gobbo can. Hah, it's the only thing he's useful for. Cummon now, Gobbo, me ould son, play the figgle an' sing for yer supper, as a thank-ye to the Abbo."

Gobbo twanged the string once. Satisfied with the tone, he sang the quickest ditty that any Redwaller had ever heard.

"Wot's in a name, a Gonfelin name,
would ye really like to know?
Now just you wait an' I'll tell ye, mate,
they all ends with *o* . . . oooooh, there's
Robbo an' Dobbo an' Bumbo an' Bobbo,
an' Gobbo of course, that's me.
There's Glibbo an' Fibbo, an' Nokko, too,
our great Pike'ead is he.
There's Slumbo an' Tumbo an' Jimbo an' Jumbo,
an' Filgo, now that's me ma,
so I've gotta mention Nokko agin,
'cos he's me blinkin' da.
We don't end in a *b* you know,
all Gonf'lins end in ooooooooooooooooh!"

Amidst the general laughter and applause, Skipper Rorgus called out to the Gonfelin leader, "Ahoy, mate, I don't mind bein' called Rorgo, in fact, ye can call me wot y'want, long as ye don't call me late for vittles!"

Nokko responded cheerfully to the Otter Chieftain, "I agree with ye there, bucko, these Redwall Abbey vikkles are the finest anybeast could sit down to, ain't never tasted scran so great. Wot do yer say, mates?"

Both the Gonfelins and the Guosim roared their approval, pounding the tables and raising their beakers. When the merry tumult died down, Tugga Bruster remarked loudly, "Huh it's not so bad, I've tasted worse!"

There was a horrified silence, then Nokko roared, "Say that agin an' I'll knock yer inta the middle o' next season!"

235

The Guosim Log a Log reached for his club. "Ye won't knock me anywhere, cheeky ragamuffin. I'm free t'speak my mind if'n I so please!"

Nokko let his paw stray to his war hatchet. "Touch that club o' yores an' it'll be the last thing ye do, sherrew!"

At a signal from the Abbot, Bosie was between the two, with drawn sword, whilst the Father Abbot of Redwall made a pronouncement. "Put aside those weapons, there will be no violence done within this Abbey!"

Nokko protested, "But did ye hear wot 'e said about yore good food, Abbo?"

The Abbot nodded. "Somebeasts have a habit of making contrary remarks. Log a Log Bruster is one of them. But that is no reason to draw weapons and fight. As our friend said, he is free to speak his mind."

Sister Violet, the jolly hedgehog, came up with an acceptable solution to the dispute. "Then why not let both beasts speak their minds, Father, how about an insulting battle?"

Nokko quaffed off a beaker of October Ale, grinning as he wiped a paw across his mouth. "Us Gonfelins are good at that, I'm game!"

Tugga Bruster curled his lip scornfully. "I wouldn't lower meself to bandy words with that scruffy object!"

Nokko thrust out his chin aggressively. "Ho, please try, sir. Ye bowlegged, snot-snouted, baggy-bottomed excuse fer a Chieftain!"

Lots of stifled chuckles were heard from the Guosim. Bruster had never been a popular Log a Log. Tugga trembled with rage. He was forced to reply, "You . . . you . . . fleabag, you thief!"

Nokko laughed lightly. "Thief? That's a compliment where I comes from. Ye thick'eaded, spiky-bellied, waxy-eared paddle paw!"

His opponent seethed, struggling for words. "Yore worse than a Painted One, smelly toad!"

Now in his element, the Gonfelin Chieftain chuckled.

"Bet ya wish yore mother hadn't dropped yew on yer 'ead when ye were little. Is that wot made ye grow daft? Ye slobnoggled, piddlypawed, ould onion bum!"

There was a gasp of wholesale shock at Nokko's language. Some parents covered their young ones' ears. Tugga Bruster was lost for a reply. All he could do was to perform a stamping dance of rage.

Nokko roared with laughter. "Hohoho! Lookit the mighty Log a Log, he even dances like an ould frogwife. He must've practiced his dancin' wid a broom, 'cos no maid could face such an ugly partner. Hahaha, mind ya don't trip up o'er yer tail, ploppypaws!" The Gonfelin tribe and the Guosim shrieked with laughter, as Nokko began tapping his paws and singing.

"Ho one two, come t'the feast,
even yew, ye awkward beast,
bow to the maids, wot's that ye say?
There ain't one left they've run away!"

With the laughter of everybeast ringing in his ears, Tugga Bruster fled, defeated. The door slammed behind him as the ill-humoured Log a Log dashed off outdoors.

Splngo winked at Dialey. "Huh, that'll teach 'im to mess wid my da, he's a champeen insulter, y'know."

Some of the Dibbuns thought the contest had been great fun; they started repeating Nokko's insults at one another. "Hurr hurr, you'm a baggity-bottum, snotty ole snout!"

"Heehee, an' yore a pigglypaw h'onion bum, so there!"

Abbot Glisam rapped the tabletop sharply. "We've heard quite enough of that language for one evening, thank you. The next beast I hear using dreadful insults will be scrubbing greasy pans for a day. Now let's forget all bad feeling and enjoy supper like real Redwall friends. Here's a toast to our new companions, the Guosim, the Gonfelins—oh, and our new permanent resident, Mister Aluco!"

The tawny owl bowed solemnly. "Thank you, Father

Abbot, and all Redwall creatures. This is a most happy day for me, and I wish you to accept this with my heartfelt best wishes." He hopped over to the Abbot's table, and placed the round, green emerald on it. Nokko was heard to gasp, "Seasons of swipin', will ye lookit that jool!"

Spingo whispered to him, "Easy now, Da. That belongs to Redwall Abbey, so keep yore eyes off it!"

Nokko patted her paw. "Shame on yer for thinkin' such a thing, darlin'."

Abbot Glisam held the shining green orb up, for all to see. "A most generous gift, friend Aluco, we will treasure it. Please accept our gratitude. Skipper, where do you suggest we keep such a treasure?"

The Otter Chieftain pondered for a moment. "I think 'twould look good in front o' Martin the Warrior's tapestry, Father. I'll put it in an empty candleholder. The light from the lanterns'll shine through the jewel nicely."

Samolus held up a paw. "I second that, a wonderful idea, Skip. What do you think, Abbot?"

Glisam smiled. "So be it, a splendid choice!"

Outside, Tugga Bruster had his ear to the door, he had heard everything. A plan began to form in the embittered shrew's mind.

25

Completely surrounded by the menacing band of crows, Dubble had the awful feeling that he would be slain in the next few moments. The young Guosim could see the stream, not far off. His only chance was to break through the cordon of fierce, black birds and make it into the water. With hungry, cruel eyes, the carrion closed in on him. Dubble did the only thing he could. Yelling the Guosim battlecry, he charged for the stream. "Logaloga-logaloooooog!"

It was a short lived attempt. Dubble got no more than a few paces when he was brought down. A savage blow from one of the predators' beaks hit him on the back of his neck. The young shrew collapsed with a roar of pain. In that same instant, several events took place in lightning-swift succession.

Yelling like a banshee, a huge black otter hurled herself upon the birds. "Eeeezaranaaaaaa!" The weapon she wielded was like a pair of sword blades, with a hilt at their centre. *Whip! Slash!* Two crows dropped, mortally wounded. Without pausing, the lithe, muscular beast threw Dubble over her shoulder, bulled through the carrion like a juggernaut and dived headlong into the deep, running middle of the stream.

Bleeding from the neck, and shocked by his sudden submersion in icy streamwater, Dubble tried valiantly to hold his breath. Dark weed fronds rushed by as the otter held her burden tight to her back with both paws. Somewhere above, Dubble glimpsed a gleam of tree-shaded sunlight. He clung grimly to his rescuer's powerful shoulders. Caught in their vortex, an errant fish struck him in the face. Dubble began to panic, his lungs could not sustain the wild underwater journey. There was a ringing noise in his head, water began running up his nostrils and forcing a passage into his mouth. He struggled as everything went dark around him. Dubble felt an energetic upsurging lunge, it thrust him out of the water, onto a hard, smooth surface. Then the otter landed on top of him with a bump, water spouted from his nose and mouth as he spluttered weakly. Trying to rise, Dubble felt himself thrust flat by the otter, who was muttering.

"Get all water out, shrew be better then, lie still, still! No fret, you still alive, shrew."

More water vomited forth, until Dubble retched and sucked in air greedily. They were under a sort of overhang, on a shelf, somewhere along the streambank. Sunlight seeping in made wavering patterns on the rock walls. The big, black otter nodded, satisfied. "You good now, what name ye have?"

The young Guosim held out his paw. "Dubble!" He gasped as the otter took his paw in a grip like a steel vise.

"Dubble, eh, funny name, I be Zaran the Black." She retrieved her weapon, and began honing the blades on the wet rock, commenting with a wave of her sinewy rudder, "This be my holt, not much, but a finegood place to hide from Wytes, carrion scum and monster snake. You see him, Dubble?"

The young shrew nodded. "Oh I saw him sure enough. Wot a giant, he scared me just to look at him!"

Zaran finished sharpening her weapon. She thrust it in a sling, which hung across her back. "Snake not hurt me,

240

I leave him well alone. Zaran slay Wytebirds, carrion, othersnakes, lizard, toad. Anybeast that come from caves of Skurr!" The white teeth of Zaran shone as she spat out the word "Skurr!"

The big otter was an awesome sight as she prowled sinuously around the rock ledges. Zaran was the strongest-looking otter Dubble had ever seen. Muscles like coiled steel springs, sinews like greased rope, lithe and fluid at every move she made.

Dubble repeated the name curiously. "Skurr?"

Her hazel-hued eyes radiated savage hatred. "Aye, Korvus Skurr. One day Zaran will kill that one. Kill him and all his creatures. They must die, Zaran has spoken, so will it be!"

Dubble was surprised at the black otter's vehemence. "Why must you kill Skurr and all his kind, Zaran?"

The otter snapped angrily, "No ask me that, Dubble. When Zaran ready she tell you." Noting the respect and awe in her guest's eyes, she changed immediately. Producing some fruit and a sun-dried trout from an aperture in the rocks, she placed them in front of the shrew. Zaran smiled briefly. "You young, eat now, young ever be hungry. Eat, Dubble, then sleep. Safe here, Zaran keep watch. We go out when nightfall. I show you. Eat, sleep, first."

As Dubble sat eating, Zaran examined the back of his neck, where the crow's beak had struck. For such a fierce creature, she was surprisingly gentle, murmuring softly to reassure him. "Hmm, not bad hurt, but hide is broken. Zaran can fix that, Dubble be still now. Dirty birds are carrion, never know where crows' beaks have been!"

The young shrew finished his meal as the black otter cleaned his wound, then applied some fragrant ointment, dabbing it on with soft moss. "Dubble live to fight another day, there, sleep now." He drifted into a comfortable slumber, watching the wavering sun patterns on the rock ledges, and listening to the soothing music of stream currents.

Night had cast its mantle over the woodlands when

Dubble wakened. Zaran the black otter was sitting silently watching him. He sat up and stretched slowly. She nodded. "You sleep well, feel better now?"

The young shrew nodded, rubbing his eyes. "Much better, thank you, is it dark already?"

Zaran hitched up the double blade at her back. "We go now, Zaran will show you the lair of Korvus Skurr. Tread soft, make no sound, follow, do as I say, Dubble. Come!"

As they left the holt by a landward exit, one thing became became abundantly clear to Dubble. His new friend was a born hunter, wise in the ways of silent travel. Zaran moved through the nightdark woodlands as though it were bright noon. Silent as a leaf upon the breeze and, at times, virtually invisible.

Dubble learned a lot from his new friend that night. How to blend in with their surrounds, to move swiftly, without seeming to hurry. To stand motionless in the shadows, controlling his body, so that even his breath could not be heard. He was amazed at how Zaran would lean, draped against a tree trunk, observing all about her, whilst ignoring moths, beetles and small nocturnal predators as they wandered over her paws and across her face.

They were following another stream course, avoiding marshground, leaving no tracks upon rock outcrops, halting frequently in the shelter of overhanging willows. After awhile, Zaran pointed ahead to a large, forested hill, which could be discerned in the half-moon and starlight. She mouthed the word *Skurr*. Having learned the lesson of total silence, Dubble nodded. He continued following Zaran, the pair of them moving smoothly as oiled silk.

Skirting a stream, they took extra caution. This was due to the presence of dark carrion birds perched in the boughs of a downy birch. The birds slept on as they stole by, some of them emitting small cawing noises as they dreamed. Zaran took an upward route, into the trees which grew thick upon the hillslope. When she judged they had gone far enough, the black otter indicated a poplar. At some time during its growth, the tree had been blown askew in a winter storm. However, it had established a new position by setting down more roots. Now it grew at an angle, sticking out oddly from its neighbours. It was not difficult to walk along the poplar trunk, to where Zaran had set up a hidden lookout platform. She pointed below.

"See, Dubble, stream, cave entrance. From here Zaran sees all, snakes, toads, carrion birds, Wytes. They come and go, night and day, but nobeast sees Zaran."

The young Guosim lay flat on the poplar trunk, staring down. It was an excellent spying post. Remembering to keep his voice low, he murmured softly, "But why do you watch them like this?"

Zaran's teeth flashed in the darkness as she spat out the words. "Each night, every day, Skurr sends them on his evil business. I will kill them all, it is my vow. Everybeast that crawls, or flies, to carry out Skurr's commands must be slain. Zaran will do it!"

Dubble did not doubt his powerful friend's word, but he felt constrained to point out a fact. "There must be far too many creatures for just one beast to overcome, even a great warrior?"

The black otter slid from the poplar trunk. "Come, Dubble, Zaran will show you."

Over the course of the next hour, the young Guosim followed his friend, awestruck at the sights which greeted his eyes. Holes, pits and deep ruts had been gouged into the steep hillside. Around rocks, between trees, wherever the earth could be dug or scraped. Every bit of the workings was disguised, by bush, rock slabs, foliage and moss.

Zaran led him back to the leaning tree, where she showed him a hidden cache of rough-fashioned digging tools, spades, picks and levering bars. She made Dubble feel her pawpads. They were deeply scored, and thickly calloused, from gruelling labour.

"Five seasons' work, but when it is the snow season all will be ready. That is how one beast will overcome many, Dubble."

The young shrew saw the grim determination in his friend's face. He shook his head. "I'm still not sure how yore goin' t'do it."

Zaran lay back on the almost horizontal trunk, gazing off into the still summer night as she explained. "Beneath this hill is a big cave, where Skurr rules over Wytes, and all who serve his evil desires. Zaran knows all about this place, many beasts from there I have captured. They tell me all, before I send them away."

Dubble knew he asked a foolish question, even as he spoke. "Send 'em away, where to?"

Zaran allowed herself a hint of a smile. "How many seasons are you, Dubble?"

The young Guosim thought for a moment. "Twelve, I think."

The black otter held up her lethal double-bladed sword, watching starlight glinting on it. "My Namur would have been twelve seasons by now." Something in his friend's eyes told Dubble not to ask who Namur was. He sat silent as Zaran continued, "There is but one entrance and exit to Skurr's lair, the one below us. Many times I search to find another, but there is only one. Zaran will make this hill move one day, it will collapse upon the entrance. Skurr and his creatures will have a living grave, and a slow death!"

Dubble understood then. "So that is how one will overcome many!"

The black otter gave a low bloodcurdling chuckle. "Trapped in there, they will die once fresh air is gone, slain by the yellow poison fumes!"

Dubble recalled being under water, when Zaran rescued him. He shuddered at the thought of being deprived of air to breathe. "What an awful an' slow way t'go!"

Zaran's eyes shone savagely. "I would like to be there,

to see it. Then I would know . . . my daughter Namur, my mate Varon, her father . . . their deaths would be avenged!" With a swift thrust, she buried the weapon in the poplar trunk, beside the young shrew. "Dubble stay here, Zaran has work to do." Gathering her crude tools, the lithe black otter vanished into the darkness.

It took Dubble some considerable effort to free the odd weapon from the tree. He lay on his stomach, watching and listening for any alien sounds in the still woodland night.

It had been a long, hard day, Dubble soon dozed off. He slumbered for a short time, then rolled over, almost falling from the poplar trunk. The sword fell to the earth, one of its two points sticking in the ground. Steadying himself, Dubble sat up, immediately alert. Somebeast was close by, and it was not Zaran. He began inching from his perch to reach the sword.

26

Dawn was banishing the dark night hours, turning the skies to a kaleidoscope of gentle, pastel hues. Woodpigeons in Mossflower's trees commenced their broody chuckling, as the first larks of day ascended chirruping joyously. None of the inhabitants of Redwall had yet broken their fast, but they appeared in force on the dew-kissed lawns. Everybeast had turned out early—even the Dibbuns—to witness the banishment of the Painted Ones to the western flatlands. The spectators crowded the walltop over the main gate.

Fully armed, Bosie led a contingent of Gonfelins, Guosim and able-bodied Abbeybeasts to the door of the Belltower.

Corksnout Spikkle stood guarding the entrance. He saluted with his huge bung mallet, knocking his cork nose to one side. Hastily adjusting it, he indicated the tower with a nod. "Ain't been a peep out of 'em all night, mate!"

Bosie returned the salute with a flourish of Martin's sword. "Mah thanks tae ye, sirrah. Off tae yore bed now, Ah'll take charge o' this wee task!"

Completely subdued, the tree rats filed out of the Belltower. Since their bath in the stream, plus the removal of their grisly body trophies, and the attendant weeds, they looked a sorry bunch.

Nokko moved them along with a stick. "Well now, ya don't look like much, eh? No more painty faces, an' trees to 'ide in. Step lively at the back there, awkward paws!"

The watchers on the walltop stood silent, as the heavily guarded rodents shuffled their way to the big front gate. Then the tiny molebabe set the Dibbuns off, with his raucous bass shouts. "Gurrout of yurr, you'm villyuns, goo on be h'off!" The Abbeybabes booed and hissed, shouting out some quite ripe comments at the sullen mob of captives.

"Hah, I cut you tails off wiv a hooj knife!"

"Yurr, et won't smell so stinky in yurr when you uns bees gone, hurr hurr!"

"H'if youse cumm back, Mista Bosy'll baff ye again. Better run very quicker!"

Abbot Glisam stood on the threshold, at the west wall centre. He waited until all the prisoners were lined up on the path, facing the flatlands on the far side of the ditch. Silence fell over everybeast when he raised his paws. Then he addressed the vermin prisoners in a no-nonsense voice.

"Hear me now: you are to be given your freedom, which is more than your tribe ever did for anybeast. But, there are conditions, under which you are released. There will be no return to Mossflower woodlands for any of you. Travel west, toward the setting sun at eventide. After one night out on those plains, you may choose whichever way you want to go. West, south, north, but not east, not back this way. I will post guards to look out from these walls. By this time tomorrow it will spell death for any they can see. Is this clearly understood?"

Amidst the silent shuffling of footpaws, Bosie paced up and down, sword on shoulder, berating the rats. "If'n certain beasties, whom Ah willnae mention, had their way, ye'd all be lang slain! Och, ye wee, ungrateful creatures, do ye not want yer life an' freedom? Bow tae the guid Abbot an' thank him right now. Come on, bow yer scruffy heids an' say 'thankee, Father,' all of ye!"

With very bad grace the tree rats bobbed swift bows, muttering thanks. Abbot Glisam nodded to his guard force, below on the path.

"That's sufficient, send them on their way now!"

Many of the rats hesitated at the edge of the ditch, but they were urged on by stern warriors, with shoves and pushes. "Come on, it ain't that deep, either climb down, or jump over!"

Nokko put his footpaw behind one or two. "I ain't carryin' youse over on my back, git goin'!"

Tugga Bruster was about to swing his iron club at Tala, the mate of Chigid, whom he had slain. However she preempted the move by leaping right across to the other side of the ditch, where she faced him, hatred and defiance glittering in her eyes.

"See me, spikeymouse, I be Tala, I killya one day!"

The Guosim Log a Log began waving his club, roaring, "I've taken enough o' this, I'm comin' over there to finish you off, like I should've done!"

The Abbot shouted from the walltop. "There'll be no killing done here, stop him!"

Dwink shot forward, grabbing Tugga Bruster in a headlock. The shrew bit his paw, tripping him and pushing him into the ditch. Nokko was on Bruster in a flash, knocking the iron club to one side. With a driving headbutt he knocked the Shrew Chieftain out cold. The Gonfelin leader smiled.

"I been wantin' t'do that fer a good while now! Cummon, young un, out ye come." Reaching down he grasped Dwink's paw and heaved.

The young squirrel tried to stand, then cried out in pain. "Yowhooch! Me flippin' footpaw!"

Samolus scrambled down to his side, inspecting the footpaw. "Must've fell awkwardly, it's broken!"

Willing volunteers carried Dwink into the Gatehouse, where Brother Torilis hastened to attend him.

Up on the threshold rampart, Abbot Glisam watched the

freed vermin wandering willy-nilly, as if in no particular hurry. He turned to Skipper Rorgus. "Is that a bow you have there, friend?"

The otter proffered the weapon. "Aye, Father, 'tis."

Glisam selected an arrow from the Skipper's quiver. Laying the shaft upon the string, he drew back and let fly. The arrow fell just behind the back vermin rank. Glisam raised his voice in command. "Right, all archers prepare to shoot on my order. Ready . . ."

Without turning to ascertain the threat, the vermin took to their heels and fled in disorder. Sister Violet watched the receding dust cloud, remarking to Skipper, "I didn't know Father Abbot was such a fine bowbeast, that was a splendid shot!"

Glisam did something quite out of character for the Father Abbot of Redwall. He winked roguishly at the astonished Sister, mimicking a rough otter voice. "Haharr, there's a lot ye don't know about me, matey, ain't that right, Skip?"

Skipper Rorgus returned the wink.

"Aye, right as rain, me ole shipmate!"

Inside the Gatehouse, Dwink stifled a yelp as Brother Torilis gave the injured footpaw an experimental waggle. The gaunt-faced Torilis pronounced solemnly, "More than one bone fractured. Some poultices to prevent swelling, a firm dressing, lots of rest and you should be up and about by autumn."

"Autumn?" the young squirrel cried. "I ain't layin' round here 'til then, we've got to go an' find Dubble!"

Torilis gave him a wry glance. "We? If you mean me I have no intention of going searching for a shrew, and you, sir, are certainly not going anywhere. Huh, we!"

Dwink explained with a pained expression, "I didn't mean you, Brother, I meant Bisky, Spingo and Umfry Spikkle. We vowed to help Dubble."

Bisky and Spingo wandered into the Gatehouse. The

249

Gonfelin maid smiled cheerily at Dwink. "How's the ole hoof, Dwinko?"

Brother Torilis looked up from a draught he was mixing for the patient. "The old hoof, as you so quaintly put it, is fractured in two places. So, miss, you and your friend can take yourselves off, and allow me to care for the injured."

Dwink shrugged helplessly at them. "Sorry, mates."

Bisky patted his friend's bushy tail. "Don't worry about it, me'n'Spingo will find ole Dubble. You'll have Umfry for company, though. Corksnout Spikkle left word that he can't leave the Abbey 'til he's finished up the job we started out to do. Cleanin' out the cellars, an' tidyin' all those barrels, remember?"

Dwink nodded. "That seems like a long time ago now. Anyhow, you two take care of each other, an' good luck with the search. I hope ye find Dubble safe."

Friar Skurpul was kindness itself to both young searchers; he packed them a haversack apiece. "Yurr naow, Oi put in summ gurt vikkles for ee. Hunnycakes, dannyloin'n'burdocky corjul, candied chesknutters, parsties an' ee few o' moi speshul 'efty dumplin's!" The good old mole gave a rumbly chuckle. "Ahurrhurrhurr, Oi wuddent go a-swimmen arfter eatin' wun o' moi dumplin's. Loikely you'd be a-sinken, daown to ee bottum. Hurrhurrhurr, they'm not a-called 'efty furr nought!"

The pair thanked Skurpul, and quit the kitchens in high spirits, feeling a great sense of adventure for their coming trip. Striding across the sunlit Abbey lawns, Spingo encouraged Bisky to get into step by lustily singing a Gonfelin marching song.

"Ho, away over the hills, mate,
from dawn through to night,
an' don't trip over yer paws now,
Left left right!

Marchin' out is great on a fine summer day,
luggin' a bag o' vittles along
to scoff upon the way.
As long as you got mateys
to pace along with you,
whilst there ain't no storms a-blowin'
an' the sky stays blue.

Ho, away over the hills, mate,
from dawn through to night,
an' don't trip over yer paws now,
Left left right!"

Perrit, the young squirrelmaid, opened the main gates for them; she smiled and waved them through. "Goodbye, friends, good luck!"

Tugga Bruster was sitting on the path outside, looking dazed as he nursed a lump on his forehead. The surly Guosim Log a Log glared at the happy pair. "An' where d'ye think yore off to, eh?"

Bisky politely sidestepped the shrew as he scrambled upright, answering him curtly, "We promised to go and search for Dubble."

Tugga Bruster blocked their way. He was looking for a quarrel. "Dubble, huh, that worthless scrap o' fur got himself lost again has he. Right, if'n ye find him, fetch him back t'me, I'll teach him t'go runnin' off without my permission!"

Bisky was about to reply, when Spingo confronted the irate Log a Log. "You'll do nothin' of the sort, ugly mug, I'm glad you ain't my da, ya big bully!"

Tugga Bruster grabbed Spingo by her paw, his face was twisted with rage. "Yore father was the one wot knocked me down, ye hard-nosed snippet."

He was raising a footpaw to kick Spingo when Bisky struck. He swung his haversack, catching the shrew a mighty belt between the ears. Tugga Bruster went down like a felled tree. Bisky was shaking slightly at the prospect of having struck a Shrew Chieftain. He laughed nervously. "Er . . . ha ha . . . one of Friar Skurpul's hefty dumplin's must've got him!"

Spingo curled her lip as she stepped over the shrew. "Shouldn't never be a Pike'ead of Guosims, that un. Nasty piece o' work, ain't 'e. Can't leave 'im 'ere, though. Yore healer, wotsisname Toreerlilero, he'll need to treat 'im, after two bumps on the noggin."

They lugged the senseless shrew across to the main entrance, banged on the gate for attention and hurried away giggling. It was Foremole Gullub who opened the gate. Looking down at the unconscious shrew, he shook his velvety head.

"Gurt seasons, ee'm musta knocked on ee gate wi' his 'ead, t'get loike that. Yurr, Mizzie Perrit, lend Oi ee paw t'get this gurt foozle h'inside."

Dwink lay on the big bed in the Gatehouse, trying to stop himself dozing off—it was after all, still early morning. However, he could not resist the potion which Torilis had administered. It took rapid effect. Bright summer day ebbed into the distance; sounds of birdsong, Dibbuns at play and the customary hum of Abbey life receded.

Sprawled on the big, soft Gatehouse bed, Dwink entered the odd realm of dreams. He saw Martin the Warrior materialise out of the mist. His voice was both strong and soothing, his eyes kind and wise as he delivered a message to the young squirrel.

"The eyes of the owl must watch the eye of the snake. He must watch for other eyes which covet the green one. Trust not the beast who is the friend of nobeast. Redwall will gain the raven's eye from a thief, but the rest you may seek. Return to the door, the door with no key, which holds the key. On, on, and on for one. For one can give you all!"

Dwink was rudely awakened in warm noontide. Three Dibbuns, Dugry, Furff and the very tiny mousebabe, landed with a thump on the bed. Dwink sat up abruptly. "Rogues, ruffians, watch out for my footpaw!"

The Abbeybabes ignored his warning. Leaping over Dwink they burrowed under the counterpane. The mousebabe popped his head out, twitching his snout at Dwink like a fellow conspirator. "Uz playin' hide'n'seek wiv Mista Bosie." Seeing this had no effect on the young squirrel, the mousebabe growled savagely, "Dwink, don't tell 'im where us are, norra word, or I choppa tail off!" He vanished beneath the counterpane, from where muffled giggles emerged.

The Laird Bosie suddenly strode into the Gatehouse. He sniffed the air, looking around dramatically. The bumps moving about beneath the embroidered covering, coupled with the noise of chortling Abbeybabes, were a real give-away. The lanky hare winked at Dwink. "Have ye no seen three wee rogues aboot?"

The young squirrel kept a straight face. "Three, ye say? No sir, I've been fast asleep here since I fell into the ditch an' injured my footpaw." As he was saying this, Bosie was beckoning him to move aside, which Dwink did, rather gingerly, being very careful with his bandaged footpaw.

Bosie then announced loudly, so that the fugitives could hear, "Och, well, if ye should see them Ah've nae doubt ye'll tell me forthwith!" He strode noisily toward the open door, then tippawed swiftly back to the bed. With lightning speed he bundled all three Dibbuns up in the counterpane, swinging it over his shoulder. "Hah, Ah've caught ye, mah bonnies. Sister Violet's waitin' wi' lots o' sweet-scented soap, an' a tubful o' guid, warm water. It's bathtime for ye!"

Dwink chuckled. "You mean they weren't playin' hide-an'-seek?"

Bosie gave the wriggling bedspread a firm shake. "Be

still, ye villains! Mebbe they were playin' games, but Sister Violet isn't. She sent me tae find these babbies. They've been dodgin' her since breakfast. How is yore footpaw farin'?"

Dwink shrugged. "Oh, I'll live, thank ye. Bosie, would you do me a favour, please? Tell Aluco I'd like to see him."

As it happened, the owl in question was at that moment passing the Gatehouse doorway. With him was Brother Torilis, heading a party of Guosim shrews, who were assisting Tugga Bruster up to the Abbey Infirmary. Leaving them to go on their way, Torilis and Aluco popped in to see Dwink.

Torilis inspected the footpaw dressing, assuring his patient, "I've an old wheelchair which you can use to get back up to the Abbey. I'll have it sent down, after I've dealt with that silly Guosim. Can you imagine it, being knocked senseless twice in one morning?"

Aluco stayed after Torilis and Bosie had left. The owl focused his huge, tawny eyes on Dwink. "Is there some way I can help you, friend?"

Having recalled his dream in full detail, Dwink related it to Aluco. Ruffling his feathers, Aluco hopped onto the bed, where he settled down fussily.

"I understand that when your warrior spirit sends a message, it is wise to heed it. So, I will gladly keep watch on the green stone which I donated to Redwall Abbey. Rest assured of that."

Dwink returned his feathered friend's stare. "But what d'ye make of the rest of Martin's message?"

The owl swivelled his head, almost right around. "Well, obviously I'll be watching for any creature who looks as if they're envious of Redwall possessing the green jewel, but I can't think of any immediate suspects, can you?"

"No, but I haven't given it any serious thought yet. But the other part of Martin's message, where he said that Redwall would gain the raven's eye from a thief. What d'you make of that, Aluco?"

The tawny owl swivelled his head back and forth. "I would be hard put to narrow it down to a single beast, Dwink. After all, there's a whole tribe of self-confessed thieves visiting the Abbey at this very moment. The Gonfelins!"

Dwink scratched his bushy tail as he mused, "Of course it's hard to choose from a whole band of the rascals, they're all so proud of being thieves."

Both creatures sat in silence for a moment, pondering the questions which Martin's message had posed. Dwink felt his eyelids beginning to droop once more. Aluco took his cue from the young squirrel. The owl was quite partial to frequent naps. He ruffled his plumage, settling his beak into it. Peace and quiet reigned in the Gatehouse as it fell into deep noontide shadow.

It was however, short-lived. Dwink and Aluco were roused by a racketing, rattling, whooping and shouting. Surrounded by a cloud of dust, Umfry Spikkle came stampeding into the Gatehouse, furiously pushing an ancient wheelchair, with Perrit as a passenger. He dragged it into a swerving halt, narrowly missing the bedside, laughing and shouting.

"Whoohoho! 'Ow was that, miss, fast h'enough for ye?"

The pretty squirrelmaid leapt from the chair, brushing dust from her apron. "Whew! That was faster'n I've ever been, yore a good chairpusher, Umfry." She turned, smiling, to Dwink. "Brother Torilis sent us with this wheelchair, we're to take care of you. Poor Dwink, does your footpaw hurt you a lot?"

Dwink blinked several times, then shook his head. "It doesn't feel too bad now, thank you. Great seasons, don't know wot Brother Torilis puts in his medicine, but it's enough to knock out a regiment o' badgers. He says I'll be well by autumn, with plenty o' rest."

Umfry sighed dreamily. "Wish it was me, h'imagine bein' able to rest for that long!"

255

Perrit giggled. "I'm glad you can't, with the way you can snore you'd drive everybeast in the Abbey mad!"

Dwink sympathised with the huge, young hedgehog. "Is Corksnout working you hard, or have you finished tidyin' up the cellars?"

"Oh, there h'aint much tidyin' up left, h'I've almost finished the job now. Ole Corksnout gave me time h'off, t'be yore chairpusher. C'mon, Dwink, h'is there anyplace ye want me to shove ye to?"

Dwink recalled that he had not eaten that day. "I'm blinkin' well starvin', is afternoon tea finished yet?"

Perrit replied, "They're having tea in the orchard whilst the weather's fine. Look, this is a big ole chair, there's room enough for two of us on that seat. Unless of course Umfry's too weary to push us there."

Flexing his paws on the chairback, Umfry assured his two friends, "Whenever vittles h'is mentioned h'I don't feel weary h'anymore. C'mon, you two, let's go for tea."

"What about Aluco?" Perrit looked toward the owl as he opened his huge eyes.

"I will make my own way at my own pace, thank you." As the owl settled back to sleep Dwink was out of bed and seated with Perrit in the ancient wheelchair.

Umfry justified the squirrelmaid's judgement of him as a good chairpusher. Putting all his considerable force into the task, the big, young hedgehog whizzed them across the lawns with lightning speed.

They skirted the apple and pear trees, rattling and clattering into the orchard, amidst raucous cheers from the Dibbuns. Panting for breath, Umfry called to Friar Skurpul, "Three more for tea h'if ye please!"

Sister Violet served them, loading plates with plum tart, almond slice, honeyed nutbread and fresh fruit. She topped up their beakers with dandelion and burdock cordial, chilled from the cellars. As they ate, Dwink related what Martin the Warrior had said in his dream.

Perrit lowered her voice, trying to contain her excitement. "Listen, Umfry, if you're still working in the cellars, you'll have to investigate that door again, give it a good looking over."

Dwink nodded his agreement. "Aye, I'll wager there's more clues to be found. Maybe a riddle, or some secret writing!"

Umfry muttered in embarrassment, "Er, that might be a problem, mates. Y'see h'I ain't much good h'at readin'. Words just look like squiggles t'me."

Perrit patted Umfry's hefty paw. "Don't worry, I'll come with you, I'm a good reader, always have been since Abbey School."

Dwink looked from one to the other. "Pardon me askin', but wot about me?"

Perrit stifled a giggle. "You can come, too. That's if you can go charging down a full flight of stairs in a wheelchair. . . ." She saw the doleful look on Dwink's face and regretted what she had said. "I'm sorry, mate, but that contraption wasn't built for stairs an' steps. It looks like you'll have to wait at the top of the stairs. I'll take some parchment an' charcoal down there, if there's anything to record you'll be the first to see it."

Dwink was getting painful little twinges in his footpaw He scratched at the bandaged poultice, which Brother Torilis had bound on. "Righto, when is all this supposed to be happenin'?"

Perrit rubbed her paws gleefully. "As soon as we've had tea, no sense wasting time."

Brother Torilis approached, opening his satchel. "Best let me take a look at the footpaw, young un. Is it paining you?"

The young squirrel sighed. "Aye, 'tis a bit, Brother." He whispered to Umfry and Perrit, "You two go an' look at the door. Leave me here, but come straight back if there's anythin' to report."

Brother Torilis had Skipper lift Dwink from the wheelchair to a blanket spread on the ground. Seeing Dwink was in some discomfort, the good Brother administered more of his potion. Dwink began to feel drowsy again. Meanwhile, the Dibbuns commandeered the wheelchair, calling to the Laird Bosie eagerly.

"Us wanna ride, Mista Bosie, cummon, you be a pusher!"

Demolishing a sizeable portion of fruit pudding and meadowcream, the lanky hare obliged good-naturedly. "Right, mah bonnies, all aboard an' hauld tight. Och, but dinnae blame me if'n mah speed affrights ye." With four Abbeybabes sitting in the seat, and four more perched in various positions, Bosie took off like an arrow from a bow, yelling, "Awaaaaay Bowlayneeeee!"

The Dibbuns squeaked, but not from fear. "Wheeeeeee! Fasta, fasta! Redwaaaaaallll!"

Brother Torilis looked up from his task. "I suppose my next patients will be several Dibbuns and a foolish hare, judging by the reckless speed of that old contraption."

Friar Skurpul merely chuckled. "Sumtoimes ee can be a roight ole mizrubble beast, zurr. Still, Oi supposen it keeps you'm 'appy."

Being an owl, Aluco was not overfond of sunlit afternoon teas—he preferred the indoor shadows. Moreover, he had also vowed to guard the big emerald, in its candle sconce, by Martin the Warrior's tapestry. The Abbey building was practically deserted, most Redwallers having taken themselves outdoors, enjoying the summer day. Aluco visited the kitchens, choosing his own afternoon tea: a small wooden bowl filled with candied chestnuts, and a wedge of hazelnut and celery cheese. A little flask of old elderberry wine proved too tempting, so he took that also. Making his way to Great Hall, the tawny owl sought out the corner where the legendary Redwall tapestry hung in serene splendour. Green lights emanated from the fabulous orb of the emerald, which had once belonged in one of the eye sockets of the Doomwyte idol. It was displayed in a candle sconce, directly in front of Martin's likeness.

Aluco loved the tranquil solitude of the deserted hall. In its centre, the worn floorstones were softened by varying pastel hues of sunlight, pouring through the high, stained crystal windows. The tawny owl found a shadowed niche alongside one of the immense sandstone columns. Settling down there, he did full justice to his improvised tea, emptying the bowl, and draining the wine flask. Through the hallowed silence, he caught far-off echoes from the orchard. It was Sister Violet, accompanied by Bosie's fiddlelike instrument. She was singing a beautiful old summersong of sentimental love.

"Far away from noise and bustle I would be,
where sun doth kiss the blooms and warm the stone,
by still green lakes I'd wander peacefully,
'midst their mossy banks I'd wait for him alone.

Watched only by small birds and butterflies,
with humble bees to drone their little tune,
in some tranquil glade where purple shadow lies,
dreaming through the sunlit halls of afternoon.

Oh, willow bending low so gracefully,
all in quiv'ring raiment standing there,
let breezes part thy boughs that I may see,
my love smile on the face he holds so fair."

The combination of good food, wine and sweet song was fast closing Aluco's eyes. Then a rustling sound passed close to him. The tawny owl blinked as he wandered dozily out of his niche. "Hullo, who is—"

A figure, heavily hooded and cloaked, laid him low with a single blow. Aluco fell stunned to the floor. The verdant light of the Doomwyte emerald was extinguished, as the phantom figure stowed it in the folds of its robe. As the thief stepped over the fallen bird, something dropped by Aluco's side. The intruder padded swiftly off, leaving the empty sconce, and the owl, groaning softly as he tried to rise.

27

In his anxiety to grab Zaran's sword, Dubble made a snatch in the dark. He fell from the poplar trunk, onto the hillside. Whatever his attacker was, it fell upon him. The young Guosim could not help letting out a yelp as he and his assailant rolled down the slope, locked together. They crashed into a bush. Dubble had not managed to get the sword, but he began battling tooth and paw to free himself. The thing did not put up much fight, but its size overwhelmed him—he was smothered by a dark, feathery mass. Dubble gave a muffled shout as it enveloped his face. Panic swept through him, the suffocating bulk robbed him of breath.

As suddenly as it had started, his ordeal ended. The thing was heaved from him, and he found himself lying flat on his back, staring up at the dark, savage face of Zaran, the black otter. She nodded curtly at the dark bundle lying nearby.

"Only crow, 'twas almost dead." Zaran made a twisting motion with her powerful paws, and a clicking sound issued from her mouth. "Crow dead now, Zaran make sure of that!"

There was a commotion of cawing and flapping from down at the cave entrance. Dubble followed Zaran to a place where they could see what all the upset was about. Even in the dark of night, a number of dead and badly injured birds could be seen. Some were draped about the branches of the downy birch, others lay limp in the stream. Wide-eyed, the young shrew turned to his companion.

"What is it, what's happenin'?"

The otter pulled him to her side; gripping the back of Dubble's neck, she directed his gaze to where the small stream swirled around the rocky entrance. "See. . . . It is Baliss!"

The young shrew shuddered as he saw the tail of the reptilian bulk sliding slowly into the passage of the subterranean lair.

Veeku, leader of the carrion crows, stumbled into the rear cave, one wing hanging useless at his side. He crowed weakly, "Craaak, Baliss is here."

Korvus Skurr emerged from the shadows, mounting the rock above the deep, cold pool, where his monstrous fish, Welzz, dwelt. He stood impassively, trying to hide his fear as he awaited Veeku's full report. Korvus had hoped, against hope, that the big snake might not reach his caves. From the messages that had reached him, he knew Baliss was badly hurt, and acting strangely. But all the Lord of the Ravenwytes' speculations had been in vain. The giant adder had not succumbed to illness, or suffered further injury. It was inevitable, the massive reptile was akin to a force of nature. Baliss was unstoppable, and now he had finally arrived at the threshold of the Doomwytes' realm.

Favouring his broken wing, Veeku nodded back to the entrance tunnel. "Yaaarrr, Baliss has slain and wounded many carrion crows outside, now he rests in the passage to your main cavern. I was lucky to escape with my life, Mighty One."

Showing no sympathy for Veeku's plight, Korvus Skurr stood watching the entrance between both caves. His keen eyes had not missed the smoothsnake trying to slide in undetected. The raven called out in a harsh monotone, "Raaaharr, come in, Sicariss, attend me. I will not slay you, we need counsel, my friend."

Sicariss had been avoiding her raven master for awhile. Still she had sought him out, knowing that old quarrels would be forgotten now, in the face of the ultimate peril. She wriggled forward, staying at a safe distance. "Lord of Doomwytcsssss, how can my humble counsel help? I am at your ssssservice."

There was an amount of water in the entrance tunnel, which had slopped in from the stream outside. Baliss laid his diseased head in it, trying to gain some temporary relief from the hot, throbbing pain which raged through his senses.

The giant reptile could neither smell the poisoned air, wafting from the boiling, sulphurous lake, nor visualise its immensity. Baliss lived in a world of pain, wrath and madness. The cold-water immersions were growing less effective as the infection from long-embedded hedgehog spines advanced, worsening rapidly. Truly, he could feel his once strong life starting to ebb.

The snake held his blunt snout in the shallow trough of water. Only the desire for revenge on Korvus Skurr and his creatures drove him onward, filling his crazed mind and occupying every waking moment. The narrow passage was completely blocked by the thick coils of Baliss.

From their vantage point above the entrance, the two watchers saw the end of the giant adder's tail slide out of sight, into the hill. A thought struck Dubble. "If we could only collapse this lot in right now! Just think, Zaran, all Mossflower'd be rid of that slimy monster, as well as Skurr and his gang, eh?"

The black otter shook her head ruefully. "Not ready, Dubble, too much work yet."

Together they made their way back to Zaran's retreat

beneath the streambank ledge, where Dubble began kindling a small fire with flint and the otter's steel blade. He shrugged when the otter looked at him quizzically.

"There's no need to hide away now, I don't think our enemies are lookin' to ambush us. Huh, they ain't in any position to attack anybeast right now. Fetch yore vittles out, mate. I'll cook us a nice late supper whilst we try to think up some sort o' plan. Wot rations have ye got there?"

Zaran had very little—a withered section of comb honey, a few nuts and berries and two big apples, wrinkled but still edible.

Dubble grinned at her encouragingly. "Us Guosim are great cooks, I'll soon show ye a trick or two. I'll borrow that blade o' yores, if'n I might. You put more wood on the fire."

There was only streamwater to drink, but Zaran was pleased with her friend's inventive cooking. They tucked into roasted apples, filled with berries, nuts and hot liquid honey, which Dubble had stuck on sharpened sticks.

The young shrew nibbled away reflectively, posing the question, "Isn't there anythin' we can do to collapse that entrance in? Maybe I'll help ye to dig, so we'll get done quicker."

The otter licked honey from her paw. "No faster, Dubble only get in my way."

The young shrew *hmmphed* indignantly. "Sorry I opened me mouth!"

Zaran flashed him one of her rare smiles. "I did not mean to hurt you, friend."

Dubble sipped water from a rough clay bowl. "I know ye didn't, no offence taken, mate. What?"

Zaran held up a paw to silence him; leaning toward the water, she listened carefully. Then Dubble heard the splash also. This was accompanied by a hollow bumping sound, and two quarrelsome voices.

"I told you to paddle on the other side, now look what you've done!"

"Hah, wot I've done, ya puddle-'eaded Abbeymouse, didn't ye never learn t'paddle?"

"Glubb, yuk! No, didn't you?"

"Gonfelins don't need boats, so wot's the blinkin' use of learnin' 'ow to wave an oar around, eh?"

"Oh, stop moaning an' give me y'paw before you drown!"

"Huh, me drown? Who d'ye think helped ya t'the bank!"

Jumping into the water, Dubble began wading out to the main stream. "I know who that is, come on, mate!"

Bisky was on the bank, pulling a dripping Spingo up onto the rocks, when his paw slipped and she fell, splashing back into the water.

She floundered about, yelling, "Didn't they ever teach ya how t'pull a beast out o' the water at that bloomin' Abbey. . . . 'Ey, wot? Leggo! Gerroff me!"

But the black otter lifted her, spluttering, onto the bank. "I am Zaran, friend of Dubble, you safe now, stop shouting!"

Dubble moored the capsized Guosim logboat to the shore. "Wot'n the name o' fur'n'feathers are you two doin' here?"

Bisky waved cheerily to him. "We've come to save you, in case you were in trouble!"

Dubble shook his head in disbelief. "Me in trouble? Oh, an' where did ye get the Guosim logboat, who said ye could borrow it?"

Spingo stamped her paw irately. "That was ole bright snout's idea, we found it up a sidestream, with some others. But I wish we'd left it where it was now, flippin' useless thing!"

Dubble gave the slim craft a sharp heave, tipping the water out and setting it upright. He retrieved the paddles, throwing them in the logboat. "Well, at least ye picked the pride o' the fleet. That's Tugga Bruster's vessel, he won't let anybeast near it!"

Spingo giggled. "Oh, I'm glad it was that ole sourface's boat I pinched. Shame we never sunk it for good."

Bisky went a few paces down the bankside and retrieved their haversacks, which were safe and dry. "Good job I slung these ashore before we were shipwrecked. Anyone for a bite o' supper?"

Dubble winked at Zaran. "Oh, I think we could manage a bite or two, especially if'n those vittles come from Redwall. Come on, ye can get dried out by our fire."

The searchers sat around the fire, steam rising from them as they listened to the account of Dubble's travels. A Redwall supper was much appreciated. Zaran took an immediate liking to Friar Skurpul's hefty dumplings; the rest, including dandelion and burdock cordial, went down exceedingly well. Bisky brought Dubble up to strength on the news from the Abbey prior to their departure, finishing with their encounter with Tugga Bruster. Dubble averted his face from the firelight, obviously embarrassed.

"I don't blame ye for what ye did to Bruster, mate. I know he's me father, but I've never liked him. He's always been a bully an' a slybeast. D'ye know I used to look at other young Guosim, whose dads had been killed, or gone off missin', an' I wished I was like 'em. Awful thing t'say, ain't it?"

Spingo nudged the Guosim shrew playfully. "My da always sez ye can't choose yore family, but ye can choose yore friends. So never mind, Dubbo, ye've always got us, we're as good as family!"

They sat in silence, gazing into the flames, until Zaran noticed them yawning. "Sleep now, I keep watch. Dry and warm here, you sleep!" The otter brought some moss and dried grasses from the back ledges, spreading them around. Dubble curled up next to his friends.

"Aye, sleep, an' while y'do, try an' think of an idea that'll help Zaran an' me to collapse that entrance in. Redwall wouldn't be troubled agin by Wytes an' that big snake if'n ye could."

Watching the shifting water patterns cast by the firelight on the ledges, listening to the peaceful gurgle of the night streamwater as it played along the bankside, the three young creatures fell asleep, each with their own thoughts and dreams.

Starlight twinkled along Zaran's double-bladed sword. She sat outside on the rocks, ever watchful, determined that the tragedy which had befallen her own family would not be visited on her new young friends.

BOOK THREE

Baliss

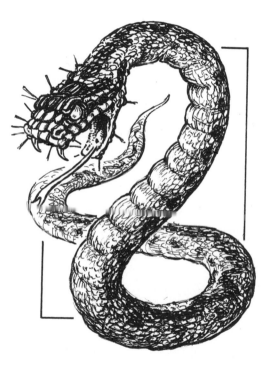

Could nothing slay the giant?

28

Afternoon tea was about over in Redwall's orchard. Dishes were being cleared onto trolleys when the Redwallers heard the tawny owl's hoots of alarm. At first, nobeast seemed to recognise the distress call for what it was. Furff, the Dibbun squirrelmaid, clambered onto Skipper's shoulder. She was giggling. "Heeheehee wot's dat funny noise goin' wooowooooowoohoo!"

The brawny Otter Chieftain smiled. "I don't know, liddle missy, let's go an' see." With Furff still perched on his shoulder, Skipper ran from the cover of the orchard hedge. Once he was out on the open lawn, it was clear to see the main Abbey building door. There was Aluco, staggering about, with both wings folded on top of his head. As he stumbled to and fro, the owl was hooting for all he was worth. Placing Furff down on the lawn, Skipper broke into a run, shouting back to the others in the orchard, "Somethin's wrong, mates, Aluco looks hurt!"

Within moments, Aluco was being cared for, with a crowd of Redwallers on the wide stone walkway pressing around him. Brother Torilis soaked a towel with pennycloud cordial, still cold from its storage in the cellars. He held it on the feathered head, making a compress. "Lie quite still please, looks like you took a bad tumble there. How did you come to trip?"

Aluco was made of stern stuff, as most owls are. Shrugging Torilis aside, he held the towel himself. "Why do you assume I tripped, owls are not in the habit of tripping and falling about. I was struck over the head by somebeast. Father Abbot, I think you'll find that your emerald has gone."

The news struck like a thunderbolt; everybeast was talking at once, most of them repeating the same thing.

"Gone, you mean stolen?"

"And you were struck over the head!"

"Who'd do such a thing?"

"Did you see who did it?"

The clamour rose, until the Laird Bosie roared, "Hauld yer weesht, ye daft, noisy bunch. Silence!" Abbot Glisam sighed gratefully as the mountain hare took command, with fine military precision. "Clear those dishes off yon trolley, an' get the poor, braw bird on it. Stand back an' stay oot the way, all of ye. Right, ma bonnies, let's go tae the scene o' this rascally outrage. Sister Violet, control these wee beasties, can ye no keep these babbies frae under mah paws? Skipper, Samolus, hurry ahead an' guard the scene o' the crime!"

Even before they had reached the tapestry, Aluco scrambled from the trolley, smoothing his feathers with as much dignity as he could muster. "I'm well enough to get along unaided, thank you. Hah, just look at this!"

The tawny owl hurried over to the place where he had been struck down. He waved the object with his formidable taloned leg. "I think this is what the thief knocked me down with!"

Ignorant of such matters, Brother Torilis stared at the weapon. "What's that supposed to be?

The Gonfelin mouse, Gobbo, supplied the answer. "Huh, ain'tcha never seen a sambag afore?"

Samolus took it, weighing it with one paw. "Aye, 'tis a

sandbag sure enough, a good, well-made one, too. Sort of thing a Gonfelin might use."

Amidst angry growls from the Gonfelin mice, Gobbo faced aggressively up to Samolus. "Aye aye, ould un, wot's all this, are yew tryin' t'say it was one of our lot who clobbered that owlburd, eh?"

The Abbot interceded. "No, no, not at all, my friend. All Samolus said was that the sandbag is normally a weapon favoured by your tribe. I don't suspect one of you Gonfelins for a moment."

Tenka, a young Guosim shrew, stepped forward, paw grasping the short rapier at his belt. "An' wot about us Guosim, eh?"

Brother Torilis sniffed audibly. "Oh your tribe aren't to blame, neither are these Gonfelins. I suppose the emerald took it upon itself to strike Aluco down, then it just rolled off, for fun!"

Skipper slammed his hefty rudder hard upon the floorstones. His eyes were cold and angry. "Stop all this silliness! The Abbot ain't accusin' nobeast. But the Doomwyte Eye is gone, an' that's a fact. Now not another word from anybeast. . . . Abbot?"

Glisam bowed to the Otter Chieftain. "Thank you, Skipper Rorgus. I'll talk to the leaders of the Gonfelin and Guosim, perhaps they might shed a little light upon the problem."

The Abbot looked around both groups. "Er, has anybeast seen Nokko, or Tugga Bruster?"

Brother Torilis pointed upstairs to his Infirmary. "I have the Guosim Log a Log in my sick bay. A most unpleasant beast, I'm treating him for two minor head wounds. You may interview him, should you so wish, Father."

Filgo, who was one of the Gonfelin Pikehead's wives, ventured further information. "My Nokko's up in Prince Gonff's ole room, takin' a nap. Said he had a headache, just afore tea."

The Abbot appeared puzzled. "Prince Gonff's old room?"

Samolus interrupted, "Er, that's my fault, Father. Nokko kept pestering me about which room Gonff used to occupy. I didn't know, but he kept on and on about it. So I chose the first attic room, above the dormitories. Who knows, Gonff might have stayed there at some time. I meant no harm, really."

Filgo smiled. "Well, it's pleased my Nokko no end. He loves that liddle room like it was his own."

In company with Samolus, Skipper and Bosie, Abbot Glisam followed Torilis up to the sick bay. Tugga Bruster was lying in bed, propped up by three pillows. He gave the visitors a surly glare. "Well, what d'ye want, come to persecute me some more, have ye?"

When he needed to be, Abbot Glisam could be quite formidable. This was such a moment. He gave the Guosim Chieftain a haughty stare. "I haven't come to bandy words with you, about alleged tribulations you have received during your stay here. I'm going to ask you some questions, to which I need straight answers!"

Tugga Bruster adjusted the bandage on his brow, and gave a sigh of obvious boredom. "Ask away then, but don't take all day. I need me rest."

Glisam came straight to the point. "Brother Torilis tells me that he brought you up here this morning. Have you moved from this room for any reason?"

The Log a Log shrugged. "Why should I, that un there, yore Healer, said I was to lie still an' rest. So that's wot I've been doin, ain't moved nowheres."

Torilis nodded. "That's true enough, Father Abbot."

Glisam turned to the Brother. "And you were with him all the time he was here?"

The Infirmary Keeper nodded. "Yes, I was here, except for going to take afternoon tea in the orchard."

From a stool next to the bed, Bosie picked up a dark green cloak with a hood attached to it. "What's this thing supposed tae be?"

Samolus answered, "Oh that, it's one of the old habits. Sister Violet an' myself found a pile of them in an old chest. So we made them into dressing gowns or bedjackets. Some of these rooms can get a bit draughty in the winter season."

The Abbot paused a moment, then gave further instructions. "Samolus, take me to Nokko's room, I'll speak to him next. Skipper, would you and Laird Bosie kindly search this room from top to bottom."

The Gonfelin Pikehead was roused from his sleep by Samolus and the Abbot knocking on his chamber door. Placing a paw on his bandaged brow, he called out grumpily, "Go 'way, an' give a porebeast some peace, will ye!"

Without further ceremony the two Redwallers entered.

Nokko smiled feebly. "Sorry, mates, I was right inna middle of a nice ole snooze then. So, wot can I do for ye, come an' siddown on me bed."

The pair remained standing as Samolus came right to the point. "What ye can do for us, Nokko, is to tell us where you've been since teatime this afternoon."

The Gonfelin looked from one to the other. "Why, wot's up, mates, wot's botherin' ye?"

Abbot Glisam placed both paws in his habit sleeves. "My friend, you'd help us by answering the question."

Sensing that it was a matter of some import, Nokko replied promptly, "Well, d'yer remember that sherrew, Bruster? I put 'im down with a good ole butt, just after 'e slung young Dwink inta the ditch earlier t'day. I tell ye, Abbo, that Bruster must 'ave an 'ead like a boulder. Ye can't see it, but under this bandage I've got a right ole bruise, an' a lump like a duck egg. I missed afternoon tea through it. Me skull began to ache somethin' fierce, so I came up 'ere to Prince Gonff's ole room, just to rest me pore 'ead. Afore I knew it I dropped off t'sleep on this liddle bed. Good job ye woke me, or I'd 'ave missed supper, an' snored through until tomorrer!"

275

Samolus nodded. "So this is where you've been all afternoon."

Nokko grinned guiltily. "That's right, Samo, mate. Why?"

Feeling rather embarrassed, the Abbot answered, "Because the green Doomwyte Eye has been stolen, and Aluco was assaulted by whichever beast did it."

Nokko leapt from the bed, a look of shock on his face. "Ye don't think I did it, do ye?"

Shaking his head hastily, Abbot Glisam assured him, "No, my friend, something tells me that you could not find it in yourself to do such a mean act. However, an investigation will have to take place. Would you be willing to take part in it?"

Picking up the dark green hooded cloak, which had been folded neatly at the bottom of the bed, Nokko donned it. "Of course, Abbo, lead on!"

Bosie met them on the stairs to Great Hall. "We've searched yon sour-faced shrew's room, but there was nought tae find. What now, Father?"

Glisam bowed to Nokko. "Excuse us a moment, sir." Drawing to one side, he went into a huddle with Samolus and Bosie. After a whispered conference, Bosie favoured Nokko with an elegant bow.

"Ah hear ye've no' had afternoon tea, let me take ye to the kitchens whilst we remedy the situation forthwith. We'll take tea teagether, eh?"

The Gonfelin Pikehead was pleased, but puzzled. "Thank ye kindly, mate, but 'ave'nt yew already had yore tea?"

The gluttonous hare struck a noble, but long-suffering pose. "It fair pains me tae see a braw beast eat alone. Ah'll force mahself tae endure another helping the noo!"

The venue chosen for the enquiry was at the scene of the crime. Samolus elected to set the stage, clearing the mass of onlookers to one side. Aluco was now back to his former self, having spurned all offers of aid from Brother Torilis.

276

The tapestry of Martin the Warrior provided the backdrop, as Samolus issued instructions. "Silence, everybeast, thank you! Now, Aluco, would you take up your position at the spot where you were when you first saw the intruder."

The tawny owl made his way to the niche, twixt column and wall, where he had begun his surveillance. "I was right here, just dozed off slightly, after a drink and a bit of afternoon tea."

Samolus turned to the Abbot. "We're ready now, Father."

Having finished their repast, Bosie escorted Nokko to the candle sconce where the emerald had rested. The hare left the Gonfelin standing alone there.

Samolus put the question to the owl. "Is that the creature you saw earlier today?"

Aluco peered at the dimly lit figure in the late afternoon shadows. "Hmm, it could have been, tell him to turn his head slightly toward me, please." Nokko did as asked, without any instruction. Aluco stared hard, declaring, "Aye, it could well have been the beast. I can see a touch of bandage showing from under the hood. Aye, I remember now, the beast was wearing a bandage around his head. I caught a glimpse of it as I was knocked down!"

Nokko's pretty wife, Filgo, called out in protest, "All us Gonfelins are thieves, just as Prince Gonff was. But we ain't sly villains, my Nokko would never steal from friends, or commit evil acts. It ain't fair, that's wot it ain't!"

Bosie interrupted her tirade. "Ah'll have tae ask ye tae be silent, marm, there'll be no interferin' wi' this investigation, ye ken. So hauld yer wheesht an' be a guidbeast, or Ah'll have tae banish ye tae the orchard."

Nokko smiled fondly at his pretty wife. "He's right, me ole darlin'. Leave it to our Redwall mates, they'll git t'the bottom o' this."

Angry words erupted across Great Hall, from the stairs. It was Tugga Bruster, who was being hauled to the scene by Skipper. The Log a Log was blustering and struggling in the Otter Chieftain's firm grip.

"Git yer paws off'n me, riverdog, yew can't make me go anyplace where I don't wanna go!"

Skipper kept tight hold of the dark green habit that the shrew was wearing. "You come along quiet now, mate, there's nothin' t'fear from a few questions if yore innocent."

The Guosim Log a Log clapped a paw to his bandaged head, slumping back as though he was fainting. "Leggo, can't yer see I'm injured?" He caught Skipper unawares, sliding free of the flowing habit and kicking him hard in the stomach.

The otter responded with surprising speed. Falling backward on the stairs, he lashed out with his hefty rudder. Tugga Bruster received a thwack on the back of his neck which sent him tumbling down the remaining steps. He hit the floor facedown. There was a noise, like a pebble dropping, as the round, green emerald popped from his belt purse. In the silence which followed, it rolled slowly over the stones, coming to rest in front of the Abbot.

Tugga Bruster sprang upright, avoiding Skipper's paws. He stared desperately about, yelling, "It's a trick, that riverdog planted it on me!"

Bosie confronted him contemptuously. "Ach, ye canna' dress a worm up as a warrior. Yer a miserable robber wi' no a scrap of honour tae yore name!"

The culprit ducked around Bosie, grabbing the short rapier from the belt of a nearby shrew. He called to his tribe, "Rally t'me, Guosim! We'll teach these stupid Redwallers a lesson afore we leaves this place. Logalogalogalooog."

The battlecry went unheeded. Not a shrew moved. Turning cold faces from their shamed leader, they stared at the floor in stony silence.

Lacking his iron club, Tugga Bruster slashed the air with the rapier blade, shaking with rage. "Wot's the matter, have ye got soil in yer ears? Charge 'em, that's an order from me. I'm Tugga Bruster, Log a Log of all the Northern Guosim!"

One of the older shrews, Garul, shook his head. "Not anymore you ain't, run whilst ye still have the chance, Bruster. Guosim don't know ye anymore!"

Hatred flashed from the deposed Chieftain's eyes. He flung the rapier, catching Garul in the shoulder, then he sped from Great Hall. Roaring in anger, the Guosim tribe chased after him.

Skipper curled his lip scornfully. "Let the coward go, an' good riddance to him."

Garul looked up from the floor, where Brother Torilis was tending his gashed shoulder. "Stay out of it, sir, Guosim deals out their own justice!"

Abbot Glisam bowed his head at Nokko. "Please accept our apologies, my friend, we were wrong ever to suspect you."

The Gonfelin Pikehead laughed the whole thing off. " 'Twasn't yew t'blame, Abbo. Anybeast who took on a tribe of thieves as guests would be crazy not to suspect 'em if'n anythin' went missin'. The main thing is that ye got yore nice, green jool back agin, ain't that right, Filgo me beauty?"

The Gonfelin wife agreed. "Aye, that's right enough, Father Abbo, wot belongs to Redwall should come back to Redwall. I think ye might get a nice surprise shortly. Who knows, another pretty stone could turn up, I'm thinkin'. Right, Nokko?"

Her husband began waffling. "Er . . . er . . . I don't know wot yer talkin' about, me liddle honeyplum."

Further discussion was cut short by the return of the Guosim. Nokko changed the subject hastily, by asking them, "Well, did ye get ole Bruster?"

Tenka, a young shrew, shook his head. "No."

Garul looked perplexed. "Y'mean he escaped?"

Tenka explained, "Oh, he never got away. Bruster ran like wolves was chasin' him, we couldn't catch up. He threw those front gates open, an' dashed out o' the Abbey, onto the path. Hah, that was when she popped up. . . . "

Bosie was overcome by curiosity. "Who's she?"

Tenka continued, "That Painted One, you remember, the beast whose mate he slew. Tala, I think 'er name was. As Bruster was crossin' the path, she jumps right out o' the ditch, all scraggy an' mad lookin', armed with a big, pointed tree branch. Afore he could wink an eye, she stabbed 'im, right through the 'eart. Then she dashes off cacklin' an' laughin', shoutin', 'I swore I'd get ye! When ye gets to Hellgates tell 'em Tala the Painted One sent yer!' "

Samolus was restoring the emerald to its former position, he turned to Skipper. "So, Tugga Bruster's wicked ways finally caught up with him. Got what he deserved, I think."

Abbot Glisam addressed Garul, the older shrew. "Will you take over as Log a Log of the Guosim?"

Garul shook his head. "Only as a deputy, until the proper one turns up."

Samolus chipped in, "An' who, pray, is the proper one?"

Garul answered without hesitation, "Young Dubble, who else? He's the next Log a Log by birth an' bloodright. Aye, an' I'm sure he'll make a far better Chieftain t'the Guosim than his father did!"

"Well, 'e couldn't make a much werse one," Nokko commented. "Er, Abbo, mate, d'yew know who's got my sambag?"

Abbot Glisam produced the sandbag from his broad habit sleeve. "Sorry, here it is, sir, it was being held in evidence. Tugga Bruster must have stolen it whilst you were sleeping, just to implicate you." He tossed the sandbag to the Gonfelin Pikehead. "Take it with my best wishes, it's rather a good, well-made sandbag."

Nokko hefted the object fondly. "My young Spingo made it fer me. A Gonfelin Pike'ead needs a sturdy sambag, to whack any o' the tribe who gets outta line. Aye, that's wot any Chieftain needs, a sense of humour, a wise mind, fairness in all things, mercy an' forgiveness, too . . .

an' a good, ould sambag t'deal with any upstarts. I'll ask Spingo t'make young Dubble a sambag, fer when he becomes Log a Log."

Samolus chuckled drily. "That's if Bisky an' Spingo ever find him, goodness only knows where he is this moment!"

29

It had become clear to every bird or reptile that dwelt in the caverns beneath the hill that their fate was sealed. Sealed in more ways than one, with the monster, Baliss, blocking the exit tunnel. As yet, the snake had not entered the main cavern, he lay in the passage. Sometimes half-conscious, but often hissing wildly, writhing and smiting the passage walls as the infected wounds grew more agonising. The huge reptile's head had become a grotesque vision of ugliness. Swollen and bloated, with broken hedgehog spines, the lips and nostrils inflated with poisonous secretions. Even the blind, blue-white eyes suppurated, leaking poison which was not natural snake venom.

All the inhabitants of the main cave, with its boiling pool and sulphurous atmosphere, crowded into the rear cavern. Their fear of Korvus Skurr, the Doomwyte Chieftain, was overcome by the terror of Baliss, whose abhorrent head could be seen lurking in the tunnel. Korvus Skurr was now a leader only by his size and savage fighting skills. The reptiles, snakes, lizards and toads concealed themselves in corners and crannies of the inner cave. Already they were being used as a food source by the army of carrion birds, who could no longer hunt outside for their needs. The only hope Korvus cherished was that the snake would finally die in the tunnel, and not enter his caverns. He perched on the rock above the bottomless, dark lake, with the smoothsnake Sicariss at his side.

Sicariss knew that the only safe place to be was by the big raven. He was her sole protection, with so many scavenging carrion about.

Korvus peered into the watery depths as he asked his smoothsnake, "Kaarh! Where is the Welzz, I would hear what it has to say."

Sicariss watched the surface of the lake, commenting, "Welzzzz musssst be offered food!"

Without looking up, the Doomwyte tyrant issued an order. "Haaraak, bring food for my Welzz!"

None of the carrion moved from their perches.

Korvus looked up then, raking the birds with his fierce eyes. "Yakaaar! I said bring food, any reptile will do. Quickly!"

Still there was no movement from within the feathered ranks. Veeku, the crow leader, was nearby, his damaged wing hanging uselessly. Drawing himself up, Korvus towered over the wounded crow.

"Haaarrr! Tell them to do as I command!"

Veeku bowed his head. "Korrah! Lord, why should these birds find food for a fish? If they cannot leave to hunt outside, they will need the reptiles to feed upon."

Korvus lashed out with his wicked talons, felling his once-faithful servant. Overtaken by rage, the big raven struck Veeku a barrage of blows with his heavy, lethal beak, crying harshly, "Rakkachakk! I will be obeyed! I am the Great Doomwyte!"

Crows, rooks, jackdaws and choughs flew screeching harshly from their perches, seeking the upper rocky crags close to the ceiling. Korvus placed his talons on the dead Veeku, calling to them.

"Yakaaaar! Death to all who disobey me. This one will feed my Welzz, watch, and witness the wrath of your Great Doomwyte!"

Dragging the dead crow leader to the lake, he flung Veeku into the water. The carcass floated on the dark surface momentarily. Then the water exploded as Welzz came rushing upward and engulfed the offering.

Korvus strutted over to Sicariss. "Hayaak! Now you will speak to Welzz. Ask if Baliss will die soon!"

If indeed the voracious fish could have spoken, it might well have mentioned what was going on above the Doomwytes' realm. Bisky and Spingo had elected to help Dubble and Zaran with their task of collapsing the cave entrance. Once they had been told of the black otter's plan, plus the fact that Baliss was also inside with the reptiles and vermin, they volunteered eagerly. Zaran was less enthusiastic, giving them her reasons tersely.

"This is my task, Zaran does not need others. Revenge upon Skurr and his creatures is my vow. There is much danger, I would not forgive myself if young ones were killed or hurt."

Being a Gonfelin, and seldom lost for words, Spingo reasoned with the avenging otter. "Enemies is enemies, my da always sez. Yore our friend, so your enemy is ours. Lissen, mate, ye won't get a better chance than this. Not only is Skurvybottom an' his mob in those caves, but now y've gorra chance t'get them an' that big ould snake, too. Aye, an' why should the likes of us get hurt an' killed, eh? We ain't gonna scrap with 'em paw't'paw. All we're doin' is blockin' 'em in, so that we don't have ter look at their ugly mugs agin!"

Bisky seconded the pretty mousemaid. "Spingo's right, marm. Besides, four pair o' paws should get the job done quicker!"

Arming themselves with Zaran's tools, they set to work on the hillside. The black otter shrugged. "It is not the work of one day or ten. Do not expect this hill to collapse soon, young friends!"

"Oh, we know that, don't we, mates? You jus' tell us

where t'dig, an' we'll get the job done, no matter 'ow long it takes!" Spingo assured her.

Zaran indicated a massive slab of rock, protruding from the side of the slope. "I think we dig that out, then balance it careful."

Dubble nodded. "Righto, then when the time comes a good push'll send it down in front o' the entrance, with any luck."

There was a big old beech tree growing alongside the slab. A lot of its root network had to be hacked away as they excavated into the uphill side of the ponderous stone. Zaran took her double-bladed sword, attacking the big beech roots. Bisky commenced digging at the back of the slab, Dubble took the side opposite the beech tree. Spingo threw all her energy into excavating the front side of the ponderous stone. They laboured steadily, the three young ones digging, and Zaran severing the thick root tendrils which impeded the task.

Dubble stopped to take a drink of water, as he straightened up he was hit by a pile of soil. Spitting earth and wiping at his eyes, he complained loudly, "Ahoy there, Bisky, watch where yore throwin' that stuff, will ye!"

Popping his head up over the rear of the slab, Bisky protested, "It wasn't me, mate, I'm chuckin' my soil backward. Watch out, here comes some more!"

Dubble ducked, just in time, as a shovelful of loose earth came sailing over. Zaran looked up from working on a weighty root. She pointed to the front of the stone, sidestepping more soil. "Young maid, working like wildbeast!" The black otter carried on working, whilst Bisky and Dubble climbed out of the meagre holes they had dug. They went to the front, to see what progress Spingo had made.

She could not be seen, but they could hear her grunting as she dug. The industrious mousemaid had burrowed a tunnel, she was practically underneath the slab. Bisky ducked to one side as more loose earth came flying from Spingo's excavation. He called down the long hole.

"What'n the name o' fur'n'tails are you doing down there?"

Another pile of loose earth shot out of the tunnel, followed by Spingo's reply. "I'm gittin' the job done, mate, that's wot I'm doin', 'ow are you'n'Dubble gettin' on?"

Dubble stared in amazement at the hole. "Not half as well as you are, miss, are ye sure none of yore ancestors were moles?"

Bisky interrupted his friend. "Spingo, come out o' there, it looks dangerous!"

More soil flew from the hole, then Spingo answered, "I'll just finish off down 'ere, then I'll come up for a drop o' water. Thirsty work, eh!"

Nobeast could have predicted what happened next. Spingo's shovel could be heard striking against the bottom of the huge slab, as she gouged out more earth. Zaran hacked through the last of the heavy root she was working on. Without warning the entire slab moved. The black otter leapt from the stone as it sank, settling down into the hillside. Bisky fell flat on his stomach, scrabbling at the stone-filled hole as he yelled, "Spingo! Spingo!"

Dubble and Zaran joined him, digging away with their bare paws at rock and earth, roaring, "Stay where ye are, missy, don't move, we'll get ye out!"

The slab moved a fraction more. Zaran pulled Bisky and Dubble away from it. She tapped against the stone several times, holding up a paw for silence. After what seemed like an age, they heard the shovel striking rock, somewhere below. Bisky gripped his shovel so tight that it hurt his paws.

"She's alive, did ye hear her? Spingo's alive!"

Zaran dug with her sword, between the hillside and the edge of the slab. It moved, settling down another fraction. They heard Spingo, banging urgently away with her shovel. Dubble waved his paws furiously.

"Stop, don't dig anymore or we'll crush 'er t'death!"

A horrific thought struck Bisky. "She might be suffocatin' down there, what'll we do?"

Rushing to the beech tree, Zaran chopped off a long branch with a few strokes of her double-bladed weapon. "We try this. I work fast!"

Swiftly lopping off any side shoots and leaves, she sharpened a point on the thinner end of the branch. Now she had what looked like a long javelin. Pushing it into the earth alongside the slab, the powerful otter started twisting the pole, whilst pushing her weight down on it. The beech spear sank deeper with each turn and push. Bisky and Dubble hurried to assist Zaran, but she shoved them aside. "No no, too much force will snap this wood. Zaran will do it. See!" The beech pole moved up and down freely. She withdrew it, cupping her paws over the hole, and calling down into it, "Spingo, you hear Zaran?"

A faint, pitifully thin voice answered, "Aye. . . . I c'n breathe now. . . . Don't dig anymore . . . y'll bring the stone down on me!"

There was a moment's awkward silence, then Zaran called gently down the tiny airhole, "We hear you, don't worry. I make another hole, you'll breathe better. Be silent now, stay still."

The black otter repeated the pressing and twisting process with the sharpened beech rod. Working away she muttered to herself, "Never should let young ones dig, too much danger. All my fault—"

Dubble cut in sharply, "Lissen, mate, stop talkin' silly. It ain't nobeast's fault. We should be puttin' our brains on 'ow t'get Spingo out, so quit blamin' yoreself. Now, wot'n the name o' Guosim are we goin' t'do? Tenscore like us couldn't lift that bloomin' big stone, an' if we dig it'll only sink an' crush pore Spingo. So, wot d'we do, any ideas?"

The brain wave hit Bisky like a lighting bolt. "I know! Moles, that's what we need!"

Zaran repeated the word. "Moles?"

Bisky warmed eagerly to his plan. "Aye, moles, what else? Redwall Abbey has a Foremole an' a mighty crew of moles. What they don't know about diggin', tunnellin' an' shorin' up isn't worth knowin'. Right, we've got a logboat, too."

A glimmer of hope shone in Zaran's dark eyes. "You can get moles here quickly?"

Dubble became suddenly fired by the plan. "You stay with Spingo, mate, keep 'er spirits up, an' tell 'er this. Me'n' Bisky are goin' to bring a full molecrew to git 'er outta there! Aye an' they'll be travellin' like the wind in a fleet o' logboats, with the best Guosim paddlers in Mossflower to speed 'em on their way. Right, Bisk?"

Bisky seized his friend's paw, shaking it hard. "Right, Dubble, let's go to Redwall!"

Below in the darkness, Spingo crouched beneath the massive slab. Zaran had informed her of the plan, so she tried to keep up her spirits by inventing a little ditty.

"O 'tis dark down 'ere,
but I'll never fear,
with mates to 'elp me out,
good friends an' true
an' I've got one or two,
who'll come if I just shout.

So come to my aid,
I'm a liddle Gonf'lin maid
Just longin' to be free.
I'm stuck down an 'ole,
just waitin' for a mole,
t'drop right in for tea. . . ."

Spingo could not think of another line, so she lay there in pitch blackness, with the mighty stone pressing down . . . and wept.

30

Down in the cellars of Redwall Abbey the quest for clues was on. Perrit and Umfry Spikkle descended the small flight of steps, and unbolted the little door. Holding a lantern, the squirrelmaid watched her burly young hog friend withdraw the bolt. He touched the door cautiously. "H'it's a good repair job, the hinges don't even creak no more. Nice, strong bolt, too."

Sensing his apprehension, Perrit nudged his back gently with the lantern. Umfry uttered a startled squeak. "Yeek! Don't sneak h'up on me like that."

She chuckled. "'I'm with you, mate, open the door and let's take a look. Don't be afraid."

Umfry bristled, his spikes stood up indignantly. "Who's h'afraid? Not me, miz! Right then, you go first, 'cos you've got the lantern."

Once they were in the tunnel, Perrit closed the door behind them. Umfry complained in a loud whisper, "No, don't close the door, miz, leave h'it h'open. H'anything could 'appen down 'ere!

The squirrelmaid held the lantern up, scanning the back of the old door. "I want to take a better look at this, here." Taking a pinewood torch, which had been left on the floor, she lit it from the lantern flame. The resiny wood flared immediately as she passed it to Umfry. "Mayhaps you'd like to explore the tunnel a bit more, there may be more clues."

The timid hedgehog took no more than two paces before deciding it was not a good idea. He stayed close to his companion, muttering excuses. "Huh, no point h'in doin' that, me'n'Skipper an' the rest h'already did h'it. There's nought t'see down there. Pore Dwink's h'on 'is h'own we'd best get back to 'im h'up there. Nearly dinnertime, y'know."

Perrit replied absently as she inspected the door, "Stop carrying on like a dithering duck, Umfry. Dwink's probably napping in his wheelchair. . . . These two nails sticking out here, I wonder what they're for?"

Umfry held his torch closer, inspecting the pair of broad-headed nails, which had not been fully driven into the woodwork. "Mister Samolus said that was where the Doomwyte h'eye was placed. There h'aint no more t'see h'on this door, miz, let's go."

Perrit, however, was not looking at the door any longer. Her attention had been distracted by something else higher up. "Umfry, can you lift me up, I want to take a quick peep on top of the door lintel."

Putting aside his torch, the burly hedgehog swung Perrit up to the lintel with ease. "Keep messin' h'about down 'ere, miz, h'and we'll get no dinner."

The squirrelmaid sighed wearily. "Just hold me still please, we'll get dinner as soon as I get this thing loose." She gave the object a mighty tug, it broke away, sending them tumbling backward.

Umfry helped her up. "H'are you alright, miz, wot h'is that thing?"

Perrit could not resist a smirk of satisfaction. "A piece of slate with something drawn on it. Let's get upstairs, I promised Dwink he'd get first look at anything we found. You can go to dinner if you wish."

Umfry pursued the sprightly maid up to Great Hall. "Not afore h'I've seen wot h'it says!"

Dwink could not wait to give them his news. "There's

been a real kerfuffle up here, mates. Aluco was knocked down, and guess wot, that horrid Guosim, Tugga Bruster, he's dead. Aye, killed by a Painted One, so Samolus told me. We'd best get in to dinner, did you find anything?"

Perrit waggled the flat slate fragment at him. "I'll show you it at dinner. All of a sudden I'm starving. Good fresh bread and cheese is what I need right now, eh, Umfry!"

Umfry Spikkle took on a superior tone. "Dearie me, h'eatin' is h'all you can think of, miz!"

There was bread and cheese aplenty at the dinner table, with some tasty vegetable soup, a selection of pasties, a fine summer salad, plus damson and pear crumble for dessert, with the option of a honeyed plum pudding. Dwink, Perrit and Umfry huddled round like conspirators, studying the piece of slate as they ate dinner. Their privacy was short-lived, though they did not object when Samolus and Sister Violet joined them. Umfry was consumed with curiosity.

"Wot's all that writin' h'and those drawin's h'about? C'mon, Dwink, read h'it to me."

Samolus tweaked Umfry's snout. "You wouldn't have to ask other beasts if'n ye'd learned to read, would ye? Dwink looks a bit dozy still, Perrit, would you like to read what's on the slate?"

The squirrelmaid obliged willingly.

"What's mixed will thicken, there's the place!
Is it there or has it gone?
Framed above a Friars Grace.
On, on, I. The middle one."

Umfry interrupted, through a mouthful of plum pudding, "Oh, no, h'another blinkin' puzzle!"

Perrit glanced up at him from the slate. "D'you mind, Umfry Spikkle, I'm not finished yet."

Suitably chastened, the young hedghog fell silent as Perrit read out the remainder of the clues.

"Where to seek a raven's eye?
What's not sad, yet makes one cry,
with what a plum has at its middle?
The Prince of Mousethieves set this riddle."

Sister Violet sipped at her mint tea thoughtfully. "I agree with you, young Umfry, it is a blinkin' puzzle. 'Wot's mixed will thicken, there's the place.' Goodness me, whatever is that supposed to mean? 'Tis all gobbledygook to me, my dears."

Samolus helped himself to a pasty. "Well, o' course it is, marm, that's how puzzles are supposed t'be, right, Dwink?"

The young squirrel sat up straight in his wheelchair. "It sounds t'me like that first line is narrowin' things down to the area where we should look. What's mixed will thicken. I think it's one of those anagram things again. What's mixed will thicken . . . hmmmm, maybe it's *what's* and *will* jumbled together, eh, Perrit?"

The squirrelmaid shook her pretty head. " *'Twill, swat, still, slats, shawl.* No, there's far too many possibilities, I think the word *thicken* is a better idea."

Sister Violet winked slyly at Perrit. "That's 'cos you've already solved it, young missy. Well go on, don't keep us all a-waitin'."

Perrit smiled. "There's only one sensible word I can make from *thicken. Kitchen!*"

Umfry chuckled with delight. "Kitchen, there's the place. Come h'on, last one t'the kitchen's a fried frog!"

Dwink shook his head. "Hold on, mate, we can't just dash off because we've solved one word."

Perrit began pushing the wheelchair away from the table. "There's no harm in going t'the kitchens and taking a look around. Maybe it'll help us with the rest of the puzzle."

Friar Skurpul welcomed them into the Abbey Kitchens cheerfully.

"Coom in yurr, eee guddbeasts, you'm cummed to say noice things about moi cooken?"

Sister Violet curtsied. "Oh, no, Friar, though there ain't a better cook nowhere, yore dinners are always the best."

The good mole beamed from ear to ear. "Thankee gurtly, marm. Hurr, then may'aps you'm cumm to 'elp with ee washen up?"

Dwink explained, "No, Friar, we're trying t'solve a riddle. We're lookin for something that might be here, or may be gone."

Skurpul laughed. "Hurrhurr hurr, naow that do bees a riggle. Summat as moight be yurr but maybe gone'd. Boi okey, an' wot moight that bee, young maister?"

Perrit attempted to make things a bit clearer. "Listen to this, Friar: 'Is it there or has it gone? Framed above a Friars Grace. On, on, I. The middle one.' We'd be grateful if you could throw any light on it, sir."

Wiping floury paws upon his apron, Skurpul commented, "Oi'd be grateful if'n Oi cudd throw any light on et, too, missy, but Friars bees only clever at cooken. Sorry Oi can't 'elp ee, zurrs'n'marms, but you'm welcumm to search these yurr kitchens, long as ee puts things back as ee foinded 'em." Leaving them some candied fruits to nibble on, Friar Skurpul continued with his work.

Dwink whispered to Samolus, "Well, that wasn't much help was it, we still don't know what a Friars Grace is."

Samolus watched the old mole rolling out pastry. "Don't be too hard on Skurpul, cookin' is wot he does best. With an Abbeyful of creatures to cater for, the Friar doesn't get time for other things."

Dwink immediately felt sorry for what he had said. "Aye, yore right, sir, let's look for a Friars Grace."

Perrit suggested helpfully, "We know what Abbot's grace is. Abbot Glisam says a different one before every meal. Maybe it's something similar, what d'you think?"

Umfry smiled brightly. "I know, let's h'ask the h'Abbot. Wait 'ere, h'I'll go'n get 'im."

Sister Violet selected a crystallised strawberry. "Young Umfry ain't as slow as he looks."

Abbot Glisam was only too glad to be of service; he put forth on the subject. "It's odd you should ask me about Friars Grace. We Abbots are constantly composing different graces, for meals throughout the seasons. But Friars Graces are pretty few and far between. However, last night I was looking through the Abbey Records, to see if I could gather more information on Gonff. I did notice something which stuck in my mind. At some point during Gonff's lifetime, there was a hogwife who acted as Friar, very good she was, too. Her name was Goody Stickle. Not only was she an excellent cook, but Goody was also an expert at crafting earthenware. It was noted in the Records that she would make bowls, flagons, dishes and beakers from clay. Goody would bake them in the ovens until they came out as fashionable and useful earthenware." Glisam turned to Skurpul, who had just finished putting the final touches to a batch of latticed apple pies. "Friar, have you ever heard of a creature named Goody Stickle? A long time ago she was cook here. She also made earthenware things."

Placing his pies on beechwood oven paddles, the old mole began sliding them into the ovens. He paused a moment. "Guddy Stickle, ee say, zurr, hurr, you'm bees castin' yurr eye o'er this." Skurpul reached down a honeypot from the shelf. It was a fine piece of work, elegantly shaped to look like a small, round beehive, decorated all round with bees and cornflowers. He passed it carefully to Glisam. "That'n bees made boi Goody Stickle, zurr, she'm wurr a gurtly clever-pawed 'edge'og. See yurr, this bee'd 'er mark!"

It was a tiny, and beautiful, picture of a hedgehog. Probably sculpted on the wet clay with a knifetip, and baked hard as a permanent signature. The friends admired it, and Perrit enquired further, "It really is splendid, Friar, do you have any more of Goody Stickle's work to show us?"

Skurpul placed the honeypot carefully back upon its shelf. "Oi 'spect thurr's a few bits, likkle missy. May'ap many got broken o'er ee long seasons. But you'm lukk for ee dishes'n'such bearin' yon mark. Them'll be Goody's, mebbe still ee few abowt."

The search began in earnest then, Abbot Glisam joined in enthusiastically. Piece by piece, more of Goody Stickle's work was discovered. Sister Violet turned up a little beaker, half-full of dried sage herbs. "This un's got a liddle hogmark on its base, my, ain't it a pretty thing!"

Dwink rolled his wheelchair across to inspect it. "Pretty I'll grant you, Sister, but it doesn't look like any Friars Grace. What's that you've got, Umfry?"

"Dunno really, h'it's a sorta puddin' basin, h'I think."

The friends rooted and rummaged through cupboards and drawers, shelves and crannies, to little avail. They found many examples of the long-ago cook's ware, but not what they were seeking. Outside, daylight was fading to purple evening haze as the Abbey bells tolled for the day's final meal.

Friar Skurpul finished supervising kitchen helpers, who had loaded up their trollies. Removing his cap and apron, the jovial mole enquired, "You uns be a-goin' in for ee supper?"

Pushing his tiny crystal glasses up onto his brow, Abbot Glisam massaged his eyelids gently. "You go on, Friar, we'll join you presently."

Dwink waved a paw at the assembled earthenware. "Well, we've scoured these kitchens from top to bottom. Just look at all these cups, beakers, plates, bowls and jugs. All made by Goody Stickle, and not one of them any use to us, friends."

Perrit quoted a line from the puzzle. "'Is it there or has

it gone?' Huh, gone I think, and if it's an item of earthenware, probably broken many seasons ago. We may as well go to supper."

Brother Torilis entered the kitchens. The Abbot nodded to him. "Not taking supper this evening, Brother?"

The gaunt-faced Herbalist bowed slightly to Glisam. "Far too busy I'm afraid, Father, some of us still have work to do. Sister Ficaria and I are preparing a splint for young Dwink. He can't sit in that wheelchair for the rest of the season. I've decided he should be up and about. A splint will help his footpaw, but he'll have to go carefully on it."

Dwink felt that he had to say something. "It's very good of you, Brother Torilis, missing your supper on my account. Sister Ficaria, too."

The Infirmary Keeper gave Dwink what passed for one of his rare smiles, a mere twitch of the lips. "Thank you for your concern, however, my assistant and I have no intention of missing supper. We'll eat upstairs in the sick bay as we work." He picked up a covered tray, on which Friar Skurpul had already set supper for two.

Sister Violet eyed the tray. "Beggin' yore pardon, Brother, but wot's that tray made of, is it earthenware?"

Without looking at the tray, Torilis answered, "Yes, it's earthenware, with a wooden frame."

Umfry blocked his way. "H'earthenware y'say, let me 'ave h'a look at it, Brother."

Torilis backed indignantly away. "I certainly will not, this tray belongs to my Infirmary, it has nothing to do with you!" Umfry grabbed out, snatching the cloth cover away from the tray. Torilis shot him an icy glance. "How dare you . . . you . . . beprickled savage, get out of my way, this very instant!"

Umfry ignored him, crowing triumphantly. "See, h'it's a tray, a h'earthenware one, with writin' on h'it!"

At this point, the Abbot stepped in. "Brother Torilis, I

apologise if we're causing you any bother, but could you let me see that tray, please? Place it down there and empty the food from it."

Torilis was loath to take orders from anybeast after being affronted by Umfry in such a manner. He tried blustering his way out of the kitchens. "Really, this is most insulting. Can you not let Sister Ficaria and I carry on with our work, and take our supper in private!"

It was very seldom that Glisam showed temper, but when he did, the dormouse was the equal of anybeast. "I'm not stopping you from eating supper, Brother. In fact, we'll carry it up to the Infirmary for you. But I must inspect that tray, so stop acting like a sulky Dibbun and empty the food from it!"

The saturnine squirrel was left with no alternative. With bad grace he quickly cleared the tray contents onto the table, slamming the tray down hard on the oven top. "There! Inspect the thing as you please, then will you kindly have the goodness to reload my tray, which is Infirmary property, and allow me to leave here!"

The tray was really a wall hanging, with holes for a hanging cord drilled at either side. The back was a thin board of knotted elm, in an oval shape. On top of the wood, Goody Stickle had fashioned an earthenware faceplate. It was the Friars Grace.

Dwink read out the words, which were inscribed in neat script.

"All that grows in our good earth,
harvested by Redwall beasts,
to test a simple Friar's worth,
at Abbey board or seasons' feasts.
Thanks to the sun, the wind and rain,
and those who toiled with loving care,
my Friar's skills be not in vain,
to cook fine food and honest fare."

Umfry sounded slightly disappointed. "Huh, h'is that all h'it says?"

Perrit traced her paw around the raised earthenware border. "That's all. Apart from these artistic decorations. See how they're raised up from the rest? There's a pattern of mushrooms, dandelions, damsons, chestnuts, mint leaves. All repeated cleverly, right around the words to form a frame."

Dwink stared hard at it for a moment. Then he took the slate fragment from the side of his wheelchair cushion. Looking from the Grace to the slate, his lips moved silently. The Abbot watched him intently.

"Dwink, what is it, have you found something?"

Words tumbled from the young squirrel. "Hah, I knew it! I knew that was it!"

Umfry scratched his headspikes. "Was wot?"

Dwink replied with two short words: "An onion!"

Brother Torilis looked on, mystified. "An onion?"

Dwink pointed a paw at the Friars Grace. "Perrit gave me the clue. All those things, mushrooms, dandelions and so on, repeated in a clever pattern. But look there, right at the top, in the middle. An onion, that's the answer!"

The squirrelmaid touched the embossed vegetable. "But why is it the answer?"

Tapping the slate with his paw, Dwink explained, "Listen. 'What's mixed will thicken, there's the place'! Right, that's how we came by the word *kitchen*. Here's the rest. 'Is it there or has it gone?' Well, we searched the kitchen, but it was gone. Until Brother Torilis walked in here and picked it up. You see, it had gone, from the kitchen to the Infirmary. Didn't you say it was Infirmary property, Brother?"

Torilis nodded. "Sister Ficaria told me the tray had been at the Infirmary for as long as she could recall. Mayhaps it had been taken from here to the Infirmary long ago, and never returned."

Dwink nodded agreement. "Now, look at the last two

lines: 'Framed above a Friars Grace. On, on I. The middle one.' Suddenly it jumped out at me. *On* is the first word, *on* is the second word. But the word *I* that's the middle one, see?"

Brother Torilis repeated the line in the correct order. "On I on . . . on I on. Of course, it's onion! Now what happens, are there further clues?"

Taking the slate, Abbot Glisam read out the second verse.

"Where to seek a raven's eye?
What's not sad, yet makes one cry,
with what a plum has at its middle.
The Prince of Mousethieves set this riddle."

Umfry's face lit up with a broad smile of understanding. "A h'onion's not sad, but h'it makes you cry when you peel it. I know, 'cos h'I've peeled h'onions afore. An' wot does h'a plum 'ave at h'its middle? A stone!"

The Abbot picked up a big copper ladle. He tapped it on the earthenware onion. "So, friends, d'you think this plum, or should I say onion, has a stone at its middle, a raven's eye?"

Brother Torilis waved his paws in agitation. "No, Father, please, you wouldn't, that tray is Infirmary property!"

The Abbot's old eyes twinkled mischievously. "Correction, Brother, it's kitchen property. Redwall kitchens, in fact, and I'm the Abbot of Redwall!"

Crack! He hit the onion a sharp tap with the ladle. There amidst the broken shards of earthenware was an object, wrapped in a scrap of linen. The Abbot smiled, bowing to Dwink. "Be my guest, sir!"

The young squirrel needed no second bidding. He unwrapped the linen. It was an awesome ruby, one eye of the Great Doomwyte raven statue. It glowed with deep crimson fires, a thing of awful beauty.

Perrit stood, transfixed by the fabulous stone. "Oh, just look at it, Dwink, look at it!"

But Dwink was scanning the small remnant of linen. "Aye, splendid, ain't it. I'll take a proper look once I've read the message from this bit o' cloth. It says here how t'find the serpent's green eye!"

31

Zaran the black otter kept up her vigil at the side of the huge slab of rock, which had slipped and sunk into the hillside. Spingo was trapped beneath the stone, in total darkness. All the Gonfelin maid could do was to keep very still. She breathed lightly, trying to conserve the small amount of air which filtered in through the thin holes Zaran had bored with the sharpened branch of a beech tree. Every now and then, Spingo felt loose, sandy earth sifting onto her paws. Each time it did, the unwieldy slab settled a minute fraction more. Zaran called down through the narrow, tubelike holes to her.

"Spingo, hold on, moles come soon from Redwall. I make another hole, give you more air, yes?"

The reply came back, faint but urgent. "No . . . don't make any more holes, mate, y'might cause a cave-in. . . . Leave well enough alone!"

The black otter put aside her beech branch, but continued talking, in an attempt to lift the young maid's spirits. Zaran said anything in the hope of comforting Spingo. "When moles come they have you soon out of there. Bisky said his Abbey has many moles. Best diggers in all the land, whole army of moles. Hah, you will drink cold water from stream, wash dust from yourself, feel good, fresh!"

Spingo licked soil from her lips. "That'll be nice. . . . Wish they'd hurry up. . . ."

Speeding downstream in the Guosim logboat, Dubble suddenly backed water, drawing his paddle inboard. The sharp action caused Bisky to topple backward—he hit his head on the vessel's stern. The young mouse sat up, calling irately to his companion, at what he thought was an unwarranted halt.

"Wot d'ye think yore doin', mate? We're supposed to be goin' full speed for Redwall."

Pulling into the bank, the young shrew turned to face Bisky. "Aye, an' so we are, but we'll get no place fast with you as paddlin' crew!"

The Redwaller thrust out his chin aggressively. "Wot's wrong with my paddlin'?"

Dubble was forced to tell him, in no uncertain fashion, "Yore goin' to turn this boat over, with the way yore flailin' that paddle around. Lissen, mate, there's an art to paddlin'. We're travellin' downstream, see, so ye let the current do most o' the work. You prob'ly heard the sayin', more haste, less speed. Well it's true. Now, d'ye want to git to yore Abbey quickly?"

Bisky readied his paddle. "Of course I do, we've got t'save Spingo. Go on then, you show me wot t'do an' I'll try my best to help."

They pulled the craft off into midstream, with Dubble working the prow, calling back instructions to Bisky at the stern end. "Easy now, bucko, watch the way I do it. Don't try t'go fast, steady does it. Lean forward, dig that paddle deep, feel the current an' go with it. Feather the paddle blade a bit to one side on the upstroke, see, just like I'm doin'."

Bisky obeyed, surprised at how the logboat glided swiftly along, picking up speed. Every once in a while he missed the stroke, calling out, "Sorry!"

Dubble replied, "Y'know, when you go marchin' with

otherbeasts, sometimes they sing a song, just t'keep in step. Right, I'll sing ye a simple shanty, the chorus is easy. It'll help ye to keep yore stroke." For a young Guosim, Dubble had a rich baritone voice. He sang out lustily.

"I cut me teeth on a Guosim paddle.
Hey hi ho! Hey hi ho!
Took to it like an ole duck waddle.
Hey hi ho! Hey hi ho!
Now run that river down the flow,
where we'll anchor I don't know.
Sing hey hi ho my matey oh,
that's the Guosim way to go!

Our logboat sails just like a dream.
Hey hi ho! Hey hi ho!
On sea or river, creek or stream.
Hey hi ho! Hey hi ho!
No room for idle paws on board,
don't scrape yore keel now, mind that ford.
Sing hey hi ho my matey oh,
Ye'll feel me boot if you go slow!"

Had it not been for the urgency of the situation, Bisky would have enjoyed the experience greatly. But he kept his eyes on Dubble's every movement, concentrating his efforts on keeping a steady paddle, and a smooth course.

In the caves beneath the forested hillslope, Korvus Skurr had begun to realise he was not the tyrant anymore. With no Raven Wytes to command, he was facing open mutiny. Several times he had ordered that all his subjects, both birds and reptiles, move to the large, sulphured cavern. Not a single creature obeyed. He had hoped that they would, to provide him with a buffer in case Baliss moved out of the tunnel. The carrion birds crowded the rocky walls of the inner sanctum. They ignored him, scrabbling, squawking and fighting amongst themselves. Crows, choughs, jackdaws, rooks and magpies were seized by a feeding frenzy. No reptile was safe from their voracious beaks, they hunted the cave relentlessly. Frogs, toads, lizards and snakes—the grass snake, slow worm and smoothsnake—were being rooted out from their hiding places in rocky niches. Beaks stabbed, and talons raked, as the dark birds fought amongst themselves every time a reptile was caught. They battled savagely for the squirming creatures, often tearing them to pieces.

Sicariss cowered beneath the big raven, fearful of the carrion packs, who eyed her wickedly. A crow called Fagry, who seemed to have taken over from the slain Veeku, called harshly, "Raahakkah! What does your Welzz tell you now, slimecoil, more lies for Skurr to hear?" Without waiting for an answer, the birds flocked off, in chase of some reptiles. These had scuttled off, hoping to find better hiding places in the main cavern. The insect-riddled heaps of filth which mounded against the walls in there provided odious cover from the rapacious birds.

In the relative reduction of noise in the smaller cavern, Korvus Skurr bent his head, staring down at the smoothsnake. "Haaarrr! So what does Welzz say now? Or do you have to think up more lies to placate me?"

Sicariss did not move to the pool's edge. "Fagry iss the one who speaksss liessss, Mighty One. Even if Welzzzz did not talk, I alwayssss gave you good advice, you lisssstened to my counssssel."

The murderous eyes of the Doomwyte tyrant bored into Sicariss. The truth was now out. "Yaggaaah! I was a fool to believe you ever could speak to the Welzz, you were only serving your own interests!"

The snake knew she was in a perilous position. However, she had always thought she could outwit Skurr. Coiling up onto the raven's head, she took her crowning position, whispering sibilantly, "You were never a fool, Lord of Doomwytesssss. I tell you truly, I can sssspeak to Welzzzzz. I have ssspoken to him many timesssss, believe me."

Korvus Skurr moved to the edge of the cold, bottomless lake. He inclined his head slightly. Down below in the icy depths, the monster fish could be seen, making its way slowly upward. "Hakaar! I believe you, my faithful Sicariss. Will you speak to the Welzz for me now?"

The smoothsnake swayed gently, satisfied to be back in favour. "Command your ssservant, Lord. What would you have me sssssay?"

Korvus inclined his head closer to the water. "Haykkarr! You said to me that I was no fool. Now tell it to the Welzzz!"

Without giving time for Sicariss to coil around his neck for balance, the raven gave his head a powerful flick, sending her into the pool. The gargantuan fish broke the surface in a shower of spray, catching the snake in its gaping mouth, then vanishing back into the fathomless waters.

Baliss had wakened in the passage to the main cavern. Driven insane by agonising pain, one thing became uppermost in the giant snake's mind. To seek cool water, the only thing that could relieve the persistent torture. Driven by the desire to immerse his head in cooling water, Baliss slid gradually into the fetid air of the big cave.

32

Redwall Abbey's twin bells tolled gently for the midnight hour. A soft, golden midsummer moon presided over the tranquil scene. Hardly a breeze was about, to stir the leafy tree canopy of Mossflower woodlands. On the terrace outside the Abbey building, Abbot Glisam and Perrit pushed Dwink in the rickety old wheelchair. Glisam breathed the scented night air fondly.

"Ahhhh! This is one of life's simple pleasures, a quiet stroll in Redwall's grounds on a summer night. There's nothing quite like it."

Dwink chuckled. "Try telling that to Umfry and Sister Violet. Did you see them, Father? Once we'd finished supper they couldn't wait to get off to their beds. A pair of champion snorers, I'd say."

Perrit steered the wheelchair toward the Belltower. "They don't know what they're missing. I don't suppose Brother Torilis was interested in a little stroll, either. Did you see the face on him, Father? He stormed off without a word after you broke open that earthenware onion."

Dwink snorted. "Aye, I noticed that, too. Blinkin' stiff-necked old misery, had a face on him like a wrinkled sour apple. Property of the Infirmary indeed, huh. You put him in his place, Father!"

The Abbot shook his head. "It gave me no pleasure to address him in that manner. We mustn't be too hard on Torilis, he's an excellent Herbalist, and a dutiful Infirmary Keeper. Trouble is that he lives by his own rigid rules. I must make things up to him somehow, soothe his wounded pride. Dwink, what was the message on that scrap of cloth, remind me."

The young squirrel had already memorised the clue which Gonff had scrawled long ago, in the dim, distant past. He repeated it from memory, word perfect.

"To find the eye of the serpent,
to the morning sunrise roam,
where death may visit those that fear,
in the wild sweet gatherers' home."

There was silence, except for the creak of the chair wheels. The Abbot turned the ancient vehicle. "Come on, you two, that's enough for one night. I think the beds beckon us. No doubt you'll be up and about at the crack of dawn. Questing for the wild sweet gatherers' home, which you're bound to do."

Perrit speeded up her pushing, all agog. "Oh, can we really, Father what an adventure it'll be!"

Dwink moved his injured footpaw, testing it. "I won't need this bloomin' chair tomorrow. Brother Torilis is making a splint for me, I'll get along just fine on that. We'll be alright, Father, don't you worry!"

The Abbot opened the main Abbey door, allowing them inside. "Oh, I'm not too worried, young un, there won't be just two of you going alone."

Perrit pouted slightly. "Oh, why's that, Father?"

Glisam patted her paw. "Well, miss, one of the lines in the clue said, 'where death may visit those that fear.' In view of any possible danger, I've decided to send Skipper Rorgus and Foremole Gullub Gurrpaw. A warrior and a wise head shouldn't go amiss, do you agree?"

Dwink seemed quite happy with the arrangement, "That'll be fine, Father, but what about Bosie?"

Glisam explained, "Bosie isn't too familiar with this area, and he can be a bit of a harum scarum at times. No, I think Skipper and Foremole would be more fitted to accompany you."

Perrit giggled. "Harum scarum, I like that. Hare um scare um! What d'you think, mate?"

The young squirrel grinned. "Bosie is enough to scare anybeast, just by the amount he can eat. We'd better not mention it to him, though, I wouldn't like his feelings to be hurt."

Glisam ruffled Dwink's ears. "Well said, young un!"

Skipper was always up and wide awake in the hour before dawn. Feeling responsible for the security of Redwall, he would take a brisk patrol. The Otter Chieftain checked outside the Abbey building, ending up with a march around the walltops. Completing the full circuit of the parapet and battlements, he ended his routine by going to the kitchens for an early breakfast.

Friar Skurpul greeted him. "G'mawnin', zurr, you'm bees a wanten yore zoop?"

The otter twitched his whiskers at the tempting aroma. "An' a good mornin' t'you, Friar. Is that my very fav'rite watershrimp an' hotroot soup I can smell, bubblin' away there?"

The kind Friar began ladling a bowl of the soup out. "Aye, that et bees, zurr, jus' 'ow you'm loikes et each mawnen!"

They were soon joined by Dwink and Perrit, who came, pulling a dozy Foremole between them. Gullub Gurrpaw nodded sleepily to Skipper. "H'on moi loife, Skip, these yurr rascals turned Oi out o' moi bed afore daybreak. Et seems us'ns bees h'off a-questin'."

Skipper looked up from his bowl of soup. "Aye, mate, Abbot woke me last night with the news, I 'ope you've packed us lots o' prime vittles, Friar, questin's a hungry business."

The Friar's homely face wrinkled with pleasure, "Oi surrpintly 'ave, you'm woant go 'ungry, zurr. Though you'm moight 'ave iffen ee zurr Bosie wurr along with ee. B'aint no feedin' that un!"

Foremole thanked the Friar, then he and Skipper listened as Perrit read out Gonff's clue.

"To find the eye of the serpent,
to the morning sunrise roam,
where death may visit those that fear,
in the wild sweet gatherers' home."

Skipper tapped his rudder against the floor. "Well, mates, that's a poser, an' no mistake! I can't make tail nor whisker of it. Any ideas?"

Foremole Gullub answered with his irrefutable mole logic, which, as anybeast knows, must be heeded. "You'm best not maken tails'n'whiskers of ought. Us'ns knows wot to look furr, a surrpint's h'eye. Read Oi ee second loine, likkle missy."

Perrit repeated the second line once more. "'To the morning sunrise roam,' what does that mean?"

Foremole Gullub Gurrpaw quatted off a bowl of hot comfrey tea at a single gulp. Smacking his lips with relish, he trundled off to the door. "Hurr hurr et means we'm abound outsoide, to see sunroise, leastways that be wot Oi thinks!"

Dwink grabbed a few hot scones from the kitchen table. "Just wot any sensible creature'd think. Right, mates, outside it is. . . . Ooof!" The young squirrel winced as he tested his newly splinted footpaw.

Friar Skurpul took a stick from the window ledge. It was T-shaped. He gave it to Dwink. "Yurr, young maister, take moi window prop. Oi uses it t'keep ee window open on 'ot days, may'ap 'twill surve ee as a crutcher."

309

The makeshift crutch could not have suited better had it been made personally for Dwink.

The four questers made their way over to the gatehouse, where they stood in the murky grey light which precedes day. Perrit sat on the wallsteps, peering up at the sky. "So, this is where it begins." As the squirrelmaid spoke, dawn's first pale light beamed faintly over the Abbey rooftop.

Dwink called out eagerly, "There it is, the sun comin' up. This is the way we go, eh, Skip?"

The Otter Chieftain shrugged the haversack full of supplies into position on his back. "Aye, young un, the sun ain't never risen in the west, as far as anybeasts know. So 'tis east we're bound. Though how far we'll be travellin' is a question yet t'be answered!"

The little party marched off in a lively manner. Across the lawns, around the Abbey building, through the vegetable patches and the herb garden. Up on the walltops, Corksnout Spikkle had begun his daily perambulation, which he termed the afore-brekkist walk. He saw Foremole unbolting the small east wallgate, and called to him.

"Where are ye off to so early in the day? I thought ye'd be lendin' a paw in the cellars. There's a pile of apples needs pressin' t'make cider!"

Foremole waved a hefty digging paw. "Us'ns off on ee search furr ee surrpinks h'eye."

Corksnout adjusted his false nose, which had slipped over onto his left cheek. "Well, I 'opes ye enjoy yoreselves. Huh, apple pressin' is an 'ard task for just one pair o' paws!"

Skipper replied, "I gave young Umfry a shake early on, but he just turned over an' kept on snorin'. May'ap he'd like to help ye. Oh, will ye bolt this gate after us, mate?"

Corksnout wandered ponderously down the east wallsteps, ruminating to himself as he made for the gate. "Hoho, sleepin' his life away an' missin' a quest, is he? Well, that young grand'og o' mine is about to git a rude

310

awakenin'. Aye, an' he can pass a profitable day, learnin' t'be an apple presser!"

Out in the summer vastness of Mossflower Wood, the searchers pressed forward slowly, looking for any possible clues. Dwink stumped along on his crutch at a comfortable pace. He caught up with Perrit, who was slightly ahead of the others. "How do we know that we're going east? It's easy to wander astray in these woodlands."

The squirrelmaid pointed. "Keep going this way. See the moss growing on the side of that sycamore? Make sure it's on your left. Moss gathers on the north side of trees. Also, you must check that the sun is in your face, then at high noon it'll be overhead. After that the sun will be going west, so keep it at your back. That's the best way to travel east."

Dwink was surprised by his pretty companion's knowledge of woodlore. He pressed her further. "But how'll we know when we're at the place where death may visit those who fear?"

Perrit treated him to her sweetest smile. "Oh, I suppose we'll just carry on until we're feared to death of where we are."

Dwink laughed nervously. "I suppose you're right!"

The Laird Bosie McScutta of Bowlaynee was not best pleased that Redwallers had left the Abbey, without the benefit of his protection. Gathering pawfuls of food from the breakfast table, he picked up the sword of Martin and sped off in a huff, berating all and sundry. "Och, 'tis a sad thing when a sworn protector cannae do his duty. Ah'm bound tae catch up with yon puir beasties an' offer them mah services!"

Watching the lanky hare lope off across the dewy lawn, Aluco remarked to the Abbot, "Act in haste and repent at leisure, eh, Father?"

Abbot Glisam nodded. "Indeed. See, he's gone out of the main gate, and they went east. Oh dear, I know he means well, let's go and tell him."

Out on the path, Bosie was gobbling hot scones and oat biscuits, peering left and right. "Now, which way have they gone?"

Samolus came yawning and stretching out of the Gatehouse. "Which way have who gone? Yore the first to use this gate today, sir. Who are ye lookin' for?"

Bosie ignored him. Spying two distant figures emerging from the woodlands to the northeast, he sprinted off toward them. "Och, that'll be two of 'em, Ah'll wager they've come back tae ask for mah help already. Hi, there!"

It was Bisky and Dubble. Having left the logboat, they were running pell-mell for Redwall. Samolus and Bosie met them. Gasping for breath, the pair informed them of the perilous situation Spingo was in.

Redwall bells tolled out the general alarm, as Abbeybeasts, Gonfelins and Guosim flooded outside to hear the news. Everybeast wanted to help, for awhile it was complete chaos. Then, after a quick consultation with the Abbot, Samolus arranged a rescue party, under Bosie's command. Samolus called for order.

"Listen now, goodbeasts, from what I've been told there's not a moment to waste. We need the Guosim shrews' swiftest paddlers, a full molecrew and some Gonfelin warriors. I know you all want to help, but there's not enough room for everybeast. So I'll let the leaders pick out their own squads, then we'll have to get moving without delay."

In place of Foremole Gurrpaw, Friar Skurpul deputised. "Hurr, Rooter, Soilclaw, Burgy, Frubb, Grabul an' Ruttur, yore moi crew. Gett ee kwippment an' stan' boi ready!"

Nokko selected his most warlike Gonfelins. "Duggo, Fraggo, Bumbo, Tungo, Flaggo an yew, Gobbo. Arm yoreselves up. An' yew, Gobbo, button yore lip an' do as I tells yer. Right!"

Garul, the Guosim Elder, deferred to Dubble. "Yore Log a Log now, so choose yore paddlers."

Dubble was perplexed. "But where's Tugga Bruster?"

Garul took him to one side. "Tugga ain't around no more, I'll tell ye as we go. Better pick yore crews quick, Guosim!"

The young shrew's jaw tightened, he turned away. "You choose 'em, old un, I'll go along with ye!"

Bosie shouldered his sword, and stood impatiently in the open gateway. "If'n we're tae save the wee maid there'll be no hangin' aboot. . . . Double march!"

Crowding the walltops, the remaining Redwallers cheered the rescue party off.

"Goo' lukk, zurrs, you'm 'urry up naow!"

"Aye, an' may the wind be at yore backs!"

"You bring that liddle maid safe back here!"

Abbot Glisam watched the dust cloud as they rushed off into the woodlands. "May fortune speed your paws, friends!"

The very tiny mousebabe latched onto the Abbot's robe. "I wanna go wiv them, Father!"

Glisam picked him up. "Maybe next time, little one."

Dugry the molebabe nodded sagely. "Hurr, an' Oi bees a-goin' nex' time, zurr."

Sister Violet smiled at the Dibbuns. "An' so you shall, next time. But meanwhile, who's to guard the Abbey and keep us all safe?"

Furff, the Dibbun squirrelmaid, narrowed her eyes ferociously. "Us'll do dat, marm!"

Aluco gave a hoot of mock relief. "Thank goodness we can all sleep safe tonight!"

33

Still trapped beneath the rock slab on the hillside above the caverns, Spingo had lost all count of time. Crushed into a shallow depression by the stone, the Gonfelin maid could feel her consciousness fading. She concentrated on one thing, the effort to continue breathing. Water and food were unimportant, but air, fresh air, was precious.

The atmosphere in the confined space was stifling. Sandy soil trickled softly in the darkness, decreasing the area within. Only the sparse amount of air coming through the two narrow holes made by Zaran were keeping her alive. However, even that was not enough—Spingo could feel her senses gradually slipping away. Though she fought the desire to sleep, it was becoming more pressing in her failing mind.

The black otter Zaran continued her vigil on the hillside. It had been quite a time since the Gonfelin maid's misfortune. Zaran did not know whether Spingo was dead or alive. However, she leant close to the little holes she had made with her beech stick, whispering constant encouragement to the young mouse entombed below.

"Spingo, help will soon be here, your friends will return, with many others. Answer if you can hear Zaran, do not give up hope, my friend."

But no reply was forthcoming, and the otter could not help any further. She knew that if she tried digging to reach Spingo, the movement might shift both soil and stone, smothering Spingo forever.

The Redwall contingent dashed gallantly through the woodlands, brushing aside or flattening everything in their way. None could travel faster than Bosie, who kept running from one end of the column to the other, roaring encouragement as he brandished his sword. "Come on, mah bonny beasts! Hasten tae the rescue! Move now, ye braw runners! Bowlayneeeee!"

With Nokko, Dubble and Bisky in the lead, they rushed onto the bankside of the creek, where the Guosim logboats lay moored. Everybeast was hurried aboard, with the moles arriving last, for as anybeast knows, moles are not the greatest runners in Mossflower.

There were four shrew paddlers to each craft, with Gonfelins and moles seated amidships. Bosie occupied the stern seat of the lead vessel, along with Nokko, Bisky, Dubble, Samolus and Garul. The logboats manoeuvred their way out of the creek, into the mainstream.

Garul shouted to Dubble, "What course do we take?"

"Straight on, an' don't take no sidewaters. Keep paddlin' in the midstream, 'til ye see the big wooded hill ahead, that's where we're bound!"

But Nokko had other ideas. "Us Gonfelins knows the lay o' the land round 'ere. I know a faster way, wot'll bring youse up be'ind that big mound!"

Bosie patted the Pikehead's back. "Very guid, mah friend, get yoreself for'ard an' tell 'em the way tae go!"

Scrambling over paddlers and passengers, Nokko made his way to the prow, where he gave orders. "The quickest way is to take the next slipstream on yore right. There 'tis, the one wid the big ould willow over'anging the bank. There's a few rapids, but that'll get us there a bit faster!"

315

Dubble was paddling alongside Garul. He took the time to enquire, "Wot happened to Tugga Bruster, tell me."

The older Guosim kept his eyes on the stream as he told Dubble of his father's fate.

When he had heard the whole disgraceful story of his father and the former Log a Log's shameful end, the young Guosim wiped a swift paw across his eyes, then breathed deep as he pulled on his paddle.

"I know he was my father, but I can't bring myself to grieve heavy over him. Tugga Bruster was never a lovin' parent, aye, an' he wasn't much of a Log a Log, either. But you knew that. Our tribe deserves a better Chieftain than him."

Garul backed water as they turned into the slipstream. "Aye, Dubble, these Guosim think you'll make a good Log a Log, they all like you."

Bending to avoid the overhanging willow branches, Dubble met the older shrew's gaze. "No, mate, I'm finished with the Guosim life. Once this is over I'm goin' to live at Redwall. I've not had much experience of the Abbey, but I know I'll find peace an' happiness there. One day, maybe, I'll forget the shame of Tugga Bruster."

Garul was bewildered by Dubble's decision. "But wot about our tribe, wot's to become of us?"

The young shrew released his paddle long enough to grasp the older beast's paw warmly. "These Guosim will do just fine with you as their Log a Log. You've always been a good an' wise ole paddle whomper, Garul. You'll make a better Log a Log than I ever could!"

The news echoed swiftly from boat to boat. All the Guosim raised their paddles in salute, roaring, "Garul! Garul! Logalogalogaloooooooog!"

The little flotilla hit the rapids, the logboats shot along. Shrews guided them skilfully, fending off rocks, banks and shoals as they sang.

"Ho, look out for the shallows now,
watch how fast yore goin',

316

you'll never beat a Guosim shrew,
paddlin' or rowin'.
Hi to me rum drum toodle hey,
wait for me, my darlin',
go set the skillet on the fire,
'cos I'll be home by mornin'.

Oh, watch her on the banksides now,
rapids an' white waters,
here's a health to all our wives,
an' our pretty daughters.
Hi to me rum drum toodle hey,
throw me out a line oh,
or a bowl o' stew, an' a drink or two,
would suit a Guosim fine oh!"

Bosie had put up his sword, he was feeling rather nervous as he clung to the prow. Spray soaked his whiskers as the logboat leapt and bucked along the rapids. Keeping a brave face, the Highland hare muttered aloud, "Och, will ye no look at this mad stream. Ah tell ye, Ah dinna know what they're singing for."

Having been told by Dubble, Bisky already knew. "Singin' helps 'em with the paddle beat, an' it keeps the logboat on an even keel."

Bosie slacked his grip upon the prow, standing up slightly, he tried a quick smile. "Oh, verra guid, that's the stuff, mah buckoes, keep the song goin', Ah like it just fine!"

However, Friar Skurpul and his molecrew did not care for the lively jaunt. Throwing themselves facedown in the boats, they gave voice to their fears.

"Ho, corks, Oi wish't Oi'd never left ee h'Abbey!"

"Hurr, we'm surtink to get sunken unner ee water!"

"Ho, woe bees Oi, Oi'll never leave ee land agin!"

Now the bankside trees were shooting by as the logboats picked up more speed. Guosim left off paddling, to fend off the rock-faced sides. Samolus gnawed his lip anxiously. "Er, Mister Nokko, are you sure this is the right way to the wooded hill?"

The Gonfelin Pikehead scowled. "Of course I'm sure, I knows this neck o' the woods like the back o' me own paw. D'yer think I'm goin' the wrong way 'cos me best young daughter's in trouble, ye daft ould bat!" The logboat scudded over a gravel rift, causing Nokko to sit back hard. Samolus helped him upright.

"Forgive my stupid remark, sir, I'm certain we're on the right course."

Nokko shrugged. "Ah, don't take any notice o' me, mate, I shouldn't 'ave spoke to yer that way."

Gobbo interrupted, "Aye, me da's just worried about Spingo, so don't take no notice of 'im."

Nokko latched onto his talkative son's snout, twisting it sharply. "Who asked yew t'put yore paddle in, gabbygob? One more word outta yew an' I'll stuff yer tail down that mouth an' pull it out yer ear, me son. So purra nail in it, right?"

Gobbo rubbed his snout ruefully. He was about to have the last word with his da by muttering a smart reply, when Bosie called out from the prow, "Ah think yon's the hill we've been seekin'!"

Sure enough, as the rapids subsided into smoother waters, the broad, tree-covered hump could be seen. It rose up ahead on the port side of the logboats. Dubble squinted hard at it. "Doesn't look familiar t'me."

Nokko explained, "That's 'cos this is the back part. I figgered it'd be safer landin' on this side. Those carrion birds guard the other side. I've seen 'em meself, perched in the trees. Huh, feathery scumwytes, that's wot I call 'em!"

No sooner did the logboats nose in to moor at a small inlet, than Bisky leapt onto the shore. He raced off uphill as the rest gathered on the bank. Friar Skurpul stamped his footpaws, grateful to be on solid ground once more. "Burr, ee young Bisky bees in a gurt 'urry."

Drawing his blade, Bosie pointed uphill. "Aye, he's hurrying tae save the wee lassie, just as we should be doin', ye ken. Garul, you an' yore Guosim help yon molebeasts tae transport their tackle. Come as fast as ye can. Hearken, the rest o' ye, follow me, up an' o'er the hilltop after Bisky. Stay silent, for we dinnae know what awaits us. Come on, mah braw buckoes. Charge!"

Nokko and Dubble kept pace with Bosie, they thundered uphill. Lances, bows and slings at the ready, Gonfelin warriors, silent and grim-faced, followed them in a life-and-death race to save their Chieftain's daughter.

34

It was noontide in east Mossflower, with scarce a vagrant breeze to stir the thick, green foliage. Skipper Rorgus called a halt beneath a massive old beech. Dwink, thinking it was for his benefit, protested. "I don't need to rest my footpaw, I can travel on quite a bit yet, Skip."

Unshouldering the big provision haversack, the Otter Chieftain sat with his back against the trunk. "Can ye now, Master Dwink, well, I'm pleased to hear it, 'cos I can't. Foremole an' me ain't young uns no more. We likes to rest when we can."

Foremole nodded agreement. "Boi 'okey we do, zurr. If'n you'm young uns bees so fulled of h'energy, may'aps ee'd loike to surve us'ns sum vittles."

Perrit placed a paw beneath her chin, and gave a charming little curtsy. "As you wish, O ancient and weary ones."

Foremole's face creased in a friendly smile. "You'm a h'imperdent likkle villyun, miz!"

They dined on soft, white cheese, preserved hazelnuts and beechnuts and a flask of coltsfoot and pennycloud cordial.

Dwink ruminated as he sat, watching a bee exploring his footpaw dressing. "Well, there's over half a day gone since we left the Abbey, with nothin' to show for it."

Skipper reassured him. "But we've stuck faithful to the clues, aye, an' searched high'n'low."

Dwink swiped idly at the bee, as it tried to burrow under his paw dressing. "So we have, Skip. Once we've eaten an' rested, we'll carry on an' search some more. I suppose that's wot a quest is all about, eh? Yeeek!"

Foremole blinked. "Wot's um matter, maister?"

Dwink was sucking furiously at his paw. "That bee, he stung me!"

Skipper corrected the young squirrel. " 'Twasn't a he, that were a she. Only female bees carry a sting. Here, mate, let me look at it." Working on Dwink's paw with a wooden splinter, the otter shook his head. "You shouldn't have hit it, the bee didn't mean ye no harm, she was prob'ly just attracted by the smell of Brother Torilis's herbal salve. There, that's got it! Rub a dockleaf on yore paw an' it I'll be good as new agin."

Dwinked complained indignantly, "But I never hit the bee, I just swiped at it, you know, to shoo it off."

Foremole chuckled. "You'm never can tell with ee bumblybees. Hurr hurr. . . . Yoooch! Naow Oi been stunged!"

Perrit clapped a paw to the side of her neck. "Eeeeh! Me, too, we must be sitting on top of a nest or something!"

Skipper never shouted out, but he jumped as he was struck on the rudder. He nipped the object out with the splinter he had used on Dwink. Inspecting it, he gathered up the haversack. "Let's hoist anchor out of 'ere, mates, afore those bees sting us t'death. Come on!"

They followed Skipper, who cut off at an angle into the trees. He ran for awhile, then halted in a willow grove on a streambank. Throwing aside the haversack, he beckoned the others to him, then spoke in a whisper. "Dwink, that was a real bee wot stung ye, but it wasn't a bee that got me!"

Foremole, who had extracted an object from his stomach where he had been hit, held it out to them. "No, nor Oi, Skip, lookit yurr."

"Hold still, missy!" Skipper swiftly removed something

321

from the side of Perrit's neck. He compared all three before giving a verdict. "These are thorns from a gorse bush. If'n I ain't mistaken, they're tipped with some sort o' juice. No bee could've done that, we was shot at!"

Dwink whispered back, "Shot at! By who?"

The Otter Chieftain unwound the sling from about his lithe waist. "I don't know, mates, but I aims t'find the rascal. Stop 'ere, an' don't stir 'til I gets back. Oh, an' miz Perrit, bees live in hives, they don't make nests."

Skipper vanished into the trees, like a wraith of smoke on the breeze. Sometimes crouching, crawling on his stomach, alternately hiding behind tree trunks or any available shelter, the otter hunted their foe. He was close to the spot where they had previously stopped, when he heard the voice, low and grumbly. Immobile, Skipper watched from the shelter of a sycamore.

There the creature was, holding a conversation with herself, wagging a blowpipe at her surroundings. A small, scraggly, thin hedgehog, with prickles greyed by age. She was adorned with stems of sphagnum moss, and garlanded by belts, necklaces and bracelets of dead bee husks, all strung together. From his vantage point, the otter listened to her tirade.

"Yeeheehee! Learn they must, you see, a painful lesson. Nobeast trespasses on Blodd Apis's land, you see. They scream with pain, they run away, that's how it should be, you see!" She danced off, laughing to herself. However, her joy was short-lived.

As the skinny hog jigged her way past the sycamore, she was caught by Skipper Rorgus. A looped sling landed neatly about her neck, and a javelin prodded her in the back. The otter bellowed at his prisoner, "Move a single spike an' it won't be no gorse thorn that'll strike ye, it'll be my javelin!"

Perrit had climbed up into a willow to spy the land. She called down to Dwink and Foremole, "Oh, corks and caterpillars, just wait until you see what Skipper's bringing to tea. Hah, you'll never believe this!"

The Otter Chieftain had his captive on a tight lead, urging her along with his javelin tip. Skipper tied the sling end to a branch, tethering the hedgehog. He showed Dwink the blowpipe, and a small pouch of darts, which he had taken from her. "This is our stingin' bee, a right nasty liddle piece o' work if'n ye ask me!"

Perrit stared pityingly at the old creature. "That sling is too tight about her neck." She approached the captive in a friendly manner. "Let's loosen it a bit, shall we."

Foremole was just in time to pull Perrit back as the hedgehog leapt at her, exposing a mouthful of filthy, snaggled teeth in a vicious snarl. "Foolish ones, ye soon will be dead, you see! Release Blodd Apis now, or die!"

Skipper leant on his javelin, ignoring the creature's threats. "Blodd Apis, eh, that's an odd sort o' name."

She gagged as she stretched the tethering sling, trying to grab at the otter with dirt-encrusted claws. "Streamdog, I am Blodd Apis, Queen of the Wild Sweet Gatherers. Ye will die the Death of a Thousand Stings if ye do not let me go, you see!"

Dwink whispered to Perrit, "Did you hear that, the Wild Sweet Gatherers. That's part of the clue, I think we should question her!"

The young squirrel addressed Blodd Apis sternly. "Listen, marm, you don't frighten us one little bit, an' yore not in a position to kill anybeast right now. So you can stop all that spittin' an' snarlin' an' answer a few questions!"

Blodd Apis went into a dance of rage. "You trespass on my land, hold me prisoner! Queen of all bees does not answer questions. You see, until I have your eyes stung out, Blodd Apis will make you plead for death, you see!" Dwink drew back, surprised at the savagery of her outburst.

Skipper winked at him knowingly. "She's tryin' to scare ye, mate, leave this t'me. I can be pretty scary in a scarin' bout, watch this!" He smiled mockingly at Blodd Apis. "Ahoy there, granny, I reckon yore mouth needs washin' out, ye naughty liddle pincushion."

This seemed to drive Blodd Apis berserk. She threw herself about, spitting and foaming at the mouth as she hurled invective on the heads of her captors. "You see! You see! I will make you scream for mercy! My bees will fly down your ears and sting your brains! Down your mouths and sting your guts! Blodd Apis will turn your bodies into slobbering lumps of agony! You see, you see!"

Skipper retaliated then. Bounding forward, with slitted eyes and bared teeth, he brandished his javelin in her face, bellowing, "Sharraaaap, ye stupid ole mud beetle! I'm the baddest beast that ever was born! Hah, you see, you see? I'll tell yer wot I see, silly spikes! I see me hangin' ye over a fire an' roastin' yore prickles off, then I see me slittin' ye open with me javelin, packin' yore insides with rocks an' sinkin' ye in a deep, muddy swamp! That's wot I see, see! Aye, an' I'm just the bucko who can do it! Like this, an' this an' this! Hahaaaarr!"

As he shouted, Skipper began jabbing with the javelin point all about Blodd Apis, missing her by a mere fraction each time. Foremole covered his eyes, whilst the two young ones held their breath, astounded by Skipper's barbaric outburst. It was a case of the bully being outbullied. Blodd Apis shrank to the ground, whimpering in terror.

"Aiee, mercy! Spare me, spare me, I was only joking, you see!"

Skipper Rorgus slammed the javelin point down in the ground alongside her. He growled roughly, "Hoho, jokin', were ye? Well, I ain't jokin'. Now, you've got a den 'ereabouts. Don't argue, take us there right away, afore I really lose me temper!"

Turning to his friends, he showed them a wide grin, and a broad wink. "Foremole, you take 'er lead. Come on, you, up on those paws, an' mind yore manners!"

Blodd Apis led them on a complicated route through the

woodlands. As they went, bees travelled with them. A few at first, but building up, until they had a huge mass of the insects buzzing in their wake. Foremole's tiny eyes widened. "Hurr, may'aps she'm truly ee Queen of bumblybees."

The old hog's den was an arresting sight. It was situated in the dense heart of the woodland. Backed by protruding sandstone ledges, two incredibly ancient yew trees spread their girth, like an annex to the ledges. In the forks of both trees, extending up into the branches, were hives piled upon hives. Some old, some deserted, but many newer ones, showing signs of habitation and great activity by the industrious wild bees. The ground surrounding the bower was thick with scent and colour. Pink bush vetch, red clover, late bluebell, sweet violet and golden tormentil. The air resounded with soft, humming drones of bees, gathering pollen as they sipped nectar.

Perrit spread her paws joyously. "What scents, and the floor, it's like, like a . . ."

"Coloured carpet?" Dwink suggested.

Blodd Apis took them into her den beneath the ledges—it was dim and cool. Skipper sat on a low ledge, taking the sling halter from Foremole.

Gullub Gurrpaw settled himself down gratefully. "Yurr, 'tis vurry peaceable, ee gudd get to loike this place, marm."

Blodd Apis had become almost fawning, following her verbal defeat by Skipper. Dwink sat facing her.

"Now, marm, about those questions. I take it that this is the home of the Wild Sweet Gatherers?"

She nodded her grey-spiked head. "Always has been, you see. Wild bees can be very dangerous, but they know their Queen, you goodbeasts are safe whilst ye stay in my company, you see, safe with me."

Dwink noticed that there were lots of bees buzzing around the ledges. "Well, that's nice to know. Tell me, have you ever heard about the eye of the serpent, does it mean anything to you?"

The old hedgehog gave no sign of recognition. "No ser-

325

pents on Queen Blodd Apis's land, you see. Snakes do not come around here."

Perrit interrupted, "He's not really talking about a live snake. The eye of the serpent is a stone, like a pigeon egg, but it is green."

The aged hog showed her snaggle teeth in an ugly grin. "No, young missie, you see I have never seen such a thing. Why do ye seek it?"

Skipper interrupted, still playing his role as the rough bully, "If'n ye've never seen it then wot does it matter to ye what we want with it, eh?"

At the rear of the ledges, Dwink noticed a number of large pottery urns, covered by woven reed mats. "What's in those big vases, marm?"

Blodd Apis sounded evasive. "Nothing, young sir, nothing, you see."

Foremole clambered to the back of the ledge. He heaved one of the urns out. "Hurr, nuthin', you'm say, marm, then let's take ee lukk at wot nuthin' looks loike!"

He took off the covering, revealing a quantity of scented amber liquid. Dipping in a sturdy digging paw, the mole licked it. Licking his lips, he smiled. "Et tasters gurtly sweet!"

Their captive hastened to explain, "It's what a Queen lives on, you see, I need no other food but that. I make it from bee honey, try some. It's very pleasant, you see." She pointed to a number of beakers nearby. "Please, I know ye'll like it, 'tis quite harmless and delicious to drink, you see."

Skipper set out five of the beakers, but he filled only one from the urn, placing it before Blodd Apis. "There y'are, missus. If'n that stuff's quite 'armless, then let's see you drink it!"

Without hesitation, the skinny old hog took a sip from the beaker. She was about to put it down, when the Foremole held a paw under the vessel.

326

"Yurr, drink et all oop loik a guddbeast, cummon, marm!"

They watched as Blodd Apis happily drained the beaker. "More please, I like it, you see!"

Perrit giggled. "Well, there can't be much wrong with the honey drink if she can swig it down like that!" The squirrelmaid filled all the beakers, by dipping them in the urn.

Dwink took a sip, proclaiming, "Great seasons, this is delicious. What did ye say this was made from, marm?"

"Just honey from my bees, an' fresh springwater, nought else, you see," replied Blodd Apis, raising a full beaker. "But 'tis not to be sipped, you see. The right way is to drink it in one go, like this." The curious old hedgehog drained the beaker with a single draught, smacking her lips as she cackled, "Just like that, you see!"

Her four guests did likewise, each giving their verdict. "Bo urr, ee'll 'ave to tell Oi the ressipery furr ee hunny drink, marm. Ole Corksnout wudd h'enjoy et!"

"Oh, it's wonderful, I've never tasted anything like it!"

"I told you, Perrit, absolutely delicious, eh, Skip?"

The Otter Chieftain refilled all five beakers. "Ye can say that agin, young Dwink, a real pretty drop o' stuff. Well, mates, good 'ealth to one an' all!" They quaffed their drinks down swiftly.

Dwink took the beakers. "Hahaha! My turn now. . . . Oops!" He chuckled as he dipped the drinking vessels into the big urn. "Nearly toppled in! Hahaha, that'd be a good idea, it'd save havin' t'fill these beakers up. We could all jump in for a drink!"

The drinks were downed with alacrity. Skipper refilled them, commenting, "Yore shore 'tis only made of honey an' springwater, missus, nothin' else?"

"Nay, nought but honey and springwater, just as I said, you see."

Blodd Apis topped them up again. Perrit took a good swig. She blinked owlishly, staring into the urn. "Funny an' stringdaughter, eh, very nice!" She hiccupped as she supplied them with more.

Dwink slopped liquid down his front, swaying to and fro, he sighed happily. "Y'right, Ferrit ole mate. S'nice, veryveyveyvey night. Hahahaha! G'night. . . ." Letting the beaker slip, he curled over, asleep.

Perrit hiccupped again, then giggled. "Heehee, Drink's dropped his dwink. Wait, tha's rot, night. Heeheehee. Whoooogolly me!" Flopping down alongside Dwink, Perrit closed her eyes. Within moments, she was snoring in the most unmaidenly manner.

Skipper staggered about, eyes rolling as he tried to focus on Blodd Apis. Grabbing his javelin he wagged it at the ancient hog. "You . . . you did sump'n to that drink, didn't ye? Hah! If'n anythin' happens t'my mates, I warn ye, missus." The Otter Chieftain took a step forward, tripped over his own javelin and fell flat, banging his head on the sandstone ledge. He lay there, senseless to the world.

Repeatedly, Foremole tried to rise from a sitting position. Each time he slumped back clumsily. He watched Blodd Apis removing the leather sling halter from her neck. "Yurr, marm, bein' ee h'assistant cellarbeast at ee h'Abby, Oi'm a-knowen 'bout drinks."

Taking Foremole's half-filled beaker, Blodd Apis finished it off in one swallow. "Then ye know 'tis not poison. Never heard of mead, have ye? Mead is just honey an' springwater mixed. When it's been sealed up for a season, mead becomes strong, you see. Aye, the longer 'tis stored, the stronger it gets. I gave you an' yore friends my Special Ten Season Mead. I've lived all my life on mead you see, so I'm used to it. Hah, but otherbeasts aren't, 'tis far too strong for 'em!"

Foremole blinked blearily, his head dropped. "Hurr, marm, you'm an 'ole villyun, aye, a gurt trickybeast. Fie on ee, you'm maked uz drunken!"

From her garlands of moss and festooned bee carcasses, Blodd Apis drew forth a woven grass bag. She emptied

328

the contents of the small receptacle onto the ledge. There were two objects: one, a hollow reed tube, stoppered with beeswax at either end to contain the liquid inside. The other was the pigeon's egg–shaped emerald. It glowed with fabulous green light as she stroked it covetously. "Fools, this is no serpent's eye, 'tis the Green Star of the Woodlands. Only a Queen may possess it, you see!"

Foremole raised his head with an effort. "Ho no, marm, that'n bees ee surrpint's eye, an' et doan't berlong to ee at all, burr nay!"

Blodd Apis hastily stowed the emerald in her bag. Foremole was still trying to rise, when she kicked him back down. There was a wicked glimmer in her eyes. "Stupid soildigger, do ye think the Queen of Wild Bees would let anybeast take the Green Star from her? Both you and your friends will be dead by sunset, you see. Now you will know what it is to feel the Death of a Thousand Stings!"

The threat of all of them being slain immediately lifted the mead-induced stupor from the good mole. However, he decided not to let the malignant old hedgehog know. Sprawled on his back, he blinked feebly at her. "Burr, you'm wicked rarscal, wot bees you'm plannen?"

Crouching close to Foremole's face, Blodd Apis showed him the hollow reed tube. She shook it, so he could hear the liquid inside. "You see this, it is the juice of many wood ants. They are the enemy of my bees. If I were to splash you with just a drop of this juice, you would be attacked and stung to death by my bees, you see!"

Foremole gave a gentle, rumbling snore, as if he had fallen into a drunken slumber. Blodd Apis kicked him scornfully. "Hah, sleep on, mudbrain, ye will soon wake for the last time, very painfully, you see!"

For such an ancient creature, the hedgehog was surprisingly strong and resolute. Foremole watched, through half-lidded eyes, as she dragged each of his friends clear of the ledges and surrounding yews into the open. Skipper, being the biggest, was the most difficult. About midway between her den and a small stream, Blodd Apis ceased hauling the otter by his rudder. Next came Perrit, she was a lot easier to lug along. Foremole's brain was racing as he saw her tugging Dwink along by his long, bushy tail. An idea came to him when he spotted Dwink's crutch, which had fallen at the foot of the sandstone ledge. He began crawling toward the slumped forms of his companions, muttering aloud drunkenly, "Burr, Oi must foind moi friends, whurr do they bees, mus' foind 'em, hurrrr!"

Blodd Apis stood over him, sniggering. "Well, you see, here's one I don't need to drag along. Come on, soildigger, here's your friends, you see, over there. This way!" Prodding her victim with one paw, she carefully held up the hollow reed vial in the other.

Foremole crawled clumsily forward, stumbling over the shallow ledges as she goaded him on. "Clumsy oaf, not that way, over there, you see?"

Foremole Gullub rolled over the final ledge, then lay flat on his stomach, hiding the crutch, which he had grabbed, under him. Closing his eyes, he snuffled, and commenced snoring once more.

This peeved the old hedgehog. Bending down, she cuffed the back of the mole's head. "Don't ye go asleep on me, there's your friends, over there, you see!"

Knowing his life and the lives of others depended on him, Foremole acted swiftly. Rolling over, he struck out with Dwink's window-prop crutch. The blow landed hard and true, smashing the reed tube in the hedgehog's paw, splashing her with the deadly liquid. A few drops fell on his paw. The buzzing noise was beginning to fill the air as Foremole scurried wildly to the stream and threw himself in.

The screams of Blodd Apis rose to an insane pitch as her bees descended upon her. Hundreds upon hundreds of the maddened insects attacked her savagely, diving, buzzing, stinging.

Foremole popped his head out of the water, to take a breath. Blodd Apis was not to be seen, she had vanished,

330

still screeching, under the swarming masses of enraged bees. Foremole scrambled out onto the bank. He ran to his friends, splashing water upon them, and smacking out with hefty digging claws.

"Wake ee oop, zurrs! Skip, mizzy Perrit, Dwink, rouse you'm selfs. Oh, do 'urry! Yooch!" Stung on the ears, Foremole was forced to dive back into the water. A small cloud of bees hovered, humming, over the spot where he had gone down.

Skipper sat up groaning, his face wet with bankmud and streamwater, and his snout smarting from Foremole's digging claw. "Ahoy . . . wot's goin' on? . . . Wake up, mates, look at that thing yonder!"

Foremole's head broke the surface again. He spat out water and a bee, bellowing, "They'm slayin' ee ole 'ogwife, get ee away!"

Whilst they had not yet been stung, Skipper shook Dwink and Perrit into wakefulness. "We'd best weigh anchor sharpish, mates, those bees have gone crazed!"

Dwink sat up, nursing a pounding headache. "Ooh me head, what's all that noise?"

Perrit was up on her paws—the squirrelmaid was horrified. "Oh, fur'n'blood, is that Blodd Apis?"

The ancient hedgehog was trying to crawl away, moaning hoarsely, completely covered by bees.

Ever resourceful, Skipper sprang into the stream. Dragging Foremole to the surface, he covered him with his own body, allowing him breathing space from the hovering bees. Dwink began limping to the den between the yews.

Perrit chased after him, she was bewildered. "Surely you're not going back in there?"

Dwink winced. "Don't speak so loud, please."

The squirrelmaid protested, "I've got to, or I wouldn't be heard over all this buzzing. Surely you're not going to drink more of that honey drink?"

Dwink was shoving one of the big pottery urns out into the open. "I'm not going to drink it, but mayhaps the bees might like a drop or two. Let's get this out where they can scent it!"

Between them, the pair managed to get four of the pottery mead vessels close to where the bee swarms were still crawling over the now-dead hedgehog. Hurriedly they tipped the urns over, sending the strong, sweet nectar cascading over the grass. Within moments, the bees caught the heavy, aromatic scent. Dwink and Perrit joined Skipper and Foremole in the stream.

The Otter Chieftain clapped their backs soundly. "Well done, mateys, that was a clever ruse an' no mistake. Come now, young uns, dunk yore 'eads in the water, 'twill freshen ye up!"

Dwink and Perrit took the otter's advice—he was right. Several duckings in cold streamwater was a wonderful cure for their headaches.

Feeling quite chipper, they emerged to sit on the bank. Skipper attended to Foremole's stings with a poultice of cool mud and crushed dockleaves. Patting the dressing with a huge digging claw, the mole grinned cheerfully. "Oi wager Oi do lukk gurtly funny wi' this lot on moi 'ead. Hurr, but et doo's feel noice, zurr!"

Perrit left off fluffing her saturated tail. "Noticed anything, mates? The bees aren't bothering us at all now!"

Dwink went over to retrieve his crutch; he flicked a bee with the tip of it. The fuzzy insect rolled over on its back, where it lay humming happily. Dwink could not help chuckling. "They won't bother anybeast for awhile, not as long as they're drunker than we were."

Perrit touched her brow. "Don't remind me, from now on I'll take mint tea, or just water. My golly, that honey drink was strong enough to knock a tree over."

Foremole wrinkled his velvety snout. "Hurr, they'm bound t'be sum gurt likkle 'eadaches round yurr cumm noightfall. Dwink, moi friend, ee old hogwife has what we cumm a-lookin' fer, do ee get yon surrpint's eye, an' let us'ns begone from yurr!"

332

Gingerly turning the body of Blodd Apis over with his crutch, the young squirrel winced at the awful sight. The whole length of her, from snout to spike end, was a mass of red, swollen lumps. Looping the crutch into the woven reed bag fastener, he pulled it clear.

They admired the green-fired emerald orb awhile, then Skipper popped it back into its container. "We should bury her, mad though she were. Let's seal her up in her old home."

The friends left the old one to her final rest. "Well, buckoes, 'twas a successful search, an' I'm sure all at Redwall will agree when they sees it."

Foremole nodded sagely. "That bees two greeny uns, an' one red un been founded. Wot doo's ee say t'that, Maister Dwink?"

Finding he no longer needed the crutch, Dwink shouldered it, assisting Foremole to his footpaws. "I say let's go back to Redwall Abbey, mates!"

35

Evening had fallen over the wooded hillside above the caves of Korvus Skurr, but its tranquil charm was lost on the black otter. Zaran alternated anxiously betwixt the spot where Spingo was trapped beneath soil and stone, and her lookout post on the sloping poplar trunk. Sword in paw, she perched, peering fretfully for signs of any assistance arriving. Thumping her rudderlike tail on the tree trunk, Zaran hurried back to the two air vents she had made, her fierce eyes creased with worry as she whispered to the Gonfelin maid entombed below the earth and rock. "I think they will be here soon, Spingo, hold on!"

Lack of air was taking its toll on Spingo. She could hear Zaran's voice, as if from far off, though she was drifting into blackness, cramped almost double now, pressed in on all sides by sandy, sifting soil, and the mighty sandstone slab. Avoiding thoughts of her inevitable fate, the young mousemaid pictured images. Her father, Nokko, the Gonfelin Pikehead; Filgo, her mother; Bisky, the young Redwaller who had become her dear friend. Special moments of her brief life, feasting in the Abbey orchard, surrounded by happy creatures. A tear squeezed out onto her dusty cheek at these fond memories.

Then the voice came, soft as misty summer morn.

"Friends are near, live to enjoy life in my Abbey with one who cares for you."

Hearing no reply to her words, Zaran called louder, "Spingo, hear me, I am Zaran, your friend. Speak, say something!"

"I've brought help, Zaran, is she still alive?"

The black otter turned to see Bisky, flanked by Nokko and Dubble, emerging from the trees behind her. She cautioned them, "Stay clear of the airholes I have made. I cannot get Spingo to answer me."

Nokko bit down hard on his lip. "She's me daughter y'know, marm, she's got t'be alive, d'ye hear me, Spingo's too precious t'lose!" He made a move to shout down the two tiny vents.

Dubble locked his paws about Nokko, lifting him clear. "Stay clear, sir, leave it t'the molecrew, they'll soon be 'ere."

Bisky sat down on the ground, staring westward at the last scarlet tinges of a descending sun. Zaran stared curiously at him—his eyes seemed distant. "Friend, are you alright, what is it?"

The young Redwall mouse blinked, coming out of his sudden trance. He grabbed the black otter's paw. "She's alive, I know it, Spingo's alive!"

Zaran pulled him upright. "How do you know this?"

Friar Skurpul came trundling onto the scene. "Hurr, prob'ly 'cos Marthen ee Wurrier spake to 'im, marm. Naow, all you'm guddbeasts coom out'n moi way!"

Without enquiry or question, Bisky, Dubble and Zaran moved aside as the molecrew came in, with Guosim shrews bearing their digging gear. Skurpul moved rapidly about, marking the earth with a small pawpick.

"Roight, naow, iffen ee maid bees stuck unner thurr, we'm gotten to be diggen two long, slopen tunnels. Lissen naow, yurr's moi plan."

Nokko was not very familiar with moletalk. Bisky could see how anxious he was about Spingo, so he translated

335

Skurpul's scheme to the Gonfelin Chief. "Friar Skurpul plans on having his crew dig two tunnels, one from the left, the other from the right. Owing to the soft earth, they'll start a short distance away. The tunnels will slope gradually, instead of going straight down, with molecrew shoring up the holes as they go. Spingo will be reached from both sides when the tunnels are completed. Do you see the oak tree on the left, and the big sycamore on the right, sir?"

Nokko looked from one tree to the other. "Aye, I sees 'em Bisko, are they part o' the plan?"

Bisky nodded. "Right, sir, the moles will attach two of their longest ropes, one to each tree, as a safety measure, that way they'll be able to haul Spingo, and themselves, back out again. Don't worry, if anybeast can reach your daughter it'll be Friar Skurpul and his molecrew. There's no better diggers in all Mossflower!"

By now, the full complement of Guosim and Gonfelins had arrived. Nokko turned to Skurpul. "Is there anythin' we kin do to 'elp youse?"

The black otter Zaran answered for the Friar. "We help by letting moles do their job. If you need something to do, then arm yourselves and watch the cave entrance below. Danger could come from that place. Baliss is in there, and Wytes, carrion birds, many reptiles also."

Garul, the new Log a Log, drew his rapier, nodding to Nokko, who was stringing a bow. "Wot d'ye say, Pikehead, shall our buckoes stand sentry?"

Nokko fitted a shaft onto his bowstring. "Right, mate, an' if'n just one snotty snout pokes outta there, we'll show 'em the meanin' of slaughter!"

The long ropes were in place, secured tightly to both trees. Bisky saw the debris of loose earth, pebbles and broken roots, showering out from two directions as the molecrews commenced their dig, Rooter and Soilclaw from one side, Grabul and Ruttur from the other. Friar Skurpul assisted Frubb and Burgy, dashing from one tunnel to the other, with pawsful of green willow boughs. These were quickly fashioned into rough frames, and forced into the sides of the diggings, shoring them against any sudden collapse.

Spingo was wakened from her semiconscious reverie by heavy snuffling, and a paw scraping her back. The Gonfelin maid squeaked in alarm as loose earth began cascading in on her. Then the reassuring rumble of a mole voice made itself known.

"Yurr, likkle miz, doan't ee be a-frettin', we'm soon have ee owt o' yurr!"

The huge stone slab shifted above them, dropping lower as another mole enquired from the other side of Spingo, "Yurr, Grabul, have ee reached ee pore creetur yet?"

Grabul spat out sandy soil, gathering in the slack of the rope on his side. "Burr aye, she'm been a-sufferin' down yurr. Oi'll just get ee rope abowt ee, missy, doan't ee be afeared, young un!"

Soilclaw burrowed through from the other side. In total darkness he fumbled about until he found Ruttur and Grabul. Soilclaw passed them the other rope. There was a rumble as the rock slab slipped even lower.

Realising there was no time left for further manoeuvre, Friar Skurpul dug furiously, pulling himself along by the rope from the left, hawking soil and bellowing, "Get ee owt! Save ee maid an' you'm selves!" His last words were drowned out as the entire hole collapsed inward, soil, sand, stone, roots and the massive rock slab.

Pandemonium reigned in the vast, sulphur-clouded cave. Baliss was on the loose within. Crazed with agonising pain, the monster reptile charged around like a juggernaut, scattering heaps of bone and slime widespread, lashing the filth-encrusted walls with a whiplike tail. Insects and small reptiles were crushed beneath the thrashing coils as the adder went on in a quest to find cool water. All else

337

was wiped from the snake's senses, only water, to rest the hideously infected head in. Cold water to ease the torment of embedded hedgehog spines, suppurating pus from nosrils, mouth and blind eye sockets.

Regardless of the sanctity of Korvus Skurr's inner retreat, frogs, toads, lizards, grass snakes, smoothsnakes and slow worms slithered into the rear cavern. Korvus Skurr, the great raven Doomwyte, was powerless to stop anything now. He cowered behind the broken stalagmite which had once been the perch he ruled from. From the other cavern he could hear Baliss charging about insanely.

Then an unearthly sound rent the air, something like a hissing screech. The snake had found water, but it was neither cool nor soothing. Baliss had dipped briefly into the boiling pool, recoiling swiftly, badly scalded. Storming off with lightning swiftness, the mighty adder came rushing into the rear cave.

Birds and reptiles stopped in their tracks at the sight of the disfigured snake. Then a strange occurrence took place. Baliss halted, the blind head reared, turning slowly back and forth. It was as if some sixth sense had taken over, letting the great reptile know relief was close by. Baliss came forward then, still weaving from side to side, but slithering inevitably toward the icy cold of the bottomless lake. Korvus Skurr watched, his beak pointing forward in anticipation, as he saw salvation from all his problems. The inevitable was about to happen. This was indeed the answer he sought.

Baliss found the water. At the first touch of its soothing, cold caress, the monstrous snake lowered its head deep. Korvus Skurr hurried out of range, as the coiled scales wrapped around the stalagmite he had been hiding behind.

Seeing food, Welzz moved at eye-blurring speed. The giant black catfish struck its prey, seizing the serpent's head in a remorseless grip. Baliss went rigid, the snake's tail anchoring itself tight about the rock as it heaved upward. There was an almighty splash, then a loud flop, as the fish was hauled clear of the surface, only to dive back down again.

Baliss repeated the process with ferocious strength. Yanking the fish clear of the lake again, the snake sought to release the hold Welzz had on its head, pulling back sharply as the fish tried to dive a second time.

An enormous slap echoed as Baliss slammed Welzz down hard upon the rocky cavern floor. The force of the impact caused Welzz to release its hold; the big fish flopped about, seeking to reach the safety of its watery lair. But Baliss was on it, like a hawk upon a dove. The eyes of Welzz popped wide, as reptilian coils closed around its body like a vise. The snake's fangs sank deep into the smooth body.

Korvus Skurr saw his hopes dashed by the snake's triumph. However, there was an alternate plan already forming in his fertile mind. He went, half-running, half-flying toward the big cavern, calling to the carrion, "Haaayaaaakkah! The tunnel is free to the outside!"

They followed him in a rush to leave the caves. Out from the gloom of the rear chamber, into the polluted atmosphere of the main cavern they went. Every inhabitant of that underworld who valued their lives rushed out to fresh air and away from Baliss. They were halfway through the sulphurous smoke when the roof caved in.

36

On the hillside, the earth suddenly collapsed into a deep depression. Bisky found himself unwittingly sliding in with it. He yelled, "Aaaah. . . . Heeeelp!"

Bosie was there like a flash. Throwing himself flat he grabbed the young mouse's paws, yanking him back to safety. But the earth was still moving, the bowl-shaped implosion growing wider and deeper. Everybeast had left the lookout posts, hurrying to see the cause of Bisky's alarm. Bosie pulled further back, calling out orders.

"Back now, all of ye, stay clear!"

Nokko strained to get past Bosie. "Wot's goin' on, mates? Me daughter, the molecrew, where in the name o' blazes 'ave they gone?"

Another warning tremor shook the hillside as the Highland hare pushed the Gonfelin Chief back. "Och, Ah dinnae know where they are, stay clear unless ye want tae follow them. Wait, Ah've got an idea!"

Grabbing one of the molecrew's spare ropes, Bosie lashed it around his middle. He tossed an end to Nokko. "Take the strain, mah bonny beasts, Ah'm goin' tae take a look. Hang on tight tae the rope now!"

Paw over paw, the gallant hare lowered himself into the depression. The debris of sandy soil, pebbles and torn roots slid along with him. Then, with alarming speed, he disappeared into the shifting mass.

Nokko roared to the band of helpers, who were holding the rope, "Pull 'im outta there mates, cummon! Heave away!"

Backs bent almost double, the rescuers strained, shuffling backward. Bosie came out suddenly, like a cork from a bottle, leaving a hole, through which shot a small column of sulphured steam. The hare hopped, jumped and skipped his way back to firm ground. He expelled a mouthful of soil.

"Phwooff! Gi' me mah sword!" Seizing the fabled blade, he sliced the rope from himself in a single slash, shouting hurriedly, "Och, there's nae time tae gossip, a charge is the only thing for it. We've got tae get inside those caves below. Arm yersel's an' follow me. Quick as ye like, buckoes, there's no a moment tae be lost!"

They thundered down the hillside en masse, with Nokko and Bisky tearing alongside Bosie. As they went, Bisky was yelling, "What is it, what did ye see down there?"

Bosie rushed on, grim-jawed as he muttered, "Ye'll see for yerself soon enough, mah friend!"

It was a breakneck charge. Stumbling, dodging, they reached the bottom of the big wooded hill. Some leapt onto the streambank, others went straight into the water, but they recovered quickly, charging into the entrance tunnel.

Bosie, leading the way, was whirling his blade like a drum major, roaring out his warcry. "Eulaliaaa Bowlaynee! Eulaliaaaaaa!"

Bisky swung a loaded sling, Dubble waved his rapier and Nokko held the shaft on his bowstring at the ready. Behind them, the beasts of Gonfelin and Guosim came, everyone armed to the teeth, blood racing, pulses pounding.

They poured out into the big cavern, straight into a mass of carrion birds and reptiles coming the opposite way. As both sides clashed, Bosie pointed through the green fog, calling to Dubble, Bisky and Nokko, "Over yonder, d'ye see? We've got tae help them!"

Bisky felt his stomach churn as he viewed the sight which had driven the hare on with such urgency.

Two ropes dangled from the cavern roof, which was so high that the length of the ropes only reached halfway to the floor. Hanging from the ropes were Soilclaw, Burgy and Frubb, holding on to the limp form of Spingo. On the floor, atop a soil heap, lay the still forms of Rooter, Grabul, Ruttur and Friar Skurpul. Unable to hold on to the ropes, they had fallen through the hole in the cave ceiling.

Nokko cast a quick glance upward, his face tight with fear. "Lookit, that big stone's stuck up there, but it's gonna come down any moment now!"

Sure enough, the huge, flat sandstone slab was lying on its side, held in the hole by the rubble, either side of it. But the loose earth was raining down, still widening the hole.

Nokko clapped a paw to his brow. "They're stuck up there, wot are we gonna do?"

Dubble shook his head despairingly. "Nothin' much we can do, mates, they're too high up t'be reached, an' that big stone's about to drop. Fur'n'blood, wot a terrible mess."

Behind them, a war to the death was raging, as birds and reptiles tried to break out through the ranks of Guosim and Gonfelins. Bisky faced the problem in front of them, blotting out the sounds of combat from his mind. He concentrated on saving those hanging upon the high ropes.

Suddenly he was acting. Even as the plan formed in his mind, he ran to the hill of rubble, which had fallen from the hole above. "Help me, mates, move these poor moles off this pile of earth, quickly now!"

All four moles were obviously dead. Bosie lifted Friar Skurpul gently, placing him to one side. "Och, the guid old beast, 'tis a cryin' shame!"

Even though there was a huge lump in Bisky's throat, he

managed to speak firmly. "Time to cry later, Bosie, leave him now and start shoring this pile up. Move!"

Under Bisky's direction, they pushed the pile into one mass, gathering loose material from around it. Flattening the top off slightly, the young mouse looked upward, gauging the distance.

Dubble looked up aghast. "Yore not thinkin' of tellin' 'em to drop down onto that, are ye?"

Bisky found himself roaring at the hapless shrew. "Well, what do you think we should do? Leave them hangin' up there until that big slab falls down on their heads?" He immediately felt sorry that he had spoken like that to his Guosim friend, and apologised. "I'm sorry, mate, but we've got to do something quickly, there's not much time."

Bosie was keeping one eye on the battle over by the tunnel. "Och, but what d'ye intend doin'?"

Bisky explained, "We'll pile this hill of soil a bit higher and flatten off the top. They might stand a chance if they drop onto to it one at a time."

Nokko, who had remained silent so far, peered up at the creatures hanging from the rope. "But four of 'em are already dead from fallin' that high. Wot chance 'as me daughter an' those three brave moles got?"

Bisky replied, having worked it all out in his mind, "The four who died fell right from the ceiling, but our friends up there are already halfway down, they don't have so far to fall. The soil heap should soften the impact, as long as they come down singly."

Nokko began levelling off the top of the heap. There was a grating noise from high up; the big stone slab was slipping as more soil leaked away from its sides.

Cupping his paws around his mouth, Bisky yelled, "Burgy, Frubb, drop Spingo down to us!"

The two moles were glad to lose their burden. They released the Gonfelin maid. Bisky and Nokko threw themselves flat on the sides of the heap. Spingo plummeted through space, still senseless as her limp body thudded onto the soil, sending up a cloud of dust. Bisky and Nokko carried her aside.

Bosie nodded his approval. "Ah think the wee lassie took no hurt, 'tis a guid plan. Hi there, Frubb, wait'll Ah smooth this heap again, yore next!"

Moments later, the mole came hurtling through the air, his eyes tight shut as he thumped onto the makeshift cushion. "Hurr, Oi did et, zurrs, Oi did et!"

Burgy came next—he, too, made a safe landing.

Bisky shouted up to Soilclaw, the last of the molecrew, "Come on, mate, let go of that rope!"

Soilclaw clung on tighter—he was far too scared to release his hold. "Ho, woe am Oi, zurrs, Oi'm gurtly afeared o' heights. Oi'd loike to letten go of ee rope, but Oi can't, 'tis a turrible long ways daown to ee floor!"

Dubble realised that the only way Soilclaw would release his hold would be through shock. So the young Guosim screeched up as loud as he could, "The big rock's fallin' on ye, mate, leggo o' the rope!"

With a panicked bellow, Soilclaw let go. "Whooo-uuuurrr!" Shooting through space like a furry cannonball, he landed bottom-first on the heap. He stood up, dusting himself off as if nothing had happened. "Thurr naow, that diddent hurt Oi!"

Nokko lifted his unconscious daughter, draping her across his shoulders. "Got t'get my liddle darlin' out inter the fresh air an' wet 'er face with cold streamwater."

Bosie took over. "Right, we'll make a path for ye. Bisky, Dubble, get either side o' him, we'll fight our way through tae the tunnel. Eulaliaaa Bowlayneeee!"

Turning, they charged straight into the fray.

Reptiles, birds, Guosim and Gonfelins were locked, tooth to claw and beak to paw, in the tunnel mouth, driving one another back and forth in a wild melee. A sharp-billed chough fluttered down, about to stab its beak into Spingo. Bisky lashed out, breaking its skull with his stone-loaded sling. The Laird Bosie McScutta of Bowlaynee forged gal-

lantly ahead, the light of battle in his eyes as he swung
the blade of Martin the Warrior like a scythe, mowing a
slaughtered lane through the foebeast. Dubble thrust left
and right with his rapier, his battlecry mingling with those
of his comrades.

"Logalogalogaloooog! Gonfeliiiin! Redwaaaaallll! Give
'em blood'n'vinegar! No quarter, no surrender!"

Bisky fought on in a crimson haze, biting, kicking, swinging his rock-loaded sling. The only thought uppermost in
his mind—to get Spingo out, into clean air and safety.

Now they were into the tunnel. Slow worms, grass
snakes and smoothsnakes hissed and snapped viciously
in their struggle to escape the caves, only to be met by
Zaran, the black otter.

She stood where none could pass, her double-bladed
sword dealing out death and destruction to the creatures
of Korvus Skurr. Any servant of the Doomwyte who ventured in range of her avenging blades was sent screaming
to Hellgates with savage fury.

Bisky managed to shout to her above the hubbub, "We've
got Spingo, she must get out of here, Zaran!"

The otter slashed her way through to Bosie's side.
"Come, friend, get the young one out, then we come back
and finish this thing forever!"

The Highland hare laughed recklessly. "Och, yer a lassie after mah own heart. Aye, let's do that, mah braw
bonny!"

Dawn rushed in with a warm breeze, and a sky as blue
as speedwell blossoms. The little party broke out of the
fetid cavern fumes into a bright summer's day. Nokko
tripped and fell into the stream, dousing both himself and
his daughter. Bisky and Dubble waded in to help them out.
Spingo, wakened by the sudden shock of cold streamwater, yelled out.

"Whaaaa. . . . Phlooooey. . . . I'm bein' drownded, 'elp!"

Bisky grabbed her paw, pulling her up onto the bank.
He was shaking all over, and grinning foolishly.

Nokko spat out a jet of water, scowling. "Worra yew laughin' at, cheeky gob?"

The young Redwaller held a paw to help him out. "It's a good day t'be alive, isn't it mate?"

Nokko suddenly realised that Spingo was standing smiling at Bisky, awake and well. He accepted Bisky's paw and waded to the bank. "Ha ha, ye can say that agin, bucko! Aye aye, where are ye off to, we've just got out!"

Bisky and Dubble joined Zaran and Bosie. Now that his warrior blood was roused, the Laird of Bowlaynee was trembling for action. "Stay here an' care for yore bonny daughter, mah friend, we've got a battle tae attend to!"

The Gonfelin Pikehead sat Spingo carefully down on the bankside. "Are ye alright, me darlin'?"

She smiled prettily. "I'm fine, thank ye, Da!"

He pulled a thick driftwood billet from the stream and gave it to her. "There now, that's me beauty. You rest 'ere an' break the 'eads of any foebeasts ye sees comin' out o' there." He cocked an ear to the tunnel entrance, scowling. "There goes that Gobbo agin, can't keep his big trap shut fer a moment. Right, let's go t'war, mates!"

Yelling blood and thunder, the five warriors charged back into the tunnel. Spingo picked a pink purslane flower, sniffing it daintily as she wielded her club and sat guard over the tunnel entrance.

Korvus Skurr was the Leader of Doomwytes, he had ruled his underworld domain with a stern claw. It had seen many seasons of his tyranny, but now he could see it was all finished. The big raven Doomwyte was many things, but he could never be called a fool. His cunning mind was ever at work, thinking up fresh ideas, devising new plans. The one uppermost in his self-centred mind now was survival—to escape Baliss, and get clear of the caves. His fear of the giant adder knew no bounds, he had seen what it could do. Any creature who could slay the Welzz, that dark monster which haunted the bottomless

346

lake, was worthy of the fear of even the Doomwyte. A bird of his size and ferocity could establish himself anywhere outside, even beyond the bounds of Mossflower. When he saw the invading forces of woodlanders charging into his caverns, he knew a swift change of plans was called for.

Urging his creatures forward to the attack, Korvus Skurr did what he deemed to be the wise move. He sent them at the foebeast, strategically withdrawing himself. Once the struggle was decided, one way or another, it would be the work of a moment to make a flight for freedom and the outside world. But there remained the problem of Baliss, how to avoid the snake, until he could effect his escape.

The raven's keen eyes searched around, until he found the answer. There! About a third of the way up the cavern walls was a recess, half-disguised by scabrous growths of fungus and lichen. As everybeast from both sides was locked in battle, it was not too difficult to go unnoticed. One lightning swoop took the Doomyte raven straight up to the hiding place.

Unfortunately, he found it already occupied by a jackdaw. Seeing the great Korvus Skurr, the grey-hooded bird moved aside to make room. Korvus settled next to the jackdaw, indicating the struggle below with a wave of one wing.

Garraaak! Why are you not fighting alongside your companions? Do ye fear those earthcrawlers?" He noticed an ugly swelling on the bird's face as it turned to him. It had difficulty replying.

"Kurrrh! Lord, I was wounded by a slingstone. My mate was slain by an arrow, she lies down there."

Korvus stared down at the arena of combat. "Where?"

The jackdaw dipped its beak toward the edge of the boiling pool. "Over there, see?"

Pretending he could not see, Korvus got behind the jackdaw, as if to look over its shoulder. "Harraaah! Where is your mate? I cannot see."

The jackdaw bent its head, indicating the spot. "Korrah!

347

By those two fallen magpies. See the arrow sticking out, she was a good mate."

Korvus stuck the jackdaw through the back of its neck with his murderous beak. With a wrench of his strong head, he sent its body plummeting downward in a whirl of black and grey plumage. "Yakkaaah! Go and join your mate, fool, there is space for only one up here!"

He settled down to watch the outcome of the battle, keeping one eye on the entrance to the rear cavern. Sooner or later, Baliss would come out of there. Korvus hoped it would be later, some time after he had made his escape.

Though the woodlanders had the element of surprise on their side, they were outnumbered by reptiles and carrion birds. Urged on by Bosie, Nokko, Bisky and Dubble, they fought fiercely. The main area of combat centred round the entrance to the tunnel. Gonfelin and Guosim archers and slingers kept up constant barrages at the carrion, who swept down on them in dark clouds through the yellow fog of sulphur fumes.

Bosie and several shrews were hard put, slashing with their blades at the horde of reptiles, snakes, toads, frogs and lizards. These were not fighting, merely trying to leave by the tunnel. They pressed the woodlanders in seething masses, threatening to bring them down with overwhelming force.

It was Bosie's injury that decided the outcome of the struggle. Flailing about with his sword like a madbeast, he let his aching paws drop for one unguarded moment. A big chough swept down and attacked him. The foebird's curved pointed beak drove a furrow across the hare's head, piercing his right ear. Bosie roared in pain. The chough latched its talons into his brow, screeching madly as it tried to extricate its beak from his ear.

Nokko leapt on Bosie's back; grabbing the chough, he slew it with a swift dagger thrust. Bosie was still bellowing as he flung the slain bird from him, then he charged, his eyes clouded red in a berserk rage.

"Eulaliiiaaa! Ye durty auld featherbags! Ah'll make ye rue the day ye broke yore eggshells! Ah'll send ye all tae Hellgates an' potscrapin's! Face me if ye dare, Ah'm the McScutta, Laird o' Bowlayneeeeeee! Eulaliiiiaaaaa!"

Such was his fury that the enemy broke, scattering widespread. The Highland hare's wild charge sent fresh energy into the woodland ranks. Howling warcries, they threw themselves anew into the fray.

Bisky found himself with a gang of Gonfelin slingers, whipping stones off, hitting birds and reptiles like a sudden thunderstorm.

A voice rang out. "Cummback 'ere, yer scummybummed, onion-snouted blaggards, stand an' fight! Yowch! Wot didyer do that for, Da?"

It was Gobbo. Bisky could not resist a chuckle as he saw Nokko cuff his errant son's ear again.

"Less o' the shoutin' an' more o' the slingin', gabbygob. Sticks'n'stones, remember?"

Bisky and Dubble broke off to charge a group of lizards, who were scurrying around the soil mound. As the fight became more widespread, the activity at the tunnel entrance waned. Some crows took advantage of this, to scramble off down the tunnel. Zaran spotted the birds and went after them.

Korvus Skurr did not see the black otter depart. He was watching Bosie, who was driving several carrion to the far side of the cavern. Something caught the Doomwyte raven's eye—he turned sharply in the opposite direction. Two magpies, who had fled into the rear cave, came flapping out, with Baliss pursuing them. Now was the time to leave, whilst the woodlanders were scattered, and the hare was well clear of the exit. Korvus launched himself from the perch, gliding silently down.

Outside, two of the crows had escaped, but Spingo had settled for one with her club, and Zaran caught another with her double blade as it tried to flap off skyward. The black otter nodded to the Gonfelin maid.

"Spingo is feeling better, yes?"

She leant on her makeshift club. "Much better, thank ye. How are me da an' Bisky doin' in there?"

Zaran shouldered her sword as she walked back to the tunnel. "They fight like warriors. I think it will soon be over in there. Stay here and rest."

Inside the tunnel, Zaran had not gone far when she saw the pale, flickering light in the gloom. It could be only one thing, a Wyte. The black otter swung her double-bladed sword high, every sinew in her powerful frame tensed. The moment had arrived to avenge the death of her family.

Korvus Skurr was flying low and fast—he did not see the twin blades gleam until too late. Zaran felt the big raven's talons grip her as she slashed out and thrust into the Doomwyte's plumage.

Spingo saw them both tumble out into the stream, a wild melee of dark fur and feathers. They plunged into the water, shooting under the surface. The Gonfelin maid hurried to the spot, trying to look into the clouded depths. There was a momentary silence, then Zaran surfaced in a rush of water.

Spingo gasped. "What was that?"

Streamwater swirled red as the otter dragged the bedraggled carcass of the Great Doomwyte up. Zaran released the slain raven; she watched stony-eyed as it floated off with the current. "Now the kinbeasts of Zaran will rest easy!"

Baliss was loose in the big cave. The giant reptile resembled a living nightmare as he roved the sulphurous mists. The huge coils flexed and curled, the hideous head shuddering uncontrollably in the grip of agonised infection. Birds flew high to escape death, reptiles fled everywhere, to crannies and any holes they could find.

With their instinctive fear of adders, the Guosim were almost petrified. The Gonfelin were little better off at being confronted by such a monster.

Bosie seized Nokko and Dubble, shaking them soundly. "Och, ye've good reason tae be afeared o' yon serpent, but don't just stan' there tremblin'. Gather yore crews an' get oot o' here. Move yersel's, buckoes!"

Bisky began pushing all and sundry toward the tunnel. "Bosie's right, no beast could face that thing. Let's move while we're still able to. Get going. Now!"

Zaran re-entered the cavern, immediately taking in the scene. She stood with Bosie and Bisky at the tunnel entrance, as the woodlanders hurried by them. Keeping an eye on Baliss, who had started gorging upon the slain, Bosie tried summing the situation up.

"A score o' warriors'd be nae good against yon beastie. Aye, but once we're out o' this place, how d'we stop it comin' after us?"

Zaran had a suggestion. "Once all your creatures are out of here, could you not block the entrance?"

Bisky shepherded the last of the Guosim out of the cavern. "We could try. I'm sure our moles could look at it, they're the ones who'd know about such work."

Trying deliberately to appear casual, Nokko strutted by, entering the tunnel. "Righto, mates, everybeast's clear now!"

Baliss left off his grisly feast. Hissing and slobbering, he wriggled off to search for water. As the snake's noise began afresh, Nokko took to his paws and shot off down the tunnel.

Bosie put up his sword. "Ah think yon mousey has the right idea. Let's be off!"

Whether it was the sound of the retreating woodlanders, or a faint breeze from outside, nobeast could tell. But Baliss turned aside from returning to the rear cave and headed for the tunnel.

37

Spingo ran to join Bisky, splashing through the shallows to meet him. The young Redwaller did not hide his pleasure at seeing her so well and sprightly.

"Hello, mate, yore looking pretty chipper!"

Spingo smiled. "You don't look too bad yourself. What's happenin', did we whack 'em?"

Nokko ruffled his pretty daughter's ears. "Ye could say that, though there's still that blinkin' adder to deal with yet."

Soilclaw surveyed the tunnel frontage, shaking his velvety head dubiously. "Burr, ee'm mostly 'ard, solid rock, zurr. B'aint a gurt lot us'ns can do abowt that, hurr, nay!"

Gobbo interrupted, "Why can't ye, yore supposed t'be moles, why can't youse block up the 'ole, eh?"

Nokko glared at his garrulous son. "Hoi, bucketmouth, give yer gob a rest, or I'll boot yer tail straight inter that stream!"

Burgy waved a hefty digging claw. "Leave 'im be, zurr, ee young maister got a point. Yurr, Frubb, us'll take ee lukk further in. Coom on, zurr, may'aps ee can 'elp uz."

Gobbo was not very taken by the suggestion. "Who, me? No, mate, I don't know nothin' about blockin' tunnels!"

Nokko grabbed him firmly by the ear. "Ho, don't yer now, seems like yer had enuff t'say about it just now. Well, me son, ye can either go an' 'elp those good moles in the tunnel, or stay out 'ere with me while I duck yer in the stream. Please yerself, the choice is up to you!"

Dragging his tail, and sticking out his lower lip, Gobbo skulked into the tunnel with Burgy and Frubb. "Huh, wot choice is that, eh? It's not fair, Da!"

Nokko winked at Bosie and grinned. "I'll tell yer wot else isn't fair. The stuff on a bird, that's not fair, it's feathers. Ha ha . . . fur, feathers, get it?"

The ghost of a smile touched Bosie's lips. "Och, very droll, Ah'm sure, mah friend. Er, by the by, did anybeast mention breakfast, ah'm fair famished!"

Garul, the elder Guosim, called to some shrews, "Set up a fire an' we'll see wot we can do."

Whilst preparations were being made to serve food, Bisky and Spingo joined the Gonfelins, to gather firewood.

Gobbo came hurtling out of the tunnel, like a stone from a slingshot. He was gabbling uncontrollably. "Quick quick runrun the addersnake's comin' down the tunnel runrun or we'll all be ate alive!"

He was leaping about, waving his paws frantically. Nokko tripped him neatly, sending him headlong into the stream. "Take a drink an' get yer breath back, me ould son. Is the snake really comin', mate?"

Frubb nodded. "Ho aye, zurr, that ee bees, though the way ee surrpint is throwen' itself abowt, 'twill take summ toime. But ee'm a-cummen sure enuff!"

Dubble tried hard to stop himself trembling.

"W . . . w . . . wot'll we do?"

Surprisingly, it was Gobbo who came up with the answer, summing up his solution in one word: "Fire!"

Nokko beamed as he hauled his son from the stream. "That's the first sensible thing ye've said in yer life. Fire, nobeast can face heat an' flames!"

Bisky began piling brushwood and twigs into the tunnel outlet. "Come on, mates, all paws to work. Spingo, get a light from the campfire!"

Shortly thereafter, everybeast was dashing about gathering anything that would burn, deadwood, dried rushes, moss, old ferns, twigs, branches and rotten bark.

Dusting off his paws, Gobbo stood, paws akimbo. "Hah, that should stop the scummy ould villain. Just let 'im poke 'is snout inter that. He'll gerra good roastin, I kin tell yer!"

Bosie watched the blaze, nibbling on an apple he had found. "Aye, but fire'll no last forever, mah friend. What then?"

Zaran took up her curious sword, nodding to Bosie. "Come with me, I have a plan." Something in her voice told the hare that he could trust to Zaran's judgement. The black otter turned to Garul, who was standing by her side. "You must stay here, keep that fire alight. Bosie, come now, bring your fine sword."

They set off uphill at a smart trot. Zaran glanced back and saw Spingo following them. Not only that, but the mole, Frubb, was also trailing Spingo. The black otter halted. "Go back, friends."

The Gonfelin maid had a resolute gleam in her eye. "I want t'see wot yore up to. Don't worry, I promise I'll stay out o' yore way, an' I won't get trapped under any big rocks. I'll behave meself."

Bosie pointed at Frubb. "What about you, mah braw beastie?"

Frubb's homely face creased with smiles. "Ho, doan't ee fret abowt Oi, zurr, may'ap you'm guddbeasts might need ee mole along with ee!"

Zaran nodded. "Come then, but do as I say."

Reaching the spot where the hillside had collapsed, they stood at the edge of the hole. Yellow vapours were still pouring out, as Zaran peered into the depression. Bosie stirred the rim with his swordpoint. He watched the sandy soil silting downward, into the cavern below.

"See, yon big slab hasnae fallen, 'tis still hangin' there. Though Ah dinnae know what's holdin' it up. So, marm, what's the plan?"

Zaran explained, "I am closer than ever before to doing what I set out to do. Korvus Skurr is slain, now I must destroy his lair."

Bosie took another look at the hole. "Aye, but even if yon auld stone drops, it won't destroy the place. Ye told me tae bring mah sword, why was that?"

Zaran nodded toward the big sycamore above the collapsing area. The molecrew's rope was still attached to its trunk. "All this ground is not safe anymore. If that great tree were to fall. . . ."

Spingo interrupted eagerly, "It'd cave the whole lot in, a tree that size!"

Bosie's head tilted back as he stared up at the massive height of the sycamore. "Skin mah scut, d'ye want me tae chop that thing doon wi' mah sword?"

Zaran faced him impassively. "We have two swords, you and I, we will work together." Without further ado, she went to the sycamore and began chopping.

Bosie sighed in resignation. "Och, this is no task for a Laird who hasnae been properly fed, but Ah'll do mah best!" Drawing the legendary sword of Martin, he stood opposite Zaran and swung the blade. Then Frubb walked in the way of the swinging blades. Both beasts had to bring their swords up sharply, to avoid slicing through the mole.

Zaran spoke through clenched jaws. "Please, friend, stay out of our way!"

Frubb did not seem at all put out by his close shave. Leaning against the tree, he shook his head with disapproval. "Nay, nay, marm'n'zurr, you'm going abowt et all wrongwise. The way you'm a-goin', you gurt tree'll prob'ly fall back'ard an' flatten ee both. Ho urr aye, take et frum Oi!"

Spingo liked Frubb, so she backed him up stoutly. "I'd lissen to that good mole if'n I was you. Moles saved my life, they're very sensible beasts!"

Frubb bowed, tugging his snout, a sure molesign of respect to another. "Whoi thankee, likkle mizzy!"

Zaran shrugged impatiently. "Then tell us what to do."

Frubb held up a paw for silence. He paced around the sycamore, sniffing, scratching the earth and tapping on the trunk with his powerful digging claws. Whilst he performed this curious ritual, he could be heard muttering odd calculations to himself.

"Hummm, wind'ard drift . . . soil spillage, ho urr aye, must a-member that . . . taken into 'count ee lay of land . . . h'angle of 'illside . . . fallen west'ard an' 'arf point north, Oi'd say. Burr aye, that should do urr noicely, Oi reckern!"

Moving to a point on the trunk directly opposite the hole, he measured two pawspans slightly left. "Cudd Oi burrow ee wepping, zurr?"

Wordlessly, Bosie passed him the sword. At about the height of his snout, Frubb notched a mark in the bark. "Start choppen yurr if'n you'm please!"

They began hewing with both blades at the sycamore. Initially their strokes were a bit disjointed, until Spingo made a suggestion. "Mayhaps if I sing a Gonfelin dancin' song it'll keep ye both in time. Right!"

Bosie spat on his paws, gripping the sword tight. "Sing out then, bonny lass, Ah'm game tae try it."

Frubb clapped his paws in time to the tune as Spingo sang; Bosie's and Zaran's bladestrokes matched the rhythm.

"Can I come a-courtin', sir,
an' can I woo yore daughter?
Aye ye can try as others have,
but nobeast's ever caught her.
Dance around an' tap tap tap,
d'ye think ye stand a chance?
Many a swain has lost his heart,
to a pretty maid at the dance.

356

Round the floor now hop hop hop,
whirl her round just like a top!

Swing her high but hold her light,
an' don't ye try to kiss her,
four big beasts are watchin' you,
an' she's their little sister.
Keep on dancin' don't dare stop,
wot a fix yore in, sir.
Yonder stands her stout ole ma,
a-twirlin' a rollin' pin, sir.

Skip'n'jump now one two three,
through the window an' yore free!"

Bosie was blowing like a bellows with the pace. "D'ye not know any slower songs, bonny lass, mebbe a soft lullaby, or an auld funeral march!"

Spingo giggled. "Oh, come on, Mister Bosie, a big, strong beast like yourself shouldn't be bothered by an overgrown twig like that. Let's see wot ye can really do, with those muscles an' that blade! Or are ye goin' t'be beaten by an otter lady, eh?"

The lanky hare went back to his task like a creature possessed. Bark, wood chips, leafsprouts and twigs scattered widespread as he plied the sword blade.

Frubb caught on to what Spingo was doing. He called to Zaran, "Hurr, ee'll take summ catchin' marm, boi okey ec'm will!"

The black otter also knew what was going on, but she winked at the mole, and twirled her twin blades. "Do you think so . . . then watch this!" With muscle and sinew toughened by gruelling seasons of work on the hillside, Zaran was unstoppable. She hewed at the great tree with awesome energy. Soon there was no need of encouraging work songs, Bosie and Zaran were hacking at the tree in swift unison. *Chack! Thock! Chack! Thock!*

Frubb watched until he judged the moment right, then called a sudden halt to the task. "Stoppee naow, guddbeasts, stopp Oi says!" After listening with his ear to the sycamore trunk, the mole nodded sagely and made his report. "Hoo arr, she'm ready t'go naow!"

Bosie leant wearily on his sword pommel. "Och, pray tell, sirrah, how d'ye know that?"

Frubb wrinkled his snout, lowering his tone confidentially. "A 'coz ee'm tree told Oi, zurr, stan' asoide naow. Mizzy, will ee untie ee rope frumm t'uther tree?"

Spingo hurriedly loosed the rope from the oak on the left, as Frubb undid the other rope, which the molecrew had tied during the rescue attempt. He gave Bosie and Zaran a rope each.

"Roight zurr'n'marm, you'm must fasten ee ropes furmly round ee tree. Far oop as ye can reach!" Taking the other ends of both ropes, Frubb bade Spingo to follow him. They went uphill until he judged the distance straight, and just right. "Hurr, bees you'm a gud treeclimberer, mizzy?"

Scooping up some soil, Spingo rubbed it on her paws. "Huh, good, me? You show me the tree wot needs climbin', then stand clear, matey!"

The mole indicated two wych elms, either side of him. "Farsten wun to each, gudd'n'igh up."

True to her word, the Gonfelin maid was an agile climber. She scaled both elms with ease, securing the ropes high, one to each tree.

Returning to the sycamore, Frubb outlined to Bosie and Zaran what was an extremely perilous operation. "You'm takes three more chops apiece at ee tree. Then 'urry back up'ill. Climb up yon h'elms, an' wait moi signal. Then chop ee ropes, get ee daown an' run furr you'm loives to yon 'illtop!"

Bosie nodded, putting up his sword. "That sounds clear enough, mah friend, but why do we have tae hurry?"

The mole chuckled. "Hurr hurr, 'cos ee h'entire

neighbor'ood bees goin' to cullapse daown ee 'ole, an' you'm doan't wants to goo with et, do ee, zurr?"

Bosie appeared quite indignant at the very idea. "Och, Ah should say not, Ah've seen enough o' that reeky auld cavern, thank ye. Right, mah bonny tree-fellin' friend, three chops apiece, eh!"

The half-dozen blows were promptly delivered, then they clambered uphill to the wych elms and climbed to their positions, blades ready, close to the ropes. Spingo and Frubb carried on upward, until they reached the crest of the vast wooded hill. The mole turned, watching the woodlands at their back.

Spingo whispered, "Wot happens now, mate?"

Frubb did not take his eyes from the panorama below. "We'm wait, mizzy, wait an' watch east'ard."

From his wych elm perch, Bosie called across to Zaran in the other tree, "Ah'm glad hares dinnae have tae live in trees. Thanks tae mah mither Ah wasnae born a squirrel."

The black otter managed one of her rare smiles. "Aye, me, too, I hope our friend gives the signal soon."

The hungry hare tasted a leaf and spat it out. "Och, there's no' even an apple or a pear growin' up here. Ye'd think a tree would at least have the decency tae grow a few nuts for a beast tae keep body'n'fur taegether whilst he's waitin'!"

Frubb saw the distant treetops beginning to wave. He murmured, "Yurr she cumms, mizzy, ee wind we'm a-waiten on!"

In another moment, Spingo felt the breeze sweep over them. It all happened so quickly. Down below the taut ropes thrummed under the easterly wind.

"Chop ee roooooopes!"

Bosie and Zaran heard Frubb loud and clear. All it took was two sharp slashes, one from each blade. Both beasts scrambled down hastily, with the creak and groan of the sycamore in their ears. It made a noise like a massive rusty door swinging on its hinges. *Krrreeeeeaaawwwwwwkkkk* . . . *craaaack!*

It toppled slowly for a moment, seeming to pause for a breathless space. Then the huge sycamore fell.

A shuddering tremor hit the entire hillside, almost knocking Bosie and Zaran flat as they fled for the summit. Spingo watched, openmouthed, as the treetop thundered down the depression, straight into the hole. Loud, sharp cracking noises reverberated around. Branches were snapped from the mighty trunk as it plunged downward through the hole. There was a resounding *boom* when the slab hit the ground in the cavern below. The hillside collapsed with a dull, nerve-numbing rumble.

Zaran grabbed Spingo, hauling her backward as long, running cracks began raking the hill, leaving deep, forbidding slits in the ground. Accompanied by the sounds of rock striking rock and boiling, bubbling liquid, a whistling jet of sulphured steam shot skyward. Then there was silence.

At the tunnel entrance, Nokko, Garul and Dubble were loading fuel into the fire. They were supplied by a constant stream of creatures, carrying any material which might prove flammable. Garul flung a bundle of dried ferns into the flames. Leaping back, he shielded his face from the backblast of searing heat. "I keep sniffin' t'see if'n I can smell roasted serpent in there. Wot d'ye think, mate?"

Nokko held a paw to his nostrils. "That's my scorchin' whiskers yew kin smell, bucko. Nobeast'd be daft enough to try gettin' through that tunnel. It must be hotter'n ten ovens in there!"

Dubble threw a length of old spruce bark into the blaze. He turned away, wiping bleary tears from his eyes. "Then tell me, wot's the point of keepin' a fire goin' if'n there ain't no snake in the tunnel, eh?"

Nokko bit a splinter from his paw and spat it out. "T'stop that ould addersnake from comin' out 'ere an' scoffin' us, that's the point! Aye aye, lissen t'that, sounds like a spot o' thunder t'me."

He ran back a few paces, glancing uphill. The summit gave a shuddering tremor, and a blast of yellow steam shot skyward. The earth convulsed suddenly under Nokko's paws. He raced sideways, bellowing, "Gerraway, that hill's comin' down! Get back, everybeast, go t'the left or right, gerrout the way!"

Inside the cave, Baliss had been stuck in the tunnel. Badly burnt, the maddened snake freed itself, retreating from the inferno. The giant reptile coiled like a corkscrew, writhing madly in the throes of a macabre death dance. It thrashed about, heedless of what was happening.

The massive slab of rock fell from the ceiling, striking the cavern floor with an earsplitting slam. Cackling, screeching and hissing, the remaining birds and reptiles scattered for safety. There was, however, no place left to go as their world collapsed over them.

Bringing the entire cave ceiling with it, stalactites, earth, roots and rocks, the sycamore trunk plunged down. It struck the eyeless Doomwyte statue, driving it deep into the boiling pool. Scalding green sulphur water vomited forth to be met by gushing torrents from the overflowing lake in the rear cavern. Under tremendous pressure, it was forced through the tunnel. Picking up speed in the narrow passage, the thundering mass smashed through the firewall.

The watchers on the hilltop and those on the ground below were witness to an unbelievable sight. A veritable river of steaming mud and stone shot forth across the stream into the woodland, demolishing several trees in its path. It ran on for quite awhile before it slackened off. Now there was just a slow-moving ooze issuing from the tunnel. From both sides, creatures ventured gingerly forth, to stand either side of the morass.

Everybeast was at a loss for words, with the exception of Gobbo. "Yow! Wow! Whooo! I never saw nothin' like that in me bloomin' life! Never!"

For once, Nokko did not cuff or silence his astounded offspring. "Yer right there, me ould son!"

With the mole and her helpers trailing her, Zaran joined the others at the awesome scene. Bisky clasped her paw.

"Ye did it, marm, by thunder, ye did it!"

The black otter pointed to Bosie, Spingo and Frubb. "We did it. I could not have done it without my friends."

Bosie was about to start speech making, when he was halted by a sucking noise and a faint plop from the tunnel mouth. He recoiled in horrified disgust. "Guid grief, 'tis the auld monster himself!"

Practically filling the width of the tunnel mouth, the swollen carcass of Baliss oozed slowly out into the light of day. It slid forth, coated in mud and slime, far more revolting in death than it had been in life.

Gobbo prodded it with a stick. "Ha ha, anybeast fancy a cob o' roasted reptile?"

This time it was Bosie who took the liberty of cuffing his ear. "Ach, come awa' frae that thing, ye might catch a plague by even touching it!"

Nokko winked at the hare. "Thank ye, sir, feel free t'give the wretch a slap anytime ye like, it'll save the wear'n'tear on my ould paws!"

Soilclaw watched the waste matter run out to a trickle, commenting with solid molesense, "Given a cupple o' seasons, 'twill all go a-minglin' with ee stream. Hurr, thur'll be a gurt, foine watery meadow all round yurr. Peaceable, with watery lilies, an' flowers, dragonflies, fishes, too. You'm wull see, this'll be a noice place for ee to visit!"

Zaran sat down on a rock, staring out at the spreading mess, as it joined with the stream. The black otter bowed her head, speaking slowly. "It would be pleasant to see, I will visit here someday, to relive my memories."

Bisky held out his paw to her. "We'll come with ye, friend. Come on, let's go home now, to Redwall Abbey. We need an otter lady there."

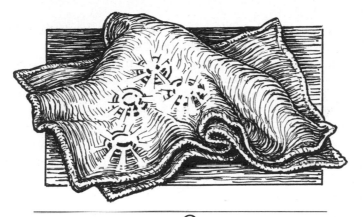

38

Homecomings can be coloured by many emotions. Abbot Glisam tried to touch on them all, as he addressed everybeast. It was after sunset, Great Hall was lit by candles and lanterns. Garlands of summer blossoms draped the columns, in honour of the returning visitors. Zaran sat alongside Skipper Rorgus, who had been fascinated by the black otter from the moment he set eyes upon her. Dwink and Perrit sat side by side, constantly together since their adventure in the woodlands. Next to them, Bisky and Spingo shared the same platter.

The feast was splendid. Redwallers were wondering who had produced many of the new dishes. It was Bosie who found out. "Och, would ye credit it, young Dubble seems tae have taken charge, Ah'm thinken he should be Laird o' the kitchens, seein' as the job hasnae been offered tae me."

Brother Torilis cocked a severe eye at the gluttonous hare. "That would be like leaving baby minnows to be nursed by a hungry pike!"

Glisam left them happily feasting, until he judged the right moment for his speech. Signalling Umfry Spikkle to ring the table bell, the Father Abbot rose. "Redwallers, Guosim, Gonfelins, friends. First allow me to thank you from my heart, for making our Abbey and Mossflower Country safe from evil—Doomwytes, predators and the dreadful Baliss, who created fear and terror for long seasons. However, each triumph has its cost. Words cannot describe our sadness at the death of four loyal and faithful moles: Rooter, Grabul, Ruttur and our beloved Friar Skurpul.

"Alas, their bodies were never recovered, but they will live in Redwall memory as long as anybeast can record or recall their bravery in saving the life of a Gonfelin maid. Such is the way we honour friends at this Abbey."

There was a prolonged silence, punctuated by lots of sobs, particularly from Foremole Gullub and the remainder of his crew.

Abbot Glisam sighed, and took a deep breath before continuing. "Now, on to more cheerful things. Our thanks is due to Aluco, for finding the first Doomwyte Eye. Then to Dwink and Perrit, whose endeavours helped greatly in the recovery of the other two eyes."

Removing the cover from a bowl, the Abbot turned the three stones out onto the table. A gasp of admiration arose from the onlookers as two round emeralds and a single blood-hued ruby were revealed. They lay on the table, reflecting the candle and lantern lights, sparkling with their own strange fires. The Abbot shook his head ruefully.

"Alas, that is where the trail ends, there are no clues as to the location of the final Doomwyte's Eye. The missing ruby may never be found."

Bisky was smiling as Spingo stood up, calling out aloud, "Oh, yes there is, I know who's got the red stone. Aye, so does Bisky. . . . An' so does another beast I could mention. A Gonfelin sittin' 'ere at yore table, Father." She turned her accusing glare from the Abbot to Nokko. "I don't mean that Father, but this Father—you, Da!"

Nokko squirmed under his daughter's stern eyes. "But . . . but that's ours, me darlin', booty, pawpickin's, loot. It belongs to our tribe."

Spingo's paw was pointed like a spear at her hapless

parent. "Our tribe are Redwallers now, Da, there'll be no more lootin', swipin' an' thievin'. We're good, honest creatures now. So come on, cough it up!"

Nokko hesitated a moment, then Bisky whispered, "Do the right thing, sir, make yore daughter happy."

A mighty cheer went up as Nokko produced the ruby and placed it with the others. He smiled sheepishly. "Ah well, as long as it makes me darlin' Spingo 'appy. Add that un to yore collection, Abbo!"

Abbot Glisam picked all four of the Great Doomwyte's Eyes up, he held them aloft. "What has come from evil will return to evil, in memory of four goodbeasts who lie there. Foremole, take your crew and bury these on what is left of that hillside in honour of our fallen friends!"

Everybeast raised their drinks.

"In honour of fallen friends."

Bosie McScutta, the Laird of Bowlaynee, had the final word. "An' now, back tae the feast, mah braw beasties. Bowlayneeee! Eulaliaaa! Redwaaaallll!"

39

A noontide nap can be a tranquil pleasure. Nothing to do, nowhere special to go, happily captured in the enchantment of a high summer day. The old mouse allowed his paw to drift in the idle flow of the water meadow. Lounging comfortably on a pallet of moss and dried ferns, he had released his hold on the tiller, allowing the raft to wend its own way through the proliferation of water lilies, bulrush reeds, sundew, gipsywort and comfrey which carpeted the cool, dim water meadow.

Closing his eyes, the ancient one took in the sounds. Snatches of songs and conversation from his companions, mingling with the squeals and chuckles of Dibbuns playing in the shallows. The buzz and hum of bees in the background, an occasional plop from a leaping trout. Distant birdsong, reed warblers, dippers, chiffchaffs and migrant firecrest, competing with their own careless raptures. Old Samolus moved his eyelids lightly, trying not to twitch his nose as a beautifully patterned marsh fritillary butterfly landed on it.

Perrit whispered to her mate, Dwink, "I think that butterfly might wake old Samolus."

The insect flew off as the ancient mouse spoke. "Old

Samolus is awake, thank ye, marm, wonderin' when afternoon tea will be ready."

Skipper Rorgus yawned cavernously. His mate, Zaran, called to their little son, who was frisking in the water nearby, "Rorzan, go ashore and see if tea's ready yet."

The young one waved his chubby rudder. "Hurr, Oi'll do thart doireckly, Mum!"

Bisky laughed at the otterbabe. "That's a very good mole voice he's learned!"

His daughter, Andio, replied, "Ho yuss, wee'm all a-talken loike that, b'aint us, Mumm?"

Bisky's mate, Spingo, answered their daughter in mole dialect. "You'm surrpinkly are, moi dearie!"

Perrit and Dwink's little one, a tiny squirrelmaid they had named Mittee, was of a different mind. "Och, weel, Ah'm no' goin' tae speak like a mole, Ah want tae be a hare like Laird Bosie!"

Aluco, the tawny owl, twirled his head almost full circle, blinking in mock alarm. "As long as you don't learn to eat like him!"

Friar Dubble called out from the bank, "Ahoy, raftbeasts, tea's ready!"

Bosie joined him, shouting hopefully, "There's no hurry, bonnybeasts, stay oot there if'n ye be enjoyin' yersel's."

Skipper Rorgus grabbed a paddle, yelling a reply. "Ye great, famine-faced glutton, don't touch a single crumb 'til we're ashore, somebeast stop him!"

Umfry Spikkle, who in the last couple of seasons had attained his full growth, and was bigger even than his grandhog, Corksnout, assured Skipper from the bank, "Don't worry, Skip. I'll keep a h'eye on Mister Bosie. Shall h'I sit h'on 'im for ye?"

From beneath a sunshade of bushes, Brother Torilis wheeled Abbot Glisam out to join the diners. Fully renovated, and running smoothly, the old wheelchair was now the aged dormouse's main means of getting about. Glisam

367

often shed a tear for little Sister Ficaria, who had gone to sleep peacefully two winters back, never to wake again. The Father Abbot of Redwall would pat his chair fondly, saying, "My friend Ficaria wanted me to have this chair, as a reward for all those morning strolls. I think it was the damp grass which got to my old footpaws."

It was a memorable afternoon tea. All the food, which had been transported from Redwall kitchens, was prepared to perfection by Friar Dubble. Soilclaw sat sipping a beaker of cider, made from last season's good russet apples. He gestured up at the curving, wooded hill, which skirted the bank as he explained to the Dibbuns, "Oi a-members sayin', jus' arter ee caves bee'd curlapsed, that this'n yurr'd make a gudd watery medder. Hurr, Oi wurr roight."

Zaran nodded. "Indeed you were, sir. Look at it now, what beast would think that we, and our young uns, could get so much pleasure from a place that was once an evil lair?"

The Abbot had become rather partial to seedcake; he selected a slice, but paused before tasting it. "You're right, marm. I was just thinking, it's nice when things change for the better, and certain things do have to change eventually."

Corksnout had known Glisam for more seasons than he cared to remember. Adjusting his false snout, the old Cellarhog stared hard at his friend. "Yore about to say somethin', ain't ye, Father?"

Glisam placed the seedcake on his plate, returning Corksnout's gaze. "Aye, and I hope you'll all take it sensibly. Listen, friends, I've had a long and happy time, ruling our Abbey, but I think 'tis high time another took on the office. I'm heavy with seasons now, and my old bones are tired."

He looked around at the anxious faces, then chuckled. "Oh, don't worry, I'm going to be around for at least as long as Sister Ficaria was, so there's still many more seasons left to me yet."

Quite out of character with his stern demeanour, Brother

Torilis clasped his Abbot's paw—he was visibly moved. "Father, I will take care of you as I always have."

Glisam patted the saturnine Herbalist's cheek. "I know you will, my good friend. Perrit, would you come over here, please."

The young squirrelwife hurried across. She crouched in front of the wheelchair. "Father?"

Glisam smiled fondly. "So pretty, so practical. I've watched you grow up, Perrit, always there, dutiful and kind. Now look at you, with a fine mate like Dwink, and a lovely little daughter. Now you must tell me, do you think that there is enough on your plate, or would you like to help me? Think, now, you do not have to answer right away."

Perrit looked puzzled, but answered promptly, "I don't have to think, Father, if it concerns you, or the Abbey, I would do anything cheerfully."

Glisam cupped her face fondly in his old paws. "Would you like to become Mother Abbess of Redwall?"

Dwink rushed forward, hugging Perrit. "Of course she would, my Perrit'd be a great Abbess!"

Sister Violet was holding little Mittee. She scrambled from Violet's lap, flinging herself upon her mother. "My mammee d'Abbiss. Yeeheeeee!"

Dwink swung his little daughter in the air, laughing. "Can't argue with that, can ye? Hahahaha!"

Bosie was heard to murmur to Foremole Gurrpaw, "Och, it grieves me sad tae say, but that's two guid positions Ah've lost now, Friar an' Abbot!"

The mole muttered back consolingly, "Burr, but you'm b'aint losted yore h'appetite, zurr!"

The Laird of Bowlaynee sniffed into his lace kerchief. "Thank ye, sir, Ah've always had a braw appetite, that's why mah grandfather banished me from Bowlaynee Castle."

Perrit stayed crouching by Glisam's chair, feeling bound to ask the question, "Are you sure this is what you want, Father?"

He replied without hesitation, "I'm certain! Oh, and from now on you can forget my titles, I'm just plain old Glisam, to you and all your Abbeybeasts."

The pretty squirrelwife pondered his words. "All my Abbeybeasts? That's a great responsibility. But what will you do now, Father . . . er, Glisam?"

Again, there was no hesitation with the answer. "I'm going to be the Abbey teacher, it's always been a dream of mine, to educate our young ones. Aye, and some of the not so young. Umfry Spikkle!"

The big hedgehog saluted. "Ye called me, sir?"

The old dormouse took Umfry's paw firmly. "Your education commences when we return to the Abbey. I'll instruct you in reading and writing. Is that clear?"

Umfry nodded dutifully. "H'aye, sir, when'll that be?"

Glisam shrugged. "'Tis not my decision anymore, ask your new Abbess, she'll tell you."

Umfry turned to Perrit. "Mother h'Abbess!"

She felt like giggling as he made his request. Umfry was three seasons older than Perrit, yet he was calling her Mother. Perrit composed herself, speaking calmly. "Hmm, we've been here three days now, what d'you think?"

Feeling much like a counsellor, Dwink scratched his bushy tail thoughtfully. "Oh, another two days would be good."

Little Mittee tugged at her mother's pinafore. "Free days, us stays annuver free days, Muvver!"

Unable to resist, Perrit hugged her baby. "Three days it is then, miss. Any more questions, is everybeast happy with our decision?"

Dubble left off brewing fresh mint tea. "Mother Abbess. Log a Log Garul and his Guosim left three seasons ago. But Garul promised to visit Redwall five seasons hence. That means he will be coming to our Abbey this coming winter. Abbot Glisam said they could, will you still honour the arrangement?"

Perrit was very fond of the young Friar; she took his

paws affectionately. "But of course, it goes without saying, Friar Dubble. Anybeast, no matter who, providing they are good at heart, is welcome to visit the Abbey. They may stay as long as they please. Our gates are open to all who come in peace, anytime. It has always been the custom at Redwall, and I fully intend to honour it!"

Glisam settled back in the wheelchair and closed his eyes. Dozing off in the warm noontide sun, a feeling of peaceful contentment fell over the old dormouse. He had chosen well. His beloved Abbey was in good and wise paws.

EPILOGUE

The following is an extract from the Recorder's Annal. It was found in this gatehouse, by the granddaughter of old Abbess Perrit.

Wisdom comes with age I know, for life has taught me
   thus,
those early wild and clouded rivers,
now flow calm and clear to us.
Tolerance replaces haste, rage gives way to reason,
our young ones grow, to learn and know,
as Season follows Season.
Lessons of truth and honesty,
from creatures, far more bold than me.
I tried my best, and played my part,
to be amongst the brave of heart.
Mayhaps I failed, though now it seems,
that I've become the Teller of Tales,
the scribe, and the Weaver of Dreams.

Umfry Spikkle.
Gatekeeper and Recorder of Redwall Abbey
in Mossflower Country.